The Missing Pieces

Fiction Novel

to Stephanie
Hope you Enjoy

By

DEBORAH HENDERSON

The Missing Pieces

Tellwell Talent
www.tellwell.ca

ISBN
978-0-2288-1154-1 (Hardcover)
978-0-2288-1153-4 (Paperback)
978-0-2288-1155-8 (eBook)

Dedication

This book is dedicated to my children
Cynthia and Richard, the loves of my life.

Acknowledgments

I would like to thank the following people for their help and support in the creation of this book.

Thank you, Diane Dugas, for your art direction and digital media. I sought a photographer, and I found a friend.

Thank you, Hristo Kovatliev, for your ability to capture the essence of my story with this amazing book cover.

Thank you, Chantal Cooper, for encouraging me to publish this story and helping with the first round of editing.

Thank you, Roger Cusson, my husband who has supported me with lots of good advice and encouragement. I couldn't have done it without you.

Thank you, Marion Henderson, my dear sister, for reading my half-finished story and encouraging me to complete and publish it.

Thank you to the rest of my family and friends. Your encouragement has made this book a reality.

Chapter 1

The dolphins were more playful than usual today. They performed acrobatics and played tag with me for what seemed like hours. The water was a very light shade of turquoise and crystal clear. The visibility was amazing, and I could see everything in this breathtaking underwater paradise. The coral reef in all its glory and all the different ocean species were picture-perfect. The warm water caressed my skin as I started slow dancing with my aquatic friends. Bodies intertwined as we weaved our way around the brightly-colored coral. A couple of sea horses joined in the celebration. The eels played hide and go seek between the sea grasses and algae. Schools of tiny, beautifully-colored fish played follow the leader as they darted in and out through the tentacles of this live coral maze. I stopped mid-twirl to take a closer look at a beautiful little starfish lying in the sand, and unintentionally disturbed a giant manta ray as it lay there camouflaged.

"Come back! Oh no! I'm sorry! Please don't go!"

He swiftly flapped his large magnificent wings and gracefully took flight away from our watery playground. As I watched him fly overhead, I felt sorry that I made him flee his resting place. He had as much right to be there as we did.

As I looked up toward the heavens, I could see the rays of sunlight shimmering like diamonds on the surface of the water. It was almost hypnotic. I could watch them for hours. Time seemed to be non-existent during my adventures. Who knew there was such beauty beneath the surface of our vast waterways? Suddenly, bringing me back to reality, I was distracted by one of my little friends who gave me a nudge on the shoulder. I guess it was his way of asking me for the next dance. He must have thought I had given up on him or something; the party wasn't over yet. I turned and grabbed onto his fin and off we went, twisting and turning, head over heels. Mr. Fred Astaire… I called him Fred for short. This guy really loved to groove. He also liked to show off in front of all the others. He was quite the acrobat. One more pass and then we headed straight up to the surface. I loved it when he did this. I enjoyed flying through the air with him and then splashing back down into the water. Just as we got to the surface, I lost my grip. Damn… I hated when that happened. It wasn't a problem though because I knew that he would come right back around and check on me; he always did.

I stayed at the surface for a moment and looked around me, but it was not something I enjoyed very much. From above the water you don't find the same sense of security. You don't see the beauty below. You fear the unknown, desperately treading water to keep your head above it, terrified about what might be lurking below.

I could feel my anxiety level mounting. My imagination had a tendency to blow things up way out of proportion. Well, considering my past… anyway, I did not want to let that happen, so I quickly turned around and faced the other way. I instantly started to feel more relaxed. Before me now was my beautiful new home. Well, home away from home I guess you would call it. It was my brand spanking new sailboat. She was a beauty. I had bought her a few months ago.

Oops, I was so distracted by her magnificence that I had almost forgotten about Fred. He jumped out of the water and crashed down in front of me. He wanted to play some more. Before heading back down, I glanced at my regulator. Noticing that my oxygen level was getting low, I decided I would just do a quick dive back down to the reef with him to say goodbye to my friends for the day. I grabbed his fin again and down we went. It was almost like he could read my mind sometimes; he was so smart. He seemed to know that our playtime was over and that I would soon be heading back up and out of the water to my floating palace.

I loved being down here. I would have stayed forever if I could, because it was the most peaceful place on Earth. I felt so safe and comfortable surrounded by my new friends. After my goodbyes, Fred brought me back up to the surface, waited till I climbed the ladder, and then off he went to rejoin the others.

The sun felt warm on my skin as I stood on the deck and watched Fred disappear below the surface.

Now, this is what life is all about, I thought. The sun was radiant, the sky was blue as far as the eye can see, and there was not a speck of land in sight. It was like being alone in my own safe little world, without any worries.

I put away my diving gear and dried myself off a bit. It was still early, so I decided to lie down on deck for a while and relax before dinner. First, I got a glass of wine from the bar and put some music on. Then I made myself comfortable, closed my eyes, and took in all the wonderful sounds of the sea.

The waves along the sides of my sailboat were tapping in rhythm with the music. The sounds of the seagulls flying overhead, mixed with the aroma of the salty sea air, were just what the doctors had ordered. This was heaven, and I had finally found it after all those years of hell. I was not bitter. I was very happy to be alive and able to enjoy the rest of my life to its fullest. I was finally free and at peace with myself, but occasionally I still found it hard to deal with the past pain and suffering I had been through, both physically and mentally.

The sea, the sail, and my underwater friends were a very good escape for me, but every once in a while, deep down inside of me, I could feel those painful memories still nibbling away at my soul, like piranhas, trying to devour every little morsel. I tried hard not to dwell on them, but they were always there, tucked away in a little drawer in the back of my mind, just waiting for something, or someone, to pry it open.

My doctors said that only time could heal my wounds. A good part of my life had already been stolen from me, so I needed to make the most of the time I had left. Writing had always been a passion of mine and they told me that putting my thoughts and memories down on paper would probably be very therapeutic. Denying my past and trying to bury it could be more damaging. So, as you can see, I decided to take them up on that.

There were still a few missing pieces to the puzzle of my life, but I figured with a little time and patience, they would all come back to me, good and bad. I had to learn to accept my past and look forward to a wonderful future.

Chapter 2

My eyes shot open. There were red lights flashing on and off all around me. The sound of the sirens was deafening. I couldn't figure out what was happening. The bright lights were making it hard for me to see where I was. I tried to focus through my squinting eyes. I saw something, my dresser, no it couldn't be. Yes, it was, and there was my closet door. This was not possible! Where were all the lights and sirens coming from? Those damned sirens, they were piercing right through my mind. I felt like screaming. I couldn't, though; no sound would come out. I put my fingers in my ears to try to block the noise and closed my eyes. Everything went dark and silent. I was awake though, I was sure of that… well, at least I hoped so. I removed my finger from one of my ears, and then the other. Nothing. The sirens were no longer blaring. I opened one eye, and then the other. No more lights; it was dark and quiet. I heard a scream, which brought me back to reality.

They are at it again, I thought. It was not unusual for me to wake up to the sound of yelling and fighting, but this time it seemed different. There were loud banging noises, painful screams, and the sound of glass breaking. Their arguments didn't usually get this violent. I was getting very worried. I couldn't imagine what was going on down there. This was not their typical drunken dispute. This went on for quite some time, then everything stopped. I focused hard, but still, I couldn't hear anything. Strangely though, the sound of nothing was unbearably loud.

I put my fingers in my ears again and began to stress. My heart started pounding so loudly that I feared somebody would hear it, if there was still anyone in the house. I was so tensed up that I could hardly breathe. It was like something was wrapped tightly around my chest. I tried desperately to pull some air into my lungs but not much was getting through. I just lay there breathless and wide-eyed for what seemed like forever, staring at my bedroom door and praying that it was all just a bad dream, but I knew it wasn't. I kept hoping that whoever it was or whatever it was would have already left the house. My imagination was running wild. I was in such a panicked state that I could barely breathe, and then I started to feel light-headed. A buzzing noise in the room kept getting louder and louder... Then everything went black.

I don't know how long I was unconscious, but when I came to and opened my eyes, the house was still quiet. I was still fixated on my door. I had no idea what I should do. I couldn't just lay there; I had to go and find out what had happened. That is what my mind kept telling me, but my body wasn't cooperating. I didn't move; I couldn't. I seemed to be glued to my bed. I needed to stay calm. I tried to take in some deep breaths again. My chest was still a little tight, but I managed, and it seemed to help.

Just as I was trying to work up enough courage to get up and go downstairs to investigate, I heard some voices. I listened hard. They were strange voices that I'd never heard before. What was I to do? Where was I to go? I listened closely so I could pinpoint exactly where they were, inside the house. They didn't seem to be coming from the kitchen where all the commotion was before. I trembled as I realized that the sound of their voices was getting closer and closer. I held my breath as the tears started running down my face. I couldn't figure out who these people were or how many of them were down there, and I didn't have a good feeling about this whole situation.

Suddenly, a stream of light came from under my bedroom door. Someone had turned the hall light on. I heard the creaking sounds of footsteps coming up the old staircase. They kept echoing loudly in my mind. I wanted to cry out, but I didn't know what they would do to me if they found me. I had never been so scared in all my life.

I decided that the safest thing to do was to hide. It took everything I had to slide out from under my blankets; they felt like they weighed a ton. I placed them back carefully, so it wouldn't look like someone had been sleeping there. I started to tiptoe across the room to get to my closet, but it seemed to be getting farther and farther away. I was terrified; I could hear their footsteps getting closer.

Why can't I move any faster? I thought. It felt like I was walking in quicksand.

I finally reached the closet, went in, and quietly closed the door behind me. I was hoping that if they came into my room and saw that the bed was made and had not been slept in, they would leave. Again, I held my breath as my bedroom door slowly creaked open. I quietly watched them through a crack in the old broken-down closet door.

They stood, for a moment, in the entrance. They didn't turn the light on, so I couldn't see very much. With the little bit of light that was streaming through the doorway from the hall, I could see that there were two of them. From the sound of their voices, I knew that they were both men. One stayed closer to the door while the other's footsteps grew louder as he entered my room.

"What a fucking shit-hole," he said, "I wouldn't let my dog sleep here. I can't believe they are keeping her in this junk room. They are such fucking assholes."

I didn't recognize him at all. He was wearing a cap and it cast a shadow over his face. I could see that the guy at the door was getting really agitated. He kept pacing back and forth. He kept whispering, quite loudly, "Come on man, let's get the fuck out of here. Nobody else is in the house!" He banged his fist on the door frame as he kept moving in and out of the room. The guy inside the room was getting very impatient with him and quietly kept telling him to shut his mouth. They broke out into an argument, quietly at first, but gradually it got much louder.

"Let's get the hell out of here before someone sees us!" the man at the door yelled as he stormed into the room and grabbed his friend by the arm. "We've been here too long as it is. This has gone a little too far! I did not sign up for all this shit. You are out of control!"

Oh my God. Yes… yes... yes, they must leave, they must leave before someone sees them; oh please leave, please do. I just kept repeating this to myself, willing them to get out of here.

"Shut the fuck up!" the man said, as he pushed his friend aside and freed himself.

"I thought I heard something. I am not leaving until I am sure that there is nobody left in this house that can identify us. There wasn't supposed to be anyone else here but I'm not so sure anymore. I am not leaving any loose ends."

I stayed as still as a statue. I did not move a muscle. I prayed to God that they would leave, but my prayers were not answered. He started looking through my things.

"I know that she's in here somewhere," he said. "I can feel it. I won't leave until I find her. Something got screwed up somewhere, and it's too bad for her. She is the one who is going to have to pay for it now. I'll have to deal with the consequences later."

"What do you mean, she's here? How do you know? You told me nobody was going to be home. I can't believe this is happening. Don't tell me you are going to..." He paused to catch his breath and yelled at the top of his lungs, "I can't believe I let you drag me into this mess!"

Oh my God, he knows me! I thought. *How could that be? I don't recognize his voice at all.*

"Didn't I tell you to keep your fucking mouth shut? I can't hear anything with you squawking like that. Honestly, I didn't know she was going to be here, but it doesn't change anything, she has to be silenced too."

They kept on arguing. I thought they would get into an all-out brawl at some point, but the guy who had been waiting at the door backed down. He turned and went back to the doorway.

Oh my God… what did they do? Why do they have to silence me?

"That's right... now get the hell out of here and wait downstairs if you can't handle it! I'll take care of this one all by myself."

His friend left the room and the crazy one turned and walked over to my bed. He just stood there for a moment staring at it. I watched in fear, as he slowly reached out for my pillow and put it up to his face. He took a deep breath.

"I can smell you, baby girl, and you smell delicious. I know you are in here, somewhere."

I saw him put one hand down to his crotch and start rubbing and squeezing it.

"I can play this game, you know; it's very arousing. Come out… come out… wherever you are."

He sat on my bed and a deranged smile came over his face. He bent forward and lifted the blankets to see if I was hiding underneath it. To his disappointment, there was nothing under there but a few dust bunnies and an old pair of slippers. He groaned and got up.

I watched him as he stood and turned around, hand still groping himself, and then he scanned the room. Then the inevitable happened. He saw the closet door. I saw a creepy smile slowly come over his face again. He was looking right at me. He knew I was here, like as if the door had disappeared and he could see me, curled up on my knees, looking through the little crack in it.

He started to move forward, getting closer and closer to where I was hiding. The fear was building up inside of me again. I knew, right then and there, that I had no chance in hell of getting out of this alive. He was going to kill me, among other things. I knew he was; 'no witnesses' he had said. There was no doubt in my mind. He reached for the door handle, and I watched in disbelief as it started to turn.

Suddenly, the room lit up with those flashing red lights again and those damned sirens. They were really loud, but I welcomed the sound. Help was on the way. I watched as he looked around him. He didn't seem worried. He started to laugh hysterically.

"Oh no you don't!" he yelled.

He threw his arms in the air, and the lights and sirens faded out. I watched in horror as he again took hold of the handle. I couldn't hold it in any longer. I started screaming at the top of my lungs.

Chapter 3

I awoke suddenly and felt like I had jumped out of my skin. I was huddled in the upper corner of my bed against the wall and wrapped in my blankets that were dripping with sweat. My teeth were chattering, and I could feel the tears streaming down my face.

"Please stop this!" I cried in desperation. "Please just stop! I can't handle this anymore. I really can't."

My hands shook uncontrollably as I reached out to turn on my bedside lamp. I looked around wildly, but everything was a blur, so I grabbed a tissue and wiped the tears from my eyes. It was comforting to see that I was safe and in my own bedroom. I stayed put for a few minutes and tried to calm down. I felt like a little child, afraid to get out of bed for fear that there might be a monster hiding underneath it. I got up slowly, and then moved my feet swiftly away from the edge of the bed. I knew there was nothing under there, but hey… sometimes your imagination is stronger than your common sense.

I made my way to the kitchen of my small apartment. With trembling hands, I filled the tea kettle and fixed myself a cup of calming chamomile tea, as I did almost every night after I had my crazy dreams. I didn't know how much longer I could go on having these terrifying nightmares and staying up half the night afterward. They were almost totally consuming my life. My nerves were shot, and I was a total basket case.

I was extremely tired at work and my boss, Mrs. Blair, was very concerned about my fatigue and mood swings. I was lucky though, because she was very thoughtful and understanding. She often took me into her office on my breaks and tried to console me when she saw that I was having a bad day. She tried hard to encourage me to seek counseling. She kept telling me that I had to do something about the nightmares that I was having. She thought that I would have a nervous breakdown if I didn't take care of them soon.

Counseling? Nervous breakdown? Here we go again, I thought.

I spent half my life in counseling. It was devastating for me to think that I would have to go back for more. Two years had passed since I left the psychiatric wing of the New York State Women's Correctional Facility. All those years spent locked up for something I didn't even remember anything about. I just knew what they had told me, but that was a whole other story, one that I preferred to not even think about.

At that moment my problem was those crazy nightmares that I kept having. They had started about three weeks ago. Before that, everything in my new life seemed to be going just fine. I was given my freedom, I had a new life, and I had a job. Well, it wasn't great, I was only a dishwasher, but I liked it very much. I had met a lot of interesting people.

One of those very interesting people was my best friend and neighbor, Carla White. I called her Whitey, which was very amusing because she was African American. She called me Looney Tunes when we were joking around. I didn't mind because I knew that she was only kidding. To me, she was the nicest person in the whole world... an angel, if there was such a thing. She kind of adopted me, I guess. She had recently broken up with her boyfriend when I met her, and I think that she wasn't used to being alone, lucky for me. The last time I had a nightmare, she came over to check on me to make sure that I was okay.

I was so deep in my thoughts that I almost didn't hear the tapping outside my door. I ran over and looked through the peephole. Sure enough, it was Carla.

As I opened the door, she smiled and said, "Hey Looney Tunes, we have to stop meeting like this. These midnight rendezvous, you know, people are going to start talking."

She always joked around to try to make me feel better, but it didn't work this time. I threw my arms around her and started to cry uncontrollably. She sat down with me and tried to console me. She was always very good at that. She was very calm, and soft-spoken, and sometimes she even sang to me. She had a wonderful voice, the voice of an angel.

"These dreams," I cried, "they are all too real! I don't know what to make of them! They are scaring the hell out of me!"

She got up, took me by the hand, and led me back to the kitchen. She sat me down in front of my cup of tea and went to the counter and fixed one for herself.

"I am very worried about you," she said. "You can't go on like this. I am not a psychiatrist, but I am a nurse, and I know that if this keeps up, you will end up right back where you came from."

I didn't like the sound of that at all, but she was right. I had to do something about these dreams soon, before they got the better of me. I did not want to end up back in that loony bin again. This was the only life I knew because I still didn't remember any of my life before I went there. I was happy in my new life and I wanted to keep it.

I loved my little apartment; it was small but cozy. It had one bedroom, a kitchen, a living room, and a bathroom. Compared to what I was used to in prison, it was a palace. I had it nicely decorated and painted in pretty pastels. I felt really at home here. It was in a nice quiet neighborhood in the suburbs. I liked my neighbors too, the ones I got to know a bit. They were very friendly and always had a smile and a hello when we crossed paths in the corridor. Even so, I never opened up to any of them. I didn't know anyone else in the area. I kind of kept to myself. Carla was the exception though.

She was a few years younger than me, but she acted like she was my mother. I loved her from the very first day I met her. There was something very special about her. I didn't have any parents, none that I could remember anyway, so it felt good to have someone who took an interest in me and who cared so much about me. I knew right away that she was someone that could be trusted. Someone I could share my deepest and darkest secrets with and not worry about pushing her away. Deep down inside I always thought of her as my guardian angel. Since the very first day I met her, she had always been there for me.

"What are friends for?" she would say.

It was more than that, though; she went above, and beyond being a friend. There was nothing that she wouldn't do for me. I remember our first encounter so vividly that it seems like it happened just yesterday. I met her at work, two years ago, when I was released from the psychiatric ward. I got a job doing dishes in St. Mary's Community Hospital. Carla was a nurse there. She had worked there for many years. I took a liking to her right away.

I was just like a scared child when I started working there. I had just finished doing my time and I had set out to start a new life for myself. The ward psychiatrist helped me get this job, and she also got me settled into my apartment. I met Carla the very first day I started work. She was having a really bad time. She worked in the pediatric ward. She walked into work that afternoon and found out that one of her patients had died unexpectedly and she wasn't taking it very well. Her heart was too big, and she cared too much about everyone. She was very upset. When she had a break, she came down to the kitchen to talk to Lou, the head chef.

He was a very friendly and understanding person. He was good friends with almost everyone at the hospital. He was also, one of those people that when you meet them for the first time, you knew that you would have a friend for life. He welcomed me with open arms that morning and showed me what my job required.

I watched her as she walked into the kitchen. She didn't see me; she was looking the other way. She called out Lou's name. I didn't say anything at first. I was kind of hoping that if she didn't see Lou, she would turn and walk away. She called his name again. Finally, I got the nerve to speak up, and I told her that he had already gone home for the day. She jumped; I guess I startled her. She turned to me with a very puzzled look on her face and asked me who I was. I told her that I was new and had just started that day. She introduced herself and then asked me what my name was.

Timidly I answered, "My name is Roberta Hansen, but most people call me Bobby."

"I am very pleased to meet you, Bobby," she said, and she gave me a big hug. I was a little taken aback, but when she told me what had happened to her patient, I returned one.

From that day forward, our friendship kept growing. We clicked right away. It was like we had known each other for years. She never judged me, not even after I told her that I had done time, and she never pried into my past. She loved me for the person I was. That was what I always admired about her. She very rarely passed judgment about anyone. She accepted everyone for who they were, not what they did in their past.

"Hey Looney Tunes… Looney Tunes... What planet are you on? Earth to Bobby..."

"Oh my God! I'm sorry. I don't know what planet I was on, but I'm really sorry. My mind just keeps on wandering off."

"What I was trying to tell you, Bobby, while you were way out in some other galaxy, is that I have been thinking a lot about you lately, and all the nightmares that you have been having. I have a friend that I would like you to meet. Now before you say no, just listen; hear me out, okay? I have invited this friend over for dinner, and I want you to come too. This way, you can see for yourself what a nice guy he is. No expectations, and then you can decide what you want to do next."

"I don't get it… before I say no? What do you mean, it will be up to me what I do next? You aren't telling me everything, are you? Okay, is there a catch here?" I asked suspiciously. "What is he, a shrink? You wouldn't be trying to set me up or something, would you, Carla? Please tell me that he is not a psychiatrist."

"Set you up?" she said abruptly. "I'm just trying to help you out. He is a good friend of mine, and I told him a little about what has been happening to you. He doesn't want to treat you. He is just curious. Just a little friendly conversation, that's all he wants.

Personally, I think it would be good for you to get another person's perspective on this whole mess. Just give him a chance. Meet him, and then you can decide if you like him or not and can trust him enough to confide in him."

"He will lock me up!" I cried, feeling my anxiety rise. "He will say that I am crazy, and he will send me back to that loony bin. What are you trying to do to me? Do you have any idea what it is like to be locked up?"

"I am doing my damnedest to try to help. I don't know what else I can do for you. This is way out of my field of expertise."

"God damn it, Carla, I don't want to go back. I won't survive if I do."

"You know what? I'm sorry, but you are crazy. Do you really think that I would let something like that happen to you?" she said angrily, as she turned and put her cup in the sink and headed for the door.

"I care too much about you to just sit back and watch you suffer this way."

She stopped in the doorway, turned, and looked back at me.

"Get a hold of yourself, Bobby," she said, "his name is Tyler Murphy, and we are having dinner tomorrow night at six, with or without you. I really hope that you will have come to your senses by then. It won't hurt you, you know; you might even like him. Give it some serious thought, okay? Now try to get some sleep."

Chapter 4

Oh my God! I thought. *This is not going to be easy. It's time to take a break.* I closed my eyes and took a deep breath. I had embarked on this sailing journey as a way of dealing with my past and trying to fill in the still missing gaps. Dredging up those memories was a frightening and painful process. They seemed to draw me right back in as if they were still happening.

I opened my eyes again and tried to relax. I thought about Carla, and a smile came across my face. Carla was a great friend and we had some wonderful years together. I really missed her company. A tear escaped and rolled down my cheek. *Here I go again.*

It was getting late to be focusing on my writing, so I shut down for the evening.

The night air temperature had dropped a few degrees. I was feeling chilled, so I put on an extra sweater. The sun was just starting to set on the horizon. What an extraordinary scene. I had to squint my eyes as I watched this big, bright orange ball make its descent. Like a beam of light, it reflected on the water, right up to where I was standing. Bowsprit pointing directly into the target in front of me. It really looked like I was going to sail off into the sunset. I liked the sound of that.

I turned and the whole deck and sails were bright orange from the sun reflecting off them. I had to close my eyes for a second; it was so intense. I'm sure another ship could have spotted me ten nautical miles away; it was that bright. The sun slowly faded, and the sails were barely visible now, with just the sound of them gently swaying in the wind. Oh... my magnificent sailboat, she was so beautiful. I bought her about six months ago, after my whole crazy life unraveled. It was my rebirth, the start of a new life for me. I have been sailing ever since and enjoying every moment of my renewed freedom.

I made my way to the galley and prepared some dinner. After that I went back up on deck and put on one of my favorite Angel Forrest CDs, nothing like some beautiful blues to help me unwind after a hard day of writing. The moon was not quite full, but very bright. It was a clear night and there didn't seem to be a cloud in the sky. It was completely covered with stars. They seemed so close that I could almost reach out and touch them.

Chapter 5

I really loved lying in a nice hot bubble bath after a hard day's work. It seemed to take the edge off. Of course, staying up half the night didn't help matters. I was so upset about my fight with Carla that I couldn't get back to sleep. Those sleepless nights had a way of catching up with me. At work today, Carla didn't even come down to the kitchen to see me. I guess she wanted to give me my space and let me decide on my own about the supper tonight, without any influence from her.

The warmth of the hot water and the softness of the bubbles were just what I needed to help me relax. They made me feel like I was floating around on a cloud in heaven. My eyes were closed, and I was so relaxed and calm that it felt like I wasn't even there. I went with the flow and let myself be carried away.

I imagined that I was flying around gracefully, through the atmosphere, without a care in the world. An angel, flying through the heavens. I opened my eyes. There were beautiful white doves flying alongside of me and a colorful rainbow on the horizon. The majestic mountains in the distance reached up into the heavenly skies. I had never seen a more beautiful sight in all my life. The rays of sunlight streamed in all directions. I could feel the warmth of them on my skin.

I closed my eyes for a moment, inhaled deeply, and then sighed as I exhaled. I was so relaxed and in a meditative state. I waited a few seconds, then again, I inhaled, but something was different this time, like the air was changing. I quickly exhaled and then opened my eyes again and looked around me. The air temperature was starting to drop. I crossed my arms in front of me to stay warm. A chill ran up and then back down my spine. I could see something dark in the distance that looked like it was coming this way, and very fast. I started to get nervous. Suddenly there was a loud crack of thunder. It sounded like a gunshot.

The graceful white doves that were following along turned into large black crows that started squawking loudly and swirling all around me. Those dark gray clouds rolled in at a tremendous speed and covered the beautiful blue sky. The rainbow disappeared into blackness. Lightning streaked across the sky in all directions, and then the rain started coming down, slowly at first, but then it became cold and fierce. It felt like bullets piercing through my skin. The pain was unbearable. I cried... I didn't know what to make of all of this. My heavenly place had been transformed into what looked like a scene from hell, right before my eyes.

Another loud crack of thunder.

Somehow, I came to my senses. I remembered that I was just imagining this. I was still safe and sound in my bathtub at home. All I had to do was open my eyes and I would be right back in my warm bath. I tried, but something was holding me back. I concentrated hard; I needed to open my eyes and get out of this place. I was relieved when my eyelids started to separate, but I quickly closed them again, because when I looked down, the water was scarlet red.

This was not my tub. This was crazy. It was not possible. It couldn't be happening. I closed my eyes again, hoping that this would all go away as fast as it came, but when I opened them again, nothing had changed. I started screaming at the top of my lungs: "Get me out of here... Get me out!"

I fought like hell to get out of the tub, but I just kept slipping and sliding in the thick, red, cold blood that I was lying in. It kept pulling me down and there was nothing I could do to keep my head from going under. I was almost drowning in it. I kept choking and splashing around and there seemed to be no way out. I was gagging from the iron taste in my mouth. My stomach was turning, and I was sure I was going to throw up.

I got hold of the edge of the tub, but my fingers were too slimy to hang on. I tried closing my eyes again, hoping and praying for this nightmare or whatever it was, to be over. Suddenly, to add to my shock, something grabbed hold of me and wouldn't let go no matter how hard I tried to escape. I opened my eyes and I couldn't see what it was because of the darkness. I was so scared that I just kept on thrashing around in my bath full of blood.

I was fighting a losing battle though; my body was aching, and I was overcome by exhaustion. I didn't think I could go on any longer. I closed my eyes again and just gave up. I didn't want to, but I didn't have a drop of energy left inside of me. I let myself go.

Faintly, I could hear a voice in the distance. It scared me. It kept getting closer and closer. I got my second wind and started thrashing and screaming again.

"Leave me alone... Let me out of here... Please let go of me!"

"Bobby... Bobby... It's me, Bobby... It's okay; I've got you... Stop fighting me... You're okay now... You were only dreaming… Open your eyes and you will see... Bobby, open your eyes… Now!"

I opened my eyes and saw poor Carla holding onto me with all her strength to try to keep me from drowning myself. There was water and bubbles everywhere: no darkness, no blood, just water.

"My God, Carla," I said as I gasped for air. "You… you won't believe what just happened to me. I was la... laying in the nice warm bubble bath and all, of a sudden, it got co… cold and I wanted to get out and it turned into blood and it was dragging me under and it wouldn't let me g… go and it was terrible and I was all red and I was screaming and I couldn't get out of that damned b... bathtub, I just couldn't, and here you are and I am still in the bathtub, only this time it has bubbles and before it was all bloody… Oh so bloody, oh please get me out of here… Oh God, please get me out… Please get…"

"It's okay… I've got you… Calm down…"

Carla lifted me out of the tub. I could hardly help her out at all, I was so weak. She laid me gently on the floor, went to the linen closet, grabbed a big towel, and then wrapped it around me. She held me in her arms and tried to comfort me. I was trembling so much that my teeth were chattering. I tried to speak but I couldn't say another word. I just stayed there in her arms for a while and didn't move. It took a long time for me to calm myself and when I finally did, I looked into Carla's eyes and started to cry.

"My dear Carla," I pleaded. "I am really sorry about last night." She looked at me, puzzled. "You know, the dinner invitation that went south. Please help me, Carla! That was too damned real, and it needs to stop! I can't go on like this! I can't take it anymore! I am going crazy… No, not really… I'm already there! Please make it stop, Carla. Please make it go away!"

"Shh," was all she said, then she took me by the arm and led me down the hallway to my bedroom. She started to sing, as she had done many times before when I needed consoling. The sound of her voice always made me feel safe. She sat me down on my bed.

She looked through my closet and found something nice for me to wear. I didn't go out much, so I wasn't what you would call a very fashionable person. She pulled out my lacy maroon blouse and a pair of black pants. It wasn't hard to choose. That was about all I owned that looked half-decent. Carla had bought the blouse for me last Christmas. She had very good taste in clothing and she loved to shop, contrary to me.

I watched her as she carefully took the clothes off their hangers and laid them on the bed. She looked so beautiful. She had on a long dress with a gorgeous floral pattern and a lace collar. Her thick black hair was all pulled back tightly into braids. She had makeup on that accentuated her dark eyes. Her large hoop earrings dangled almost to her shoulders, and around her neck, she wore the large crucifix that her mother gave her. Carla loved to wear lots of jewelry.

She helped me dress and she never said a word to me; she just kept on singing. I was like a helpless child and I didn't like feeling that way. Yet somehow Carla didn't make me feel vulnerable while she helped me. She took my hairbrush off the dresser and started to untangle and dried my hair. Then she opened my makeup pouch that she had bought me and proceeded to work on my face. I didn't say a word; I just sat there and listened to her calming melody.

When she finished, she looked at me and smiled.

"You know, Bobby, you are a very pretty woman when you fix yourself up."

She brought my little mirror over and held it in front of me. I looked at my reflection and smiled. She was a very good artist and had painted me up beautifully. My long brown hair flowed down past my shoulders with a slight wave. The makeup brought softness to my face and highlighted my deep green eyes. The lipstick was natural looking but added a soft glow.

"You should take better care of yourself," she said, "You have your freedom now, and you should be going out and meeting guys and having the time of your life. You need to get your head together and start living the life that you deserve. You need to stop reliving your past. Take care of it now, tonight. Come over and meet Tyler. You'll see he is a really great guy."

"I was planning on it, Carla, I really was. I was going to take my bath, get dressed, and go over. Oh my God, my bath! Damn it, Carla, I wish you would have seen it. I'm sure it wasn't a dream. It just seemed too real."

Carla tried to reassure me that it wasn't real, and that if it wasn't a dream, then I had a very wild imagination.

"I'm sorry, but it was not my imagination," I blurted out before she could say another word. "Nobody in their right mind could imagine something so gory and frightening."

"My point exactly!" she said in retaliation.

"Oh shit!" she yelled as she looked over at my alarm clock to see what time it was. "Tyler will be here soon, and I still have so much to do. Hurry up, let's go; you have to help me now."

She grabbed me by the arm and practically dragged me next door to her place.

I was so happy when she decided to move into the apartment next to mine. My old neighbors moved out about six months ago. Carla was not happy anymore where she was living and decided to take their apartment.

She used to live a couple of blocks from here. She was still living in the apartment that she had shared with her boyfriend. It was larger than this one and after he left, she said it sometimes felt a little empty to her. I think she was trying to hang on to the good memories by staying there, the memories from way back when, before he changed. I guess she really loved the guy.

She told me that they had a wonderful relationship at the beginning, but he got involved with a bad crowd and started partying and drinking all the time. She said that when he was sober, he was a wonderful, loving partner, but when he was drunk, he became very abusive. It was a Jekyll and Hyde scenario. As the drinking became more frequent, the abuse became more violent. He would go out and cheat on her and then come home and beat on her.

One day she went home to an empty apartment. All his things were gone and some of hers too. He didn't leave her much. She was devastated. He must have found someone else to beat on; lucky for her. Leaving was probably the best thing he ever did for her. She loved the man he used to be, but he was not that man anymore. She was heartbroken for quite some time, but I guess I helped her through it. I think that is how we became so close. Now we are even closer since she lives next door.

She had her place so clean that you would have thought she was expecting royalty. I didn't know what she was so nervous about because everything seemed to be under control. The table was all set up, the lasagna was in the oven, and all that was left to do was prepare the salad and cut the crusty loaf. Tyler wasn't going to be there for another forty-five minutes, but even so, Carla put me right to work and we were done in no time at all.

"There we go, Whitey," I said. "All done and time to spare. I don't know what you were so worried about."

She thanked me and gave me a big hug. She opened a bottle of wine and poured us each a glass. I was glad about that because I had the feeling that I was going to need a little something to take the edge off. I was starting to get a little antsy about meeting Tyler. What was I going to tell him? Where was I going to start? My life was such a jumbled mess that I didn't even know who I was, so how was I supposed to tell someone else? I started to pace the floor. Carla could see that I was getting a little flustered and told me to relax and have a seat. She said that Tyler was not going to be there for another ten minutes or so. In other words, "Get a grip."

I sat there on the barstool at her kitchen counter, nervously watching the clock. Deep down, I was almost hoping that he wouldn't show up, but I knew that even if he didn't, I would have to talk to him eventually. It was best to get it over with tonight, especially since Carla went to all this trouble to make this a very special evening.

The doorbell rang, and I practically jumped out of my skin.

"Well, what do you know? He's right on time. I had a feeling he would be. Bobby, would you get the door for me please?"

I was so nervous that my body was frozen like a statue and I just sat there with my mouth open and stared at the front entrance.

"Well, get the door, silly," Carla said impatiently. "Don't keep the man waiting."

"Get your own damn door, Carla. It's your house, and besides, I don't know the guy. I'm sure that even he would prefer to see a familiar face when the door opens."

"Please, Bobby, can you get the door for me? Come on," she said as she pointed to the entrance and motioned me to get out of the kitchen. "I just want to check on everything, one more time. I want this meal to be perfect."

I slowly walked into the living room and the bell sounded again. "Just a minute," I said, and I picked up the pace.

I reached for the handle, turned it, and slowly opened the door. I was so nervous that I just stood there and stared at him. He was really quite handsome. He was tall, with short, clean-cut, dark hair, big, beautiful green eyes, and a smile that went from ear to ear. He didn't look much like a doctor to me; I don't know why. I guess it was because he looked so young and casual and down-to-earth and… did I mention good looking?

He wore jeans and cowboy boots with a dress shirt and a sport jacket. He looked very nice. It suited him well. Suddenly our eyes met, and I realized that he was also standing there staring at me and not saying a word. His eyes were gazing straight into mine, almost as if he were looking right through me and into my very soul. He had a smile on his face and didn't even blink, like maybe he was stuck in a daydream. I had to turn away because I started to feel so vulnerable.

"You don't have to leave him in the doorway, Bobby. You can ask him to come in," Carla yelled from the kitchen.

"I'm so sorry," I said shyly. "I'm just a little nervous. My name is Roberta, but my friends call me Bobby. You're Tyler, I presume?"

"Tyler Murphy, at your service," he said, "and you don't have to be nervous with me. I don't bite; well, at least not too often, though I am pretty hungry."

He had good looks and a sense of humor too; what more could you ask for? He seemed like a perfect gentleman. He even brought flowers and wine. He handed me the beautiful bouquet and took me by the arm, and we headed into the kitchen.

"You ladies look stunning," he said as Carla turned and came over to greet him. "If I would have known this was going to be a formal dinner, I would have dressed up."

Carla smiled. "Don't be silly; you look great. You always did."

She gave him a big hug and thanked him for the wine, then she found a vase for me to put the flowers in. While I arranged the bouquet, they went into the living room and talked about old times. I couldn't take my eyes off him. There was just something about him: the way he laughed, the way he talked, the way he looked at me, I don't know. I couldn't quite put my finger on it.

My thoughts were interrupted by the sound of the oven timer. Carla came back to the kitchen and started to prepare our plates. I turned the oven to broil and put in the slices of crusty bread that I had already covered with garlic butter. By the time I served each of us a bowl of salad and put them on the table, the bread was ready. The slices of garlic bread were a perfect golden brown. I took them out of the oven and put them in a basket. I put a napkin over them to keep them warm and brought them to the table. Carla had already brought out the plates. We looked around at each other and then we all dug into what turned out to be a wonderful meal.

Carla and Tyler started right back up where they had left off. It was nice to listen to them reminisce about old times, and all the fun they had together as kids. Sometimes I wished that I could just think back and remember some of the good things that happened in my past. I'm sure there were some. Who knows?

"Well, Whitey," I cut in, "you've outdone yourself again. It tastes like more; you don't mind if I help myself, do you? You are an amazing cook. Every time you invite me to dinner, it's always the best meal that I have ever had. You should have been a chef."

"Yeah right, Looney Tunes," she said sarcastically. "You ate hospital food for twenty years. I work in a hospital and I know exactly what that is like. You're just too easy to please. Go ahead and help yourself to some seconds, and you can get some more for Tyler too, if he wants. If I remember right, Tyler had a bottomless pit when he was young; I don't know about now. By the way, Bobby, I could strangle you. You look like a beanpole and you're a bottomless pit too. I don't know where you put it all. You must have two hollow legs or something. I just have to smell the food and I gain five pounds."

Tyler laughed as he brought his plate into the kitchen so I could serve him seconds. I guess he did have a good appetite too. All the while I was serving him, he never took his eyes off me. I tried not to look but I was so drawn to him. It felt very strange.

"Do you think it is possible that we both have hollow legs?" he asked with a wink.

"Maybe… but she always says that because she's just jealous that she can't have seconds," I replied and started to giggle.

I finished serving our plates and he escorted me back to the table. Carla gave us both a funny look. I guess she noticed that there was something going on between us.

Finally, Carla and I started joking around as we usually did, and we all started to feel a little more at ease. Tyler jumped right in too. He was quite the character.

"Why are you looking at us that way, Whitey?" I said with a smirk.

I picked up my fork, cut into the lasagna, and swirled it around in front of her.

"Do you want some more... just a little bit?"

"Ha... ha... ha... real cute, Looney Tunes; have some more wine."

Then she snorted like a pig and we all laughed.

"I can't believe you did that, Carla," he said. "I remember you doing that when we were kids."

"Seriously?" I said.

"Yup, you know what? I don't recall ever seeing her eat."

Carla crumpled up her napkin and threw it at him and we all cracked up.

I watched as he laughed and carried on and I started to feel quite comfortable with him. I still couldn't take my eyes off him. He was quite the character.

Carla was having a really good time too. I think the wine was starting to kick in. She was a really cheap drunk. Two glasses of wine and she was almost done for. I only had one glass because I was not much of a drinker. I didn't want to get in the habit. Two or three drinks was usually my limit, but most of the time, I stopped at one. It would have been too easy to drown my sorrows in a bottle. I didn't want to create more problems for myself. Anyway, tonight I wanted to stay in control. I wanted to keep my guard up just to be on the safe side.

"Seriously, Carla," I said, "this is amazing. I am so full you might have to call a tow truck to get me home."

We all laughed.

"It was nothing special, Bobby; like I said before, all those years of hospital food."

Tyler looked at me and said, "Twenty years? That's a long time. You must be glad to be out of there. I can't imagine what it must have been like. I hope they weren't too rough on you on the inside. Do you remember anything at all about your life before that, where you lived, or your family, or friends?"

The question took me by surprise, but it was okay; I could handle that one.

"Nothing," I said. "Absolutely nothing. It is like I never existed. I only know what they told me. Is it true? I don't know. I guess it must have been, or they wouldn't have put me away for so long."

Tyler looked at me, very puzzled, and asked, "Do you mind very much, Bobby, telling me what you did? I mean what they say you did, that landed you in a prison cell?"

I knew that our conversation would head that way, the question was inevitable, but knowing that didn't make it any easier. I took a deep breath, sat back in my chair, and started to feel a big lump forming in the back of my throat.

I watched him as he sat there and waited patiently for me to put my thoughts into words. I still had trouble saying it aloud. That was because I still, deep down inside of me, couldn't believe that I had done those things that everyone said I had. It was too horrifying to be true. I didn't understand what could have driven me to do something so terrible. Something as cruel, senseless, and unimaginable as that just sent shivers down my spine.

What kind of a monster was I, and was I still capable of doing such a thing again? The thought scared the hell out of me. My eyes started to fill with tears. I did not want to cry, not at my first meeting with Tyler. I really did feel like I could eventually open up to him, but it wasn't going to happen tonight.

"I'm so sorry, Bobby; I shouldn't have asked. We should get to know each other before you trust me enough to confide in me."

Carla could also see the emotion building up inside of me and said, "Hey, Looney Tunes, that's enough about you. Let's get back to the business at hand."

I looked at her, puzzled. "Business at hand?"

"Yeah! Guess what I made for dessert? It's your favorite."

Carla knew exactly what to say and exactly when to say it. She knew that our conversation was going nowhere fast. It was time to change the topic. Tyler also looked relieved when Carla cut in. I don't think that he had a clue how emotional I would get when faced with a question that would reveal how much of a monster I was. I had kept it a secret from Carla for the longest time before I felt comfortable enough to talk about it with her. Obviously, she didn't tell him anything, or maybe he was trying to see how much I would open up.

"You know, Bobby," Tyler said finally, "you are one lucky lady. You are best friends with the nicest person in the world. I'm jealous. I bring the wine, I bring the flowers, and what do we have? Your favorite meal and your favorite dessert! Oh… what the hell! My curiosity is killing me. I love sugar. What's for dessert?"

Carla and I looked at each other and burst out laughing. What a nut! He sat there, looking like a little kid waiting to open a big present or something.

"Yummy, yummy, cherry cheesecake," Carla said to Tyler teasingly.

"Mmm… Mmm..."

Tyler smiled at Carla and said, "Well? What are you waiting for? Don't just sit there! Go and get it."

We laughed at him again. He was worse than a child. Carla got up and went to get the dessert. His eyes were as big as quarters when she came back with the plates. It was delicious as usual. It was true, though; I really was lucky. Carla was a wonderful friend and she did spoil me a lot.

We cleaned up and went into the living room. Carla was humming to herself. Tyler sat down and asked me to join him.

"Hey Carla, I'm sure that you must have some nice jazz music? A friend of mine really loved her jazz. We used to listen to it all the time."

He turned and looked at me.

"What do you think, Bobby?"

"I love jazz, and blues too; they're my favorites. Sounds good to me."

Carla slow-danced all by herself and sang with the music. She looked like she was in her own world. She was very relaxed and, oops, very tipsy. I got up and grabbed hold of her as she started to stagger a bit.

"I'm good… I'm okay," she said, "just getting into the music."

She took my hand and spun me around; I almost fell over myself.

"Come on, Bobby, you can do better than that! Show me what you've got."

She grabbed me by the hips and swayed them from side to side, very sexy-like. Tyler laughed along. He had a beautiful smile on his face.

"Oh my God, Carla, what in the hell."

I freed myself and went back and sat down with him. Carla kept dancing.

Her two glasses of wine went straight to her head. You would have thought that she drank a whole bottle, the way she was carrying on. Tyler and I couldn't get over how crazy she was acting. She made us laugh till we cried. I hadn't had that much fun in a long time.

All we did for the rest of the evening was joke and fool around.

Tyler didn't ask me any more questions, and that was fine with me. He was right, though, it was going to be easier for me to talk to him about everything once I got to know him a little better.

I really didn't want to call it a night, but it was getting late and I hadn't gotten much sleep the night before, so I was starting to feel very tired. I would have liked for the evening to go on forever, but I was dead on my feet. I told Carla, who was still staggering around, that I had really enjoyed myself, but I was exhausted and was going to head back to my apartment.

Tyler looked at me with his big, sad, puppy eyes and said, "So soon?"

"I know," I said sadly as I got up, "but I didn't get much sleep last night and I am really beat, all of a sudden. I a great time, though, and I hope to see you again soon."

He didn't argue; he just got up from his chair and walked toward me. I didn't know what to expect. When he got close to me, he reached out and gave me a friendly hug. He held me close for a moment and told me that he had a wonderful time tonight, and that he would really like to see me again. He felt so warm and I felt so secure in his arms. As he retreated from our embrace, he moved the hair away from my neck, revealing an old scar. I pulled back, embarrassed, and he went blank. His eyes were fixed on me, but it was like he wasn't there.

"Are you guys okay?" Carla asked.

He immediately turned to her and responded, "I'm sorry; I guess I'm tired too."

He apologized for upsetting me at the dinner table, then he walked me back to my apartment. He gave me a peck on the cheek and said goodnight. He was a perfect gentleman. I said goodbye and closed the door behind me.

My head was in the clouds. I had never felt this way before. I had butterflies in my stomach and I just couldn't stop smiling. I felt very happy. Was it possible that something good was going to happen, in my nightmare of a life?

I was getting ready for bed, when I heard a knock at the door. I was in my pajamas and was a little nervous about opening it. At first, I thought it might be Tyler. I didn't want him to see me like this. Then it dawned on me that it was probably Carla. I guess that she wanted to check on me before she turned in.

"How was your evening?" she asked as I opened the door and stared at her curiously.

"Okay… okay…" she said, "I'll cut to the chase. What happened with you and Tyler? I saw how you two were looking at each other. I think he likes you. Did he kiss you? Oh… I'm sorry, I shouldn't ask… Well did he?"

"Oh my God, Whitey; you're nuts. You and your two glasses of wine are totally berserk. Well, to tell the truth, I had a blast. He seems like a really great guy. I think he likes me, too. He kissed me on the cheek; do you believe that? He really kissed me. I feel strange, like my feet are not touching the ground, and my stomach is all fluttery. I've never felt like this before, at least not that I know of."

We sat for a while and talked about our wonderful evening with Tyler. We both really enjoyed ourselves. Carla knew that I was tired, so she told me how happy she was that the evening turned out good for me, then she gave me a hug and told me to get some rest. I thanked her for a fantastic evening and said goodnight.

Chapter 6

I could feel the warmth of the sun on my face as I woke to the sound of the birds chirping outside my window. I opened my eyes and saw that in all the excitement last night, I must have forgotten to close my blinds.

I felt so lazy that I just lay there anyway, closed my eyes again, and listened to the sweet sounds of spring. I hadn't heard those sounds in a long time. Glorious music, sung by Mother Nature, brought a smile to my face.

I finally had a good night's sleep. I don't remember dreaming at all; I felt so relaxed. I hadn't felt like that in a while. I started to think about last night. To be honest, I was thinking about Tyler. Was he for real, or what? We had a great time together. I felt very comfortable with him. I was really hoping that he meant it when he said that he would like to see me again. I knew for sure that I really wanted to get together again with him.

After a little more daydreaming, I decided to get my lazy butt out of bed and get dressed. I felt so good, and I was anxious to go out and enjoy the beautiful sunshine. I went over to Carla's apartment to see what she was doing. I was sure that she would be awake by now, but I knocked very lightly on her door just in case she was still sleeping. The door swung open and there she was, all dressed and smiling from ear to ear.

"How is my little Looney Tunes today?" she said as I walked past her. "Must be good, because I think we finally both got a good night's sleep, thank you very much. Am I right?"

"You sure are," I replied. "Slept like a baby. I haven't felt this relaxed in months. Man, does it feel good. Hey Carla, it is such a gorgeous day that I thought it would be nice if we could go out to breakfast together like we used to, and then go out and enjoy a little sunshine. Would you like to join me? It's my way of thanking you for last night. That is, if your head is okay. You were a little tipsy, you know."

"Hey! I'm okay! I was just having lots of fun, all right? And yes, I would love to join you. We haven't done this in quite some time. I used to love our Sunday morning breakfasts together. Anyway, you owe me, big time. You two make a great couple."

She grabbed her purse and her keys and off we went. We walked down the street to Stella's, the little diner on the corner. We used to go there often until I started lying awake half my nights from the bad dreams that I was having and wanting to sleep in every chance I got.

I liked it at Stella's, because it was small and cozy, and the owners were very friendly. They were unusually busy this morning. It must have been the beautiful weather. We saw only one table available at the far end, so we hurried and sat down before someone else got to it. I was very hungry, so I ordered a big breakfast of blueberry pancakes, yummy. Carla only wanted toast and coffee.

She never ate very much. She was always worried about gaining weight. It was true, though. It didn't make sense. Carla always said that it wasn't fair. She ate like a bird and she gained weight, and skinny people like me ate like a pig and stayed thin. I guess maybe she was right about the hollow legs.

As we ate, we joked around and laughed about the wonderful evening we had with Tyler.

"You know what, Carla? You were so right about Tyler. He is a great guy. I don't know what it is about him. He felt like an old friend and I was so comfortable being with him. He's very friendly, he's good looking, he's funny, he's good looking, he's a perfect gentleman, and did I say that he's good looking?"

Carla and I both cracked up laughing.

"Cute… real cute. Well, I'm thrilled that you liked him. I knew you would."

"Seriously though," I said, "I felt a very strong connection to him, as if I've known him for a long time. Was it the way he looked at me, the way he smiled? Maybe it was the way he embraced me at the end of the evening. I really don't know what it was, but there was something, and it felt wonderful."

"I saw that connection, Bobby. He never took his eyes off you, and he had this look of pure joy on his face the whole time. I am very happy that you two hit it off."

"Me too, Carla. I haven't stopped thinking about him since."

Carla suddenly got a weird look on her face. Her eyes seemed to be looking at something above my head. She did not look happy.

"Hi Carla," said a voice from behind me. "How are you doing today? Aren't you going to introduce me to your friend?"

I looked over my shoulder to see who it was. I couldn't place the guy, but he looked vaguely familiar. He extended his hand, but I didn't respond. He didn't seem friendly, and Carla's reaction made me wary of him.

He was very tough looking. Rough around the edges, if you know what I mean. His hair was long, wavy, and uncombed. His skin was really tanned and leathery. He had a scar across his left cheek, a battle wound, I imagined. It looked like he hadn't shaved in a couple of days. He resembled someone who might have worked outdoors. Maybe in construction or something. His eyes were narrow and somehow threatening. He looked very strong, and when he reached out his hand to me, I noticed the large tattoo on his forearm of a snake wrapped around a sword.

I didn't like the way he looked at me. It gave me the willies. I turned back to Carla. I did not want to look at him anymore.

She looked at me, kind of rolled her eyes, and said, "Bobby, this is David… David, Bobby. Now if you will excuse us, we were having a private conversation and I don't recall inviting you into it."

"Well, excuse me," he said, then nothing. He just glared at us and then turned and went back to his booth.

I couldn't believe my ears. I had never heard Carla talk to anyone like that before. She was very cold toward him. That really piqued my curiosity. I waited for a few minutes to see if she would voluntarily tell me why she was so mean to him, but she didn't. It was obvious that she did not like the guy. This was not like her. Carla was nice to everyone.

"What the hell was that all about?" I said quietly so he wouldn't hear me.

"Never mind," she whispered. "I'll tell you later when he's not around."

Carla got pretty quiet after that. Her mood changed completely. She looked like she was getting uncomfortable being there. I hurried up and finished my breakfast so we could leave. I didn't bring up the subject again. He didn't take his eyes off us as we walked up to the cash and paid, and then left. I was very happy when we walked out onto the street and I didn't feel his eyes boring a hole into my back anymore.

It was such a beautiful day, so I tried to put him out of my mind. I asked Carla if she wanted to go for a walk in the park. She smiled and said that a walk would be nice. I guess a lot of people had the same idea, because the place was full. Some were walking, cycling, jogging, rollerblading, and skateboarding. Others were just sitting on park benches or lying on the grass relaxing and enjoying this unusually warm spring day. We decided to just walk around a bit.

There was a big beautiful fountain in the park. I used to go there often. It was very relaxing. There was something about the sound of the flowing water that would just carry me away to places where I had no cares or worries. Ever since I moved there, whenever I was feeling depressed or lonely, I found that taking a walk to the park was a big help. Of course, I always ended up sitting on the bench in front of the fountain with my eyes closed, listening to the trickling of the water. I couldn't get enough of it.

Sadly though, it was closed in the winter, so this was my first time back in the park this year.

As we walked down the jogging path, I turned and looked at Carla and asked, "Do you think that the fountain will be running yet?"

"How should I know? I haven't been in the park since last summer."

We couldn't see it from where we were because it was on the other side of the old historical building that the town had transformed into a museum. As we rounded the corner and walked toward the front of the building, I saw it in all its splendor. The water was splashing out around it. I was overcome with joy.

I was so happy that I started to run toward it. I yelled back at Carla to keep up. I think I was still on a high from the night before. When I reached the fountain, I didn't waste a moment; I didn't even wait for Carla to catch up. I just sat there on the bench in front of it, closed my eyes, and listened to the familiar sound that I loved so much. I could feel the warmth of the sun on my face and the fine mist from the splashing water. I could hear the sounds of the birds frolicking in the air above. It didn't take long before I was gone. I had forgotten how wonderful this felt.

Off I went on my little journey. It felt good to be back. Everything looked so familiar. Unchanged and unspoiled. I was so excited.

In my mind's eye I could see the enchanted forest with a river running through it. The current was quite strong and the water flowing through the rocks and branches made a wonderful relaxing sound. A tree lay across the river which made it possible to sit right in the middle of this magnificent water symphony. I remembered last fall just lying there for what seemed like hours in the center of my little paradise. For today, I guess I was just going to hover above the treetops and take in all its splendor.

The reflection of the sun filtering through the trees sparkled on the rippling water like jewels. Downriver I could see a family of beavers whittling away at their latest masterpieces. Busy as a beaver,

I guess that is where that expression came from. I was sure they wouldn't give up until they were done. Through the branches to the left of me I spotted a doe with her fawn making their way through the dense majestic pines. The rainbow trout basking in the sunlight at the shallow end of the river were also taking advantage of this beautiful spring day. Paradise, if there was such a thing. I was completely mesmerized by the sights and sounds that surrounded me. The overwhelming fragrance of trilliums…

"Bobby! Where are you? Yoo… hoo! Come back to Earth!" Carla said, as she stood there waving her hands in front of my face. "What am I going to do with you. You are always daydreaming."

"Oh man! I'm sorry! I did it again, didn't I? I need to stop wandering off into outer space like that. I'll try not to do it again, I promise; please forgive me."

I gave Carla a hug and she sat down next to me on the park bench right in front of this glorious fountain.

"This is my most favorite spot in the whole world," I said. "I came here last fall when you were gone on vacation." I looked at the water splashing for a while, closed my eyes, and then just sat there and listened and relaxed. "You know what, Carla? To tell the truth, I wasn't really in outer space before. I didn't think to tell you this last fall because by the time you came back, the fountain was closed, and I didn't really think about it again.

"Today, when we were heading toward the park, it all came back to me. Just now, when I sat in front of the fountain and closed my eyes, it all happened again. The same as it happened last year. I don't know what it is, but there is just something about this fountain. It seems to magically carry me away to a very special place in the woods where I am at peace with myself and I don't have a worry in the world. I feel right at home there, surrounded by earth's natural beauty."

"That is really strange," Carla said. "Do you always go to the same place?"

"As a matter of fact, now that you mention it, I think I do. Is that weird or what? I guess I didn't question it last year because I only went there a few times, but now that I think about it, it doesn't seem like it could be a coincidence that I daydream the same scenario over and over again. Now, with all the crazy things going on in my life these days, like those recurring nightmares and everything, I'm starting to wonder. This is like a recurring daydream, but the one difference is that it is fabulous. I enjoy being there so much that I never want to leave."

Carla looked at me with great enthusiasm and said, "You know what, Bobby? This could mean something. This could be a piece of the puzzle. It might be a part of your life that has been unknown to you for all these years. The sound of the water splashing in the fountain could be triggering a memory. This is great."

"You might think so, but I don't," I said, my emotions rising. "This place I wander off to seems like heaven. When I am there, I don't even want to come back. I don't believe that I have ever been in a place like that before. How would someone end up in jail for twenty years if they had such a peaceful life?" Tears began to roll down my face.

"Shh..." Carla said abruptly, cutting in. "Wipe away those tears and please stop being so negative. Even if your life was hell, there had to be a few good memories in there somewhere. It couldn't have been all bad; I am sure of that. Oh shit! Look who's coming our way. Let's get out of here!"

She grabbed me by the arm and we quickly started walking away from the fountain. I didn't question her. I just went along with it. I didn't even know who she was talking about and I never had a chance to look back because we turned a corner and she started to run. We didn't slow down till we were out of the park. I tried to look back a few times to see if someone was following us, but nothing...

Carla finally turned around and said, "I think the coast is clear... let's go home."

I didn't say a word; I just followed her lead. She was walking again but at a quick pace, looking back every few seconds just to be on the safe side. She kept me hanging in mid-air and didn't say anything till she was darn good and ready. We were almost at our building when she finally spoke up.

"I'm sorry, Bobby, about keeping you in such suspense. It is really not a big deal," she said as we started climbing the stairs to our apartments.

"It's David. He was the one I saw coming through the park. I am so afraid that he will find out where we live. There is just something about that guy that doesn't feel right. He is new at work and he's a kiss-ass, if you know what I mean. He works in maintenance. He tries to suck up to the bosses and I don't like that."

I opened the door to my apartment, and we went in.

She continued, "The other day I saw him sneaking around in my locker and when I confronted him, he said that it was open, and he was trying to find out whose it was, so he could tell them. I know damn well that I did not leave my locker unlocked; I never do. I don't know how he got inside it, but somehow he did."

"What did you do then?" I asked.

"Well, I went to the supervisor and told her, and she told me that I should be more careful and make sure that my locker is secured. She also told me that he was a very good worker and that she did not think that he had any interest in snooping around in anyone's locker."

"Oh, you know, I thought he looked familiar," I said. "I was sure I had seen him before, but I just couldn't figure out where. I think I saw him talking to Lou the other day in the hallway at work. It's the hair that threw me off. He must tie his hair back when he's at work."

"Yeah, I see him talking to Lou every once in a while. I am surprised that you haven't met him yet. He was asking me questions about you the other day. I don't know why. Maybe he is interested in you. I didn't tell him anything; I just told him to leave us both alone. I guess he didn't get the picture because he still seems to be hanging around. I seem to see him everywhere I go these days. Don't you ever get friendly with him, Bobby. I don't think he can be trusted. I usually have good intuition about people. He rubs me wrong for some reason."

I told Carla not to worry, that I wasn't planning on it, especially after what she just told me about him. Carla was always a good judge of character, and if she thought he was bad news then I was taking her word for it. I didn't need any more problems.

I fixed us both something cold to drink and we sat on my balcony to take in a little more of that beautiful sunshine. At least here we could have a private conversation without any interruptions. We started talking about the water fountain again. What was it about that fountain that made me feel so safe and comfortable?

"You know what, Bobby? I think that the fountain or even just the sound of the flowing water is the key to your past. It is just a small part of the puzzle that has been missing for all these years and is trying to come back to you. I'm not an expert, but I really do think it is possible."

"Oh God, Carla, I'm so confused. I'm not sure that I really want to know about my life back then. Right now, I don't believe that it is possible that I could have done the things that they said I did. If I ever start remembering everything and find out that I am the monster that I was accused of being, then I don't know what I would do."

"Monster? You are not a monster! I would stake my life on it. I don't ever want to hear you say that again! Unless you have been possessed by someone else and the old Bobby doesn't exist anymore, which is ludicrous, then I think that they must have made a big mistake. They weren't there to see those things happen and I think it was just speculation on their part."

"Please, Carla, can we just get off this topic now? I really don't want to talk about it anymore. I really would like to enjoy the rest of this gorgeous day, so what do you say we get onto something a little more cheerful."

Carla waited for a few seconds. I could see the wheels turning, and then she looked up at me, smiled, and said, "What about Tyler, again? How about we continue our conversation from where we left off earlier, before we were so rudely interrupted? I guess I've got your undivided attention now, because there's that smile from this morning. You know, you are so beautiful when you smile. I love to see you like this."

"Oh Carla, do you know that last night was one of the best evenings that I have had in a long time? I am so sorry about all the trouble I caused between us the night before. I was worried for nothing. Tyler seems like a really nice guy. He was lots of fun. Oh, and you were lots of fun too: you and your two glasses of wine. I can't thank you enough."

"Could you not remind me of that!" she said, blushing. "I must have been tired or something, because that wine really got to me fast for some reason. Anyway, you know what the nice thing about Tyler is? He is a very good doctor and he can help you sort your life out. But you know what the best thing about him is? He is single, and I think, no, I know he took a liking to you. You are one lucky girl! He has never looked at me the way he looked at you last night. I think he always thought of me as more of a sister than anything else."

Now it was my turn to blush. I could feel the heat rising up to my face, and I knew that I must have been as red as a beet. I was very infatuated by Tyler, and Carla knew it too. She was very happy for me. We talked for a little while longer, then we said our goodbyes and she went to her apartment. I spent the rest of the day cleaning my apartment, listening to my favorite jazz, and daydreaming about Tyler. *Could it be possible that we could live happily ever after?* I had butterflies in my stomach just thinking about him.

Chapter 7

I had trouble getting to sleep that night. I tossed and I turned and my mind kept wandering. Of course, I was still thinking about Tyler. All these scenarios of what our next meeting would be like were going through my head. Then, when I was finally starting to doze off, I was awakened by the sound of someone knocking at the door. I didn't get up right away, because I thought maybe I was only dreaming.

A few minutes later, the knocking started again. I got out of my bed, threw on my housecoat, and quietly walked to the door. If there was someone out there, I didn't want them to hear me till I could see who it was. If it was someone I didn't know, then I could just back away from the door and pretend that there was nobody home. I didn't usually have people knocking on my door this time of night. Then again, I thought maybe it was Carla and there was something wrong.

I put my face against the door so I could see out through the peephole. I didn't take chances at night by opening the door to just anyone. I was not afraid to live alone but you never know. Bad things do happen sometimes. I couldn't make out who it was. All I could see was their shoulder. They were a little off to the side. I waited a bit. I was getting nervous. If it was Carla, she would have said something by now, or she would have stood in front of the peephole where I could see who it was. But she had her own key, so that didn't make sense either.

I still couldn't see anything, then suddenly the knocking began again. It scared me, and I jumped and made a sound. So much for pretending I wasn't there. Finally, I heard him speak, "Bobby, is that you?" It was Tyler. I remembered his voice from last night. I couldn't imagine what he was doing here at this late hour. I slowly opened the door and to my surprise, I saw him standing there dripping wet. He looked like a drowned rat. I guess it had started to rain outside after I went to bed.

I told him to come in and quietly closed the door behind him so as not to wake up the neighbors, if we hadn't done so already. I told him to hang up his jacket and I went to the linen closet to get him a big towel so he could dry himself off. I glanced at the clock as I went past the kitchen and saw that it was only midnight. For some reason, I thought it was a lot later than that. I handed him the towel and told him to come into the kitchen and I would fix him some coffee or tea to warm him up.

"What are you doing here at this time of night?" I said as I tried hard not to yawn in his face. I was really sleepy and still in a little bit of a daze.

"I am really sorry," he said. "I don't normally do things like this. I couldn't do anything at all today, because all that I could think about was you. I had a really wonderful time last night. Oh God, this is ridiculous. Please forgive me. I should not have come over this late. To tell the truth, I didn't even realize what time it was. I was visiting a friend who lives just a few blocks north of here. I could not bring myself to drive by without stopping in to say hi. I wasn't even thinking about the time. I should really leave now and let you get back to sleep."

"No, no, no, it's all right!" I said as I turned towards the counter to fix us each a cup of tea. "I don't have to work tomorrow so I don't need to get up early. To be honest with you, I thought about you all day too. It kind of scares me. I am used to keeping my heart closed up tight, with a lock and key.

"You know, I was furious with Carla when she set up our meeting. I don't know if she told you about this, but I got very upset with her and we had a big fight. Just the mention of a psychologist, psychiatrist, or even therapy or counseling makes me flip out. It seems like all I have done my whole life is try to talk to people about a life that I don't remember anything about.

"Anyway, after I saw you standing in the doorway of Carla's apartment, I immediately felt attracted to you. I don't know why. Maybe it was the way you looked at me. The sincerity in your smile or... whatever... who knows. Ever since then, I can't get you out of my mind either. I would really like to get to know you better and spend time with you, but it is all new to me. I haven't really had a relationship with anyone before and I don't quite know how to go about it."

"Bullshit!!!" an angry voice yelled out from behind me. "You lying little slut! Have you been fuckin' around behind my back again with someone else? How many times do I have to tell you that you are mine and nobody else's? I take care of you, so you need to take care of me. When is that going to sink into that stupid, thick little skull of yours?"

I practically jumped out of my skin. I quickly turned around to see what was going on and Tyler was nowhere to be found. Instead, there was this big, ugly old man staring down on me. My heart just about stopped beating. I didn't even breathe. I just stood there staring at him, wide-eyed and scared half to death. I was so confused. I couldn't understand what was going on.

"Why you little shit! You want to fuck around with boys? I'll show you what fuckin' around is. You are mine. I've told you that before. What is your problem; I'm not good enough for you anymore, you little tramp? Well, it looks like I am going to have to teach you a lesson that you will never forget for the rest of your life!"

I was paralyzed as I looked at this man in horror. I wanted to vanish into thin air. I wondered where Tyler had disappeared to.

Just as I contemplated making a run for it, he reached out his hand and grabbed me by the hair. I cried and pleaded for him to leave me alone, but he wouldn't. He just kept yelling as he dragged me by the hair out of the kitchen and down the hallway to my bedroom. I could hardly keep up with him and I kept falling on the floor. It felt like he was going to rip the hair right off my head, roots and all. He yanked off my housecoat, threw me on my bed, and stood there towering over me, shaking his head.

"Now, you see what you've done?" he said angrily. "It's all your fault, you know, and now I have to give you a beating so that you don't screw around on me again."

I sat in the corner of my bed, trembling and crying and begging for him to stop, but he didn't. I held my breath as he extended both his hands and started to reach out for me. Violently, he grabbed my nightie and tore it right off my back. I pulled my blankets up around me, but he ripped them off too. I felt so exposed and so terrified as I watched him unbutton and remove his shirt. The sight of him disgusted me. He was big, fat, old, and ugly. I kept pleading for him to stop but it just made him angrier. He grabbed me and turned me on my stomach. I heard him unbuckle his belt. I gasped as he started lashing me with it. I could feel the leather ripping through my skin. He came at me with his belt again, and again; I thought the pain would never end.

Finally, he stopped beating me and threw the belt across the room. My body was numb from shock and pain. I found the strength to roll over and edged away from him. I didn't dare look down at my tortured self. I was afraid of what I might see. I watched him as he picked up his shirt and wiped the sweat from his face. He removed the rest of his clothing. I felt nauseous, but I held it in. Throwing up was probably not a good idea. It would have made him angrier. His hands were shaking, and he was huffing and puffing as if he had just run a marathon. I just lay there and didn't say a word.

He started to come towards me, wiping his face again with his shirt. I noticed that he wasn't wiping sweat off his face; he was wiping tears. I couldn't believe my eyes.

"I'm so sorry, baby!" he said softly as he laid his old, ugly naked body down next to me. "You know that I love you and I don't like to hurt you this way. You shouldn't do things to make me angry like that. It's your own fault, you know. You should know better than to disobey me. You brought it on yourself. Now give me some lovin' again, and I will forgive you like I usually do. Come on, you know what to do. Don't make me tell you."

I just lay there numb and in shock as he gently turned me on my side to face him and then slowly moved his hand onto my breast. I couldn't move, I couldn't talk, I couldn't do anything. This was just too crazy. He was just about to kiss me when I came to my senses. I didn't know what I should do but I had to get out of there somehow. He said that he loved me then closed his eyes and began kissing the side of my cheek. I was thoroughly disgusted and felt the urge to vomit again. I managed to swallow it back, but I could taste it in my mouth.

I did not want to find out what was going to happen next, so I decided that it was now or never. I conjured up every little ounce of energy that I had left in my body and kneed him right in the groin. He abruptly let go of me, letting out a yell and putting his hands down between his legs. Now was my chance, so I jumped up and tried to make a run for it. He was quicker than I was though because he managed to grab hold of my leg as I jumped off the bed. I crashed down onto the floor face-first. Without letting go of my foot, he twisted my leg and made me turn over onto my back. I could feel the blood from my nose start to drip down the side of my face, and I could taste it in my throat. I was sure he was going to kill me, so I closed my eyes and started to scream at the top of my lungs. I don't know how long I screamed, but it seemed like forever.

Suddenly, I opened my eyes and saw Carla. She was trying to calm me down. Thank God she was there. Frantically, I looked around the room to see where he went to, but like Tyler, he was nowhere to be found.

She picked me up off the floor and helped me back into bed. I held her with all my might. I couldn't speak; I was disoriented and confused. I think she knew because she didn't even ask. I saw blood on my hands and realized that my nose was really bleeding. She told me to sit tight for a second so she could go get something to clean up my face. I did not want her to go. I begged her to stay. She told me that everything would be okay and there was nothing to fear.

I eventually gave in, but I made her look under the bed and in my closet to make sure that there was nobody hiding there. She did that, even though she knew it was just a terrible dream, and then she left the room. She came back a couple of minutes later with a face cloth. She cleaned me up and then began to rock me gently in her arms. I pointed to my blood that was on her pajamas, and she just half-smiled and shook her head. She started to sing. My head was aching so bad that I could hardly stand it. I felt cold and stiff all over. Chills were going up and down my spine. My nightmare kept replaying over and over again in my mind. I wished so much that it would stop. I trembled uncontrollably. My jaw was clenched so tight that I didn't think that I would ever be able to open my mouth again. Still, Carla never let go of me. I concentrated hard on her singing so I could put this horrible ordeal that I had just experienced out of my mind. This seemed to go on for hours. The gentleness of her voice and the warmth of her caress eventually made me feel more relaxed. I did not want to close my eyes for fear that this craziness would start all over again. I don't think I could have handled an experience like that a second time around. No matter how hard I tried to stay awake, though, I couldn't fight the exhaustion that I was feeling. I was totally drained. My eyes began to feel very heavy. They would close, and I would force them open, then they would close again, and I would force them open again… and again… and again… and again… Her wonderful voice seemed like it was going farther and farther away as I drifted out of consciousness.

Chapter 8

I opened my eyes and realized that it was morning. What a night! I just lay there for a while, staring up at the ceiling and trying to sort out everything that had happened. The one thing that I was grateful for was having Carla around to watch over me. I was very happy that I had given her the key to my apartment when she asked me for it. She wanted to be able to come in if there was something wrong so she could check on me. It's a good thing, because she had rescued me from many crazy dreams in the last little while. My guardian angel. That's what she was.

Then I started to wonder what had happened to her. I didn't remember her leaving; I must have blanked out. Then I turned around onto my side and there she was, wrapped up in my blankets and sleeping like a baby. I couldn't believe that she had stayed with me all night. *What would I do without her?* I thought. I tried very carefully to get out of bed without waking her up. I figured I should let her sleep some more because I was sure that she didn't get very much sleep last night.

I tiptoed out of the room and quietly closed the door. Poor Carla. I was the one having nightmares and she was the one losing sleep. She was a good friend. I thought I should do something nice for her, so I decided to make her a beautiful breakfast.

I looked in my fridge to see what I had to work with. I found some leftover boiled potatoes which would be great for home fries, and I had some eggs. I didn't have any bacon, but I had some sausages, so that was going to have to do. I also had some fresh fruit that I bought at the market the other day. This was going to be a great breakfast after all.

I started slicing up the different kinds of fruit and putting it on a little platter. I cut up the potatoes, so they would be ready to fry. I found some gourmet coffee in my freezer that I had put aside for a special occasion, and I started up the coffee machine so that it would be ready when she got up.

I looked out the window. It was a very dark, dreary day. The rain was coming down so hard that I could hardly even see across the street.

It wasn't too long before I heard the bedroom door open. Carla walked into the kitchen with her arms stretched out into the air and yawning.

"Something smells good," she said as she rubbed her eyes and tried to get them into focus. "What are you doing?"

"I thought I would make you a special breakfast since I kept you up half the night. Well, actually it's more like a brunch; it's almost noon."

"That's sweet of you, Bobby, but you didn't have to go to all that trouble."

She reached into the cupboard, took out two cups, and poured us each some coffee.

"How are you feeling, anyway?" she asked as she sat down at the table. "Your nose looks ok; there's a little bit of swelling and redness but I don't think it's broken. You really took a tumble last night. You had me worried."

"Maybe my nose will be okay, but I feel like shit. That was a really crazy one, and please don't make me talk about it right now. I would prefer not to think about it if that's alright with you. Let's just relax a bit and have this fantastic breakfast that I am preparing for you to thank you again for being such a wonderful friend. I promise I will fill you in later."

Carla agreed that it was probably a good idea, but she made me promise to spill my guts out after we finished eating. Carla pitched in and helped me finish cooking breakfast. Soon, everything was ready and we sat down to eat. Our little brunch turned out to be as fantastic as I said it would be. Carla appreciated it very much. It was the least I could do.

"That wasn't bad at all," she said.

"What do you mean, it wasn't bad? I worked hard, you know."

"Sure you did, and it's a good thing I helped you… we both know that you can't boil water."

"What?" I yelled and threw a dish towel at her.

She got it right in the face.

"Whoa, girl, I'm only kidding. Looks like you are back to your normal self."

We both laughed.

We started to clean up the table. Carla brought some of the dishes to the sink and I followed with more. I guess she didn't realize that I was behind her and she turned to go back to the table, and we crashed face to face. I yelled and dropped the dishes, grabbed my nose, and then fell onto the floor.

"Oh my God," she said, and put her hand over her mouth.

I looked up at her and started to laugh.

She burst out laughing too.

"I'm sorry, Bobby. Don't make me laugh; it's not funny. Are you okay?"

"Don't make you laugh? Who do you think you're kidding? You covered your mouth so I wouldn't see you laughing."

"Oh, shut up, you are laughing too. It was pretty funny."

She sat down next to me, unable to contain herself. I guess we were both a little giddy from our lack of sleep.

We were really starting to have fun when I heard a knock at the door. We both stopped laughing and looked at each other, very puzzled.

"It isn't me," she said then we both burst out laughing again. I got up from the table and staggered to the front entrance, still giggling. I could hardly contain myself either. I stood for a second beside the door to try to regain my composure.

I took a deep breath, took hold of the door handle, and opened it slowly. I was suddenly paralyzed. I seriously think that my heart stopped beating for a moment. There he was, just like in my dream, soaking wet and standing in my doorway.

When my heart jump-started again, it was beating faster and stronger than ever. It felt like someone was inside my ribs and trying to break through them with a sledgehammer. I held my hands to my chest as if to prevent it from exploding. I started trembling and I felt a growing uneasiness in the pit of my stomach.

My body felt like it was starting to go numb. I tried very hard to speak but my mouth wouldn't move. I wanted to close the door, but my arms were not cooperating either. I did not want to relive that nightmare. I managed to close my eyes, but when I opened them, he was still there, dripping wet, just like last night. I could see that Tyler was speaking to me, but I couldn't hear him. I could only see his lips moving.

Oh my god, the horror, his face was changing. It wasn't him anymore, it was that crazy old man from my dreams. I closed my eyes and hoped he would go away, and to my surprise, Tyler was back. This was not possible, I was going completely insane. I looked away to see if anyone else was around, but the hallway was empty. I turned back just in time to see that disgusting old man reaching out to grab me. I tried to scream but no sound came out of my mouth, not even a whisper. I couldn't move, and I couldn't breathe. I started to feel tingling in my arms and hands and there was a kind of buzzing in my ears. I felt a little dizzy, and I don't know how, but I managed to reach out and grab the door frame. I got a quick glimpse of Tyler again before I hit the floor. Everything went black.

I slowly opened my eyes to the sound of trickling water. I could smell the freshness of the warm clean air. Even though I could remember what had just happened, I felt very calm, like I was outside of myself. Outside of that crazy world that I lived in.

I could see the bright sun and blue sky through the leaves of the trees that towered over me. I looked around me and I knew exactly where I was. I was in my very special place in the woods. The place where I seemed to go when I was depressed, lonely, or upset. My safe place, I guess that's a good name for it. I lay across the tree trunk and stared up at the beautiful sky. The sounds of the rippling river and the gentle breeze swirling through the trees made me feel very relaxed. I closed my eyes and rested for a while, listening to the sweet sounds of paradise.

I could hear something from far off in the distance. It sounded like a voice. I couldn't quite make out what it was saying at first, but as it got a little louder, I realized that it was my name I was hearing. "Bobby… Bobby… Bobby... come on, open your eyes. It's me, Bobby. Wake up Bobby."

I opened my eyes and saw Carla leaning over me. I was in a little bit of a daze. I closed my eyes again.

"Bobby… come back."

I came to again and saw her patting my forehead with a cold, wet face cloth. I lay there totally disoriented for a few minutes and then asked what had happened. She told me that I had answered the door and then collapsed.

"The door?" I said. "Oh my God, it was Tyler; no, it wasn't; yes, it…. oh shit, was it?" I started to shake all over. I didn't know what to think. This was not possible. This was not going to happen again. I couldn't let it.

"He was in my dream, Carla. This is exactly how my nightmare started, the one that I promised to tell you about after breakfast. You can't let it happen again, Carla! Please make it go away! Make him go away! Where is he? Was he really here, or did I imagine that?"

The door was closed, and I looked down my hallway and saw nobody.

"He is in the bathroom, looking for some bandages," she blurted out as she frantically tried to calm me down. "Jesus, Bobby, what happened?"

"He's in my apartment? I don't have any bandages, so he doesn't need to be in there. Oh Carla, please help me. In my dream, it was late, and someone knocked at my door. When I opened it, I saw Tyler standing there, and he was dripping wet, the exact same way that he was just now. I can't believe this; it is just too freaky. What the hell is going on?"

Carla helped me to my feet and sat me down on the little seat next to the door.

"You must have hit this bench or something when you passed out, because you have blood trickling down the side of your face."

Carla lifted the hair away from my forehead to see if she could find the cut. It was very sensitive; I must have hit my head hard. First my nose and now my head. This had to stop; what in the hell!

"Tyler," she yelled, "never mind, Bobby said that she doesn't have any. I guess I will have to go over to my apartment and get some there."

"No…" I yelled, "you can't. I will be fine; I don't need any damned bandages."

At that moment, I spotted Tyler coming out of the bathroom and starting to walk towards me. I didn't know what to do. I stared at him and didn't speak. All kinds of frightening thoughts were going through my mind. He came right over to my bench, sat down next to me, and took me by the hand. I tried to pull away, but he wouldn't let me.

"I don't know what happened to you, Bobby," Tyler said softly, "but I'm here to help you. There is nothing I want more than to see you through this. Please let me be your friend."

I turned away, afraid or maybe just slightly embarrassed. My head was still bleeding a little. Carla asked Tyler to hold the cloth on my cut so she could go to her apartment to get some bandages. She was about to go out the door when I called out to her. I didn't want to be alone with him because I was terrified that he would turn into that crazy old man again. She turned and shook her head. She said that she would just be gone a couple of minutes, and off she went. I turned and looked at him for a second, and then I put my head down and saw his big beautiful hand wrapped around mine. He never let go the whole time Carla was gone. I never looked back up at him; I just closed my eyes and sat there, leaning against the wall. He didn't say a word; he just squeezed my hand every once in a while… and waited for Carla to come back.

She returned and did what she does best. I think that this was the first time she had to use her nursing skills on me. She disinfected the cut and then bandaged it up.

I finally looked up at Tyler, who was still holding onto my hand. I tried to force a smile, and he winked back at me. I was feeling a little calmer now. This wasn't one of my bad dreams; this was real. Everything was going to be okay; I was with my friends.

Carla suggested that we go back into the kitchen and she would prepare another pot of coffee. Tyler asked if I was able to get up. I told him that I would be fine. We stood up, and hand-in-hand, we walked into the kitchen. He pulled out a chair for me and without letting go of my hand he reached out and brought another chair right next to mine.

I turned to him and started to cry.

"Last night in my dreams you came to my door soaking wet, the same way that you did just now. I got you a towel from the linen cupboard so you could dry yourself off and I brought you in here to fix you something warm to drink. I had my back to you as I prepared some tea. When I turned around, you were gone. There was an ugly old man sitting in your place. He was yelling and swearing at me and calling me all kinds of names. He beat me, tore my clothes off me, and was about to rape me when Carla woke me up."

I put my head down and let the waterworks flow. He turned in his chair and put his arms around me. He told me that everything would be all right and that he would help me figure out what was going on in my head. Carla grabbed the box of tissues that was on the refrigerator and placed it in front of me. She got an extra cup for Tyler and refilled ours.

"Come on, honey, let it out," she said. "We are here to help you. Everything will be fine, you will see."

"Fine? How can everything be fine when I am totally losing my mind? I am getting crazier by the day. My whole life is turning upside down. I don't know if I am coming or going. I think I had better check myself back into another loony bin before I end up hurting someone again." The words escaped my mouth before I could stop them.

"You couldn't hurt a fly if your life depended on it, Roberta Hansen," Carla said. "Calm down and let us help you."

She turned to look at Tyler to see if he had anything to say. I watched her as she started to giggle and wondered what the joke was.

"You look like a drowned rat!" she said. "In all this excitement, I didn't even notice. What are you doing out on a day like today? It's raining cats and dogs."

Tyler looked at me and started to blush.

"Actually, I didn't have anything to do so I decided to come over and visit with you both. I really enjoyed our supper the other night and it has been on my mind all this time."

"You mean you came to visit Bobby, right?" Carla said sarcastically. "You have been thinking of Bobby all this time, haven't you? Whose door did you knock on? Certainly not mine. I saw the way you two were looking at each other. I wasn't that drunk."

"Shut up, Whitey," I shouted in embarrassment before she could open her big mouth again. "Christ, it looks like I'm not the only crazy person around here."

We all had a little laugh. It felt so good to get onto a different topic. Carla was blushing again. She told us that she was only joking and that she was very happy that the two of us hit it off so well. Tyler was still sitting right next to me and he never took his eyes off of me the whole time. I could tell that he was deep in his thoughts; you could almost see the wheels turning. Suddenly he lit up.

He started to talk about his last year of school and more specifically about a research project he had worked on for his final marks. The project was about PTSD (Post-Traumatic Stress Disorder). I had heard of that before from many doctors, but I didn't quite understand what it was. Though it wasn't his specialty, he explained it to us in great detail everything he recalled about trauma, repressed memories, flashbacks, and amnesia. He also said that the nightmares that I had been having were very possibly flashbacks from the past.

"Oh my god!" I yelled. "They couldn't be! Please tell me that was not my past! That crazy old man?"

"I'm so sorry, Bobby," Tyler said, "I didn't mean to freak you out. It's really hard to tell what is real and what is not when it comes to dreams."

I took a few good breaths and tried to calm down.

"Are you okay?" Carla asked.

I nodded my head and half-smiled again.

"How long have you been having these nightmares?" Tyler asked, and then added, "if you don't mind me asking."

I thought for a few minutes and said, "Almost a month, right Carla?"

Carla agreed and added that they were getting more frequent and more severe and that she too thought that they were memories from my past that were coming back to me. She also mentioned they weren't all bad. Well, that got Tyler's attention.

"What do you mean they're not all bad? Tell me about them."

"Come on, Bobby. Tell him what happens when you go to the park and stand by the fountain. I know there is something to that. There has got to be."

I told him about the sound of the water and where it took me. I described the forest and the river and the peace that I felt when I went there. He watched and listened very attentively. I explained that I always went there when I was feeling depressed or lonely and it always made me feel better.

Tyler had this very serene look on his face as if he could almost see and feel the peace that I felt. He listened to every single detail and I could almost see him picturing it in his mind.

"I call it my safe place," I said. "I have never really thought about it, but Carla seems to think that I really had this safe place and that it really exists, and my mind unconsciously goes back to it when I am feeling down. I'll tell you one thing, though: I am really happy that I have this place to go to, or I think I would go crazy."

"That is amazing," Tyler said. "Wow! Uhhh… I mean, I believe Carla is on the right track. If you keep going back to that same place, then maybe your past is starting to come back to you, and as painful as it might be sometimes, I do believe that this is a good thing."

"I wonder if I ever lived near a lake or a river. I just love the sound of flowing water. It makes me feel like I'm in heaven. I think that I would love to live by the ocean and listen to the sound of the water and seagulls and smell the salty air. Do you think maybe I might have lived by the ocean at one time?"

Carla jumped in and said, "I don't know about that, but I know that I would give anything to live by the ocean. I would purchase a large sailboat and I might even sail around the world. Imagine the freedom that you would feel. What a life we could have. Wouldn't it be nice if we could just drop everything and sail the world, just the three of us?"

"That sounds fabulous," Tyler said. "If any of us ever wins a lot of money, we will all quit our jobs and sail around the world. I love the ocean. I have done some scuba diving in the past and it is the most amazing thing that I have ever experienced. I would give anything to live that way."

"Well, I see we all have something in common," I said, "but we are dreaming in Technicolor. I don't mean to burst your bubbles, but in my experience, I have come to the conclusion that 'life's a bitch and then you die.' Though it does sound very appealing, I don't think that anything that great would ever happen in my lifetime."

"Quit being so negative," Carla said. "You are a very good person and good things will come to you if you would just keep the faith. You need to start being more positive."

"Oh, come on, Carla. Look at what is going on in my life right now. Look at my very sketchy past. Nothing good is going to come out of this. I can feel it."

She gave me a look and a little smack on the arm, then turned and started talking to Tyler.

We got back on track to the original topic which was PTSD. Tyler started explaining what it was all about and how it affected people, well, as much as he could remember from his project.

"The mind is a powerful machine," he said. "If someone suffers through a traumatic experience that is too hard to deal with, sometimes the mind will completely block it out. It is like a page has been torn out of their scrapbook of memories. It doesn't disappear; it's kind of like putting a document in a filing cabinet and forgetting about it. The experience can be filed away in the back of your mind for many years.

"Sometimes, something can happen that can trigger a memory. It can be something that you see, something you hear, or even something you smell or touch. It could be anything. Have there been any changes in your life in this past month? For example, maybe you bought a new perfume and without your knowledge it happened to be the same perfume you used to use."

"I don't know," I replied. "I haven't really thought about it."

"All those things can trigger memories. Maybe, unknowingly, you crossed paths with someone from your past. It could also be a sound, as we have already discovered. The sound of trickling water seems to bring you somewhere. The possibilities are endless."

I hesitated before answering, "But I don't only go to my safe place when I hear the sound of water. I also go there when I am scared and lonely. When I opened the door and saw you standing there dripping wet the same way I saw you in my nightmare, I blacked out and went right to my safe place. I feel like nothing bad can ever happen to me there." Turning to Carla, I said, "You know, Whitey? I'm beginning to believe that you are absolutely right."

"Of course I am, Looney Tunes," she said with a wink.

"No seriously, Carla, now that I think about it, it seems like a very familiar place, a place that I have been to many times before. A place where I am safe and sound."

"I understand that, Bobby," Tyler explained, "but we need to find out what is triggering all these flashbacks… good and bad. You need to start taking notes. You need to think back and try to remember anywhere new you may have been, or anyone you may have met lately. It could even be something you ate, or even purchased. Maybe it was a song you heard on the radio. Anything out of the ordinary. You need to try to replay, at least, the last month and a half of your life in your mind and write everything down. Then the three of us can go over it and see if we can help pinpoint anything that might have taken place during that time period that was different from your usual routine."

Wow… Carla and Tyler really gave me a lot to think about. We spent the rest of the day trying to put together a calendar that dated back a month and a half so I could jot down the events as they came to me. It was not going to be easy.

Chapter 9

It was going to be another sleepless night. I tossed and turned for most of it, thinking about this PTSD business that Tyler was talking about. If there was something triggering memories, I wish I knew what in the hell it was and why it was happening. Deep down, all this talk about repressed memories scared the crap out of me. If my past was so bad that my mind blocked it all out, why would I even consider trying to remember it? Why was it coming back to me now after all these years? It just didn't make any sense.

Lots of the symptoms of this PTSD that Tyler and Carla talked about sounded very familiar. You know what was really funny? All my fears about discussing my problems with Tyler were completely unjustified. Mind you, I hadn't gotten into any of my deep dark secrets yet with him, but still, he was so easy to talk to because he seemed to take a real interest in what was happening to me. He was genuinely concerned for my well-being. It got me thinking about how lucky I was to have such really great friends.

Morning came quickly, and I felt the consequences of my lack of sleep. I had trouble getting my ass in gear. It looked like it was going to be another beautiful spring day. Too bad I had to work. I was running a little late, so I jumped in the shower, got dressed, inhaled my breakfast, and hurried out the door.

I arrived at the hospital with about two minutes to spare and was almost at the elevator when I heard someone call my name. I turned around and saw Judy at the front desk motioning me to go over there and see her.

Oh boy, just what I needed to make my day even worse! I couldn't stand that old busybody. If you wanted to dig up some dirt about someone or spread rumors, she was the one to see. She hated my guts. Somehow, she found out where I came from, even though it was supposed to be confidential. At least she didn't know why I was there. I think she thought I was a thief or something because every time I went close to her desk, she always watched me like a hawk. She didn't trust me as far as she could throw me.

I looked at my watch again and reluctantly headed for her desk. I was a little bit uneasy about going back to see her because she wouldn't normally talk to me unless she wanted to blast me about something. Well, I wasn't late, so it couldn't be that. As I approached her desk, she kind of just gave me this weird look, rolled her eyes, reached over, grabbed a bunch of flowers that was lying on the edge of her desk, and slapped them on the counter in front of me. She didn't say one word; she just gave me a puzzled look then turned and went back to work. I was kind of stunned myself. I stood there for a few seconds, just staring at this beautiful bouquet with my name on it. I felt very self-conscious because people were staring and probably wondering who would have sent them to me.

I quickly grabbed the flowers and headed back to the elevator. I didn't want to look at the card until I got to my locker where I would have more privacy. When I got to the locker room, I was very happy to see that no one else was around. The curiosity was killing me, so I sat down and immediately opened the envelope. I was surprised that it was still sealed, and Miss Busybody hadn't taken a sneak-peek. I pulled out the card and read it.

Well, I should have guessed. He was so sweet. Of course, it was from Tyler. Dah!!! Who else did I know that would have sent them to me? Well, they could have been from Carla; she had given me gifts before, but usually on my birthday or something. Anyway, the note was short and sweet. It read, "Had a wonderful day. Hope to see you again soon. Your good friend, Tyler." I held the card to my chest, closed my eyes, and thought about how lucky I was. That was the second time he gave me flowers. What a sweet guy.

Suddenly I felt someone's hand touch my shoulder and I practically jumped out of my skin.

"Jesus Christ!" I blasted, then caught my breath and turned around, "Oh my God, I'm sorry I yelled like that. It's uhhh… Danny, right? You scared the living crap right out of me. You shouldn't sneak up on people like that. What are you doing here, anyway?"

"Actually, I work here, and the name is David, and I didn't sneak up on you; you were a million miles away. I saw you at the front desk. Who sent you the flowers?"

"Excuse me?" I replied, slightly annoyed by his curiosity. "What business is it of yours?"

"None at all, I was just being nosey," he said, turning away quickly and leaving the room.

After saying that and practically giving me a heart attack, he just leaves? Well, that is weird, I thought.

I put my things in my locker and brought the flowers with me to the kitchen to find something to put them in. Lou greeted me with a smile and a big hug as usual. He was very surprised to see me carrying a bouquet of flowers.

"Who's the lucky man? Are they for me, by any chance?"

I looked at him and I started to blush. "I'm not giving them to anyone," I said. "Someone sent them to me."

He started giggling. "I gathered that, silly! What I mean is, whoever it is, if you return his affection, he will be the luckiest man in the world."

"Oh, come on, Lou," I said, as I blushed again. "No one has ever seriously taken an interest in me before. I don't think that this will be any different."

"Oh, stop it, Bobby! You are a beautiful, loving person. Why, if I were twenty years younger, I would..."

"All right, Lou," I cut in. "I know, you've told me that a million times before. Enough already! I need to get these flowers in some water and get at these dishes before I get in trouble; I'm late as it is."

I never did tell him who sent the flowers and he didn't even ask. He didn't like to pry. I found a jug to put them in for the day till I could get them home, and then I went right to work.

The day seemed to drag on forever, because I was too anxious to get home and show Carla what Tyler had sent me. All day long people who passed through the kitchen were asking who the flowers belonged to and Lou told them all that I had a secret admirer. I didn't usually like being the center of attention, but it was kind of fun to see the expressions on everyone's faces when he told them they were mine. Imagine that, a man sending me flowers. The sound of that still blew me away.

My shift was finally over so I took my flowers, went to my locker to get the rest of my things, and got on the elevator. Well, guess who happened to be in that confined little space with me? It was the old busybody, Judy from the front desk. She was not happy to run into me; she never was. She was looking really uncomfortable, like she wanted to crawl into a little hole and disappear. I had heard from one of the nurses that afternoon that she was fishing around all day to try to find out who sent me the flowers. I sure as hell was not going to tell her.

"Hi Judy," I said. "How was your day?"

She just rolled her eyes and stuck her nose up in the air. I knew that she wouldn't answer me, but I always tried to be friendly with her just because I knew how much it annoyed her.

The elevator doors opened, and she practically ran me over to get out of there and away from me as fast as she could. Crazy old bitch.

I walked out of the main entrance of the hospital and started to make my way down the path that led to the street. All of a sudden, someone bumped into me from behind and I dropped my bouquet of flowers. I almost fell. I turned and realized that it was that pain in the ass from the locker room. He quickly bent down and grabbed my card before I could stop him and ran away with it.

"What in the hell are you doing?" I yelled as I tried to chase him down to take the card away from him. "Give me that back right now! It is none of your business." He kept shoving me away and running around in circles as he tried to read the card. I couldn't get near it; he kept pushing me back.

"What are you going to do," he said as he struggled to open the envelope, "kill me?"

I froze in my tracks. I didn't know what to do or say. I just stood there, terribly confused. What did he mean by that? Did he know something about me? That wasn't possible though. This could not be happening.

I needed to get out of there. I picked up my bouquet that was still lying on the ground and took off down the street. As I ran past him, I could hear him call after me.

"Here's your stupid card. What's wrong with you? Can't you take a joke?"

"Keep the damn card, you idiot," I yelled, "and stay away from me!"

I was very upset. As I hurried down the street, I kept looking back to make sure that he wasn't following me. I arrived at my apartment just in time. I couldn't hold it in any longer. I threw myself down on the couch with my flowers cradled in my arms and I broke down.

Why was he being so mean to me, and why did he say what he did? Why did people always have to ruin everything? Every time I felt good about something, someone always had to ruin it. I really didn't like that guy. He gave me the creeps. He was very nosy, and I didn't like the way he sneaked around. Did he know something about me, or was I just being paranoid?

The phone rang and startled me, and I was almost afraid to answer it. I looked over at the call display, breathed a sigh of relief, and reached over and answered it. It was Carla.

"Hi Bobby, how was your day? Why don't you come over and have a cup of tea?"

"Hey Whitey, I don't know. I'm not really feeling up to it."

"Oh, come on, Looney Tunes. What happened? Spill it. I know you; I can tell by your voice that you have been crying. Get your butt over here and we'll talk. You'll feel much better once you get it off your chest."

I stayed on the line for a few minutes and didn't say anything.

"Never mind," she said impatiently, "I will be there in a few minutes."

She hung up the phone and about five minutes later she was knocking at my door. When I opened the door for her, I was still holding onto my flowers. When she saw them, she broke into a big smile. She knew right away who had sent them to me. She was very confused about why I was so upset. I told her what happened with David and she got really mad.

"That bastard," she said. "What is his problem? I told him to stay away from you. He doesn't seem to understand, does he?"

"He even snuck up on me in the locker room and almost gave me a heart attack. There is something wrong with that guy. I don't know anything about him, but he really creeps me out. I can't stand him, and I wish he wouldn't come near me."

We went into the kitchen and I put my flowers in water. Carla started to talk about Tyler. She was really happy that he had taken a liking to me. I told her that I was very happy too. I fixed us both a cup of tea and we sat down and talked for a bit.

The phone rang so I got up and answered it.

"Hi Tyler," Carla yelled, loud enough that he could hear her. She could tell by the big grin on my face who it was.

Tyler told me to say hi to her. He asked me how my day was, but I knew that he was just fishing around to see if I got my flowers.

"Same old drag," I said, trying not to laugh. "Washing dishes is not the most glamorous job in the world, you know."

"Really?"

"Yeah, same old, same old."

"You didn't receive anything today?"

"No, not that I recall."

"Damn it, I told them to send..."

"Oh, wait a minute, I almost forgot about that; do you mean that big, beautiful bouquet of spring flowers that I received this morning when I got to work?"

"Jesus, Bobby, you had me going for a minute."

"Thank you so much, Tyler; it was the highlight of my day. You should have seen the looks on people's faces. Everyone was trying to figure out who sent them to me. I believe my co-workers were all just a little jealous. I felt like I was the center of attention, except for one asshole who tried to ruin my day."

I told him about David and how he stole the greeting card away from me. Tyler was not impressed. He said that if this David character ever gave me trouble again that I would have to point him out, and he would give him a talking to.

"Oh… I almost forgot what I was calling about. Do you want to go out to dinner?"

"Ahh… dinner, really, now, tonight?"

"No, next year, silly; yes, tonight."

"But Carla…"

I knew that Carla could read between the lines because she kept on motioning for me to say yes. She got up from the table and started to head out to the front door. I told Tyler to hang on for a second and I asked Carla where she was going. She said that she was tired anyway and was going to relax in front of the television. She said to go to dinner with Tyler and have a great time. I thanked her and said goodbye.

I put the phone back up to my ear and heard Tyler singing, "*I love rock and roll…*" a song that I could hear playing in the background.

I started to giggle and said, "Don't give up your day job. You better stick to psychology."

"You're not very nice, and to think I just asked you out to dinner. Maybe I should just forget about that."

"No, no, I was only joking. I would love to go."

He told me that he was still at the office and had a few loose ends to tie up and that he would pick me up in about an hour or so and to dress casually. There was a new little Italian restaurant that had opened close to where he worked, and he had been wanting to check it out. That was fine with me because I loved Italian food.

I put down the phone and went into the bathroom and jumped in the shower. I was very excited, and I couldn't stop smiling. I could feel the butterflies start fluttering around inside my stomach. My imagination was running wild. I felt very happy that this handsome young man was taking me out, hell, that he even had an interest in me. I rushed into my bedroom to find something to wear. It was quite an undertaking. I got dressed, and then changed, then changed again, and then changed back into the first thing that I had put on which was a pair of black pants and a blouse with a red and white print.

What the hell is wrong with me? I thought. *Am I completely losing my mind?*

I was so excited that I could hardly keep my feet on the floor. I combed my hair and then tried to do something different with it. What a mess. I was never good with hair, so I just left it down. I brushed my teeth and rinsed my mouth, and then I decided that a little makeup might help me look irresistible. Oh yeah, right, dream on, girl. I wasn't that great with makeup either.

I was all ready to go, at least as much as I could be, when I heard someone knocking at my front door. *Right on time,* I thought to myself and I ran over to let him in. I took a second to calm down a bit and then with a big smile across my face, I grabbed the handle, pulled open the door, and said, "What took you so long?"

Then my jaw fell right down to the floor. It took me a few seconds to react because this was not who I was expecting. He threw me right off guard and I froze up for a second, staring.

"What the hell are you doing here?" I yelled.

David was standing there in the doorway with my card in his hand and a very stupid little grin on his face. He passed the card to me and I gave him a dirty look and grabbed it out of his hand.

"I'm really sorry about today," he replied. "I didn't want to upset you like that. I was going to give you back the card, but you took off so fast that I didn't have a chance. I was just joking around, you know.... Wow... you're lookin' good... goin' somewhere?"

"Jesus, you're an idiot. Shut up; I don't want to hear anything from you, and, uh, how did you find out where I live, anyway?"

"I saw you come in this building one day after work, so I presumed that this was where you lived, and your name is on the mailbox downstairs."

"You know what? Really you have no business here. You could have waited till I went back to work. I don't ever want you to come here again, do you hear me? Now get out of here before you really piss me off."

He said goodbye and turned and walked away. Man, that guy was really good at messing with my head. Why in the world would he show up here with my card when he could have very easily given it to me at work tomorrow? Something was not right with him. Well, I decided to put him out of my mind. I went back to my room to take another look at myself in the mirror to see if I still looked presentable. I went to the kitchen and looked at the time. It was past the hour and Tyler still wasn't here. I thought that maybe he had been delayed at the office. I decided to give him a little more time.

Another half hour went by and there was still no sign of Tyler. I was starting to get worried. I didn't think that he had stood me up or anything, at least I hoped not, but I was concerned about what might have happened to him. My imagination started to run wild. It was always like that; I don't know why. When something was worrying me, I always got thinking about the worst thing that could possibly happen Well, maybe it was understandable, considering my past. All these bad thoughts kept popping in my head. Did he get in an accident, was he mugged, did he fall, did he get hurt somehow and couldn't reach me? Finally, the phone rang, and I was so relieved to hear his voice.

"What's going on?" I said, trying to stay calm. "Is something wrong?"

Tyler told me that everything was fine and that I was not to worry. Not to worry? That was easy for him to say. He wasn't the one going crazy here.

He went on to say that for some reason his car wouldn't start, and no matter what he did, he couldn't get it going. It was completely dead and wouldn't turn over at all. He had called a tow truck and they brought it to the garage. The driver told him that he would have to go back in the morning to find out what was wrong with it because the mechanic had gone home for the day, and he didn't work on cars, he just towed them.

"I'm really sorry," he said, "I'll make it up to you, I promise."

I was disappointed, but I knew that it was not intentional. It was just one of those things. He was sincerely upset about keeping me waiting. We talked for about an hour and then we made plans for the weekend. He wouldn't tell me what we were going to do but he said to plan to be with him for the whole day on Saturday. He was such a sweet guy. I didn't tell him about David. I just didn't want to go there and spoil our talk. I was pretty sure it would come up again. I could hardly wait for Saturday to come around. It was going to be a long week, a very long week, I was sure of that.

Chapter 10

I was absolutely right, and the week dragged on for what seemed like forever. I never thought it would end. Each night when I went to bed, I counted down the days. Carla spent a few evenings with me and that helped to pass the time a bit. When I finished work on Friday, I was filled with anticipation. Tyler called, and we talked for a while. I was very curious as to what he had planned for me, but he still left me hanging, although he did tell me to wear jeans and running shoes. That was a relief because I had wondered all week about what I was going to wear.

Finally, it was Saturday. It had been a very rainy week, but the weather forecast was looking pretty good. Tyler had told me to be ready by eight-thirty, and believe me, I was. I was awake at the crack of dawn and couldn't get back to sleep, so I took a shower, got dressed, had a little breakfast, and tried to relax. I picked up the book I had started a while back, *On the Road with Janis,* one of my favorite singers, and started to read while I waited for him to arrive. Then, just like clockwork, I heard a knock on the door. As I grabbed the handle I hesitated, remembering last Monday when David showed up at my place. I shook off the image and opened the door. It was Tyler, in the flesh, and wow… He was looking good. He was wearing blue jeans and a white t-shirt with an unbuttoned plaid shirt over top. I was so happy to see him that I jumped into his arms and gave him a big hug. I backed up, slightly embarrassed, when I realized what I had done. He started to laugh, and I gave him a smack on the arm.

"Stop it," he said. "If you could see the look on your face right now, you would laugh too."

He hesitated for a moment, then reached out his hand and took mine.

"Do you know how beautiful you are?" he said. "I am really happy to see you too. Now let's not waste any more time; I have a wonderful day planned."

We walked out of my building and onto the sidewalk, and then he led me to his car.

Wow, I hadn't even thought about what he might have for a vehicle. We were going to be traveling in style. He had a beautiful, shiny, royal blue Ford Mustang. I presumed that he had it all polished up for the occasion. The sun was reflecting off it like a mirror. He unlocked the door and opened it for me. I got in and he carefully closed the door behind me. He was a perfect gentleman. I never rode in one of these before and I felt very special. He went around to his door and got in. He started up the engine with a roar and turned down the radio that blasted when the car came to life. He apologized and put the car into gear. He rounded the corner and headed up the street.

"Nice car," I said. "Oh, by the way, did they ever figure out what was wrong with it? It seems brand new; I hope it wasn't anything serious."

He explained that for some unknown reason, there was a wire in his motor that was disconnected. That was why the car wouldn't start. He said not to worry, that the wire was reconnected and that we shouldn't have any trouble.

He still didn't tell me where we were going, and I didn't even care. I was just so happy to be with him for the day. We talked and joked around the whole time he was driving. I had no clue where we were because I had never really gone out of the city and I wasn't paying much attention to road signs. I was just admiring the beautiful scenery. It seemed like we had been driving for hours. Telephone poles became trees and highways became country roads. The bright sun was peeking through the few leftover clouds from yesterday. It was going to be a picture-perfect day.

We passed a sign that read "Rest area 3 miles" and Tyler asked if it was all right if he stopped for a bit. I had no problem with that. I was anxious to get out of the car, stretch my legs, and smell the fresh spring air. We pulled in and found a place to park. It was still early in the day and there wasn't anyone else around. Tyler got out of the car and ran over to my side before I had a chance to get out. He opened the door for me and took me by the hand again and helped me up. We stood and looked around for a bit.

The sun was warm, the sky was blue, the air was clean, the view was breathtaking, but most of all, I was with the best of company. Tyler became more appealing each minute I spent with him. What more could I want? Hand in hand we took a stroll around the property. There were picnic tables and benches and a small pathway through the flower gardens and the trees. The perennials were poking their heads up through the soil to try to catch a few rays of bright, warm sunshine.

It felt good to get out and walk around after being seated in the car for a couple of hours. Most of all, though, it felt wonderful to be out enjoying all this beauty with a new friend that I was growing more and more fond of by the minute. I hadn't felt this happy in a long time, probably never. I was thinking that Tyler had no choice but to hold my hand, just to keep me grounded.

We were almost at the other end of the lot when I started to feel so overwhelmed with joy that I felt like I was going to explode. I did the only thing I could think of. I turned to Tyler and said, "Race you back!"

We both let out a yell and started running as fast as we could. I got a little bit of a head start because he wasn't expecting that, but it didn't take long before he took the lead. All of a sudden, he tripped and fell head-first onto the ground, and I had to maneuver around him so I wouldn't fall too. I immediately stopped and turned around to see if he was alright and burst out laughing when I saw him lying there. He looked up at me, squinting in the sunlight, and shook his head in frustration.

"I'm so sorry," I said. "I shouldn't be laughing but you look pretty funny down there. You're not hurt, are you?"

I reached out my hand to help him up and the bugger grabbed it and pulled me right down on the ground next to him.

"How do you like that?" he said with a little smirk on his face. "Now you look pretty silly too."

I was so shocked. I would have never expected him to do such a thing. Well, I was not going to let that pass; I could play dirty, too. I pounced on him and we started wrestling. He rolled over on top of me and then I rolled over on top of him. Once again, he rolled over on top of me and stopped everything. I didn't know what was happening. He just sat there, on my stomach, face to face with me and didn't move a muscle. He stared right into my eyes for the longest time. I felt terribly vulnerable and didn't know what to expect. As I watched his gaze, I could see his face getting closer and closer to mine. At this point, I was starting to feel a little nervous. He put his lips so close to mine, but they did not meet. Instead he turned his head a little and slowly moved his lips down my cheek and next to my ear. My heart was racing. I felt warm all over as if there was a flame growing inside of me…

"Last one there is a rotten egg," he said as he jumped up and ran to the car.

"No fair. You're nothing but a cheater."

I got up and raced him back to the car. When I reached him, he grabbed me by the shoulders and said, "What do you think of that, Miss Roberta Hansen? Are you upset because I beat you to the car, or are you upset because I didn't do this?"

He pulled me close and paused, looking into my eyes as if he were trying to read what I was thinking. I looked down at his mouth and noticed how soft his lips looked. I could feel my temperature rising and I was sure he could feel it too because a smile came across his face. He looked down at my mouth and slowly pulled me closer till

I felt his lips touch mine. I didn't resist, but I was very nervous and started to tremble. He backed off.

"I'm sorry," he said, "I didn't mean to scare you."

"It's all right; I wasn't scared. I was just feeling a little anxious. This is all new to me, you know."

He held me in his arms for a few minutes and then he took me by the hand and turned around.

"Hop in," Tyler said as he again opened the passenger side door for me. "We are almost there."

We got into his car and drove back onto the highway. Neither of us said very much; I think we were both thinking about what had just happened. I put my head back and closed my eyes. I kept playing back our kiss over and over again in my mind. I never felt anything so wonderful in all my life. Why did I get so nervous? I didn't want him to stop. I wish he'd kept going.

As I was daydreaming, he reached over and gently took my hand. I didn't open my eyes, but I couldn't help but smile. I know he saw me because when I did, he squeezed my hand. There were a lot of good songs playing on the radio — oldies that I hadn't heard for a while. I almost started to sing along, but I decided to spare him, so I just relaxed and listened to the music.

It wasn't long before he got off the highway. I opened my eyes because I didn't want to miss the sights. The little country road was lined with flowers and trees. It was wonderful to see. Tyler had to slow down to let a couple of deer cross the road in front of us. They were so beautiful, and they were so close that I could almost touch them.

"You have to be very careful when you're driving around here," Tyler said. "There is always a lot of wildlife crossing on this stretch of the road."

"You seem to know the region very well," I said. He was giving me a grand tour of the area. We drove through this quaint little village and Tyler pointed out all the historic buildings and what they used to represent to this town. He showed me the old hotel that was converted into an office building and the old sawmill which had been transformed into a restaurant. Amazingly, nothing seemed to have been modernized. It all seemed to resemble a little frontier village in an old Western movie. It was like going back in time. I had no idea that places like this still existed.

"How come you know so much about this town?" I said finally. "Did you used to live here or something?"

"You mean you didn't know I was a country hick?" he said, laughing.

"No way," I said.

"Seriously, when I was a child, my parents brought me out here during the summer holidays to spend time with my grandparents. I really enjoyed living out here with them. I made a few good friends too. It was a very special place."

"Was?"

"Yes… was. When I was in my teens, something happened that upset me very much and I never wanted to come back. The memories were too painful. I kept in touch with my grandparents all the time, though, by phone or by email. I loved them very much, but I never returned for a visit.

"I went back for my grandfather's funeral three years ago, and then my grandmother's funeral almost four months ago, now. They always told me that one day I would have to put my past behind me and move on. I never thought I would be able to do that. I guess this was their way of making me do just that."

"Do what?" I asked. "I have no idea what you are talking about."

He pulled the car over to the side of the road, and then he reached over and opened the glove compartment and pulled out a set of keys. He squeezed them tightly in his hand. I turned to him and saw a look of sadness come over his face. I didn't know what to say or do. As he started to explain, a tear rolled down his cheek.

"At the reading of the will, I was told that their property was left to me. Their little piece of paradise which is made up of three-hundred and thirty-one acres of prime real estate is all mine. I hadn't gotten the nerve up enough yet to come out here to visit the house until the other day when you talked about your safe place. It brought back some old memories, ones that I had kept locked up deep inside my mind, hoping that they would never resurface again. See, you are not the only crazy person around here.

"At the same time, it also brought back some wonderful memories too, and there were many. This was like heaven to me for many years. The happiest moments of my life were spent out here on their property. Too bad they had to come to an end. But I know that time has a way of healing things and I think it is about time that I start dealing with my past too. I should start practicing what I preach to my patients. Already I feel like a big weight has been taken off my shoulders. I am very glad that I have come back. I thought if I brought you with me it would be good for both of us. I hope you're not upset with me?"

"Upset, are you kidding? On the contrary, I'm flattered. I am very happy to share this special day with you, and you're right, it does remind me of my safe place."

He handed me the keys to the house and put the car in drive. He drove for a few minutes and then slowed down and turned onto a dirt road. We seemed to be passing right through the middle of a forest. There were trees on both sides of the road that reached out over top of us and creating a shelter, as if we were driving through a covered bridge. There was that very familiar smell again. The ditches on both sides of the road were covered with trilliums.

"Stop the car," I shouted. "Look at all the flowers; I want to get out and pick some."

Tyler pulled over and I jumped out. There were trees and flowers as far as the eye can see. I walked off the road and into the woods. I knelt in front of a big patch of trilliums and started picking some. I had gathered a good handful when I heard a knocking noise above me. I got back on my feet and looked to see if I could find where it was coming from. It was amazing to see the tall majestic trees with their long branches reaching up to the heavens.

"This is great!" I yelled as I started to spin myself around while I was still looking up at the sky. What a childish thing to do, but I just couldn't help myself.

It didn't take long before I started to get dizzy and fell on my ass. I heard the car door open and Tyler was laughing his head off as he ran through the trees to come and check on me.

"Well, aren't you a sight for sore eyes, silly girl. Wow..." he said as he knelt over me. "You look so beautiful laying there on that blanket of trilliums."

"There it is again," I whispered. "Be quiet, listen. I was trying to see what was making that knocking noise."

"It's a woodpecker, silly, now let's get back in the car. The house is just up the road from here... but wait, don't move... hang on a second."

He turned and ran back to the car. I was still focused on the sound, hoping I could see where it was. It is amazing to think that a little bird could make that much noise. I heard the car door slam. The sound echoed through the trees. It must have startled the woodpecker because I caught a quick glimpse of him as he flew off into the heavens.

Tyler ran back, armed, and ready with a camera in his hand.

"Oh no," I whined. "I hate getting my picture taken."

"But you look so gorgeous lying there completely surrounded by all those beautiful spring blossoms. Come on, smile and enjoy yourself, please, and I promise that if they don't turn out nice, I will delete them. I'll let you decide. Now do some poses for me."

He kept snapping pictures and I kept rolling around and smiling and laughing. Actually, it was lots of fun, and he was having a great time too.

After a while he came and sat down next to me. He leaned over and gave me a kiss on the forehead. It felt like I was going to melt, right then and there. He lay down next to me and raised the camera into the air, then he snapped a picture of the two of us together lying in the flowers. I wanted to look at them right away, but he said that we needed to get going and that we could check them out when we got to the house.

He got to his feet, and I reached out my hand and he grabbed it and helped me up. He never released it till we got to the car, and then we drove off again.

I could see a mailbox ahead in the distance and wondered if we had finally arrived. Sure enough, when we got closer, Tyler put his flasher on and slowed down and made the turn. I was very excited, and I could tell that Tyler was feeling it too. The narrow driveway was also lined with maple trees on both sides. We soon came to a clearing and there it was, sitting on top of a small hill: the country home that Tyler spent his summers in. It was just beautiful. I watched him as he slowly drove up to the front of the porch and stopped the car. It was hard to tell what was going through his mind; he was being so quiet. He turned and looked at me.

"I have so many wonderful memories of my summers here with..." he said as he reached out and took my hand. A tear rolled down his face.

"You loved your grandparents very much."

I put my arms around him and tried my best to console him. He held me so tight that I could hardly breathe. After a few minutes, he loosened his grip and looked straight into my eyes.

"The past is wonderful," he said. "It is really too bad that you can't remember."

"I don't think I want to remember my past. The only thing I know is that I was a monster. How could I have any good memories?"

"I don't want to hear another word about that. You are not a monster and I don't think you ever were one. I am very sure that there are also some wonderful memories locked up in that little brain of yours. You will see. I know they are there."

He took the keys from my hand and said that we should go in and check out how the old house was holding up. I followed him to the bottom of the steps and watched as he walked up and unlocked the door. He opened the door and stepped through the entrance.

It was a classic old farmhouse, right out of a Western movie. It had a wide porch that looked like it went all around the house, with large carved posts and beautiful gingerbread trim. The house was covered with wooden clapboard that had been painted white, with green trim around the windows and doors. The windows on the second floor were adorned with shutters that were painted to match the trim. Next to the doorway was a weathered hand-painted sign that read, "Welcome to the Murphy's."

A chill went up my spine and I looked up and realized that Tyler had already gone inside.

The old stairs creaked as I started to make my way up to the porch. The sound seemed to echo in my mind. I felt very strange all of a sudden, as if I were in a dream. My heart was pounding loudly, and it felt almost like I was moving in slow motion. My eyes followed a bird that flew into the corner of the porch. I guess she had made her nest somewhere back there. I looked up and saw two hooks on the ceiling where they must have hung a swing in the summertime. I could just imagine how wonderful it must have been to sit out here on a warm summer evening with a cold drink and soft music playing in the background. How romantic.

As I stared into space, I imagined seeing an elderly couple sitting there together, enjoying life and each other. They seemed to be looking right at me. I felt warm all over and it brought a smile to my face. There was something very welcoming about this house. It almost seemed like I belonged there.

"Check this out! Just like I remember it. Hasn't changed a bit."

The sound of his voice startled me and brought me back to reality. I walked through the doorway to catch up to him. In front of me, to the right, I could see a large staircase leading up to the second floor. It had a beautifully carved spindle railing on one side and a handrail up against the wall on the other. The wall was lined with what looked like family photos from the bottom, all the way up to the top. There was a carpet runner going up the center of the stairs.

"Make yourself at home and look around," he said as he left the entrance.

At the bottom of the stairs to the right of me, there was a closed door. I slowly turned the handle and took a quick peek inside. It looked like it might have been an office of some sort. A large desk sat in front of the window and one whole wall was lined with bookshelves filled from top to bottom. Yes, it was definitely an office. There was a diploma on the wall from a medical school. Tyler's grandfather was a doctor? He didn't mention that, but I guess the topic had never come up. Tyler had followed in his grandfather's footsteps. That was pretty cool.

I left the room and went down the corridor on the left side of the stairs. It led me to the kitchen. Everything looked antique but in very good condition. There was an abundance of wooden cupboards and cabinets lining a couple of the walls. Some had glass doors and I could see very fancy dishes inside. There was a window above the sink and a couple of larger windows on the rear wall. Between them was a door leading out to the back of the house. I peeked through the window and saw a huge yard that ended at the edge of a lake. *Nice*, I thought. I turned my attention back to the kitchen. In the center of the room, there was a small rectangular wooden table with four chairs around it. The table was adorned with a fancy crocheted tablecloth and a dry flower arrangement. To the left there was another doorway. I entered and found myself in what looked like a very fancy dining area. There was an enormous dining room table that looked like it could fit about twenty people comfortably. There were large armchairs at each end of the table and smaller ones lining each side. It was decorated with a beautiful lacey-looking runner, placed lengthwise down the middle of the table, that looked like it was hand-made. There was another arrangement of dried flowers with candles as a centerpiece. Again, there were fancy cabinets filled with beautiful dishes.

There was an old cook stove in the corner that looked like it was more for decoration than anything else, and an old gramophone in the opposite corner. I walked over and opened the compartment where the old records were stored and pulled one out. How I knew that the records were in there was a mystery to me. Anyway, I think Tyler's grandparents were really into antiques. Along with a few shelves filled with knick-knacks, the walls were decorated with dried flowers, candles, photos, and paintings. It was like being in a museum. To the left was another doorway. It had a swinging saloon door. I pushed through and entered the living room. I had never seen so many books in my life. There was a whole wall with shelves from the ceiling to the floor that was filled with books. The opposite wall was covered in books too but with a beautiful fireplace as a centerpiece. It was cleaned out and looked like it hadn't been used for a very long time. There was a wrought-iron rack next to it with a few chunks of wood standing by. The mantle looked like it was made of marble and had a few more knick-knacks and candles on it. I realized, all of a sudden, that it was very quiet, and I was so caught up in my exploration that I had totally forgotten about Tyler. I looked over at the couch and saw that he was lying there, wrapped in a crocheted afghan, almost camouflaged, and looking at what seemed to be a photo album. He had a big smile on his face and was so wrapped up in what he was looking at that I don't think he even knew that I was in the room.

"What are you looking at?" I asked.

He let out a yell and jumped about a foot in the air. He closed the album immediately and got up and hurried over to the shelf unit to put it back where had he found it.

"Nothing," he replied. "Just some old pictures of people I used to know."

"I want to see them," I said as I walked over toward the shelf and tried to retrieve the album. Just as I was about to put my hand on it, he grabbed me by the arm and turned me around to face him. He put his arms around me, looked me straight in the eyes, and pressed his lips against mine. He took me totally by surprise, but it felt wonderful. His kiss was like magic. It made me feel so good. He pulled away from me and connected with my eyes again.

"But I…" I almost lost my train of thought... my mind was still in the kiss. "Oh yes, I wanted to see the pictures that you were looking at," I pleaded.

"Not now," he said. He took my hand and we looked around the house a bit more. I pushed what had just happened out of my mind. I barely knew Tyler; he didn't have to share everything with me.

The upstairs was very well-kept but not as impressive as the downstairs. The bathroom was up at the top of the stairs. It was very cool. It had one of those old-fashioned bathtubs with claw feet and a high back which looked like you could lay down in and relax really comfortably. There was also a corner stand-in shower, which kind of didn't fit in with the country theme, but hey, we all love to take showers.

There were three large bedrooms. The master bedroom and the guest rooms were beautifully decorated, like they were on display. Then there was Tyler's room. He barely let me inside the door. I got a quick glimpse, from the doorway, of posters and pictures all over the walls, then the door closed.

"Okay, you don't need to go in there," he said.

"But..."

"Let's go back downstairs; we can check this out later."

So we did. He wanted to take me outside so he could show me around the property. We turned and walked hand in hand down the steps toward the front door.

The view from the top of the porch steps was amazing. I felt like I was the king of the castle, or queen, in my case. There, lying in front of me, was a beautiful front yard, which I hadn't noticed on the way in, at least not from this vantage point. Wow, what a view. The large circular driveway was lined with trees and gardens. There was a little pond with a fountain in the center. Of course, it hadn't been running for years and looked a little worse for wear.

The house seemed to me to be in pretty good shape, like there wouldn't be too many repairs if someone wanted to live here. The old sheds and barn in the back of the property, on the other hand, needed a lot of work. The paint was starting to peel and fade, and it looked like the wind had caught under the tin roof in a few places on the barn. Some of the barn boards on one wall were broken and laying on the ground. There were some old birds' nests under the eaves and a few leftover beehives, not to mention the spider webs left over from last year. Luckily their inhabitants were still hibernating; well, I hoped so, anyway.

One of the sheds had a broken window and we saw a squirrel peek his head out but then run back in when he saw us walking by. I guess he had decided to make himself a home there, since nobody was there to evict him. The grounds looked in fairly good shape as if they may have had a gardener taking care of them at some point. I'm sure that Tyler's grandmother didn't take care of this whole property by herself after her husband passed away.

There were flower gardens everywhere and the perennials were starting to show through the undergrowth. The fresh aroma of spring was all around us. I followed Tyler down a path that looked like it led into the forest up ahead. Buds were already forming on the branches of the trees and grass had already started to weave its way through last autumn's fallen leaves. We walked through the bush for a short distance and I had that familiar feeling of déjà vu when we ended up at the edge of the lake. I looked all around. Okay, it didn't look exactly like my safe place, but it was a close second, I would say. Tyler explained that he used to come fishing here all the time, with his grandfather, when he was young. He said that they would spend hours and hours just sitting there with their lines in the water while his grandfather talked about the good old days. Tyler loved to listen to his grandfather tell his amazing stories. It didn't matter if they caught any fish, he said; he really didn't want to catch any because he didn't want to hurt them. It was the highlight of his day, just spending those precious hours with his grandfather. We climbed up onto the rock where they used to sit and drop their lines. The view was breathtaking.

I felt warm as I lay down on the rock, closed my eyes, and absorbed the sunshine.

"You know what, Tyler? I am very happy that you brought me here, and that you wanted to share this special day with me. It must be really hard for you to come back here after all this time."

"It is, but with you here, by my side, it's not as painful."

"This is a really great place. It's funny, but I almost feel at home here. Out in the woods, by the lake, you know... it kind of reminds me of my safe place a bit, the one that I told you about."

"That's right," Tyler replied, "You said something about a forest, with a stream running through it."

"You remember?" I said and smiled.

"Of course I do. I want to know everything about you. I want to help you remember, and if bringing you here helps, well, I'm glad I did."

Tyler lay down next to me and took my hand. I felt very safe and comfortable with him.

I turned my head, opened my eyes, and saw that he was looking at me. He had a big smile on his face.

"What?" I said.

"You are so beautiful," he replied.

He reached out his arm, touched my shoulder, and my hair slid off. I quickly placed my hair back where it was.

"You have quite a scar on your neck. What happened, if you don't mind my asking?"

I swallowed hard. Suddenly, I felt insecure. I trusted him with all my heart, I was sure of that, but I was afraid to scare him away. I was really starting to like him.

"Oh... Tyler," I whispered, "you don't know me. Hell, I don't know me. I spent twenty years of my life behind bars, and I barely remember anything that happened before that time. I did some terrible things; I really don't want to scare you away."

"I don't scare easily, Bobby. When I want something, I usually get it, and I really want you in my life. Please, let me help you; I'm not going anywhere."

I turned my head and looked up at the sky. I felt my chest tighten as my emotions built up inside of me. I had to tell him now, before this went any further.

"They said that I murdered my foster parents."

The words just flew out of my mouth, with no chance to stop them. I listened, but he didn't say anything. I was afraid to look at him, to see the look of horror on his face. I felt a tear escape through my eyelashes, and his hand caught it as it rolled down my cheek. I finally turned and looked back at him, and he smiled.

"You see?" he said, "That wasn't so bad... I'm still here, and I have no plans to run."

He took on an air of professionalism that I hadn't seen before. Well, being a psychologist, I guess he learned how to be objective and not react or show emotion when a patient opened up to him.

"I'm sorry, Tyler, I really am. I honestly don't remember anything. I must have been some kind of monster back then; I don't know."

"Don't be too hard on yourself. Like I've said before, the brain is an intricate machine. It can suppress memories to protect you. Who knows what your life was like? I will help you work on that; you just need to trust me. You shouldn't rush it; just take things slowly."

I brought my hand up to my neck and moved my hair back to reveal the scar. I was always very self-conscious about it. Tyler put his hand on it, and I cringed.

"Oh... I'm sorry; does it hurt?" he said, quickly pulling his hand back.

"No," I replied, "I just think that it's disgusting."

"Don't be silly, it's just a scar, everyone has them. Look here, I have one on the side of my forehead. It was very well taken care of and healed properly, thanks to my grandfather. It's barely visible. So, do you remember how you got yours?"

"Not at all. It is one of those mysteries in my life, like everything else. And you?"

He got quiet and stared into the distance. I was about to say something and...

"Shh," he said, "look."

I turned my head and saw them. A family of deer was walking past us, not that far away. They were so beautiful that I couldn't take my eyes off them. I watched till they disappeared into the forest.

I turned back to Tyler, and he was sitting up and looking out at the lake.

"Are you okay?" I asked.

"Yes, of course. I was just thinking about my grandfather."

I closed my eyes again and listened as he told me stories about his grandparents and the summers he spent with them. They sounded like wonderful people; I wish I could have met them.

Chapter 11

I opened my eyes and realized that I had dozed off. I was a little disoriented. I looked around and saw that Tyler was lying there with me and had fallen asleep too. It was getting late, so I decided that I had better go home before someone came looking for me. I sat up, put my hand on Tyler's shoulder, and woke him gently. I told him that I needed to get home as soon as possible and that I would be back tomorrow, and then I ran off into the woods. It was starting to get dark, so I stumbled around a little to find my way. I ran for a bit and then suddenly someone grabbed me by the hair and pulled me down to the ground.

"Why, you little slut! I saw you two together! Do you think that I'm blind or something? How many times do I have to tell you that I don't want you fucking around with that boy or anyone else? You want to get fucked? I'll fix that right now."

I couldn't figure out where I was or what was going on. I didn't see his face, but he had a scratchy old voice. He never let go of my hair. He reeked of alcohol. I could feel his other hand reaching up under my shirt. He grabbed my bra and yanked it off. By this time,

I was kicking and screaming. I kept calling for Tyler to come rescue me, but he didn't. The old guy kept yelling at me to shut up, but I just kept on screaming at the top of my lungs. He let go of my breast and I saw him raise his hand up into the air. It came back down full force and landed me one across the side of my face. I could hear my neck crack as my head flew sideways. My cheek felt like it was on fire. I begged for him to stop but he wouldn't. I could taste the blood that was flowing into my mouth as I watched him raise his arm and land his fist right back down on my face, over and over again. I thought it would never end. He beat me till I was so weak that I thought I was going to pass out.

"Tyler," I whispered, then I gathered up every little bit of energy that I had left in me and yelled as loud as I possibly could… "Tyler!!!"

Chapter 12

"Bobby… It's all right, Bobby; I'm here. You fell asleep. It was only a dream. I won't let anything bad happen to you ever again, I promise. Everything will be fine, you'll see. I will always be there for you."

I was shaking all over. The tears started running down my face. Tyler put his arms around me. He held me close, but I was still really scared. I was afraid to close my eyes and end up right back in the middle of that beating.

I could feel the warmth of his body as I lay there in his arms. I felt safe, but I still wouldn't close my eyes. I was starting to calm down a bit, but I didn't say a word. I looked up at him and there he was, gazing at me with that beautiful smile on his face, like he had when we first met.

"What are you looking at?" I whispered.

"You."

"It seems like you are looking right through me."

"I am," he said softly. "I'm trying to figure you out."

"I really didn't want you to see me like that, at least not right away."

"Why? What's the difference between now or later?"

"Well, I really like you, but let's face it. I am going crazy and I didn't want to scare you away before you had a chance to get to know me better."

"You couldn't scare me away if your life depended on it. Can't you see what is going on here?"

He spoke softly and I watched as his eyes filled.

"Don't you feel it when I hold you? Can't you feel it when I kiss you? Do my feelings not trigger anything inside of you?"

He took my head in both his hands and pulled it closer to his. I watched him as he licked his lips and brought them closer to mine. They met and then he pulled back, but he still stayed close to me. I did not want him to stop so I pulled him closer until his lips met mine again. My heart started to pound, and I felt that fire inside of me again. He lay down next to me and rolled me over on top of him, never leaving our embrace. The passion was building up inside of me. Suddenly I felt like I was losing control and I stopped. I pulled back a little and looked him in the eyes and smiled..

"It feels so good that it scares me," I said as a tear rolled down my face.

Tyler wiped the tear from my cheek. "It's all right, Bobby. It scares me too."

As we were looking passionately into each other's eyes, my stomach started to growl, really loud. How embarrassing. Tyler cracked up laughing and then I joined in.

"That's Bobby for you. You start getting passionate and all she thinks about is her stomach."

I blushed and gave him a playful punch on the arm.

"Actually, it is way past lunchtime and I have a surprise for you. Let's go back to the house."

He helped me up and then down off the rock. I grabbed his hand and we started to head back.

"This way, Bobby; you're going the wrong way."

"Are you sure? That's really weird, you know, because I am positive that we came from that direction."

"You're just disoriented. Follow me."

We walked back to the house hand in hand. When we got to the car, he grabbed his keys and opened the trunk. He pulled out a big basket and a blanket. He laid the blanket out on the lawn and set the basket on it. He put the music on in the car and opened the windows. He took me by the hand and escorted me onto the blanket. I watched him as he opened the basket and started to empty it. He had thought of everything: the wine, the fancy cheeses, the crackers, the fruit, salads, sandwiches…

"Oops…" he said as he finished emptying everything out of the basket. "How stupid of me. I forgot to bring wine glasses."

"I'll get them," I said, and I got up and ran into the house. As I walked through the living room, my attention was drawn to the bookshelf where Tyler had put away the photo album. I was so curious to see those pictures that had put such a beautiful smile on his face. I was just about to pull it off the shelf, when I heard Tyler call out.

"Do you need any help in there?"

"No, it's okay," I yelled. "I know exactly where they are." I left the album where it was and hurried into the dining room. I opened the cupboard door and grabbed two wine glasses, then ran back outside.

"You didn't have any trouble finding them?"

I sat back down and started to think about what had just happened. That was really weird. I didn't even give it a second thought. I knew exactly where his grandmother kept them. Maybe I noticed them when we first got there. I pushed it out of my mind. We had a beautiful picnic lunch. We talked and laughed and enjoyed the warm spring sunshine.

After a couple of hours of listening to Tyler telling more of his stories and enjoying his company, I starting to feel like I was really getting to know him.

He sat up and started to pack up what was left of our picnic. He poured us each another glass of wine to finish off the bottle.

"Now tell me about the dream or flashback or whatever it was that you had before, at the lake."

I looked at him for a moment and decided that it was about time that I started talking to him about what was happening to me. I felt very comfortable with him and I knew that he would be understanding. Maybe he could help me figure out what was going on in my head.

I told him how we were together in my safe place, and that we were lying alongside each other in the forest and had fallen asleep. Then I mentioned that crazy old man who saw us together and kept calling me a slut and tried to rape me and beat me half to death. He kept saying that he didn't want me to be with anyone else but him.

I could see Tyler's eyes start to fill with tears. He grabbed me and held me in his arms.

"I'm so sorry," he cried. "It was that bad? Was this a recurring thing? I wish I could have helped you back then. I want to help you now."

"I told you that these dreams I am having are really bad. They are very frightening, and they feel so real. What do you make of this old man who doesn't want me to be with anyone else but him? This is not the first time I've dreamed about him. He always calls me a slut and tells me that I belong to him and nobody else. Then he beats me and tries to rape me. You were in that dream too."

He released me from his arms and gazed at me.

"What's up with that? I've just met you, and all of a sudden you are in my dreams. I am confusing my reality with my nightmares."

I stopped for a moment to take a breath.

"It's just bad dreams, Bobby; they can be very confusing," he whispered.

"I do realize that dreams don't make sense half the time. I guess I have been thinking of you a lot since I first met you at Carla's. Maybe that is why you are showing up in my dreams. This old guy, though, oh my God, it seems like whoever this person was, if he is from my past, he did not want me to get involved with anyone."

Tyler paused and looked like he was absorbing what I had just said.

"Do you not recognize this person?" he finally asked.

"I don't know. It's like I kind of see him but I don't. It's hard to explain. I think that I am maybe just so scared of him that I really don't want to know who he is. I never seem to get a good look at his face. I think I block it out somehow."

Tyler never took his eyes off me as I talked about my dreams. I could see from the expression on his face that he was very sympathetic. It looked like he could almost feel my pain as I recalled the beating that I got in the woods by that madman.

"Oh my God, Bobby; that explains a lot of things. I am really sorry."

"Sorry for what? It's not your fault," I said, slightly confused. "You're trying to help me. I'm very happy about that. If I don't talk about it then I will never be able to sort it all out; at least, that's what Carla says."

"Carla is right, but we can't just dredge it out all at once. It might be a little too hard for you to handle. I believe that these are some of your memories that are coming back, and they don't sound like they are going to be very pleasant, so we need to take it slow."

"I'm not scaring you away, am I?"

"You could never scare me away, my dear Bobby. We are going to get through this, and once we do, we can start a whole new life together."

Tyler got up and put the basket back in the car while I folded the blanket. He locked up the house and we settled in the car for our long drive back to the city. We didn't speak very much on the way home. We just relaxed and listened to the music. My mind was a whirlwind of thoughts. I kept replaying our day together. Tyler was amazing, and I felt so comfortable with him. I almost wished that the day would never end.

Before we knew it, we were back in the burbs. When we got to my building, like the perfect gentleman that he was, he escorted me up to my apartment. I thanked him for a most amazing day and for sharing a piece of his past with me. We kissed and said our goodnights.

Chapter 13

I slept very well that night. I guess that all the fresh country air made me feel very relaxed. No nightmares… what a treat. It was Sunday morning and I had promised Carla that I would go out for breakfast with her again. I jumped in the shower, got dressed, and went over to her apartment. She was all ready to go and waiting for me. We walked down the street to the little diner again. It wasn't so busy this time. We sat at a booth next to the window. We ordered breakfast and then Carla asked about my day with Tyler. I thought for a minute and didn't say anything, but I must have been glowing.

"Wow!" Carla whispered. "That good, huh? Come on, Bobby… spill it, don't keep me in suspense."

Carla watched and smiled as she attentively listened to me tell her all about our wonderful outing. Breakfast came, and I kept telling my story as we ate. She laughed at the fun times and got teary-eyed at the very emotional times. I could tell that she was really happy for me.

"Couldn't happen to a nicer person," she said once I'd finished. "I am really happy that you two have hit it off so well."

"Just out of curiosity, Whitey, how long have you known Tyler? You guys have never told me anything about where you met or how long ago it was."

"Actually, we have known each other since we were kids. We pretty much grew up in the same household, but we were not allowed to associate with each other. You see, Tyler's parents were very rich and had a live-in servant. My mom worked for them all her life. We lived in the servants' quarters. Tyler's dad was a really special person and he let me play almost anywhere I wanted to on the property. He even let me play with Tyler every once in a while if no one else was around. On the other hand, Tyler's mother, well, that's a completely different story. She was a real snob. She didn't think that I was good enough to play with her son. I remember Tyler getting really mad and having these big temper tantrums when he would see me playing outside and his mother wouldn't let him go out and join me. He hated his mother so much.

"That is why every chance he had, he would go out to his grandparents' house. They were good people too, just like his father. I saw them occasionally when they would come into the city for a visit, which wasn't often. They were always very nice to my mother and me. They always had a surprise for me each time they'd come. I was always very happy to see them. I was very sad to hear that they had passed away."

I was so into her story that I almost didn't notice the waitress taking away our plates. I stopped her just as she was leaving the table and asked her to bring us some more coffee. Carla paused for a moment.

"Don't stop now," I pleaded. "You never told me about this part of your life before."

The waitress came back with refills and Carla picked up where she had left off.

"Well, the years went by and it was time to go to college. Tyler was going of course, and my mother had saved every dime she could to be sure that I could have a college education and not end up being someone's servant for the rest of my life, like she was. Anyway, this is unfortunately where Tyler and I parted ways.

"That last summer before college was different. He went to his grandparents as usual, but something wasn't right. He had changed, drastically. He had bought a motorcycle earlier that spring. His mother was furious. He was acting very irresponsibly. He drove back and forth between his parents' house and his grandparents' house. He hardly ever came to see me or even acknowledge the fact that I existed. I was very hurt.

"Then one day, I heard that he had totaled his motorcycle. He had a short stay at the hospital, but I can't remember what his injuries were. I do remember that he lost his driver's permit. He claimed that he had been shot at, but there was alcohol on his breath. Nobody believed him, of course. Afterward, he became very angry and distant. Even his grandparents couldn't get through to him. Still, he spent the rest of the summer with them. I was very concerned about him, but my mother said that it was none of our business and that I should stay out of it. I missed him so much. I wanted to know what was going on with him. Then one day, about two weeks before college, his grandparents brought him home. They couldn't do anything with him. I was told that he was clinically depressed. I couldn't understand what was happening to my dear friend. All he did was cry all day long. From morning till night, he wouldn't talk to anyone; he just cried. It was so sad to see him like that. It was like his whole world had collapsed, and nobody seemed to know what had happened.

"Then the day came when I had to leave for college. As hard as I tried, I didn't get to say goodbye to him. His mother was guarding him like a watchdog; she wouldn't let me anywhere near him. I never saw him again. The only news I had was the little bits of information that my mother told me, each time I called, which wasn't much. He had missed his first semester of college. By the time the second semester started, his bags were packed and off he went. I never heard anything more about him. There wasn't a day that went by that I didn't think about him."

"That must have been hard," I said.

"It was, Bobby; he was my best friend, and I couldn't be there for him. Anyway, I hadn't seen hide nor tail of him in all these years.

Imagine how surprised I was when we literally bumped into each other a couple of months ago at the hospital.

"I was hurrying down the hallway with my arms full of files and when I turned the corner, I ran right into him. The files flew everywhere. I didn't notice who it was right away because I was too worried about my files. I quickly bent down to retrieve them, and he did the same thing at the exact same time. Well, didn't we bump heads again. I burst out laughing and so did he. When I looked up at his face, I couldn't believe it. I knew him right away. I could never forget those eyes.

"He recognized me too and gave me a big hug. We were so happy to see each other we hugged again. He helped me pick up my files and walked with me to my station. We didn't have much time to chat. He was at the hospital to look in on one of his patients who had tried to commit suicide. Anyway, we exchanged phone numbers and made plans to go out for supper to catch up on old times, but it never happened. I was working too many hours and didn't have much time.

"When you started having these nightmares of yours, I really hated to see you suffering like that, but I didn't know what I could do to help you. I knew I needed to take the time to go and meet Tyler, to see if he had any experience with something like this and could give me some suggestions on what I could do to help you. So, I called him up and we met for supper and had a great time together.

"I was very happy to see that he had turned out to be a loving and caring person just like his father, and not a conceited bitch like his mother. I didn't ask him about what had happened that last summer before college and I never will. It is probably a part of his life that he does not want to be reminded of. We all have our secrets, I guess.

"I knew that he was going to be very sympathetic when I talked to him about you and your dreams. He showed a great deal of interest. We talked into the wee hours of the morning and that is when he told me that he would be very interested in meeting you. The night that I rescued you from your nightmare and told you about him, I had just gotten home from our evening together."

"I'm really thrilled that you ran into him, too, because I have never been happier," I said. "He is the nicest guy that I have ever met. There is just something about him that makes me feel safe and secure. I feel so comfortable with him that it seems like we have been best friends forever."

"You know, Bobby, I can see it too. There is, like, a very strong connection between you. It's really weird."

We were so caught up in our conversation that we almost forgot where we were. The waitress came to our table and asked if we wanted anything else. I guess that they needed the table or something. We got up to leave and I noticed two guys at the table behind where Carla and I were sitting. My blood started to boil. One of the guys was that asshole, David, from work.

"What in the hell are you doing here?" I yelled as I stepped towards him. "Are you following me around or something? It seems like everywhere that I go, you are there."

"Excuse me," he snarled, "but the last time I checked, this was a public place. My friend and I are allowed to have breakfast here too, just like everyone else. If you have a problem with that, well…"

Carla grabbed me by the arm and dragged me to the cash register. We paid for our breakfast and left.

"Son of a bitch, that guy is really pissing me off!" I said frantically as we passed by the window where he was sitting. He leered at us as we walked away.

"He probably sat there and listened to our whole conversation, and who was that guy with him? Jesus, not another asshole to watch out for, I hope."

"Calm down," Carla said as she tugged on my arm to slow me down. "The house isn't on fire," she said. "Relax, this is not helping you any."

"Okay… okay, I'm calm! This is crazy. I just can't figure this out. He shows up at the same restaurant for breakfast, not only once but twice. We go to the park, guess who's there. Even at work, he seems to always be sneaking up on us. He purposely bumps into me so he can grab my card to see who sent me the flowers the other day. He shows up at my apartment and I never told him where I live. Sometimes I feel like he is following me, and don't tell me I'm being paranoid, because I'm not. These are not coincidences. This is starting to worry me a lot."

We reached our building and Carla asked if I wanted to go to her apartment with her for a while and talk. I had no other plans, so I did.

"I'm glad to hear you say that you feel the same way Bobby because I thought I was being paranoid. That guy scares the hell out of me too. I didn't tell you that before because I didn't want to scare you, but he is always sneaking around. He seems to know our every move. It almost feels like he is stalking us. I don't know what we should do. We can't call the police because he hasn't done anything wrong."

"Police!" I screeched. "Are you crazy? I don't want anything to do with the police! I don't need any police! They will think that I did something wrong and I will be in trouble again! No! No police! No way! Absolutely not!"

"Okay… okay… forget I said that."

Carla tried to calm me down again. She wasn't very successful because she was pretty upset herself. What kind of a game was this guy playing, and who was the guy sitting with him in the restaurant? I had never seen him before and neither had Carla. Another mystery to deal with.

I leaned back on her couch, closed my eyes, and tried to relax a bit. I didn't need this. Not with all my crazy nightmares happening. I needed to try to ignore him and get my life back to normal.

"Hey, Carla? Maybe we are letting our imaginations get the better of us. I mean, the guy does work at the hospital with us. We're bound to bump into him once in a while. That restaurant is close to the hospital too, and a lot of people that work with us go there."

I don't know who I was trying to convince more, Carla or me. I stayed there for a little while longer and then decided to go to my apartment and catch up on some housework.

It was almost suppertime when I heard a knock at the door. I cautiously walked down the hallway, still thinking about the events of the morning, and reached for the door handle. "Who is it?" I said with a forced calmness in my voice.

"Pizza delivery."

Silly man, I recognized his voice right away.

"I don't recall ordering any pizza," I said, trying hard not to laugh.

"Are you sure, because this is the address they gave me?"

"I'm positive, but you know, it smells really good and I am a little hungry. Come on in, Mister Pizza Delivery Guy, and we can share it."

I swung the door open with a big smile on my face.

Tyler started to laugh.

"You are really good at this," he said. "You know, we make a pretty good pair; we are both a laugh a minute."

We had supper and talked about the wonderful time we had together on Saturday. When we were done, we went and sat in the living room. He sat down next to me and took me by the hand.

"Do you know how happy I am that we are finally together?" he said as his eyes met mine. "I never thought I would find happiness again."

Before I could say a word, his lips were touching mine. I could feel the butterflies fluttering around in my stomach. My temperature was rising. I could hear my heart pounding faster and faster. I held him close and I started to tremble.

"God, it feels so good when you touch me. Please don't stop."

"But you're trembling."

"I know, but I'm not scared. I don't know why it's happening. I just know that I don't want you to let go. It feels so good. I feel so safe in your arms."

We just sat there for a few minutes embracing and neither of us spoke. It was just too good for words. I was just about to say something, when I heard a knock at the door. Before I could get there, Carla walked in.

"Am I interrupting anything? Isn't this cozy? What are you guys doing sitting in the dark?"

Carla walked right past me and went and joined Tyler in the living room. I closed the door and followed her in.

"Make yourself at home, Whitey; you have really good timing."

She didn't pay any attention to what I said; she seemed a little bit preoccupied. Tyler also noticed that she was not acting like herself and asked her what was wrong.

"I really don't know," she said. "I am feeling a little bit jumpy, is all. With everything that is going on, I guess, and this morning, well, you know. Anyway, after supper, I decided to walk to the grocery store to get a few things, and on my way back, I don't know for sure, but I felt like someone was following me. I'm not sure if it was my imagination, but it is making me very uneasy."

"What happened this morning?" Tyler asked.

"Carla and I went out for breakfast," I replied. "Sometime after that, David showed up. We didn't see him come in because we were too busy talking, but we saw him on our way out. He was with some guy that we have never seen before. They were sitting at the table right behind us. That guy seems to be always around where we are. He's starting to play on our nerves a bit."

"Who is this guy, anyway? Do you know anything about him?"

"Not really. He is new at the hospital," Carla replied. "I just know that he is very annoying, and he seems to be around all the time. He sticks his nose in everything that goes on."

"No wonder you are nervous; I would be too. Tell me what his full name is, and I will see if I can do a background check on him. I have some friends on the police force who can maybe help me out. In the meantime, you should both be very careful. Don't go out walking around alone at night just in case. Maybe it's nothing but coincidences, but it is better to be safe than sorry."

We didn't know his full name, but we told Tyler that we would look into it. We figured that there must be somebody at the hospital who knew what it was. Mrs. Blair would know but I wasn't sure that I wanted to go see her about this right away. Tyler was right, though. We needed to find out what David was up to, if anything. I didn't like the thought of police involvement, but Tyler said that he would leave my name out of it for now.

It was getting late so Tyler kissed me and said goodnight. Carla left too. She had to get to work early the next morning. I fixed myself a cup of herbal tea, put some music on, and tried to relax before going to bed. All this talk about David had me a little stressed out. The soothing chamomile and the soft jazz soon had me forgetting about David and concentrating on Tyler. He was such a great guy. I was starting to think that maybe I was falling in love. The thought scared the hell out of me because I never thought that I would ever find happiness with someone. Something was bound to go wrong.

Just as I was heading to my bedroom to get some sleep, the phone rang. It was Tyler. He told me that he had had a wonderful evening and he wanted to see me again. He asked if I was free Friday night and of course I told him I was. He said that he would pick me up after work and we could go out for supper or something, and that I should put my thinking cap on and try to think of something I might like to do. I was very excited to be seeing him again; I really enjoyed his company. We said goodnight and I went to bed.

Chapter 14

I started to tremble as I peeked over the edge of my blankets and watched the door. I could hear them fighting, and I knew that it wasn't going to end well. The thought of what was about to happen next terrified me.

The light from downstairs cast frightening shadows on my bedroom ceiling. My eyes were glued to the doorway like a sniper waiting for the kill and ready to shoot his target. My ears were tuned into every little sound.

I could hear the scratching noises that the mice were making as they scrambled through the attic. Even the squirrels were active at this late hour as they rummaged through the butternuts that were drying in there. The wind made an eerie sound as it flowed past my window. I could hear my heart pounding in double-time as the tears started running down my face. I didn't want to cry anymore because it didn't help matters... it only made things worse... but I couldn't help myself. It was far beyond my control. I could feel every muscle in my body ache from being so tense. I tried to relax them, but it didn't work. I knew it was only a matter of time.

Faintly, I could still hear the arguing that was going on downstairs. As long as I could hear them, I knew I was safe, but as fast as it started, the arguing stopped. The fear inside of me intensified as I heard footsteps coming closer and closer. They stopped at the bottom of the stairs.

"Please don't come up here tonight," I whispered under my breath. "Please go away; I can't deal with this anymore."

I heard the creaking of the old stairs as he started to make his way up. I counted every step that he took. About halfway up to my bedroom he paused and started coughing. How I hated his phlegmy cough; it always made me gag. He got quiet again and started inching his way up to the top of the stairs... eleven... twelve... thirteen... fourteen...

Oh no, not again; I can't take it anymore.

On my wall, I could see the tall shadow of this monster of a man as he clung onto my door frame to keep his balance. He was pissed drunk again, and as usual, I was always the one who got to suffer the consequences. He always came up to my room when he was loaded and miserable from fighting a losing battle with his wife. She cursed his continuous drinking and him in general. They hated each other. I didn't know why they stayed together; what a way to live.

"It's just me, sweetheart. I've come to say goodnight."

He stumbled through my room then stood next to the bed and looked down on me. I gasped when he swayed, for fear that he would fall on top of me.

"Are you crying again? What the fuck is wrong with you? Now be quiet and move over."

I tried to stop, but I was not successful, and I was having trouble breathing. I kept gasping for air. He leaned over and backhanded me one on the side of my face. I could feel a burning sensation on my cheek. I didn't say a word; I just did what he said and made room for him. He lay down next to me and started to caress the side of my face that he had smacked. His hands were rough and calloused, and it stung when he slid his fingers across it. His breath stank so bad of alcohol that I thought I was going to be sick.

"Don't you love me, baby? You're my favorite little girl."

I could see his face coming closer to mine, so I closed my eyes and prayed that he would disappear. I could feel his stinky old lips touch mine and I turned my head.

I opened my eyes again, and I was safe and sound in my own bedroom.

"Oh my God, what a relief," I muttered to myself.

I was still shaking and crying but I knew he couldn't hurt me anymore. It was only a dream. I sat up and tried to catch my breath. The dream kept replaying over and over again in my head. It was horrifying. I needed to try to put it out of my mind, so I got up and just walked around the apartment for a while. I would have liked to talk to Carla, but I didn't dare wake her up; she had to work a long shift at the hospital in the morning. I decided to make myself another cup of chamomile tea to help me relax. There was no way I was going to fall asleep like this.

I grabbed a sheet of paper and a pencil and started to doodle. I was not much of an artist, but every once in a while, I did like to sit down and draw, or just write anything that came into my mind. It seemed to relax me. My most recent drawing was a sketch of a little girl trapped on a spiderweb made of yardsticks, and a big ugly hand crawling across it to catch her. I could never make much sense of my drawings or stories, but they seemed to represent sadness, fear and loneliness. It didn't matter, though, because drawing and writing always made me feel better.

I finished my tea and decided that I should go back to bed and try to sleep again. I was feeling a lot calmer. I put my cup and drawing away and got back into bed. I closed my eyes and lay there for the longest time. I couldn't seem to go back to sleep.

I opened my eyes and oh my God, you won't believe what I saw! That old, ugly, stinky man was back, and he was lying right next to me again. I tried to get away from him, but I couldn't. I started to yell out, but he put his hand on my mouth.

"Stay quiet, you stupid brat; I want to play a little stink finger. Now stop your fucking squirming and let's have a little fun."

His hand was still over my mouth and I could hardly breathe. I could feel his other hand reach up under my nightie.

"No! no!" I tried to yell out, but his hand muffled my words. "Let go of me! Please don't touch me… please leave me alone!"

I was terrified, and I tried desperately to get away. I didn't have much energy left and I was starting to feel faint. I was on the verge of losing consciousness and I couldn't think of anything else to do so I bit him as hard as I could. He let go of me and started yelling.

"Well, you good-for-nothing piece of shit; I'll show you who is boss!"

He grabbed me by the throat with one hand and raised his other hand up into the air and formed a fist with it. I watched in desperation as it plunged down toward my face.

I jumped up out of bed, got my foot caught in my blankets, and fell on the floor. Quickly, I got back up and turned my light on. He was gone, thank God. I was still terrified. I sat back down in the corner of my bed, pulled the blankets up around me, and cried. I looked around my room and prayed that he would not come back. This was unbelievable.

I couldn't even figure out what had just happened to me. The one thing I knew for sure was that I didn't want to go back to that place where I was in my dream ever again. I didn't want him to come back here either. It was just too crazy. My second nightmare was a continuation of my first one. There was no way that I was going to go back to sleep now. I was too scared to close my eyes and have it start all over again. I couldn't take any more abuse like that. It seemed so real. I was so confused.

It was almost time to get up anyway, so I got dressed and went into the kitchen to make myself a big breakfast. I figured that food would keep my mind off my dreams. I whipped up some eggs for a cheese omelet, which I threw in the oven along with a small tray with a few strips of bacon. I cut up some leftover potatoes for home fries and put the bread in the toaster. I started up the coffee machine. I was going to need a few cups to keep me awake. While I waited for the eggs to cook, I put the radio on and started singing along to "Summer of 69…" I was really getting into the music and started dancing around the table.

"Not Crazy!!!"

When my food was ready, I sat down to eat. I was almost done when I heard a very soft knock at the door. As I made my way there, I wondered who would be at my door at this hour. Of course, it was Carla; who else would it be.

"Hey there, Looney Tunes; what are you doing up so early? I could hear you singing from my apartment. Aren't we in a good mood? If you don't mind a little advice, dear, uh, don't give up your day job, eh!"

I didn't look at her; I just turned around and walked back toward the kitchen. She didn't say anything else; I think she realized that this wasn't a laughing matter. I heard her footsteps as she followed me in. I turned and faced her, and my eyes started to fill with tears.

"Jesus Christ, Carla, good mood? I don't think so; I was just trying to clear my mind. I wanted to completely shut off all my thoughts. I can't take it anymore. Something's got to give. I need to figure out what is going on, and why this is happening to me. I know that you are on your way to work so I won't trouble you with it right now, but can you please stay here with me tonight? I don't want to be alone."

"I'm sorry that you are having such a terrible time, Bobby. I wish I could make it all go away but it doesn't seem like I can. As for tonight, you can count on me. We'll walk home together after work."

She left for the hospital and I went back to finish my breakfast. I cleaned up the dishes, took a shower, and got ready for work. It was a little early and it looked like it was going to be a beautiful day, so I decided to take a walk through the park before going to work. I thought the fresh air would do me good. I was a little tired and still a little shaken up from my nightmares.

In the distance, I could hear the trickling sound of the water fountain. I picked up the pace and headed straight for it. There it was in all its glory, shimmering in the morning sunlight. I hadn't come back here since I walked through the park with Carla a couple of weeks ago. Now all I had to do was sit in front of the fountain with my eyes closed and let the sound take me away. I sat there for a few minutes and nothing was happening. I guess there were too many people walking by who were distracting me. I didn't realize that there would be so many people at this hour. I didn't give up; I kept trying. I tried to block out all the sounds that surrounded me.

I opened my eyes and there I was, back in my safe place. Something was different this time, because I was looking at it from a distance. I moved slowly toward it. As I got closer, I could see that someone else was in my safe place. It looked like a guy, but I couldn't really tell because he had his back to me. I didn't understand what he was doing there. This was my place. My safe place. Nobody else had any business there.

"Is that you, Robbie?"

I was so startled that I opened my eyes and I was sitting in front of the water fountain again. I very quickly got up, turned, and walked away. Who was in my safe place and why did he call out for Robbie?

My life was getting more and more complicated and I was getting crazier with each passing day.

I walked straight to the hospital and went to find Carla. I told her about what had happened, and she seemed pretty puzzled too. I didn't have much time to talk and neither did she, so I told her that I would see her after work and that I would tell her all about it then.

The day seemed to drag on. My mind wandered from one nightmare to another. I tried to think of Tyler but then my mind would switch to David, ugh. Thank goodness I didn't run into him.

When my shift was finally over, it felt like it had been a really long day. I was just about to grab my things and head upstairs when I turned and saw Carla come through the kitchen entrance. Lou spotted her and walked towards us, whistling away as he usually did. He was always in a good mood. He flung his arms open and hugged both of us at the same time.

"Group hug," he said. "What a way to end my day, with my two favorite women in my arms. It's a man's dream come true, you know. How are my two beautiful ladies doing today?"

At that moment, just as I was about to respond, I saw David walk in at the other end of the kitchen. He had that stupid little smirk on his face like he usually did.

"Everything was pretty good right up until now," I said.

Lou let go of me and gave me a strange look. I guess he thought I was talking about him.

"Not you, Lou; that's not what I meant."

Carla gave me a weird look too.

"I didn't mean Lou. Look behind you."

Carla turned and saw David walking towards us. I could see her face start to get red. Lou didn't know what was going on. He didn't say anything; he just watched.

"Well, hello ladies," David said as he walked by. "Aren't we looking fine? Are we all done for the day?"

"Bastard!" Carla yelled. "Leave us alone."

David laughed hysterically as he left the kitchen.

Lou turned and looked at Carla with a really stunned expression on his face. I don't think that he had ever heard her talk like that. He looked pretty funny and I started to giggle.

"What are you laughing at?" he said. "And what in the world is going on around here?"

"I'm sorry, Lou. I didn't mean to laugh at you, but you should have seen the look on your face when Carla swore at David."

We waited till David left the kitchen, and then we told Lou how much trouble he had been causing us and how we thought that he might be stalking us or something because he was always around. Lou listened attentively to what we were saying but he didn't seem surprised. He just stood there quietly for a few minutes and I could tell that he was trying to recall something.

"Come to think of it," he said, "I remember him asking me some questions about the two of you when he first started working here. I didn't think anything of it at the time. I thought that maybe he was just interested in one of you or something. I'm sorry that he is causing you trouble. Is there anything I can do to help?"

"Actually," Carla replied, "you could very discreetly try to find out his last name for us. I have a friend who knows what is going on and he is going to try to get some background information on him. He just wants to try to find out where he is from and what he's doing here."

"That's easy; it's Allen."

"What?" I didn't know what he was talking about.

"His last name. It's Allen. David Allen."

I threw my arms around Lou and gave him a big hug.

"You're the best; thank you so much."

Carla and I said goodbye to Lou and headed for home.

We were very excited about finding out David's last name, so as soon as we got home, I called Tyler to tell him. He was happy to hear the news, and he said that he would look into it first thing in the morning. Carla went to her apartment to change while I talked with Tyler. I told him that she was going to sleep over because I had such terrible dreams the night before and I did not want to be alone. He wanted to hear about them, so I sat back on the sofa and recounted my crazy nightmares to him. It wasn't hard. I remembered every gory detail as if it had really happened. I tried very hard not to get emotional, but he could hear it in my voice.

"That's enough for now, Bobby," he said. "You'll need to relax and try to stop thinking about it if you want to get some sleep tonight."

Then I remembered about the fountain. I told him about the person who was in my safe place and that I didn't really see who it was, but it was a guy and he called out for Robbie.

"What do you think about that?" I asked.

I waited for an answer and none came. Tyler didn't say a word. I knew he was there because I could hear him breathing.

"Tyler! Did you hear me? Hey! What are you doing?"

"I'm sorry, Bobby; I was just thinking. There are a lot of things going on in your mind and I will help you solve them, but you need to be patient; it takes time."

"That is almost impossible because I can't control these things that are happening. To top it all off, there's David who keeps annoying the hell out of me."

I was about to start crying when Carla walked in the door with her rubber duckie pajamas, teddy bear, and a bottle of wine.

"What are you doing, Looney Tunes? Get with the program, it's pajama party time."

I burst out laughing. Tyler asked me what was so funny, so I described to him what Carla looked like and what she had said.

"Sounds like the Carla that I know and love. Well, it looks like you're in good hands. Have fun but don't forget that you both need to get up early to go to work tomorrow morning. Behave yourselves. I will call you if I get some news about David."

We had a quick spaghetti supper and then Carla put on some rock and roll and started to dance around the room with her teddy bear.

"Are you being a party pooper or what? Get me a corkscrew and get your pajamas on now! That's an order!"

I put my hand up to my forehead, stood at attention, and saluted her.

"Yes ma'am," I replied as I walked past her and out of the room. "No wonder I'm crazy! Look who I hang around with!"

She let out a yell and started to chase me down the hallway. I tried to close my bedroom door, but I wasn't fast enough, and she pushed her way in.

"You're in trouble now!" she said as she grabbed my pillow and started hitting me with it.

"Stop it, Whitey! Okay, I give up! I give up!"

She wouldn't stop but I managed to grab her and flip her over onto the bed. I sat on her stomach and got the pillow away from her. It was my turn to show her who was boss. I kept hitting her, and she kept yelling. We wrestled for the longest time. We got laughing so hard that we were both almost in tears. Finally, we kind of both just dropped from exhaustion. We lay on the bed next to each other and just stared at the ceiling till we caught our breath.

"You're a really good friend, Carla White. You know that? What would I do without you?"

Carla rolled over onto her side, looked at me, and smiled.

"Oh, come on, Bobby, you don't get it, do you? I wouldn't want to be anywhere else. You are all I have left in this world. If it weren't for you, I would be very lonely. I love you. You are like the sister I never had. I remember when my mom passed away; well, if you hadn't been there for me, I would have never gotten through it. Now it is my turn to help you through your hard times. That's what best friends are for, don't you know that? Okay, so enough of this mushy stuff. Why don't you take a nice hot bath, and I will pop the cork on that wine bottle?"

"Bath! No way. I don't think I will ever take a bath again. I'll take a quick shower but not a bath! Remember the last time? I ended up almost drowning in that sea of blood. I will not risk going through that again, not if I can help it."

"Fine, take a shower, and come and sit in the living room after and we will talk."

When I got out of the bathroom, there were no lights on anywhere. Carla had found every candle that I owned and probably some of hers and brought them into the living room and lit them. There was soft music playing and Carla was singing along. I could see her in the dim candlelight laying on the couch with her glass of wine in her hand.

"Come on and join the party," she said softly as she sat up and handed me my glass of wine. "Now this is what I call relaxation."

I took a sip of the wine and sat down and listened to her sing with the music. "Summertime," one of my favorite blues songs was playing, and Carla was really good at singing the blues. She was right, though: this was wonderful. I sat there for a long time and didn't say a word. I felt hypnotized by the candles and the music. The flames seemed to sway and keep time to the sound of Carla's wonderful singing. I closed my eyes. The sound of her voice seemed to be getting farther and farther away.......

Chapter 15

"Sleepyhead! Hey, Bobby, it's time to get up. I made you some breakfast."

I opened my eyes and I was still lying on the couch in the living room.

"You fell asleep and I didn't have the heart to wake you up, so I blew out the candles and crawled back onto the couch. I didn't hear a peep out of you all night. I woke up about half an hour ago and decided to make breakfast. Did you sleep well?"

"Like a baby," I said as I got up and headed for the kitchen. "I'm starving, and something smells really good."

She'd made blueberry pancakes. We had breakfast and then Carla went to her apartment to get ready for work, rubber duckies and all. I headed for my room and did the same. We walked to work together.

* * * * *

The week was going by quickly, and it was already Thursday afternoon. Carla stayed with me the whole time and I slept well each night. Tyler called every night to talk to me, but he did not have any news about David.

I was almost done my shift. I just had a little more cleaning up to do, but I started feeling uneasy. It felt as if I wasn't alone anymore and someone was watching me. I slowly turned around and looked behind me, but there was no one there. I still couldn't shake that feeling. I was getting very nervous, and I wanted to get out of there as soon as possible. I finished, took my apron off and hung it up, and then walked around the corner and into the main kitchen. Someone grabbed me by the arm and I almost jumped out of my skin. It was David.

"You scared the shit out of me, you fool! What in the hell are you doing here?"

"Where is your friend Tyler? I haven't seen him around, lately. Did you scare him away? Is he not sending you flowers anymore?"

"That's none of your goddamn business!" I yelled. "Just leave me alone."

"You should stay away from him. He's bad news. Do you know that he's a shrink? He's just going to mess with your head, you know. You don't want him to know what is lost inside that little brain of yours, do you?"

"Leave me alone, you son of a bitch! What in the hell do you know, anyway! Stay out of my life and leave my friends alone too or I'll..."

"Or you'll what? What are you going to do, you little psycho bitch? Are you going to hurt me?"

Well, that did it; I completely lost control. I punched him in the face with all my strength and knocked him on his ass. Just as I was about to pounce on him, somebody grabbed me from behind. I tried to break free, but I couldn't.

"Bobby! Bobby! Stop it right now! He's not worth it! Calm down!"

I started to cry, and Lou turned me around and held me in his arms.

"He wouldn't leave me alone, he just kept taunting me, and I can't take it anymore. Why is he doing this to me? I don't know how

I am going to work in the same building as him if he keeps bothering me like this. If he doesn't leave me alone, I'm going to have to quit my job here and find something else."

"No, you're not. Don't be silly. You have been working here a lot longer than he has and if anyone is going to leave it will be him. I saw everything, and I am going to go down to management to report him."

"The fucking bitch broke my nose!" David howled.

"You better get your ass out of here," Lou yelled, "or that won't be the only thing broken, and it will be my pleasure."

David got up, grabbed a towel for his bloody nose, and left the kitchen. A few minutes after he left, Carla walked in. She freaked when she saw the blood on the floor and me crying in Lou's arms. She ran over to check on me. She thought I had cut myself or something.

"Oh my God, Bobby, are you okay?"

Lou looked at Carla and started to laugh.

"In this corner, Roberta Hansen, featherweight champion of St. Mary's Community Hospital, winner by knockout."

I sniffled and wiped the tears from my eyes and then smacked Lou on the arm.

"It isn't funny," I cried. "I can't believe I did that."

I turned and looked at Carla. She looked so puzzled that I couldn't help myself and I started to giggle too.

"Your friend here just pounded the crap out of David. That's his blood all over the floor."

Carla just stood there with her mouth open and didn't say anything. I was still a little shook up, so Lou told her what had happened.

All at once, it hit me. I had actually lost my temper and hurt someone. I started to shake all over, and my eyes started to fill with tears. Suddenly I wasn't feeling so well, and I felt like I was going to pass out.

"Bobby, what's wrong? You look like you've seen a ghost," Lou said. "Come and sit down for a minute."

"I can't believe I did that… I can't believe I did that… I never wanted to hurt anyone… I really didn't mean to do that… I really didn't…"

"Come on, sweetheart; he was asking for it. Anyone else would have done the same thing you did. Don't worry about it."

I didn't feel well at all. I didn't say another word; all I did was sit there trembling and crying.

"Carla, you need to get her home. I'll give you a ride. I'll get my car and bring it around to the front entrance. I'll see that you get home safe and sound, then I'll come back and take care of this mess."

As soon as we got home, Carla called Tyler. I just curled up on the couch with Carla's teddy bear. It wasn't too long before there was a knock at the door. Carla got up to let Tyler in. He came straight to the couch and took me in his arms.

"I'm so sorry… I didn't mean to hurt anyone… I really didn't…"

Tyler cut me off. He told me to relax and that we would talk as soon as I calmed down. He sent Carla into my bedroom to get my comforter. He unfolded it and wrapped it around me. Then he asked Carla if she knew the whole story about what happened, but she told him that she wasn't in the kitchen when it all took place. She told him that Lou was there when it happened, and he had witnessed it all, and he could probably him out. Tyler got up and called the hospital to see if he was still there. He was on the phone for the longest time. I didn't pay much attention. I just kept on replaying the whole thing in my mind, over and over again. I kept remembering the blood running down his face… All that blood.

Tyler came back and took me in his arms again.

"It's not your fault, Bobby," he said. "Lou heard everything that David said to you. He provoked you, big time. He deserved what he got. I'm sorry that he put you through all that."

"I'm so sorry, Tyler. Look at me. I'm falling apart at the seams. I'm sorry you got dragged into this mess. I really don't want to ruin your life too. I can see it now. I'm probably going to end up right back in a mental institute. That asshole is really getting to me. I don't know what I ever did to him to make him harass me like this. What scares me the most, though, is that he seems to know a lot more about me than he lets on. He said that I shouldn't talk to you because you are a shrink and you might try to find out what is lost in my brain. Somehow, he knows about my memory loss, among other things. I am sure he knows, but how?"

"Calm down, Bobby; everything is going to be okay. He's just trying to scare you. Well, he doesn't scare me. I'll take care of this."

"Here Bobby," Carla said. "I made you a cup of chamomile tea; it should help you relax."

I looked up at her and kind of half-smiled, but I didn't move. Tyler was still holding me in his arms… and I didn't want to leave them. It seemed crazy, but I thought that if I stayed close to him, he would protect me. I closed my eyes and snuggled up a little closer. I concentrated hard on the warmth and security that I was feeling in his embrace and tried to block out everything else.

Carla put my cup on the coffee table. She and Tyler started talking but I could barely hear them. I seemed to be going farther and farther away till I couldn't hear them at all. I felt like I was floating off into space.

It was dark, and I couldn't see anything, but I wasn't scared. I was very calm and relaxed. I could see a dim light in the distance. I went towards it. The world opened up before me, and what a wonderful world it was. There were farms and green meadows, flowers and trees, lakes and rivers, mountains and blue skies all around. I could see herds of cattle grazing on the fresh green grass in the pastures and horses galloping along the riverside. I followed along behind them and felt a tremendous feeling of freedom unlike anything I had ever felt before. The horses veered back out into the pasture and I kept on following the water. There seemed to be some kind of invisible force pulling me that way.

I was soaring just above the treetops when I started to slow down. I soon came to a complete stop. There was something very calming about this place. I noticed the log that lay across the river and the familiar trees and flowers that surrounded it. I realized at that moment that I was in my safe place. This was the first time that I had seen the area around it. It couldn't be real. It was just too magnificent.

I couldn't see them right away because there were branches obstructing my view, but as I moved in closer, I noticed that there were two people sitting in the middle of my log. They were in each other's arms, holding each other lovingly. A very warm feeling came over me. How lucky they were to be together in such a beautiful place.

Then it dawned on me, "What are they doing in my safe place and why am I here watching them?"

I was kind of embarrassed. I felt like a peeping tom, but I felt very drawn to them, so I moved in a little closer to see who they were. I couldn't believe my eyes. I knew for sure now that my safe place was only a dream. The loving couple on the log was Tyler and me, only we looked a lot younger. Tyler's hair was longer, and he looked so boyish. My hair was so shiny and full, and I was so thin. We carried on so playfully. It was amazing to watch them and it made me feel really happy because all I wished for in my life right then was to heal my mind and spend the rest of my years with Tyler. I was very much in love. I could hear our laughter and I could feel our passion. As I started to float away, I heard the younger me yell at the top of her lungs, "I want the whole world to know that I love you, Ty!"

I love you Ty… I love you Ty… Those words kept echoing through the forest and I kept repeating them over and over again in my mind… I love you Ty…

"I love you Ty," I whispered, then I opened my eyes and saw that I was still in Tyler's arms.

Slightly embarrassed, I pushed away from him and tried to apologize. I looked around and Carla was nowhere to be seen.

"Shh…" he said as he put his finger across my lips and pulled me close to him.

The look on his face made my heart melt. He gazed into my eyes as if he could read everything that was going on in my mind. I could see a tear form in the corner of his eye and watched as it slowly flowed down his cheek. I reached up and wiped it with my finger. He seemed to be in so much pain and I didn't know why.

"You called me Ty," he said. Then he gently pulled my face close to his and very slowly pressed his lips against mine. He pulled away again and looked into my eyes once more, as if he was puzzled about something.

My body was starting to tremble all over, and the heat was building up inside of me. I felt like I was about to explode. My heart started pounding double-time and I was starting to breathe heavily. I couldn't wait much longer. I closed my eyes, pulled him close, and wrapped my arms around him. I could feel him tremble as I very passionately moved my hands across his back. It felt so good that I could hardly control myself.

"Oh God, look what you do to me," I whispered as I pressed my lips against his neck.

I kissed my way up to his ear and caressed it for a few seconds and then I made my way back to his mouth. I could tell that he was really getting into it too because I could hear his heart pounding faster. I felt the strength in his arms as he held me close to him… so close, like he never wanted to let me go. I pulled away and looked deep into his eyes. I was on fire. I yearned so much for his affection. He pulled me back. When our lips met again, it was like nothing I had ever felt before.

The bond between us seemed to be getting stronger and stronger. I could feel it in his caress. I felt so safe and secure and loved. All that was bad in my life disappeared at that moment. I couldn't think about anything else but the passion that I was feeling. I tilted my head a little more to the side and opened my mouth slightly. I was very nervous because I didn't know how far this was going to go. I felt his tongue slide gently between my lips. It felt wonderful. He tasted so good. Our tongues slow-danced for the longest time.

For a while, it seemed like we were the only two people in this world that existed. Everything and everyone had disappeared. Then he gently pulled away and looked straight into my eyes.

"You know, Bobby? I have loved you since the first day I met you. I have never loved anyone else."

My heart melted right then and there. I don't think that I had ever felt love like that before. I wanted to tell him how I felt, but I couldn't. I was speechless. I just couldn't find the words. I was just too emotional. I felt a big lump forming in the back of my throat and

I could feel my eyes start to fill. I tried to hold them back, but Tyler could see that I was struggling.

"Oh Tyler," I whispered. "This feels so good, but it's so new to me, and a little frightening. There is so much craziness in my life right now, and I don't want to lose you, but I think I need to try to take it slow. I don't want to; really, you feel so right; oh God, listen to me; I am totally losing it. I'm sorry; I don't even know what I am saying."

Tyler put his finger across my lips. "Shh…" he said, "I'm not going anywhere."

He lay back down next to me, pulled me close, and held me firmly in his arms. He felt me tremble, so he reached for the blanket and covered us both with it.

"It's okay, Bobby," he whispered. "I'm here now."

Chapter 16

I was still half-asleep, but I could hear birds chirping, so I knew it was morning. I was so comfortable that I just lay there and relaxed for a few minutes with my eyes closed. I heard a whisper and quickly opened them. It was Tyler; he was lying next to me. He was looking at me with a big smile on his face. I was a little disoriented and I couldn't quite remember how we both ended up sleeping on the couch, or that he had even spent the night.

"What are you looking at?" I said between yawns.

"Do you know how truly beautiful you are?" he said as he ran his fingers through my hair.

"Who are you trying to kid? I just woke up; I must look like crap!"

I pulled the blanket up over my head and held it tightly.

"Did you stay here all night? I'm sorry, Tyler. I'm not a very good host; I must have fallen asleep. Did you get any rest?"

"Sleep! Are you kidding? Could you get your head out from under that blanket?" He tried to pull it down off my face. "Actually, I should have thought of that last night. It might have muffled the snoring. It was so loud that I can't understand how the neighbors can sleep."

"Ah! You liar!"

I pushed away from him and got up and headed for the bathroom. I closed the door behind me and looked in the mirror. A big smile came across my face as I started to remember a little about what went on last night. There was only one problem, though. I couldn't figure out if it was all a dream or if it had really happened. Then I heard a knock at the bathroom door.

"Come on, Bobby," he said. "I was only kidding. You didn't snore at all, and I slept like a baby."

"I'll be out in a minute," I said. Then I hurriedly washed my face, combed my hair, brushed my teeth, and rinsed my mouth.

He was standing at the door when I opened it and I pretended to be angry as I walked out. I couldn't keep a straight face for very long because he looked so pitiful.

"Gotcha!" I shouted, and I burst out laughing.

He pushed me gently against the wall and held me there. I tried to struggle just a little bit to make it look good, but I was not really anxious to be released from his hold. I might have been kidding around about being mad, but I wasn't joking about this. I wanted Tyler more than anything.

He held my arms against the wall to stop me from struggling, he looked me in the eyes, and then he kissed me on the lips. It felt wonderful, but the best part was that I knew right then and there that the events that I vaguely remembered from the night before were not a dream. They were the real thing.

"Are you alright?" he said. "I don't want to push you."

"I have never wanted anything more in all my life," I whispered.

Suddenly, I came back down to Earth and realized that I had to get ready to go to work. I didn't know if I would still have a job after what had happened yesterday. It was still early so we had time to have a little breakfast and talk about my job. Tyler tried to make me feel better by telling me that I had Carla and Lou in my corner, and that they would stand behind me no matter what. I was about to get up from the table and go get cleaned up for work when I heard a knock at the door. It was Carla; who else would it be.

"Hey Bobby, how are you doing this morning?" she said as she reached out and gave me a big hug.

"I'm as well as I can be, I guess, but I can't talk now. I need to get ready for work if I don't want to be late. That is, if I still have a job."

"Don't worry about it because I will be with you every step of the way. I have already made a few phone calls. Lou and I will take care of this mess as soon as we get there. We have a meeting with Mrs. Blair at nine o'clock sharp, and we better not be late if we know what's good for us."

Mrs. Blair was always very nice to me, but she was also very strict. If you did your work and didn't cause any trouble, you were okay. If she was not happy with your work though, she didn't mince her words. She would tell you straight out. She liked things done her way and was not liked by many of the other employees because of that.

I liked her very much, though. I had a lot of respect for her. She gave me this job, knowing full well where I came from. She thought I deserved a chance. She had faith in me, and now I went and screwed up, royally. This was not going to go over well.

Just as Carla started to say something, Tyler walked into the room. She saw him and stopped mid-sentence then turned and looked at me with a funny little smirk on her face. Well, before I turned too many shades of red, I excused myself and went to get ready. I was sure that Tyler would fill her in.

Ten minutes later we were out the door and on our way. Tyler drove us to work. He kissed me goodbye and wished us both lots of luck.

All eyes were on us as we walked into the hospital. I felt like we were at a firing range and I was the target. I could tell that everyone knew that something was going on. I could only imagine what they were thinking. I am sure that they all knew about the fight. Old Judy looked like she was just bubbling over with rumors. You could see it in her face, that stupid little grin of hers. I was sure that she was hoping I would get fired. She would have been thrilled with that outcome. We headed straight for Mrs. Blair's office. Lou was sitting outside her door waiting for us. I was very nervous, but hopefully with Lou and Carla there to support me, things wouldn't turn out too badly. It was time to face the music.

We were in there for the longest time. Mrs. Blair and all the Disciplinary Board members that I hadn't even known existed were present. They asked us to give them very specific details about any conversations or encounters that we had had with David Allen since he started working there. To my disappointment, I was up first. It was very nerve-wracking because they hardly said a word. They pretty much just sat there staring at me and taking notes. I couldn't tell what they were thinking.

When they were done with me, they turned to Carla. She tried to remember everything she could about David and the way he always seemed to be sneaking around. When she was done it was Lou's turn. Since he was a witness to the altercation in the kitchen between David and me, he was asked to recount the whole ordeal. Finally, my boss spoke up. I was glad because I couldn't take much more of their silence. The more I listened, the more frightened I was of David. The fact that I would probably lose my job because of him didn't help.

"Alright, I think that we have everything we need," she said. "Carla and Lou, thank you for your time. You need to get back to work now. As for you, Roberta, I am sending you home for the day. I'll get back to you on Monday and let you know what is going to happen with all this mess. In the meantime, I want you to do some serious thinking about your job here and what you have done. Violence is not the way to solve problems. I am very disappointed that you didn't think you could confide in me about this. That is all I have to say to you right now. Go home and I will talk to you on Monday."

"But I…"

"Go home, Roberta."

I was doing my best to hold back the tears. Since she was sending me home, I was sure that I was fired. Carla took me by the arm and led me out of the office. At the end of the corridor we crossed paths with David. I guess he had a meeting with Mrs. Blair too. He didn't look too happy.

"I'm gonna get you for this," he whispered as we walked past.

"Why you son of a…"

"No Carla!" I shouted as I grabbed her by the arm. "I won't let you risk your job too."

Lou just looked at him and shook his head. He had to get back to his kitchen, so I gave him a big hug and thanked him for his support.

I walked with Carla up to her floor. Her shift was starting in a few minutes. She did not want me to go home alone, so I called Tyler to see if he could pick me up. He said that he had about an hour to spare before his next appointment and would be happy to come and get me. Anyway, he was very anxious to find out what had happened at our meeting with my boss. He also said that he had some news that might interest me. I told him that I would meet him at the main entrance.

I saw him pull up, so I ran out and jumped into the car. Just in the nick of time too, because as we pulled away, I saw David storm out of the hospital, and he didn't look very happy. Tyler wanted to turn around and go back so he could see what he looked like, but I told him not to bother. I just wanted to get out of there, the sooner the better.

"So, tell me, how'd it go with your boss? That is all I could think about after I dropped you off."

"Oh God, I'm sure that by Monday morning I won't have a job anymore. Lou, Carla, and I told her everything that had gone on since David started working there. She and her colleagues asked a lot of questions and took a lot of notes, but what upset my boss the most was that I didn't go and see her about it. Instead, I lost my temper and beat him up. I don't think that she will be able to get past that."

"Just try not to dwell on it, Bobby. You need to try to relax and have a good weekend. We'll cross that bridge together when we get to it."

He reached over and took me by the hand. I turned to him and smiled. I was trying hard not to break down.

"Where are we going?" I asked. "You just drove past my street."

"Oh, I didn't think you should be alone, so I am taking you to the office with me, if that's okay. I just have to take care of one more patient before lunch, and then we can go and eat somewhere together.

You can wait in the conference room and read or doodle or whatever it is that you like to do until I am finished with my patient."

"Doodle? How do you know that I doodle?"

"Ahh… I don't know. Doesn't everybody doodle? I must have seen a picture lying around somewhere in your apartment. Anyway, while we are having lunch, I will tell you what I found out about David." He paused. "Well, here we are; this is my office building."

We drove into the parking lot and got out of the car. Tyler took me by the hand, and we made our way to the front entrance. He opened the door for me, and we walked in. I felt a little uneasy because I was going to meet everyone for the first time. On our way to his office, Tyler introduced me to everyone we crossed paths with. He seemed to be very well-liked. He grabbed a few magazines from the waiting area and showed me to the conference room.

"I have to go into my office and look over my patient's file before his appointment. There are drinks in the fridge, there's the coffee machine, and here are some magazines. Don't be shy. Just make yourself at home. If you need anything, my secretary is out front; her name is Carol. I will tell her that you're here. See you later, Bobby; I shouldn't be too long."

He gave me a hug and a kiss and then he turned and left the room. I decided to help myself to a cup of coffee and then sat down and leafed through a fashion magazine just out of boredom. After a while I started to feel a little tired, so I leaned back on the chair and closed my eyes.

I awoke suddenly. A woman was getting a drink out of the refrigerator.

"I'm sorry," she said. "I didn't mean to startle you. I'm Carol, Tyler's secretary, and you must be Bobby. I've heard a lot about you."

"It's nice to meet you, Carol, and don't worry about it. You didn't scare me. I wasn't planning on falling asleep. I just wanted to close my eyes a bit. I guess I must be really tired. I haven't been getting much rest lately."

At that moment, Tyler walked into the room. I turned to him and smiled.

"Well, I see that the two of you have met. God, I love to see you smiling like that, Bobby. You are so beautiful. Are you ready for lunch?"

I looked at Carol and must have turned ten shades of red.

He leaned over and gave me a kiss. He asked Carol if she could cancel his appointments for the rest of the day, and then we were on our way. I was still in my work clothes, so I asked him if he could drive by my place so I could change.

He pulled up in front of my apartment and we went inside. I started to feel strange vibes as I walked down the hallway of my building. I could see something lying on the floor in front of my door. I was starting to get very nervous. As we got closer, I noticed that the door was open a little bit.

"Oh my God!" I yelled as I ran up to the entrance. "Someone has broken into my apartment!"

Tyler grabbed me by the arm and told me to wait because he was worried that maybe there was still somebody inside. He stepped in front of me, slowly pushed the door open, and peeked inside. We couldn't hear a sound and didn't see anyone, so he cautiously walked in and I followed behind.

My belongings were scattered all over the place. I was frantic. I didn't know what to do. Tyler grabbed me and tried to get me to calm down. I kept crying and yelling that my things were all broken.

"Calm down, Bobby! You must not touch anything. We have to call the police."

That did it! One word… that was all it took to get my attention and stop me dead in my tracks.

"Do we have to? They will know that I was in prison and they will think it is my fault."

"Don't be silly," he said as he reached into his pocket and pulled out his cell phone. "I'll be right here with you."

We paced the floor outside my apartment for what seemed like hours. Finally, we heard footsteps coming up the stairs. I felt a big knot forming in my gut as I watched the policemen walk towards my apartment. Tyler greeted them, and we showed one of them in while the other one stayed at the door. Well, in at least as far as we could go. He saw how badly everything was scattered around my living room. There was barely any place to even walk. It was a disaster zone. The screen of my television was shattered, my sound system looked like it was in a million pieces, my shelf units were pulled down, and everything on them was completely destroyed. There was glass everywhere and my furniture was tossed around the room. Anything that could have been thrown or smashed, was. That was just the tip of the iceberg.

Tyler held me close to him as we carefully made our way to the kitchen. I took one look and then I broke down. Tyler turned my face into his chest and held me tight. All my cupboards were opened and every dish I owned was in pieces on the floor. I was devastated. I couldn't take much more, and Tyler knew it. He turned me around and we walked back through the wreckage in the living room and headed to the front door. The police officer followed. There was no use in going any farther. He was sure that the rest of the house would be the same. He called for a team of investigators to come take pictures and dust for fingerprints.

"I'm very sure that this isn't an ordinary robbery. It looks too personal. I get the feeling that whoever did this is very hateful towards you. Did you notice if there was anything missing?"

"Are you kidding... Oh my God, Tyler!" I yelled. "I was supposed to come home. My boss told me to go home. If I would have been here, Tyler, oh my God! He would have killed me. I know he would have. He said he would get me for this. He said it at the hospital when we were leaving. Carla and Lou were there, too. He said that he would get me back for what happened yesterday and this morning."

Tyler took me in his arms and held me tight. I couldn't imagine what I would have done if he hadn't been there with me. The policeman tried to ask me some questions, but I was shaking so badly that I couldn't even talk.

"I think that if you just let her calm down for ten or fifteen minutes, she will be able to answer all of your questions," Tyler told the officer.

The officer nodded, then he turned and went back into the apartment. After a few minutes, I came to my senses.

"I'm gonna get you for this," I whispered. "This is what he said to me. When we left the office after the disciplinary hearing, we crossed paths with David and he whispered, 'I'm gonna get you for this.' You can ask Lou and Carla; they heard him too. Carla almost jumped him. I held her back because I didn't want her to lose her job too. Oh God, I know it's him. Who else could it be? I don't know anyone else who would do something like this to me. I have no idea why he is doing these things to me, but I know that it's him."

It took a while, but after I had calmed down a bit, I answered all the questions that the police officer had about David and the way he was always sneaking around and bothering Carla and me.

The other investigators arrived and started going through the apartment. Looking around, taking pictures, touching things with their rubber gloves, going over everything with a fine-tooth comb how awful, and I felt terribly violated. Tyler decided that he should call Carla and let her know what was going on. He told her what had happened and asked her if she had heard anything more about the meeting that morning. She told him that she wasn't one hundred percent sure, but the word on the grapevine was that David was fired on the spot.

Tyler told her that she didn't need to come home right away because he was going to stay with me, but he told her that the police would probably want to talk to her at some point, and that they would probably want to question the hospital staff.

Hours passed, and we just sat on the floor in the hallway and waited for the police to finish their job. I hardly spoke. I just leaned my head back against the wall and closed my eyes. I think I was still in shock.

When Carla came home from work, we were still sitting there. I wanted to stay close to my apartment, but she insisted that we go into hers. I was starting to feel sick to my stomach and Tyler reminded me that I hadn't eaten since breakfast and that I was probably just hungry, so we ordered some pizza.

One of the officers came to the door and asked to talk to Carla. They went out into the hallway to talk privately. The neighbors gradually started coming home from work and were also being questioned. The police were not having much luck with them, because most of the people who lived in the building worked during the day.

The food finally arrived, but as hungry as I was, I didn't feel much like eating. Carla and Tyler dug in, but I just nibbled on a few pieces of crust. I was just too stressed out. I couldn't even sit still for very long. I kept getting up, walking around the room, peeking out the door, and then heading back to my chair… over and over again…

"I can't take much more of this," I said, as I stood up once again and headed for the door. "I wish that they would hurry up and get done. I mean why aren't they out looking for Da…"

I ran face to face into a man as he turned into Carla's apartment.

"…vid. Oh shit, I'm sorry. I am going crazy here. Are you almost done? What are you doing about David? Why aren't you out looking for him?"

The man bent down and picked up the notebook that he had dropped when we collided.

"Very sorry, Miss; it was my fault. I should have knocked. Miss Hansen, I presume? I am Detective Collins. I'm in charge of your case."

He was a tall man with a good build and the looks to match. He didn't smile, but there was a sincerity about him. He looked kind but very serious.

"That is an awful mess you have in your apartment," he continued. "Well, my team is almost done. They are just packing up their equipment. It would be a good idea for you to go through your apartment and sort out your things as soon as possible. I need you to try to figure out if anything is missing, but we have pretty well all come to the same conclusion. That is, that this is not a robbery. Thieves don't normally destroy everything in their path; they just take what they want and leave. By the way, Miss Hansen, I have been looking into these allegations of yours, about that co-worker."

The detective reached into his pocket and pulled out a hospital ID card.

"We think you might be right. It seems to all add up. Is this the guy?"

He turned the ID card around to show me the picture, and sure enough, it was David's.

"That's him. Where did you find that? Where is he?"

"I sent two officers to the hospital to question the people that you work with. We found it in his locker. Everyone was very cooperative, but nobody knew very much about this Mr. Allen or his personal life. Actually, we are sort of at a dead end here. The address and phone number in his file are non-existent. We will just have to put his picture in the system and see what we come up with. Hopefully we will find a match when we analyze the fingerprints we found in your apartment. Don't worry, we have an A.P.B. out on him, so he shouldn't get far."

Tyler took the card in his hand and looked at it.

"That's him?" he asked, his face going white. "Oh shit!"

"What's wrong?" I said.

"Oh… nothing," he said. "He just… I can see why you were afraid of him; he doesn't look very friendly."

I stared at Tyler for a moment, confused; something didn't seem right. I was just about to say something when the detective continued.

"In the meantime, Miss Hansen, I don't think that you should stay alone. It's probably a really good thing that you weren't in your apartment when this happened. By the looks of it, there is no telling what he would have done to you. Presuming that it was him. Anyway, I don't want you to take any chances, so you should stay with a friend tonight."

"Are you kidding? I'm scared to death! I don't plan on being alone, and I can't stay in my apartment, anyway."

"Good. Well, here is my card. If you think of anything else, just give me a shout. Oh, by the way, one of my investigators will be coming over to take fingerprints from the three of you so we can eliminate those ones."

The detective wished me luck, told me again to be very cautious, and left to go back to the station. An investigator did come to take our prints and then they all left the building together.

"Boy, are they going to have a field day when they check out my fingerprints. I can already hear them. This is far from over." I cringed.

"Oh no! I almost forgot. Uh… I need to take care of something at the office. Never mind about cleaning up your apartment tonight. I think you've had enough excitement for today. Stay here with Carla, and lock the door, and don't open it for anyone. I'll be back in a little while," Tyler said quickly.

"But I..."

Before I could get the words out, Tyler kissed me and was on his way. I locked the door behind him.

"Jesus Christ, what was that all about? What the hell am I supposed to do now?"

"Wine?" Carla blurted out. "Yep, I think that now would be a damn good time to open that bottle of wine that Tyler gave me when he came to supper, don't you?"

"Whatever," I said, as I went back and sat down on the couch.

The pizza box was still sitting on the living room table. I lifted the cover and saw that there were a couple of slices left.

"Well, I might as well stuff my face then. I haven't got anything better to do."

Carla brought the wine in and set it on the table, and then she went and put some music on. I finished the pizza. She came back to the couch and poured us each a glass. She made a toast to our friendship and to Tyler and me. She was trying so hard to make me feel better. I was still a pack of nerves. I kept getting up and walking into the kitchen to see what time it was. She kept bringing up all different subjects to try to keep my mind off of what happened. This went on for quite a while.

"Jesus, Looney Tunes, it's about ten minutes past the last time you looked. Time won't pass by faster just because you keep going into the kitchen and looking at it. Come here. Have another glass of wine."

She filled the glasses again, came and sat next to me, and took me by the hand.

"Look at you, you're all tensed up. You've got to try to relax a little."

She got up and went around to the back of the couch. She put on some soft jazz and then placed her hands on my shoulders and started to massage them. She squeezed hard on the muscles as she tried to relieve some of the tension. I closed my eyes and moaned as she worked her way up the back of my neck. She had magical hands. It felt so good. I started to feel the tension slowly disappear. The wine was going down pretty well too. I think that was helping me also. I reached for the bottle and poured the rest of it in my glass.

"Whoa there, girl! Tyler should be back soon. It would be nice if you are still coherent when he gets here."

At the mention of Tyler's name, I started to cry.

"Did you know, Carla, that Tyler told me that he fell in love with me the first day he met me? I really do love him too. I don't know what it is about him, but I feel like I've known him all my life. It just feels so good when we are together. Too good to be true it seems, with all this other shit going on. My whole sordid past is going to blow up in my face and I can't do a damn thing about it. I really don't think that he will want to be a part of that."

"Don't be such a fool, Bobby. Tyler is a good man. If he loves you, he will stick by you."

Suddenly there was a knock at the door. Carla and I both jumped about a foot in the air. We looked at each other and didn't move. My heart was racing.

"It's me, Carla; it's Tyler. Let me in."

I got up, ran to the door, and let him in.

"Where did you go?"

"I had business to take care of. Don't worry, Bobby. I won't leave you again. Is it okay, Carla, if we camp out on your couch tonight?"

Carla said that it was fine, of course, and she went and pulled out some extra blankets and pillows. I was very tired and a little groggy from all the wine I drank so Tyler prepared the couch and I followed Carla into her bedroom to see if she could find something for me to wear to sleep in. She lent me a nightie, I got changed, and went back to the couch. All the excitement had really taken its toll on me, so I lay down and Tyler tucked me in.

"I will come and join you a little later, Bobby. I will just be in the kitchen. I am going to get myself something to drink first. Try to get some rest."

Tyler left the room and went and joined Carla who was already in the kitchen. I could hear them talking but I couldn't quite make out what they were saying because the music was still playing. It didn't matter, though, because it wasn't long before all of the sounds started to fade off into the distance…

Chapter 17

It was very dark in my room even though the window blinds were open. There had been a heavy cloud cover all evening, and there was no moon or stars in sight. I could hear the thunder rumbling in the distance. It sounded like it was getting closer and closer. I couldn't hear any noises in the house. Emma must have gone to bed already and Harold was out drinking as he always did. Where else would he be on a Saturday night?

Suddenly my room lit up. A gigantic streak of lightning spread across the sky, followed by a few smaller ones. There was a big crack of thunder and then the rain started. It was hammering down fiercely on the old tin roof. I could hardly hear myself think. More lightning… Another loud crack of thunder…

All at once, I jumped up and turned on the light. I forgot that I had left the window open when I went to bed. I ran over to close it. I was too late; the floor was already soaked. I grabbed the towel that I had used to dry off after my shower and wiped up the floor. I stood there for a moment and gazed at the light show. I always wondered how something so beautiful could be so devastating.

Just as I was about to head back to my bed, I noticed headlights going down the road. I watched them, and sure enough, they turned into our driveway. I quickly ran back to my bed and turned off the light. I knew it was him and I was praying that he hadn't seen my light on. I pulled the blankets up over me and stared at my slightly opened bedroom door. I was terrified of what he might do to me if he came up to my room after he had been out drinking for half the night. The thought scared the hell out of me. I could just imagine what kind of shape he'd be in.

I kept trying to listen for him, but I couldn't hear a thing because of the rain. I could see a faint glow of light in the hallway outside my bedroom, so I knew that he had made it into the house. It was just a matter of time.

I kept my eyes glued to my door as I hoped and prayed that he might pass out somewhere for the night. Much to my dismay, the hallway lit up. I knew, right then and there, that this was not going to end well. A chill went down my spine and I started to tremble all over. My eyes started to overflow and there was that familiar knot inside my stomach. I still couldn't hear him because of that damned rain. I wished it would stop so I could figure out where he was. The suspense was driving me crazy.

The door flew open so violently that it sounded like it almost tore right off the hinges. My heart just about leaped right out of my chest. That monster of a man stumbled into my room, yelling.

"Here... Slutty, Slutty, Slutty. Come here... Slutty, Slutty. Where's my little whore?"

He could hardly stand up. I didn't do anything. I couldn't move. I was as still as a statue. I just lay there and watched. He stumbled a few more times and then started yelling again.

"Where's that god-damned light of yours. Get your slutty ass out of that bed and turn on that fucking light, you hear... What are you waiting for, damn it? Now!"

I slowly slipped out of my blankets and reached over and turned on my lamp. As soon as I saw the look on his face, I jumped right back into my bed, sat as far as I could up against the wall, and pulled my blankets and pillow back up around me. He was plastered out of his mind. He just stood there for a few seconds while his eyes adjusted to the light. He stared at me with a look of disgust, and then he turned and headed for my dresser.

"So, this is the thanks I get for everything I do for you, right? You go slutting around behind my back? You don't think I know, but I do. I hear things, you know. This is a small town, and people talk."

He threw his arm in the air and slid it across the top of my dresser. My things flew everywhere. He took one of my books and threw it into the mirror. It shattered into millions of pieces. He opened my dresser drawers and started tearing up my clothing and throwing them all over the place. I couldn't do or say anything. I just sat there paralyzed with fear. He went to my closet and repeated the same thing, cursing, and swearing, as he turned my room into a disaster area. He just about collapsed from exhaustion, but he caught his balance on the closet door.

"Son of a bitch!" he yelled. "Look what you do to me, you little whore. This is all your fault."

I started to cry as I watched him stagger his way towards me. He stumbled as he reached the bed and fell face-first onto it, right next to me. He didn't move for a few seconds. I was so hoping that he had passed out, but he didn't. He slowly turned his face towards me and tried to sit up. I was horrified. Before I could do anything, he grabbed me by the arm and pulled me towards him. He put his other hand around my throat.

"Now, my little slut, you need to listen to me very carefully! I am not going to repeat myself again! If I catch you with that little pecker-head across the bush from here, I will take my shotgun and blow his fucking pecker right off him! You hear me? Jesus Christ! What the fuck do I have to do to make you understand? You see him once more, you little whore, and he is dead meat! Dead meat, you hear?"

I couldn't say a word because I could hardly breathe. His hand was too tightly wrapped around my neck. I lay there, wide-eyed and gasping for air. Finally, he loosened his grip, but I realized that his other hand was working its way up underneath my nightie and up between my legs. Just as I was starting to kick and scream, his body collapsed on top of mine. He had finally passed out.

I stayed quiet for a moment trying to figure out what I should do. I carefully took his hand off my throat, hoping not to awaken the monster. I was pinned down, crushed by his weight, and my lungs were in desperate need of air. I lost it when I realized that his hand was still up between my legs, and I started screaming again…

"Get off of me," I screamed as I tried to push him away with all my might. "Get away from me… Get off of me… Get off…"

"Bobby. Wake up, Bobby."

"Get off of me. Get…"

"Bobby, it's me, wake up."

"Get off… Get… Oh my God, what are you doing here… You need to get out of here… I can't see you anymore… He's going to kill you… He told me so… He will kill you… Get out now, while you have the chance… Get out… Get…"

"Bobby, it's okay, nobody is going to kill anybody. It was just a dream. It's over. Calm down."

It was Tyler. He took me into his arms and held me close. Carla came running into the living room. I was still trembling from that terrible dream.

"Is everything okay?" she asked.

"I wish they would stop!" I cried. "I wish these dreams would just go away!"

The room went silent. I held onto Tyler as tight as I could. I could hear his heart beating as I pressed my ear against his chest. The sound of it was very calming.

"Everything is going to be okay, Bobby, you'll see. Tyler and I are both here to help you get through this." She reached down and patted me on the shoulder.

"Well, the sun is starting to come up, so there's no use of any of us trying to go back to sleep. I'll go to the kitchen and start making us something for breakfast. You guys just relax a bit and I will tell you when it's ready," Carla said.

I wanted to tell her not to bother but, I knew there was no use arguing with her. I never let go of Tyler; I felt so safe. I needed to tell him about my dream, but I really didn't feel like reliving it again. I wanted to wait until later. There was just too much to do. Suddenly, I thought about yesterday.

Oh my God, my room in my dream, it was completely destroyed by that monster, just like my… oh no, how could that be? I couldn't understand what was happening.

My beautiful little apartment turned into a war zone, what a mess! I had no clue where we were going to start. It didn't look like there was very much that was salvageable. I didn't say anything about it because I didn't want to ruin our nice breakfast that Carla was making.

"Hey Whitey! What the hell are you doing in there? We want to eat this morning, not next week!"

"Then why don't you get your skinny little ass in the kitchen and help me out, Looney Tunes?"

Tyler shook his head and then a big smile came across his face.

"Now there's the girl that I know and love. Why don't you go help her out? I'll clean up the living room."

We sat down and had a good breakfast. When we were done, we started to plan how we were going to go about tackling that mess. We had plenty of garbage bags, but boxes, well, not so much. Tyler offered to go to the grocery store and get as many as he could fit in his car. While we waited for his return, the phone rang. It was Lou. Carla talked to him for a little while and I cleaned up the dishes. I heard a knock at the door and ran to answer it. It was Tyler. He was back already, and he had managed to find some boxes.

"Are we ready?" he said as he stacked the boxes in front of my doorway.

"That was Lou on the phone," Carla announced. "He just wanted to know how you were doing, and what was going on. I'm ready when you are, Bobby."

"I'm as ready as I'll ever be," I replied. "It's now or never."

I gave my key to Tyler and he opened the door. I followed, and then Carla. She hadn't gone anywhere near the apartment yesterday. She had no clue what it looked like. All she knew was what we had told her. She let out a yell and I practically jumped out of my skin.

I turned to look and saw her leaning against the doorway with her hands in front of her mouth.

"Oh… my… God! Oh my! I… I… I didn't imagine that it was this bad! Oh Bobby, I'm so sorry. Oh my God!"

I walked over to the door and put my arms around her. We stood for a while hugging and then we both got busy cleaning up. Tyler lifted the shelf units and put them back where they belonged. They didn't seem to have too much damage, maybe just a little scratch here and there. The couches seemed to be okay, too. They had just been flipped over and the cushions tossed around the room. The television and sound system were destroyed. Carla and I took care of the lamps, knickknacks, coffee tables, pictures, and so on, which were pretty much all garbage. We slowly made our way to the kitchen. It was carpeted with broken glass, from one end to the other. I was starting to feel a little teary-eyed and I looked over at Carla and she was the same. She didn't say a word, though; she just shook her head and kind of half-smiled. She went right to work, carefully picking up the debris.

It looked like the table and chairs were going to be salvageable, with just a few scratches here and there. The fridge and stove weren't touched, thank goodness. The only kitchenware that wasn't broken was the pots and pans. Well, at least I had those. Anything that was breakable was broken in pieces, and all over the kitchen floor.

I heard some noise coming from the hallway. I looked into the living room and noticed that we hadn't even closed the front door, so I started to walk over there to do so. I didn't want anyone snooping around and seeing this mess.

I was almost to the door, when I heard some familiar whistling. It sounded like Lou. I peeked out the doorway, and there he was. He had his arms full of boxes.

"There's my favorite girl," he said. "I hope you don't mind; I didn't have anything better to do on my day off."

"Carla! Tyler! Look who's here." I ran and jumped in his arms and knocked all the boxes out of his hands.

"It's okay, girl, you're not alone. We'll all help you through this, whatever this is. Carla, could you go down to my car and get the big basket out of the front seat and bring it up here, would you please? I made us all a picnic lunch. Well, don't look at me that way, you were going to eat today, weren't you?"

Lou was such a wonderful man. He always knew what to say and what to do to make you feel better. I introduced him to Tyler. They had spoken on the phone, but they had never met face to face. Well, they hit it off right away. We took a break for a while and had our wonderful lunch with Lou. When we were done, he went into the hallway, got his boxes, and then came in and dug right in like the rest of us. I stopped for a moment and looked around the room at these wonderful people.

"It's at times like these where you find out who your real friends are."

"Shut up, Looney Tunes, and get back to work. This is no time to be sappy."

Carla threw a wet dish towel at me from across the room and everyone started laughing. I guess she wanted me to lighten up. It was tedious work but gradually we were getting there.

Finally, the kitchen was done, so into the bedroom we went. I hadn't even seen what the bedroom looked like yesterday.

I was kind of scared and Tyler knew it, so he took me by the hand and escorted me in. When we reached the door, we stopped and stood there with our mouths open, frozen in our tracks. This was ground zero. It was really hard for anyone to understand how I was feeling at that moment. My bed, my pillows, my blankets, and my clothes were all ripped to shreds. I felt so violated. I was speechless. I didn't move.

"Bobby… are you okay, Bobby? Bobby… come on, we'll go back to the living room. You don't have to do this. I'll take care of it," Tyler said. Carla and Lou hurried into the room to see what was going on.

"Holy Jesus Christ," Carla said, as she looked into my room.

"Carla, take Bobby and stay in the living room with her, and Lou and I will clean this up," Tyler instructed.

Carla was just about to sit me down on the couch when I finally came to my senses.

"Those were my personal belongings," I cried. "I have to do this."

Carla didn't argue. She understood. She came back to my bedroom with me.

"I can't believe she still..."

"What do you have there, Tyler?" I asked.

"Oh... uh... this little uh... chain. Uh... I found it on the floor in the corner."

I walked over to see what it was.

"Oh, that thing; I have no clue what it is. It was given back to me when I was released, along with a few other things that they said I had arrived with. I guess I was wearing it when I was arrested. Nobody could tell me anything about it."

It was a very simple but elegant heart-shaped locket on a delicate little chain. It was broken so I never wore it. There were no pictures inside. I had never figured out where it came from or what photos might have been enclosed. It didn't mean a thing to me. I didn't know why I'd kept it for all these years, I turned and threw it in the garbage bag.

"What are you doing?" Tyler yelled. "Don't throw it away!"

He quickly walked past me and looked through the garbage bag to retrieve the pendant. We all looked at him kind of strangely.

"It could be a part of your past and I don't think you should throw it away. Maybe if you work at it, the memory will come back. I'll just keep it for you in case you ever remember what it means and want it back. You shouldn't throw away anything like this. It's a part of your past for sure, and one day you might remember something about it and be very disappointed that you threw it out."

He put it in his pocket.

"He's right, Bobby," Lou said. "You never know."

Carla nodded her head in agreement.

"Alright, keep it," I said, and smiled. "You're right."

We then got back to work. Well, it wasn't hard to sort things out. Everything went to the garbage, clothes and all. All that was good was the dresser and the nightstand. Of course, I would have to replace the mirror on the dresser because it was in little pieces all over the floor. What in the hell was I going to do for clothing? We were pretty well done so I walked out of the room and went and sat on the couch. Carla came out to join me and I burst into tears.

"Somebody… shoot me… please! I have no TV, no sound system, no dishes, let's see, no bed, oh yes, I don't even have one stitch of clothing, oh, and to top it all off, I don't even know if I still have a job. *Ain't life grand!* I don't know if I can even hold it together anymore! It's too much! Just too damned much!"

I took a deep breath and let out one big, loud, long scream until I ran out of air. Boy, that got everyone's attention. In about two seconds flat, Tyler and Lou were standing in front of me. They had these very worried looks on their faces. You should have seen them. They didn't know what to think. They looked so funny. I put my hands over my mouth and tried not to laugh. They all looked so puzzled that I couldn't hold it anymore. I burst out laughing.

"Oh my God, I'm so sorry," I said as I burst out laughing again. "But you all looked so helpless with your little sad puppy eyes. Oh God... I can't believe I screamed so loud. I had no clue that I was going to do that; it just happened. Oh, but you know what? I feel so much better now. Oh yes, much better. That felt great."

"Yep, and you ask me why I call her Looney Tunes? Girl, you damn near gave me a heart attack. You could have at least warned me ahead of time. My ears are still ringing."

She stuck her fingers in her ears and shook them. "Listen, Bobby, I need to go to my apartment for a few minutes; I'll be right back."

"I'm really glad that you feel better, Bobby," Tyler said, "but you damn near gave us a heart attack too."

I told him how sorry I was, and he sat down next to me and put his arms around me. Lou went back and started to bring the full boxes and garbage bags to the door.

"There goes my life," I said, "all in the garbage."

Tyler gave me a kiss and got back up to help Lou. When they were done, Lou came over and gave me a hug.

"I'm going to head home now, sweetie. Keep your chin up. Things can only get better; you'll see. If you need anything at all, I'm here. I mean anything, you hear? I'll see you at work on Monday morning."

"But I…"

"No Buts. See you Monday morning, and don't be late."

He shook hands with Tyler and then told him to take good care of me. Tyler came and sat beside me and smiled. He pushed me down onto the couch and lay down next to me. I looked into his eyes and thought about how lucky I was to have him in my life.

"Alone at last," he said. "I thought they'd never leave."

His eyes never left mine as he very gently combed his fingers through my hair. I tilted my head back slightly as he continued down my neck. I knew that he could feel my temperature rising. With his eyes still focused on mine, he continued his descent. I could feel his hand slowly zig-zag down the front of my chest. I pushed him away. I couldn't think about that, right then and there. As much as I wanted to be in his arms, I just couldn't handle it. Not at that moment, anyway. I was too full of anger, helplessness, and don't forget… fear for my life. There were too many unanswered questions.

"What in the hell is happening to me?"

I got up and started pacing. I got thinking about my job, or lack of, and the loss of all my belongings, what little I had accumulated since I moved here. Most of all, I got thinking about David. I was sure that he was behind this mess, and maybe even right outside this apartment building waiting for me to step outside so he could finish the job. I could feel it in my gut. I had no clue why. I had no idea who this guy was and what he wanted with me. Fake name… Fake address… Fake phone number… it was like he didn't really exist. He seemed to know things about me, and I didn't know how. Maybe he was from my past. I was frantic. I was so lost in my thoughts, I didn't immediately notice that Tyler was talking to me.

"Bobby, honey… Bobby, I'm sorry… I just wanted to comfort you and take your mind off of things."

"I know you mean well, Tyler, but damn it. I can't think about that right now. I'm going crazy here, can't you see that? I am losing my mind! What in the hell am I going to do? Where in the hell is David… Look what he is doing to me. He is making me crazier than I already am! I need to do something, but I don't know what..."

I don't really remember everything I said after that, but I totally flipped out. Just as I was about to explode, Carla came waltzing into the apartment.

"Trouble in paradise? What's going on? I can hear you next door!"

"You have really great timing, Carla. I don't know, girl; you tell me what's going on. You're the smart one with all the answers. Tell me then, what in the hell does someone do when they lose almost everything they own and their whole life is falling apart before their eyes?"

I started pacing the floor again. I didn't want to snap at her like that, but I was pretty much at the end of my rope. For a few minutes, she just stood there looking at me and didn't say a word. I could tell that she was very offended and maybe even hurt. Tyler was watching me too and he didn't say anything either. Suddenly she turned and headed for the door. I felt really bad, but I, too, was at a loss for words. I couldn't understand what had come over me. She had no sooner left the apartment, when she turned around and stormed back in.

"The Bobby I know," she cried, "would jump over this hurdle, put the pieces back together, and go on with her life."

"What?" I yelled. "The Bobby you know? Well, obviously you don't know me very well! This is not the same Bobby! This one is losing her mind! I am falling apart at the seams! Can't you see that? You can't imagine what I am going through! You and your perfect world! Jump this hurdle and go on with my life? What life? I don't have a life! I don't have a job! I don't even know who I am! I am freaking tired of all this shit!"

I paused for a moment to catch my breath.

"You think you know me? How can you? Oh, you must be a genius. Okay, why don't you just tell me who in the hell you think I am!"

"You really want to know, Bobby? Well, sit your skinny little ass back down on that couch and shut your mouth and maybe I will tell you."

I was so shocked to hear her confront me that I just stood there staring at her. I could feel the rage building up inside of me. I wanted to walk right up to her and punch her in the face. It took all the willpower I had left just to hold myself back. The bad in me wanted to jump her, and what little bit of good I had left in me was fighting like hell to stop me from doing something that I would regret for a very long time.

I hated myself for the rage that was taking over my body and mind. I didn't want to do these things. I didn't want to be like this. I was about to open my mouth and speak, but I couldn't. I was so confused. I couldn't think of anything to say that could repair the damage that I had already caused. I didn't know what to do. I glanced over at Tyler. He was just calmly sitting there observing me. I looked around the room at what was left of my belongings and suddenly I felt very claustrophobic. I had to escape before I dug myself a deeper hole that I wouldn't be able to get myself out of.

I turned and ran out the door, down the stairs, and out of the building. I could hear Carla yelling and running behind me, but I didn't pay any attention to her. I just wanted out. I needed to be alone. I needed to run. I needed to escape from this life that was swallowing me up and pulling me into deep, dark places that I didn't want to go.

I was four or five blocks away when I started to slow down to a fast walk. I was never much of a runner. My lungs were bursting out of my chest. It was pouring rain, yet I was so out of touch with reality that I hadn't really noticed. I was soaked from head to toe. It didn't matter, I still kept my pace. I needed to burn off this negative energy. I kept reliving what had just happened back in my apartment and I wasn't very pleased with myself.

What had I done? I had probably just ruined my relationship with the best and only true friend I ever had. How stupid could I be? What had come over me? It didn't even feel like I was me. It felt like I was someone else, someone mean, someone evil.

My imagination started to go wild. Maybe I wasn't that mild-mannered Bobby. Maybe I was this crazy person that everyone said I was, and she had just come back to life after hiding away inside of me for all these years. That evil person who got me into all the problems I had in my past. That scared the hell out of me and I started to run again. I ran as fast as my legs could go. Maybe if I ran fast enough, I could outrun this crazy person that was taking over my body and mind.

I pushed on, faster and faster, with not even a clue as to where I was running to. The rain was still coming down hard. I was drenched to the bone. I felt like my lungs were going to explode and bring my body along for the ride, but I still didn't stop. My mind started playing tricks on me. I felt like someone was chasing me. I was hearing noises, no, maybe they were voices. Oh God, and these visions kept flashing before me. My prison cell… the old man in my dreams, oh no… I didn't want to go there… David… Tyler… dead bodies… what? No!

Those visions just kept playing over and over again in my mind. I was terrified, and I still had that crazy feeling that someone was chasing me. Who was out there?

"Leave me alone!" I yelled. "Get away from me!"

There was nobody there, though, just those crazy visions. The ugly old man… David… Tyler… my prison cell… dead bodies covered in blood… David's bloody face… Tyler… the crazy old drunk…

I stopped dead. I was in a daze. My head was spinning. It was like a dream, or rather more like a nightmare. I felt like I was moving in slow motion. There seemed to be a force that made me turn around and look back to where I had come from.

I saw something down the street in front of me, but nothing registered. It was getting closer and closer. Loud roaring noises and blinding lights… I didn't move. I just stood there frozen in my tracks. Was I dreaming? Those visions still kept popping up in front of me. That monster in my nightmares… David… my jail cell… the monster in my nightmares… David… my bloody hands… My bloody hands? Oh my god, no!

Chapter 18

Something struck me hard. It felt like every bone in my body cracked. There was a thunderous sound as I felt myself being tossed into the air, like a rag doll. Then everything stopped and there was silence.

I could feel the rain hammering down on my face. It was dark. My head was hurting. I couldn't move. There was this buzzing in my ears that wouldn't stop. I could hardly breathe. I was feeling very dizzy. I didn't know if I was awake, in a dream, or even dead. All I knew was that I couldn't feel anything except this pain in my head.

I thought I heard someone's voice, so I tried to talk. No words came out. My mouth didn't move. The voice faded away.

I heard what I thought was a police siren, but it also faded out. I was scared, so scared. I was so alone. Where was I and why was it so dark? Another voice. Who was it? Why couldn't I talk? Don't touch me. Something touched my head. Oh my God, what was happening to me? The voice faded away again. The buzzing in my brain stopped. I didn't even feel the rain on my face anymore.

I felt very strange, as if I didn't exist anymore. I felt like I was floating. These visions kept popping up in front of me and then disappearing again. Too fast to make out what they were. People… I saw people gathered in the rain… oh no wait… they were gone.

Oh, okay… there they are again… they are looking at something. Gone… oh no… there... It looks like there is someone on the ground. Oh… So much blood. Oops gone… What in the hell. Oh, there we go, coming in for a closer look. I could see the ambulance with all those flashing lights and the paramedics running towards the crowd, pushing their way in. Oh no, it couldn't be! There was so much blood, it was me!

Suddenly, there was a flash of light. I could feel the rain coming down on me again. I felt crushed, beaten, and disoriented. The pain was excruciating. Something touched my face. Was that really me I saw? How could that be? Was I dead?

I felt so scared and alone. I tried so hard to move but I couldn't. I was so afraid of what was happening. I could hear their voices, but they seemed so far away that I couldn't make out what they were saying. I was terrified and couldn't see anything. My eyes wouldn't open. I could feel the rain, the pain, and people touching me, but that was it. Where was I and who was out there past the dark place that I seemed to be confined to? What were they doing to me?

Suddenly the rain stopped, the voices faded out, and the buzzing in my head disappeared. I didn't feel any more pain. I was confused, but I started to feel like I was safe and nobody could hurt me anymore. It was still dark around me, but I could see a dim light, way off in the distance. I felt warm all over. It was a wonderful feeling. I was no longer afraid.

The crazy visions had stopped. I decided that I should make my way toward the light. It seemed so far away. I felt like I was floating as I approached it. It got larger and larger as I got closer. I could see images. I couldn't quite make out what they were, but I was not afraid. I felt like they were welcoming me. The image started getting clearer. It was a woman. She was calling out to me. As I got closer, I recognized her.

The tears started coming down my face. They were tears of joy. I could feel the love radiating from her as I approached. I couldn't believe my eyes. She was so beautiful, just like I remembered her. Her smile that would light up a room, her beautiful long blond hair, and her deep blue eyes.

"Mommy," I cried. "I miss you so much, Mommy. Please hold me. I love you, Mommy."

She seemed so close to me, but I couldn't reach her. I was sure that if I put my hand out far enough, I could touch her, but no matter how hard I tried, I just couldn't get close enough. I came to an abrupt stop. I tried to keep going but something was holding me back.

"Mommy… don't leave me again," I cried. "I promise I will be good. I really mean it. I love you, Mommy."

"I love you too, Roberta. You will always be my baby. I'm sorry for all your pain. You have a wonderful life ahead of you. Make the best of it. I will watch over you, I promise."

I couldn't believe that she was speaking to me. I was sure that she was not really there, and that I was only imagining her. I remembered her beautiful voice, though, and how it used to calm and comfort me. She was really there, just a little out of my reach, but she was really there with me. I felt like I was a child again and she was going to take care of me and protect me and love me.

Slowly, she started disappearing out of my sight and her voice was fading away. My heart was breaking. I could feel some kind of force pulling me back. There was nothing I could do to stop it. It was getting dark again. I was starting to feel scared. The buzzing in my ears and the pain in my head were all coming back now.

"Mommy… come back. I love you, Mommy. Mommy… don't leave me… please don't…"

Suddenly I heard the loud sound of sirens.

"We have a pulse," I heard someone say. "She's talking."

I opened my eyes. The light was very bright, so I closed them again.

"It's okay, Miss; you are in good hands. Try to stay calm and don't move."

"Mom," I whispered, "Don't leave me."

I slowly opened my eyes again. There was a man standing over me. He looked at me and forced a smile. He seemed very nervous. He reached for an oxygen mask and put it over my mouth. I could hear someone talking to him, but I couldn't make out what he was saying.

"We are getting you to the hospital. It won't be long, Miss; you are going to be fine. Just stay with me, okay? Just stay…"

Everything started to fade away again. The darkness returned. I was scared. I was looking around for my mom, but she wasn't there. I called out and she didn't answer. I didn't want to be alone. I didn't know what was happening to me.

Off in the distance I could see another dim light. I started to move toward it again. As I got closer, I could see blue skies with white, billowy clouds. I looked down and saw trees and rivers. I could feel the excitement building up inside of me. I was in my safe place. I couldn't have been happier. I saw my old log where I usually sat above the river. Oh no, there was someone else sitting on it. I moved in closer to see who it was. It was Tyler. I was so happy to see him. I called out his name and started to move toward him. But he kept getting farther and farther away. I kept calling him.

"Tyler, don't leave me… Tyler, come back... Tyler..."

The pain in my head… oh no, not again. The buzzing in my ears was all coming back again. I started to hear voices. They were getting louder and louder.

"It's okay, baby; I'm here. Wake up, Bobby. Don't leave me again. Hang in there. Everything will be okay."

I opened my eyes and smiled. I was so happy to see him at last.

"Stay with me, Bobby. I don't want to lose you again."

The tears were coming down his face. I wanted to hold him, but I couldn't. I was too weak. It took all the energy I had just to keep my eyes open. Everything was starting to go fuzzy again.

"We're losing her… we have to get her to surgery!"

"Bobby… Don't leave me… Bobby…"

I could hear the desperation in his voice as it slowly faded out.

Chapter 19

Into the blackness I went again, but I wasn't afraid this time. I remembered my mother's kind words. She promised she would watch over me and I'm sure she was. I could feel her love all around me in a way I'd never felt before. A bright light appeared in the distance again, and it seemed like a window to the world was opening up before me. I smiled as I watched the big, beautiful snowflakes that were slowly floating down from the heavens. I was looking at what seemed to be a street in a small town. The houses were all beautifully decorated for the holidays. It appeared to be early in the morning; there were no tracks in the freshly fallen snow. There were no signs of life at all outside. The sun was rising and shedding light on a beautiful, picture-perfect winter scene. I wasn't cold, though.

I moved along down the street a bit and stopped in front of one of the houses. I had the strangest feeling. It all looked vaguely familiar. I seemed to remember this house from somewhere. It was very old and run-down, but it looked beautiful all covered with snow. It was one of the smaller houses on the block. It had a little white picket fence all around it. I opened the gate and slowly moved up the walkway toward the house. The branches of the beautiful evergreen tree on the front lawn were weighed down from the heavy overnight flurries. I went up the front steps. There was an old toboggan and a shovel leaning up against the wall. The front door was decorated with a Christmas wreath. It was the most beautiful wreath that I had ever seen. It looked hand-made. It had popcorn, gingerbread men, and ribbons all over it.

I went through the door… Yes, right through it, like a ghost, it was incredible. I looked around. There wasn't very much furniture in the house and what was there looked very old. It was clean, though, and it seemed very cozy. Gold garlands hung on all the doorways. There was an abundance of angel and Santa figurines. Hand-made ornaments hung on a beautiful fir tree in the corner of the living room. Neatly wrapped gifts were scattered underneath. It was Christmas morning. A feeling of joy and happiness spread through my soul.

Suddenly I heard a sound coming from the hallway. I turned and saw a bright-eyed little girl heading for the Christmas tree. She looked to be around five or six years old. She was smiling from ear to ear. She had beautiful light brown curly hair and piercing green eyes. A big lump was forming in the back of my throat. I was trying to hold back the tears. *No, this can't be. It's me, oh my God, that's not possible.*

"Mommy… Mommy... Santa came, and he brought presents. Mommy… come quick."

I turned and there she was, as beautiful as ever. I couldn't believe my eyes. It was like I had gone back in time. I had a front row seat, watching me and my mom wake up to a beautiful, snowy Christmas morning.

I couldn't understand what was happening, so I closed my eyes and then opened them back up again. They were still there. This could not be real. I watched in amazement as I ran into my mother's arms, then I turned and ran back to the tree and inquisitively looked over all the gifts. I appeared very curious to know what was inside the elegantly wrapped packages, but they were so beautiful that I almost didn't want to see them opened. My mom walked over to the tree and sat down on the old rocker.

"Come on, Roberta, dig in. What are you waiting for?"

With a smile that lit up the whole room, I picked up a gift and very carefully unwrapped it.

"It is the most beautiful doll I have ever seen," I said. I ran over to my mom to show it to her, and then I went back and opened the other gifts. I looked so happy.

This was incredible. Being here and watching this.

"Santa was very good to me, Mommy."

A tear rolled down my face. I still couldn't believe my eyes. I smiled as I watched my mom sort out the gifts and pick the wrapping paper up off the floor. I turned just in time to see that I was sneaking out of the room.

"Where are you going, baby?" my mom said. "Come back and help me clean up."

A few minutes later I returned to the room with a package. I ran over to my mom and handed it to her.

"Merry Christmas, Mommy. I made it at school. I hope you like it."

Mom got very emotional and gave me a big hug. I could feel her love radiating in the room. At that moment, I remembered what it felt like to be in the warm loving arms of my mother. I couldn't help but cry as I watched them cuddle.

"It is the most beautiful candle that I have ever seen," she whispered as she sobbed.

"Why are you crying, Mommy?"

"Because I love you, Roberta. You are my special angel. You are all I have in this world. Promise me that you will never leave me."

"I won't, Mommy. I love you too".

"I have something special for you too, baby. Look in the tree, on one of the branches near the bottom. You forgot one. It is a very little box. Can you see it?"

I still couldn't believe what was playing out before me. It was just like watching a movie at a theater. All that was missing was the popcorn. It was dark all around except for what looked like a big screen in front of me, projecting a very sentimental moment from my past. A moment that I did not remember. It was a little piece of the puzzle of my life which somehow had been completely erased from my memory.

I watched as I walked over to the tree and examined all the lower branches.

"A little more to the right, sweetie."

I moved a little to the left.

"Your other right, silly," Mom said as she giggled. "We're going to have to work on that."

I turned and walked to the other side of the tree. Finally, I spotted it and gently retrieved the tiny package from its nesting place. It was perfectly wrapped in green paper patterned with miniature holly berries and topped with a beautiful little bow. I watched as I stood there for a few moments and examined it.

"It's too small, Mommy. I don't think anything can fit in here."

I giggled and thought, *how cute is that.*

"Come here, baby, and don't you worry. There is something in there for you. Something very precious that you can treasure for the rest of your life."

Mom walked over to me and she picked me up, brought me back over to the chair, and put me on her lap. She removed the bow for me and tore off the paper. She handed me back a little gold metallic box.

"Now you open it."

I was so excited that I just sat there looking at it.

"Come on, Roberta; what are you waiting for, Christmas? It's already here; open it."

Mom looked like she was about to burst. I could feel the excitement that was building up inside of her. I pulled open the lid and looked inside. My mouth opened and my eyes were as big as quarters again.

My curiosity was killing me. I wanted to get a closer look, but I couldn't. I watched them impatiently and coaxed them along.

"Come on," I said, "show me. Take it out of the box; I need to see it."

Well, it was almost as if my mother heard me because at exactly that moment she reached into the box and gently pulled it out. It sparkled from the morning sunrays streaming through the window.

It looked like a piece of jewelry or something. I was not close enough to see it very well. I started moving in a little bit. I was almost close enough to touch them. I so wanted to reach out and put my arms around them. I closed my eyes for a moment and imagined what it would be like to feel my mother's arms around me.

"It's a locket, sweetheart; you wear it around your neck."

"It's a heart, Mommy."

"I know that, but look: you can open it up, see? On one side I put in a picture of you and me, together, and on the other side I put a picture of you. When you grow up, you can put a picture of you and your husband there."

"My husband? Yuck! I'm going to stay with you forever, Mommy."

Oh my God, the locket. It was from my mother. But there were no pictures in it. What happened to the pictures? Oh, and to think I almost threw it out. Thank God that Tyler had the sense to retrieve it from the garbage and keep it. *I must get it back from him*, I thought. *I wonder what happened to the pictures? I will probably never find out.* I was in a daze. I was consumed by my thoughts when I realized that the vision in front of me was starting to fade away. I tried to reach for my mother, but I couldn't. She was slowly disappearing out of sight.

"Come back! Don't leave me again."

There was nothing that I could do or say to stop her from fading out of my life again.

* * * * *

She had no sooner faded away when the vision came back. This time, Mom wasn't there. I saw myself again. I was playing with my toys I got for Christmas, but there was someone else in the room with me. I had no clue who this person might be. I seemed to know her very well because she laughed and played with me. She was an older woman, thin, with white hair and glasses. She seemed very nice.

Suddenly there was a knock at the door. The lady told me to stay put and she got up and went to see who it was.

"Merry Christmas, Officers," she said. "What can I do for you?"

"Is this the Hansen residence?"

Police officers, oh no… the story of my life.

"Yes sir, it is, but Miss Hansen is not here at this moment. She should be back shortly, though. She had a couple of errands to do and she asked me if I would watch her daughter for a little while. I'm her neighbor, Paula Crawford. If you give me your card, I can have her call you when she comes back."

"Mrs. Crawford, is there somewhere that we can talk privately?"

"Well… sure. Roberta, be a good girl and go play in your room for a few minutes."

I watched as I left the room. *I don't have a good feeling about this at all.*

"Listen, Officer, I don't think I can help you with anything. I think you should wait for Jennifer to come home. She shouldn't be too much longer."

As I watched this play out in front of me, I could sense that something was very wrong. I could feel a lump forming in my throat and an aching in my heart.

"There has been a terrible accident, Mrs. Crawford. The roads are very slippery out there and a tractortrailer lost control in a curve just as Miss Hansen was rounding it. They had a head-on collision. She didn't have a chance. The car was totaled, and emergency crews worked as fast as they could to pry it apart to search for any survivors. By the time they got to her, she was already dead. They figure she died on impact. I'm terribly sorry."

Mrs. Crawford put her hand over her mouth and caught her balance on the wall.

"No…" I cried, as the waterworks started.

The officers helped Miss Crawford to a chair.

"Is there a Mr. Hansen?" they asked.

I couldn't move. I couldn't breathe. I just watched and listened with tears constantly flowing down my face. I couldn't believe it. How could this happen? I wanted to stay with her forever. My eyes were so full of tears that everything was a blur and then suddenly it all went black.

"No wait… This can't be happening… Come back… Please come back…"

It was very dark, and I was devastated. My heart was broken, and I was getting scared again. Scared of being left alone like this, broken-hearted and confused. Scared of this emptiness.

"Think good thoughts," I kept telling myself. "Think good thoughts."

What good thoughts… my life is shit!

I started to hear that soft, beautiful voice of my mother echoing all around me.

"Keep looking and you will find yourself… You need to remember… You need to find all those missing pieces… Don't stop looking."

The voice started to fade away.

"No… No… Don't go… Don't leave me here all alone… so alone…"

Chapter 20

"Bobby… Bobby, it's me. It's okay. I'm right here."

"Don't leave me… Please come back… Mommy…"

"Bobby… Bobby… You are only dreaming, Bobby. Open your eyes. I am right here with you."

I could hear Tyler's voice in the distance. It seemed so far away. I tried to go towards the sound. I was happy that he was close by. I was not feeling as afraid anymore. I kept following his voice. It kept getting nearer and nearer. The darkness was slowly giving way to light. I couldn't quite focus; everything was a blur.

"Oh, Bobby, honey. Thank God you're back… Bobby, can you hear me?"

I opened my eyes, and then closed them again, trying to put them into focus. The light was very bright, and it was hard to see. I tried to open them again, but it hurt, so I closed them and tried to relax.

I felt very weak and lightheaded. I couldn't figure out if I was dreaming, or this was real. I did hear Tyler's voice though, so…

"Bobby, honey, are you awake?"

I tried to respond, but my lips wouldn't move.

I felt his hand brush through my hair. I was not dreaming; he was really here.

I tried to speak again, but only managed a whisper.

"I'm here, Bobby," he said.

"Tyler," my voice cracked, and I paused. "It is so nice to hear your voice."

"Oh my God, Bobby, I was so afraid to lose you again."

He took my hand and I felt him kiss me on the cheek.

"Tyler… My locket... Do you still have it?"

"What?"

"I had a dream… My locket… My mother gave it to me… I remember…"

I managed to open my eyes a sliver. Tyler was leaning over me, so close. I could see the very concerned look on his face. He tried to force a smile, but it wasn't too convincing. My eyes were fully open now. They had adjusted to the light. I was very confused all of a sudden.

"Where am I?" I said finally.

I saw a tear overflow from Tyler's eye and start slowly gliding down his cheek. I watched and waited. It took him a few minutes to answer.

"Bobby... baby. Don't you remember anything?"

I tried and tried but all I could remember was Mom and me and Christmas…

The accident… oh no…

I started to stress as I remembered my dream.

"Oh my God, my mom," I whispered.

"She had a car accident… She died… We were having Christmas together… She left, and I never saw her again… The locket… She gave it to me… Where is it? Tyler, do you still have my locket?"

I saw him straighten up and reach into his pocket. He pulled his hand back out and held it in the air in front of me.

"Here it is. I told you not to throw it away. See, it does mean something to you."

I was too weak to move, and my arm wouldn't budge. Tyler could see that I was struggling, and he brought it down and placed it in my hand. I closed my fingers around it and cried.

My throat was so dry that I started to cough.

"Ouch… Oh my God, that hurt."

I started to cough again. The pain was unbearable. I held my chest and tried to hold my breath so I wouldn't cough.

"I'll get help!" he yelled. I saw Tyler turn and start to run out of the room.

"Don't leave me," I whispered, and I started to choke again. It felt like someone was stabbing me with a knife, right into my chest. The pain was unbearable. A young woman came running into the room. She reached above the bed and pulled down an oxygen mask. She gently placed it over my mouth and nose.

"You must stay calm, Miss Hansen. Try to relax and breathe normally."

I was starting to feel frightened. I was in terrible pain and I could hardly move. I tried to speak but it was difficult with the mask over my mouth. At that moment, as I watched the young woman all dressed in white check my vitals, I realized that I was in the hospital. I knew she looked vaguely familiar. She was a nurse at St. Mary's; I had seen her in the cafeteria. I was at St. Mary's.

"Tyler…" I tried to speak but the mask was muffling my words. "Where is Tyler?"

"You must stay quiet, Miss Hansen. Try not to speak."

Tyler seemed to materialize beside me.

"I'm right here, Bobby. You must listen to the nurse. I'm not going anywhere, I promise; just relax."

He took me by the hand again. I watched as the nurse walked around to the other side of the bed.

"I'm going to give you a little something to help you relax." I watched as she removed the cap from a syringe. I hated needles, damn it, but I didn't have the strength to argue.

"This won't hurt a bit. Just a little pinch."

She pulled the blankets down to expose my hip, and then she disinfected the target.

"Ready? Take a deep breath."

Of course I got all tensed up, which you shouldn't do because your muscles tighten and it's more painful.

"There," she said, "that wasn't so bad."

"Easy for you to say," I whispered under the mask. "You're at the other end of that needle."

She was very gentle, though, and it wasn't so bad. I didn't want to act like a baby in front of Tyler, so I smiled at her and watched as she headed for the door.

"Get some rest. The doctor will be in to see you in a little while."

She left the oxygen on me. I looked up at Tyler. He tried to force a smile again, but it didn't come close to hiding the concerned look that I observed on his face. I wanted to speak but the mask made it impossible. I wanted very much to remove it, but I didn't have the strength. I saw Tyler close his eyes and I could tell that he was fighting off the tears that were building up inside of him.

"Everything is going to be okay, Bobby," he said finally. "We will be together again, soon, you'll see."

He squeezed my hand ever so gently. I tried to smile. I was so weak, and I didn't know why. My eyelids started to feel very heavy. They would close, and I would force them open again. That happened time after time, until I finally gave up.

I could still hear the heart monitor echoing through my mind, loud at first, then gradually fading out. I could still feel the warmth of Tyler's hand around mine. I felt myself slowly start to drift away. It was very dark, but I stayed calm. I was not afraid. I was floating around in nothingness.

Strangely enough, I kept wondering what was going to happen next. With all the craziness that had been going on in my head lately, nothing would have surprised me.

It was still dark, but I could hear a faint sound in the distance. I couldn't really tell what it was. There it was again… sounded like laughter. Not sure, too far away. Oh… what was that… a hint of light, off in the distance? I heard the sounds again and followed them. They were coming from the light. It was definitely laughter. I could hear it so clearly now. It made me smile.

The closer I got to the light, the louder the sounds got. Suddenly, like a gust of wind, the whole sky lit up in front of me. What a beautiful sky it was. Baby blue, and not a cloud in it. I was almost sure that I could feel the warmth of the streaming rays of sunlight. I knew that this wasn't real; I had been wandering off in my mind so many times lately. It felt wonderful, though. Ah… There was that laughter again. I looked around me. What a magnificent view. Breathtaking. Right below me, I saw a lake. It was surrounded by a forest and some pastures. There were mountains in the background.

Again, I heard the laughter… I tried to get a closer look. I saw something move through the trees. The forest was dense, but now and then between the pines I could see them. It looked like a boy and girl, running together through the forest, hand in hand. Her beautiful, wavy, long brown hair was flowing behind her. They seemed to be so happy. They looked like they were headed for the lake. I smiled as I watched them zig-zag between the trees and bushes as they made their way there.

I was surprised and excited as I watched them arrive full speed at the edge of the lake, and without any hesitation whatsoever, they splashed right into it, clothes and all. I couldn't help myself; I had to laugh. They were having a blast. They were screaming and laughing and splashing each other. With all of that, they never let go of each other's hand.

Gradually, the splashing stopped. They looked at each other so intensely. I found myself moving in a little closer. With both hands, the girl reached up and pulled the hair away from her face. He reached out his arms, grabbed her by the waist, and pulled her close. They looked so much in love. I approached cautiously, as if I were afraid that they would see me. I felt like I was intruding on a special moment. She raised her head and looked up toward the sky as he caressed her neck. That is when I got a close look at her… I mean me... I mean, I don't know what I mean. It was not possible. How could it be? It was me, but a lot younger, and I knew instinctively that the boy had to be Tyler. He turned his head and sure enough it was. He was so beautiful. Actually, we both were. We made a really nice couple.

But why do I see us together again as such a young couple? I started feeling really confused.

Suddenly everything went black.

"No, come back! I need to see more."

Chapter 21

There was a bright flash of light. I could hear the faint beep… beep… beep… beep… of the monitor. It kept getting louder and louder. Something touched my eye. Another flash of light. I was starting to hear voices. I was back. Back in the hospital where I was before my little journey to the forest. I was still groggy from the sedative, or whatever it was that the nurse gave me earlier. I could still feel Tyler's hand wrapped around mine. My eyelids felt very heavy, but I managed to open them: a little bit at first, and then gradually all the way. The oxygen mask was gone. What a relief.

"Tyler," I whispered, "you're still here?"

He had never left my side. He stayed there the whole time. He got off his chair, leaned over, and gently kissed me on the cheek.

"The doctor is here to see you."

"Miss Hansen… I'm Dr. Blake."

I turned my head toward the voice. He was standing on the other side of the bed, towering over me, with a tiny flashlight in his hand. A big man in a white jacket. He looked more like a football player than a doctor. Well, maybe a retired football player. He wasn't a young man. His hair was all white. He was very handsome, though. He had a square, very stern-looking face. He looked like he was all business. His eyes were narrow, just barely revealing their beautiful shade of blue. I watched him as he jotted notes down in his folder.

I was trying to remember if I had ever seen him before, but nothing was coming to mind. My dishwashing job didn't really get me out of the kitchen very much, and the doctors didn't have a habit of hanging out with the kitchen staff. Maybe I had crossed paths with him in the hallway coming in or leaving work, but anyway, my brain wasn't processing anything very well right now.

"You gave us a good scare, Miss Hansen," he finally said. "How are you doing?"

"I don't know… groggy… tired… I don't really feel much of anything… I just want to sleep… what happened to me? Why am I here? Why am I feeling like this?"

"You were in an accident, Miss Hansen; do you not remember? Try to think back. Do you not recall being out on Samson Street?"

"You were upset, and you ran out of the apartment," Tyler started. "Try to remember, Bobby. Close your eyes and focus. Try to rewind, back to when you ran out of the apartment. It's important, baby. Only you can tell us what happened."

I closed my eyes. I could still feel Tyler's hand around mine, and in my other hand, I could still feel the locket. I still had it. It was real. *Oh my God, Mom,* I thought. *I wish you were here right now.*

"I love you too, Roberta. You will always be my baby. I'm sorry for all your pain. You have a wonderful life ahead of you. Make the best of it. I will watch over you, I promise."

Her words echoed through my mind.

"Please help me, Mom," I said softly under my breath. "Please help…"

Suddenly there was a flash in front of my eyes.

"Oh my God," I yelled.

"What is it, Bobby?" Tyler squeezed my hand a little.

"I just remembered the mess in my apartment. Oh my God, that was real, wasn't it?"

"Yes, Bobby, don't worry about that; it will be okay. You must think of what happened after, Bobby; keep trying."

"I'm so confused, Tyler. I don't know what is real and what is not. All these visions, they keep flashing in front of me. I don't know if I am dreaming or I am awake."

"Maybe it is too soon, Miss Hansen. I think it is probably better if you stay calm and get some rest. Tomorrow is another day."

"But my apartment, what am I going to do? Everything is destroyed. I have nothing. Why would someone do this to me? What did I do to deserve that? I don't know what to think anymore."

"Like the good doc said, Bobby… 'Tomorrow is another day,'" Tyler whispered.

Thoughts were flying through my head and I kept trying to push them away. I didn't want to go there right now. I just wanted to sleep. *Somebody, please make me sleep*, I thought. Well, it was as if someone read my mind. The nurse came in my room with her wonderful syringe full of the good stuff, and off to la la land I went.

* * * * *

I awoke to that now familiar music… the beep… beep of the monitors. It was daylight outside. I seemed to be lost in time. If it weren't for the clock, I wouldn't know what time of day it was, and even then, I was never even sure if it was a.m. or p.m. I looked around the room and I was alone. I felt uneasy. Where was Tyler, the nurse with her syringe, the doctor? I couldn't believe they had left me alone. I was hurting all over and my heart was starting to pound.

I saw the buzzer and was about to reach for it when I heard a noise. I held my breath and scanned the room. Who was it, and what were they doing in my room? I pressed the buzzer and hoped someone would come. Then, of course, the waterworks started. Great… I couldn't see anything in the room anymore. Everything was blurry. The door flew open and a nurse came running in.

"Is everything ok, Miss Hansen?" she said as she glanced at the monitors.

Right after she said that, I heard another door open.

"Bobby, what's going on? Are you okay?"

He came to my side and took my hand.

"I was scared, Tyler. I woke up and I was all alone and I was wondering where everyone was. I wasn't sure if I was dreaming and something bad was going to happen and then I heard a noise and…"

"I'm sorry, Bobby; I was in the bathroom freshening up. I won't leave you alone. Don't worry. There will always be someone here with you. I promise."

"Ok… now I feel really crazy. I'm so sorry for being such a baby."

Tyler kissed me on the cheek and said that he would be more worried about me if I wasn't scared.

"The doctor will be in soon," he said, "and he will want to talk to you again to try to find out what you remember about the accident."

Those words no sooner came out of his mouth when Dr. Blake walked into the room.

"Good morning, Miss Hansen. How are you feeling today?" He reached for my chart and scanned it quickly. "Did you sleep okay?"

I told him that I didn't even realize that I had slept a whole night. Then he went on to tell me that I had been out for a whole day and that he had seen me yesterday morning.

Ok, I thought, *never mind not knowing if it is morning or night; I don't even know which day I am in.* I was totally confused and suddenly lost in thought. I could hear the doctor asking me if I was able to recall anything more about the accident and I could hear Tyler telling me to concentrate, but they seemed so far away. I didn't know what was going on. I thought I was heading off into my dreams again with all those drugs they were giving me.

Suddenly there was a flash of light.

"I remember something," I said. "There was an argument, oh no… it was so stupid of me. Oh my, will Carla ever speak to me again?"

Tyler squeezed my hand. "It's okay, Bobby; go on."

"I stormed out of the apartment, running. I went down the stairs two steps at the time and then flew out the door and started running in the rain. It was pouring down hard. I don't know where I was going..."

I paused to try to catch my breath.

"Wait, I need to slow down a bit. Everything is coming at me too fast. All these little clippings of thoughts. I can't make out any of them."

My brain was like scrambled eggs. Everything was mixed up and coming at me from all directions.

"Okay, Bobby. You need to calm down. Take a deep breath and relax for a minute."

"Okay… Okay… I'm fine, just let me think a minute… just a minute."

I looked up at Dr. Blake. He was taking notes again.

"Okay, just let me try to organize my thoughts. I was running. It was pouring rain. I was cold and soaked to the bone. I was terrified. I remember I felt like someone was chasing me. There was nobody around, but I still couldn't shake that feeling. Then I started having those crazy visions. They kept popping in front of my face. I wanted to get away from them, so I kept running, but they wouldn't leave me alone. No matter which way I turned, they just kept exploding in front of me. Then, I don't know what came over me, but I stopped. I couldn't run anymore. I couldn't move a muscle. I remember feeling like I was in some kind of trance, and I had no control over anything. Everything seemed to be going in slow motion. Something distracted me, and I had to turn around. Everything was a blur. Oh my God!" I yelled.

Then I sat up screaming.

"Oh God. What happened to me?"

A sharp pain shot through me. I pulled my hand out of Tyler's and brought it up to my chest where it was hurting.

"Miss Hansen. You must lay down. You shouldn't be moving."

Dr. Blake and Tyler each took hold of a shoulder and gently laid me back down on the bed. The nurse came running into the room again.

"Nurse Halloway!" Dr. Blake said, then he jotted something down on a piece of paper and handed it to her.

"Hurry, we need to keep her calm."

I didn't protest. I was crying hard now. Just like a baby. Just like the day they told me that my mom was dead and that I would never see her again. I remember now how I cried and cried and cried some more, till there were no more tears left. Crazy how at such a young age you could believe that your life is over. Here I was still crying all these years later. I felt a little prick, barely noticed it, and then the nurse left the room.

"Bobby, honey, It's okay. I'm sorry, maybe you should rest..."

I cut him off before he could finish his sentence.

"There was a loud roaring noise," I cried. "I turned to see what it was."

It was very hard to get the words out because I kept sobbing.

"I saw lights in the distance; they were very bright... so bright they hurt my eyes. They were coming closer and kept getting brighter. Then it struck me. It sounded like an explosion... blew me right off my feet. I felt like I was flying through the air. I remember screaming. I... I just kept screaming... I remember..."

Suddenly, I felt so weak and I could hardly speak. I kept whimpering. I felt very lightheaded, like I was floating again.

"What did you give me?" I whispered.

"It's okay, Miss Hansen. That is quite enough for today. We'll talk about this again another time. You need to get some rest."

The doctor reached down and put his hand on my shoulder.

"I'll stop in and see you later."

"But..." I said softly. "What is wrong with me? Why can't I move? Why can't I..."

Chapter 22

Very faintly I could hear someone singing in the background. It was very relaxing. I thought there was a radio playing somewhere. As I focused a little more, I smelled some perfume. It was a scent that I recognized, L'air du Temps. I realized then that it wasn't Tyler who was holding my hand. I smiled as I slowly opened my eyes because I knew it was Carla. I should have known when I first heard the singing. The voice of an angel. That was probably why I was so calm. That voice of hers always had that effect on me. I looked up at her and saw a tear run down her face as she watched over me. She looked so sad. I smiled and squeezed her hand.

"I am so sorry, Bobby. I should never have..."

"Shh... Carla. You were right. I was so tired and upset that I just lost it. It was nobody's fault but my own. I don't even deserve to have you as a friend. I am the one who is sorry. Sorry for being such a fool. I love you more than anything in this world. We have been through so much together. I am surprised that you are here, by my side, after what I did and what I said. I don't know why I went crazy like that. Please forgive me... please..."

"There is nothing to forgive, Bobby. You were right. There was no way I could know how you were feeling with all those things that were happening to you. I should not have presumed that I did. I don't know how I would have reacted in your place. I just want to be here for you and help you in any way that I can. You are the closest thing to family that I have, and I don't want to lose you. You scared the hell out of me. God, it is nice to see you and talk to you again. Don't worry about anything. Tyler and I will take care of you till you get back on your feet."

I watched as she spoke. I couldn't help but smile. She reminded me so much of an angel. I mean, she would never have tolerated me, or taken care of me like she did, if she wasn't an angel. It made me think of my mother. I could still see her face. Her beauty. Her long, curly blond hair flowing in the heavens and her piercing blue eyes. Then it dawned on me. In my dream, when I was with Tyler in the lake, I looked just like her. Except for my green eyes and brown hair. I didn't have her eyes. I didn't know who my father was, but I must have inherited his.

"Carla," I whispered. "I don't want you to think that I am crazy, but I want to tell you something."

She looked at me curiously. "Crazy… you? Never…"

She hesitated and smirked a little.

"Sorry… couldn't help myself; you walked right into that one… go on."

"Ha… ha… come on, I'm being serious. Something happened."

Her expression changed as she focused on what I was saying.

"My mom," I said softly. "I saw her. After the accident. After I went floating into the heavens. She was there in front of me… an angel… she spoke to me. I could feel her presence, her warmth, her love. I know it was real. She said that she would watch over me; she really did."

Carla watched me in amazement as I recounted my experience to her.

"You do believe me, don't you, Carla? I was not dreaming; I know it. I felt her presence."

"I do, Bobby; I really do. I have goosebumps. You are so blessed, you know. We are all going to help you through this, even your mom; you'll see. Things will all work out for you in the end."

Just then, Tyler walked into the room. We both turned to look at him and smiled.

"Did I come in at a bad time?" he said, smiling like the cat that swallowed the canary.

"Whoa..." Carla said. "Aren't you in a good mood!"

I watched him closely as he approached my bedside. He was so beautiful. His smile lit up the whole room. I felt butterflies in my stomach. I thought of the dream I had when we ran into the lake, hand in hand. I recalled the way we looked at each other as we stood arm in arm in the water. I wanted to freeze that moment in my mind forever. We looked so happy together. Like a fairy-tale *and they lived happily ever after* kind of scene. *I wish... I really do wish...*

"How's my girl?" he whispered as he kissed me on the cheek.

"I am doing much better since I got a chance to patch things up with Carla," I told him. "As for the rest of me, well, I must be really drugged up because I can't feel a thing."

"I have a surprise for you," he said, and he turned and looked at Carla. "Did you tell her?"

"No," she replied. "Not a word."

"What have you two been up to?"

Tyler instructed me to close my eyes and open my hand. I felt something in my palm. I closed my hand around it.

"It's my locket," I said as I opened my eyes. "What's the surprise?"

"First of all," he said as he bubbled over with excitement, "I had it repaired. The latch on the chain was broken. Now here, let me show you something."

I watched attentively as he pried open the heart. It made me think back to when my mom gave it to me and how she carefully pried it open for me. I remember the picture of her and me together. If only I knew what happened to it.

He turned the open locket down toward me, so I could see what was inside. I swallowed hard and I could feel the tears starting to fill my eyes as I remembered my dream.

"Later on, when you grow up, you can put a picture of you and your husband there."

"My husband! Yuck! I'm going to stay with you forever, Mommy."

"I'm sorry, Bobby. I thought it would make you happy. Are you upset with me?"

I shook my head, no.

"Do you remember when I snapped the picture?" Tyler asked. "You and I were laying in the field of trilliums. You looked so beautiful rolling around in the flowers. I had such a wonderful time that day and I know that you did too. The picture of the two of us turned out so nice that I thought it would look good in the locket. I hope you are not too upset with me. I love you, baby, and I want to take care of you."

He bent over and kissed me on the lips. "Would you like me to put it on you?"

I smiled at him and thought about how lucky I was to have him. I raised my head a bit and he put it around my neck, the same way my mother did. I kept thinking about her too. I wanted to see what it looked like on me, so I asked if there was a mirror anywhere. Carla and Tyler just looked at each other in silence for a few moments.

Carla spoke up. "Honey, you have just had a bad accident, and I don't think it's a good idea for you to look in a mirror right now. You are badly bruised. It looks a lot worse because of the swelling. I don't want you to get upset."

Suddenly I felt scared. "Do I really look that bad? I am not going to be scarred for life, am I?"

Tyler took me by the hand.

"No," Carla said. "Give it a little time. It will all heal nicely."

I really needed to see myself, so I insisted they give me a mirror. At least I knew what to expect. Tyler rolled the little tray table over till it was right in front of me. Underneath the top cover, there was a mirror. He paused just as he was about to lift the mirror.

"Are you sure about this?" he asked.

I looked at him, then Carla, then I took a deep breath and nodded. I closed my eyes for a moment and then opened them slowly.

"Oh my Lord," I gasped. "My face... Frankenstein, for Christ's sake."

I had umpteen stitches across the top of my forehead. The left side of my face was black and blue and very swollen. My eyes were bloodshot. I looked like I came right out of a horror film.

"Bobby, honey. It is going to heal up properly. Carla promised."

My eyes started to swell with tears. They overflowed and started to stream down my face. I closed them again and Tyler let go of my hand and moved the table back to where it was.

"It's okay, baby. You will look beautiful, again. Don't worry," he said, and I heard him leave the room.

"Give it a little time, Bobby," Carla whispered.

I opened my eyes and Carla was there leaning over me. She reached out and put her hand on my shoulder.

"You will be back to your old self soon enough; just give it a little time."

"I can't believe this is all happening to me. I thought my life was finally getting better. For the last couple of years, I have been very happy. What a fool I was to think that I could get away from this hell that I have always lived in."

The door opened and Tyler came back in followed by the nurse. I saw her pull out a syringe. I didn't protest. I wanted the numbness. I didn't want to feel. I knew that I would have to face up to everything soon enough, but for now it was nice to not have a care in the world. It didn't take long. I closed my eyes, and in just a few minutes I could already start to feel the buzz.

I opened my eyes again and Tyler and Carla were still there, standing each on their own side of my bed looking down on me.

"A freak from a horror show. That is what I look like. How can you look at me with a straight face?"

Tyler started to speak, and I cut back in. "Yep, I know," I said. "It is going to heal properly, and I will be just like I was before. Just give it a little time. Do me a favor, okay? Don't let me look in another mirror until that time."

Suddenly there was a commotion in the hallway. We all turned and looked toward the door. I recognized his voice; it was Dr. Blake. He was arguing with someone.

"You can't see her right now," he ordered. "She is not strong enough yet. She has been hysterical since she came in. We have had to sedate her several times since she has regained consciousness after her surgery. Let me check on her again first."

"We need to talk to her as soon as possible if we want to start working on this case," someone said.

The voice sounded familiar, but I couldn't place it. I listened some more. I watched as Tyler turned and walked toward the door. Then it dawned on me. It was the detective that came to my apartment the day that it got vandalized. I couldn't remember his name though. It was funny that I could think about that and not get upset.

I saw Dr. Blake and Tyler walk back in and close the door behind them. Carla moved over to make room for the doctor.

"How are you doing, Bobby? You are looking much more relaxed than the last time I saw you."

"What the heck do you have me on? I'm as high as a kite." I giggled.

"We have some serious talking to do and I need you to stay calm."

I knew by the look on his face that he meant business. I felt Tyler put his hand around mine. I guess he thought it would comfort me. He was probably right. The doctor started talking. I listened carefully, though I had a little problem processing it all. This much I got. They saved my left leg, just barely. It was almost completely shattered. My left arm was broken in two places. Cracked ribs… concussion… lost a lot of blood…

"Whoa!" I said. I looked up at Tyler and then back at the doctor, and then I smiled. "Got any good news?"

Carla giggled. "Oh my God… Can I have some of that stuff?"

Tyler laughed too.

The doctor smiled. "You are going to live. Is that good enough news for you? Seriously, though, your recovery will not be easy. Your leg is badly damaged. We are talking six months to a year of therapy, maybe more; it depends on you. You will have to work long and hard and hopefully regain full use of your leg. The rest won't take as long. You are going to be here for quite a while, and you won't always be drugged up like this, so I need you to get hold of yourself. We don't want to make an addict out of you either. It won't be a picnic, so I need you to be strong and think positive. I am a good listener, if you need someone to talk to. Also, if you feel the need, the resident psychiatrist can stop in and pay you a visit…."

Psychiatrist… Funny how the word doesn't freak me out right now…

"Bobby, are you with me?"

I nodded.

"As I was saying, don't keep things bottled up inside of you. It's not healthy. You seem to have two very good friends here who are probably very good listeners too."

"Don't worry, doctor. We will try to be here as much as we can," Tyler said. "Carla and I will take turns, right?"

"Sure thing. I'm here practically every day, anyway."

There was a knock at the door.

"Just a minute," Dr. Blake shouted. "Miss Hansen, there is a very persistent Detective Collins at the door, and he has been waiting a very long time to talk to you. I have put him off, I think, for as long as I can. If you can't handle it now, just say the word and I will turn him away again, but he has informed me that he is not leaving the hospital until he speaks with you, and frankly I am getting tired of looking at him."

Dr. Blake was a good man, trying to protect me like this. I was liking him more and more. Good thing, because I knew that I was going to be seeing a lot of him in the months to come. As for the detective in the hallway, well, I figured that I should maybe give him a chance, too. They couldn't all be bad. Not that cops were bad, but if you had gone through what I did, you would be a little uneasy around them too.

"Uh… I don't know… I guess so… Might as well get it over with."

"That's right. The sooner the better. I will let him in on my way out. Try to stay calm, though. I don't want you getting upset, you hear me? I do have other patients to take care of. I can't be here all the time."

He put his hand on my shoulder, winked and smiled. "Good luck," he said, then he turned and headed for the door.

"If there is any problem at all, Dr. Murphy, come and get me. I will be in my office at the end of the hall."

Dr. Murphy… hmm… It had a nice ring to it. Dr. Tyler Murphy. I hadn't heard anyone call him that yet. Not even in his office. The people were all very friendly and casual. Everyone I met was introduced by their first name, if I remembered right.

The door opened and in came Detective Collins. You know what was weird? The name didn't ring any bells, but when I saw his face, I remembered him well. He was, in fact, the same detective that I bumped into in Carla's doorway the day my apartment got ransacked.

He was very good looking, that I remembered. He had dark hair and the eyes to match. He looked very tired though, with dark circles around his eyes. He was probably a workaholic. I would bet anything that he hadn't slept since he heard what happened to me.

He was wearing a casual suit and he looked very fit. I glanced over at Carla and she had her eyes glued on him, too.

"We meet again, Miss Hansen. I'm sorry it had to be under terrible circumstances again."

I was so lost in my thoughts that his words startled me, and I jumped. Must be the drugs. I felt like I was floating on air. Not a care in the world.

"I'm sorry, Miss Hansen. Didn't mean to startle you."

"It's okay. I was just daydreaming."

"Carla?" I said, as I turned to look at her again. "Yoo-hoo, Carla?"

She finally took her eyes off him and looked at me.

I was giggling at her and wiping my chin.

"What's wrong?" she said.

I kept wiping my chin.

"What?"

"You can stop drooling now. He's here to see me."

She gasped and put both hands to her mouth.

"I can't believe you said that. You're so bad!"

She turned away, embarrassed.

"I'm sorry, Carla; I didn't mean it, honestly."

I looked over at the detective, and he looked a little uncomfortable. He stood there and didn't say anything.

Tyler walked over to the detective and shook his hand. "She is highly medicated, and I don't know if she could be of any real help to you right now."

"I just have a few questions."

"Shoot… I mean … no… I mean don't shoot! I mean ask away." I sniggered.

Carla started to giggle, and we found out that this very stern detective's face could crack a smile after all.

"How are you feeling, Miss Hansen?"

"Better than I look, I guess."

"Can you tell me what happened to you the other day? Do you remember anything at all?"

"Let me see." I hesitated for a moment. "The day after the break-in, after we finished cleaning up, I guess I just freaked out. Everything started to get to me and I exploded. I took off out of my building and ran down the street. All these crazy things were going through my mind and I just kept running. I started to feel uneasy. I don't know why. I had the feeling like someone was watching me or… I don't know, really. I stopped running and turned around. There was a very loud roaring noise and really bright lights. I remember flying through the air… Then my mom… She spoke to me…" A tear rolled down my cheek. I was smiling but still there was a tear.

"I'm sorry, Miss Hansen, But I need to find out who did this to you. Do you remember anything about the vehicle? Make… model… anything at all?"

"All I saw was bright lights… that's all… and I remember the loud noise… I'm sorry. It was all like a bad dream."

"I'm going to be honest and tell you that we don't have much to go on, here. It was pouring rain so there wasn't much chance of collecting any evidence. There was no sign of any brake marks, so we believe that it might have been intentional. That, plus the vandalism that was done at your apartment, and the harassment... Well, there are just too many coincidences for me. A person cannot have that much bad luck at the same time. Just to be on the safe side, I have posted a guard at your door. There will be an officer on guard, twenty-four-seven. At least until we sort through this mess."

I was listening to everything he was saying, yet sometimes I felt like I wasn't really there. Like it didn't concern me. He was talking about someone else. Like it was someone else's life that was in danger. It felt very weird. Tyler and Carla listened and looked on. I could see the concern on their faces. I felt a tear come down my face again. No clue why. I closed my eyes and breathed in deeply. Damned those waterworks.

"Bobby!" Tyler reached out for my hand. "Are you okay?"

I opened my eyes again. It took a lot of effort. My eyelids were getting really heavy. I tried hard to keep them open.

"Yeah, I'm okay."

My eyes closed, and I forced them open again. "Just a little tired... Just a... a little... tired..."

Chapter 23

Everything went black. I could still hear their voices but very faintly. Tyler was still holding my hand. He pulled me close and put his arm around me. There was music playing in the background and we slow-danced. It was "Evergreen," one of my favorite love songs. I found myself humming along. I held him close and felt the warmth of his body next to mine. It felt wonderful.

The music suddenly stopped, and we stopped dancing. I started to feel uneasy. My eyes were still heavy, but I forced them open. Oh my God! It was David! He had this evil look on his face.

"I'm going to get you," he kept saying. "I'm going to get you."

I started screaming…

"Bobby… Bobby… wake up. It's just a dream. I'm here… open your eyes."

I pushed my eyes open and saw Tyler leaning over me. Suddenly, the door opened and in ran the police officer, gun in hand. On impulse, Tyler threw his hands in the air.

"It's okay, Officer," he shouted. "You can put the gun down; she was just having a bad dream."

He looked around the room and slowly lowered his pistol.

"You okay, Miss?"

"Yes… I guess… I… you scared the shit out of me."

"Likewise, Miss. Sorry, just doing my job. I'll go back to my post."

I looked at Tyler, who had since put down his arms. He looked pretty scared for a second.

"Nice to know that they are on the ball," he said, and then he yawned and started rubbing his eyes.

I watched as he yawned again. He didn't look very spry. He had dark circles around his eyes.

"What time of day is it? I have completely lost track. What happened to Detective Collins?"

"That was yesterday, Bobby. This is Tuesday morning. The accident happened Saturday night."

"That, I remember. Are you telling me that I have been in here for three days already? It really doesn't seem like it. I guess that it's because I have been sleeping most of the time. Oh my God. Have you been here since the accident?"

"Carla replaced me for a couple of hours each day, so I could go home to shower and change."

"And at night?"

"Never left your bedside."

"You can't do this. What about your patients? You are important to them. They need you too."

"I had Carol reschedule my appointments yesterday and this morning. This afternoon, I need to go in for a little while. I will come back when I am done. Carla will take my place."

"I don't need a babysitter twenty-four-seven," I said, "and besides, I have an armed guard standing outside my door, with an itchy trigger finger, it seems. I think that I'm in good hands."

"I just don't want you to be alone, that's all."

"Don't be silly. You can't sleep here every night. They will kick you out. Besides, you have a life and a job; you can't just drop everything for me."

There was a knock at the door. I looked over and it slowly opened.

"Is it safe to come in? Special delivery for Miss Hansen."

It was Lou. I was so happy to see him. He was carrying a big tray.

"I made a special breakfast for my favorite girl. No offense there, Tyler, but I saw her first."

I started to giggle. It felt good. Lou always knew how to put a smile on my face.

"Quite the guard dog outside your door. I almost didn't get in. By the way, when I told you to come to the hospital Monday morning, I didn't mean as a patient."

He put the tray on the table and wheeled it over to me. He raised the head of my bed slightly, so I could sit up a bit. It felt weird because I had been lying on my back for such a long time. I didn't remember having anything to eat since before the accident. I was feeling very hungry. Whatever it was, it smelled really good. He lifted the cover off the tray for me.

"I made you your favorite: blueberry pancakes. Now, eat them while they're still warm, doctor's orders."

He bent down and kissed me on the forehead. A tear got away from me and rolled down my cheek.

"Are you okay, sweetie? Are you in any pain?"

"I'm okay. Just a little emotional. You are such a sweetheart, Lou. Thank you. You didn't have to go to all this trouble."

"That's right, you shouldn't have," Tyler said. "I'm taking really good care of her."

I turned and looked up at him. He seemed upset, or maybe he was just tired.

"I've got this," he said.

He picked up the container of syrup and poured some on my pancakes. I reached to pick up my fork. With only one hand, and not very much strength, it was going to be tricky. I set my fork sideways on top of the stack of pancakes and pressed it down. I moved it over a little and pressed it down again. I managed to slice a small piece. I poked my fork into it and brought it to my mouth.

"Mmm… this is delicious!"

"Here, let me help you."

Tyler took my fork from my hand, picked up the knife, and cut up my pancakes for me.

"There you go, honey; now dig in. Would you like more syrup on them?"

I nodded, and he added more. Then he fixed my coffee for me.

Lou and Tyler talked while I ate. I got a few words in now and then between mouthfuls. The topic of the hour was David. Where had he disappeared to, and who in the hell was he? Nobody seemed to know.

Everyone agreed that he wasn't stupid enough to show up here, at his place of work, where a lot of people would recognize him. Everyone, including the police, thought that David was behind all this mess. He was the number one suspect. The break-in looked very suspicious; the motive was definitely not theft. They also believed that it was not an accidental hit and run. The driver knew exactly what he was doing.

"I overheard something about the accident," Tyler said. "I was in the corridor near the ER, and there were a couple of paramedics talking about it. One of them was on call that afternoon and he was recounting what had happened to his co-worker. It seems there was a man out walking his dog and he witnessed the whole thing. The man told the paramedic that he had heard a car moving at a normal speed down the street and then he heard the motor revving loudly and that the car then took off like a bat out of hell. He heard a loud scream, then a crash, and then he heard the car speed away."

"What? You mean there was a witness?" Lou and I blurted out simultaneously.

"Yes. I was close by when they were talking, but I only heard parts of the story. I didn't want to look like I was eavesdropping. You don't remember him, Bobby? He may have saved your life. Him and his dog, that is."

"he and his dog saved my life? What do you mean? I don't understand."

"This is an amazing story, Bobby. You are very lucky to be alive."

"Don't keep us in suspense," Lou said, "Go on."

"From what I understood, he had just stepped out of his apartment to walk his dog when all the commotion started. It seems that the dog stopped dead in his tracks and wouldn't stop barking. The man called out to see if anyone else was out on the street and didn't get a response, so he commanded his dog to lead the way so they could go and investigate. The paramedic recounted that the man had told him how terrified he was, because he had no clue what he was getting himself into and that he was relying totally on his dog's instinct."

"Oh… my… God! Are you telling me that the man is blind? A blind man saved my life?"

A tear rolled down my cheek.

"Yes, Bobby; isn't that amazing?"

Tyler reached over and handed me a tissue.

"That's an incredible story," Lou said. "I want to hear more."

"Well, I didn't really hear much of anything after that. There were too many people coming and going around me. Oh wait, yes, I did hear him say something about the dog's kerchief, and how he tied it around your leg to stop the bleeding."

At that moment, the nurse walked in. She caught the tail end of our discussion as she did.

"Sorry to interrupt, but are you talking about the blind guy?" she said as she came over to take my vitals.

"Yes," I replied. "Do you know anything about him?"

"His name is Thomas Fletcher, and he is the talk of the town. It is in all the newspapers. 'Blind man and his seeing eye dog miraculously save hit-and-run victim.' He saved your life, girl. If it wasn't for him and his dog, you would have bled to death on the street. They are heroes."

I was suddenly overcome with emotion again. I closed my eyes and tried my best to suppress it. While the others kept talking, I tried to imagine him and how he managed to save me without his sight. He must have felt so helpless and even terrified of what he might find. I can't even imagine what he must have been feeling.

"I need to meet them," I said without even a second thought.

"Who, Mr. Fletcher?" Lou said.

"Mr. Fletcher and his dog, if he is allowed in here."

"I will see what I can do," Tyler said.

The nurse was done so she left the room. It wasn't long before Lou had to go back to work too. Tyler and I chatted for a little while longer, and then he also had to leave for work. Before he left, he leaned over and put his arms around me. It felt so good. I really needed that. We said our goodbyes and off he went, promising to be back later that evening. I didn't rest much that morning, or even that afternoon, as a matter of fact. I kept thinking about Mr. Fletcher.

Carla came in and had supper with me on her break. I was really happy to see her. I told her all about Mr. Fletcher, but of course she had already heard the story. I guess it was the buzz all over the hospital and all over town too, for that matter.

She said that she had something for me and went out into the hallway for a few minutes. She came back with a little gift bag in her hand. She gave it to me and told me that I was going to be really surprised. I couldn't imagine what this was all about. She undid the ribbon for me, and I reached in and pulled out this beautiful black and red kerchief. I examined it carefully. It had the word "Maestro" printed on one corner of it. I looked at Carla, puzzled. She smiled and explained that it was the kerchief that Mr. Fletcher used to tie around my thigh to try to stop the bleeding. It was the dog's kerchief. Maybe Maestro was the dog's name. Nobody knew.

The nurse in the operating room heard the story and asked if she could keep the kerchief and sent it out to have it cleaned so she could return it to the owner. She gave it to Carla, thinking that I might want to give it to the owner myself in appreciation.

I couldn't believe it. Everyone was being so nice. What a wonderful gesture. I held it close to me for a moment, then I asked Carla to fold it back up again for me and put it in the gift bag. She put it in the top drawer of the bureau next to my bed, then she gave me a hug and went back to work.

Chapter 24

The days went by and before I knew it, the weekend had arrived. It was Saturday morning, a week since the accident. I still had a guard outside my door at all times, and a steady stream of visitors. Well, more accurately, the same ones over and over again. A few new ones came. Some of the staff who had never really paid much attention to me before now took an interest. To be fair, that was probably my fault, though, because I never really wanted anyone to know anything about my personal life.

Surprisingly enough, I didn't mind my new visitors. Everyone was being very nice and helpful, of course. I don't think that the hospital had ever had this much attention before. The media, constant police presence, a guard outside my door… I was getting dizzy just thinking about it.

Mrs. Blair also stopped by a few times to check on me. She was still a little upset that I hadn't gone to her for help, but she felt really bad about what happened to me, and maybe a little guilty. 'I saw the look on his face when I fired him' she said, 'I felt threatened, but he just stood up and stormed out of my office, slamming the door behind him.'

I didn't blame her, none of this was her fault, she was doing her job.

Then there was, Tyler, bless his heart, who came here every morning before work and every night afterward. Carla and Lou were no strangers either. They would visit throughout the day, whether they were working or not. I welcomed the attention. There wasn't much I could do, and they were cutting down on

the drugs a bit, so… I was in a lot more pain and of course I wasn't sleeping all day long anymore. I needed the distractions and looked forward to the attention I was getting from everyone.

I was trying to ignore my pain, and thinking I could use a visitor, when I heard a soft knock at the door. I got excited because I thought it was Tyler, but then, why would he knock?

"Come in," I said.

Nothing was happening.

"Is anyone there?"

The door started to open slowly. I was getting nervous. Something didn't seem right. Was I dreaming? The thought crossed my mind and scared the hell out of me. My imagination all of a sudden flashed back to a part of an old nightmare I had a while ago. I didn't want to go there so I closed my eyes for a second, hoping that when I opened them again, the door would be closed.

Well, it wasn't, but what a shocker. If I hadn't been laying down, I would have fallen on my ass.

"Hi, Roberta," she said, as she walked in with a big vase of flowers. The bouquet covered most of her face and she didn't move it, as if she were trying to hide.

"What can I do for you, Judy, are you lost? Oh… I see, someone sent me flowers and left them at the front desk by mistake? You could have saved yourself a trip. Tyler could have gotten them."

I was staying on the defensive. That lady always hated me so much. I didn't know what she might have up her sleeve. She put the flowers down on my bureau and turned. Finally, she looked at me. She examined me from head to toe and her face reddened. Her lower lip trembled, and her eyes started to swell with tears. I couldn't help but feel a little emotional too, but I did my best to suppress it.

"Oh my God," she said. "What have I done?" She buried her face in her hands. "I am so very sorry, Roberta. I really am."

"Okay, Judy. What in the hell are you up to?" I blurted out.

She kept sobbing and I kept getting more upset by the minute.

"I'm not up to anything, Roberta, I promise. It was him."

"Excuse me?"

"He was so friendly with me all the time and he always wanted to know what was going on around here and especially what was going on with you."

"He found the right busybody to talk to, didn't he?" I demanded angrily.

"I'm so sorry, but he always wanted information about you. He told me that you were a bad person and that he was going to keep an eye on you to make sure that you stayed out of trouble. He knew exactly what buttons to push with me, and I kept feeding him everything he wanted to know. I'm so sorry."

"It was you? That is how he knew how to find me all the time? Are you the one who told him where I live?"

"Yes, well not exactly. I didn't tell him the exact address. I just told him approximately where your apartment building was. I swear, Bobby. I didn't know that he would hurt you. He said he was undercover and investigating you. I believed him. I'm so sorry. I really am."

"You believed him, you… stupid bitch? Get out of here, Judy! He almost killed me! Are you happy now? Get out, and I don't ever want to see your face in here again!"

She turned, still sobbing, and headed for the door. Before she reached it, the guard rushed in. He had heard the yelling. Judy froze in her tracks. I told the guard I wanted her out. Without waiting, he took her by the arm and escorted her out of the room.

"Are you going to be okay, Miss Hansen?" he said before he closed the door. "Would you like me to send in the nurse?"

"No," I said. "I'll be okay, thank you. Tyler will be here soon. Just keep her out of my sight!"

That woman, I thought. *How stupid can anyone be? Investigating me? Who in the hell did she think David was?*

Tyler came in just before lunch and I told him what had happened. Of course, he already knew. He had talked to the guard at the door before he came in. He was very sorry that I had to go through that alone. He informed me that Judy had been taken to the police headquarters for questioning. He also told me that she was suspended from her job until this whole mess was sorted out. Confidentiality, especially working in a hospital, was very important. Obviously, she didn't understand that. They were worried about what other information she might have been divulging.

I was glad she was being punished, but in a way, I felt kind of sorry for her. No clue why. After all, she was the cause of all my misery at work.

Tyler and I talked and enjoyed each other's company until about twelve-thirty I was getting really hungry. I found it funny that nobody had come in to bring me any lunch. My stomach started growling, and Tyler started laughing at me.

"Hungry, baby?"

"Starved," I said. "I wonder why nobody brought me any lunch."

"Maybe they are really busy; who knows. Maybe Lou came in late this morning, and so lunch is a little late."

I must have looked puzzled, and he started to laugh.

"Just kidding… I have a surprise for you; be patient."

I smiled. "You are always full of surprises."

The door opened, and Carla walked in. It was so nice to see her. I was sure she had said that she had the day off today, and I wasn't going to see her. I had a feeling it was going to be a wonderful day after all.

"Okay, what are you two up to? I can see it in your faces that something is going on here."

Without a word, Carla turned and headed back to the door. She had no sooner left the room when the security guard came in and held the door open. Then Carla came around the corner with a huge wheelchair and a smile on her face.

"It's a beautiful day, my dear, and we are going out on the terrace. Oh, and before you say anything, it has been cleared by Dr. Blake and the good detective."

"Are you out of your freaking mind? My whole left side is totally out of commission. My left leg is tied up to a pulley, with all those metal pins through it. My left arm is in a cast, not to mention the broken ribs, or have you forgotten. Do you really think that I can get into that chair? It is bad enough trying to get my ass up onto the bedpan."

The words slipped out before I could stop them. How embarrassing. I don't know how many shades of red there are, but I'm sure that my face took on every one of them.

Carla looked at me, shook her head, and started laughing.

"A little too much information," she said.

"Oh my God. I can't believe I said that out loud, but there is no way I can get in that chair... no way."

"Don't worry," Tyler added. "The cavalry is on its way."

He barely got the words out of his mouth when the security guard opened the door and let two orderlies and my nurse in. I realized then that this was really going to happen. At first I was excited and then I got scared.

"Are, you guys crazy? It is not safe. David, what if he's around? What if he finds out that I am outside? It's too dangerous. I feel safer here with the guard outside my door."

Tyler took me by the hand. "Don't worry, honey, I won't let anything happen to you. Detective Collins has been informed and he is on his way here. He wanted to speak with you anyway. He assured me that you would be well-guarded."

They had thought of everything. The nurse told me to relax and let the orderlies do all the work. I gave in, and surprisingly enough, it went very well. The chair had a platform that raised up, horizontal with the seat, so it was almost like sitting up in bed. There was an attachment to hook the pulley on that was holding up my leg. Okay... this was definitely going to happen.

I started to get anxious to go out there and breathe in the fresh air. Carla got behind me and put the chair in motion, and Tyler led the way with the security guard.

"I hope you have your permit to drive this thing, Whitey."

"Don't worry, Looney Tunes. I got it out of a Cracker Jack box."

Tyler laughed. "Nice to see that you two girls are back to your old selves."

As we left my room, I saw a police officer. He got behind Carla and followed us down the hallway. All the hospital employees that we passed along the way greeted me with kind words. It felt good. Even though I knew I looked like hell, with all this attention, I almost felt like a celebrity. Leave it to Carla and Tyler to pull off something like this.

The automatic doors opened, and a gust of fresh air blew towards us. I could smell the wonderful aroma of the lilac bushes that were in full bloom. I knew that the hospital had hired landscapers to do some work around the terrace, but I hadn't been back here to see the results. They did an amazing job. There were rock gardens with pathways going through them, decorative shrubs, park benches, picnic tables, and a beautiful little fish pond. It was surrounded by rocks and plants and had a trickling waterfall at one end.

There was a table set up near the pond and there were two men sitting at it. One of them heard us coming and got up and came to greet us. I almost didn't recognize Detective Collins. He looked very casual today, like maybe he was not on the job and this was just a social call. He greeted me with a smile and shook my hand. I was surprised by how comfortable I was with him and I smiled back. He turned and escorted us to the table.

"There is someone here who would like to meet you," he said.

I was very intrigued. I had no idea who it could be. The man did not turn around right away. He just sat there facing the pond. Suddenly a dog poked his head out from under the table and started to whine, but at the same time, I could hear his tail banging against the table leg as he wagged it wildly.

I could see how badly he wanted to run to me, but he obediently stayed by his master.

"Maestro," the man called.

The dog got up and barked. The man stood, took hold of the dog, and then turned and walked toward me. He was quite good looking with a medium build. He had short brown hair and graying sideburns. He was wearing dark sunglasses. I knew right away who he was.

The dog barked as they got closer.

"Maestro?" I said. "Oh my God!"

He got so excited, he looked like he was going to explode.

"Miss Hansen, I presume? Heel, Maestro."

He sat back down next to his master.

"Mr. Fletcher?" Tears started filling my eyes.

I watched as he reached down and patted Maestro to try to calm him down.

I looked over at Carla who was also looking very emotional. She handed me the little gift bag with the kerchief in it. She must have retrieved it from my bureau without me noticing.

"I'll leave you two to get better acquainted," she winked. Then she left to join the others.

I looked back at Mr. Fletcher.

"Oh my God. I don't know what to say. They told me that you saved my life. There are no words to express..."

I could hardly speak. My nose was running, my eyes were running, and I was shaking all over.

"Uh... to express my gratitude. They told me that if it weren't for you, I would not have made it. I can't thank you enough. Can you come closer, please?" I reached out my hand, took his, and pulled him toward me. "I need to give you a hug... you don't mind, do you?"

I put my arm around his neck, held him tight, and thanked him again for saving my life. The dog let out a loud bark and startled me.

"It's okay, Maestro," he said as he straightened up.

He then knelt and removed Maestro's vest.

"Actually, you need to thank my friend, here. He was the one who led me to you and went for help. He even made me realize that he was wearing his kerchief, almost telling me to tie it around your leg. He is an amazing dog, and I didn't realize to what extent until that day.

"The only problem now is that he hasn't been the same since. We go for our walks down the street, and every time we pass the place where we found you, he stops and whines. He has been very sad and miserable since then. I figured that maybe if he saw you again and knew that you were okay, he would feel much better. That is why I called the detective and asked permission to come and visit you today."

Maestro sat there next to his master with his tongue hanging out and his tail wagging. He looked like he was getting ready to pounce on me.

"You're a good dog, aren't you," I said.

He let out another loud bark and up he came, with both front paws landing on the side of my chair. It kind of scared me; for a second, I thought he was going to land on me.

"Maestro, heel!"

"It's okay, Mr. Fletcher. He's not hurting me. I want to thank him too. He is my hero."

I gave him a good rub around his neck.

"You are such a good boy, Maestro. Thank you for saving my life."

He let out another loud bark; I guess it was his way of saying, "You're welcome."

Maestro couldn't keep still for two seconds, he was so excited. He would jump down, then two seconds later he would be right back up on my chair again, always staying by his master.

I had tucked the gift bag between my thigh and the side of the chair, and in all the excitement, I had almost forgotten that it was there.

"Oh… by the way, Mr. Fletcher. I…"

"We don't need to be so formal. You can call me Thomas. It's Roberta, right?"

"Actually, my friends call me Bobby, and after all that you have done for me, I'd say you are right up there near the top of that list, you and Maestro both."

He smiled and said, "Okay, Bobby it is."

"I was going to say, Thomas, that I have a surprise for you. I think you will be very happy. Really, it's for Maestro. Here you go. It's in this gift bag. Give me your hand."

He extended his arm and I handed him the bag. He fumbled with it a bit, but he managed to untie the ribbon. He put his hand in and pulled out the kerchief.

"This feels very familiar."

He kept moving it through his fingers till he came to the corner where the word "Maestro" was embroidered.

"Sure enough, this is Maestro's scarf. How did you…"

Maestro barked again and jumped down off my chair where I had been giving him a major rubdown. He jumped up on Thomas and practically knocked him over.

"Easy, boy. Yes, you know your scarf when you see it. Sit, boy, and I will put it on you."

Maestro sat down and didn't move while Thomas tied the kerchief around his neck. It looked really nice on him. He looked so happy to have it back. Thomas stood back up and Maestro started prancing around as proud as a peacock, showing off his beautiful scarf. It wasn't long before he had his two front paws back up on my chair. He kept pushing my hand with his nose so that I would pet him again.

"I think I have a new friend. Okay, Maestro, okay. You're such a good boy. Calm down, boy."

"You're sure he's not hurting you?" Thomas said. "I can put his vest back on."

"No, not at all. He's just so excited."

"Thank you so much, Miss Hansen… I mean, Bobby. Maestro seems to be back to his old self again. Coming here and seeing you is exactly what he needed. I didn't know what I was going to do with him."

"I'm glad you came too. I wanted to thank you in person. The only thing is I can't figure out how you go about thanking someone for saving their life."

"Knowing now that you are alive and on the road to recovery is thanks enough, Bobby. You are going to be okay, aren't you?"

"The doctor says that with a lot of hard work and persistence, and of course, a little luck, I should completely recover. Right now, my face is pretty bashed up. I look like Frankenstein. I'm glad you can't see me. My arm..."

He reached out both hands and moved them towards my face.

"May I?" he said. He very gently moved his fingers over my whole face, examining it carefully.

"I don't know what you are seeing, but what I am feeling is very beautiful. There is a little swelling here and there, and of course the stitches. All of your injuries are superficial. They will heal nicely, I am sure. You have a beautiful face. What else?"

I put his hand on the cast that was on my left arm.

"Broken in two places," I said.

He examined it.

"May I sign it?"

"Sure, we'll ask someone for a pen later."

"Anything else?"

I put his hand on my leg. He carefully moved his fingers along it. He looked confused when he touched the steel bar that ran along both sides of it. Then, the inevitable look of shock appeared when he felt the pins that protruded from the steel bars and went right through my leg. He pulled his hands back.

"Now that, I don't like. Those pins... Are they going right through...?"

"Right through," I said.

"Is it very painful?"

"Uh... well, not really, not right now anyway. The good doctor is keeping me pretty drugged up. When the drugs wear off, though, it's a whole other story. As long as I don't move, it's okay, but it is hard to not move. I get uncomfortable sometimes and without thinking I try to adjust myself... that can be very painful. The doctor is trying to wean me off the meds. He says that the drugs are very addictive, and he wouldn't want me to become dependent on them."

"I guess he's right; that wouldn't be good. As long as you don't suffer too much."

Maestro nudged his hand. Thomas patted him.

"May I ask you, Thomas, if you don't mind, to tell me what you recall about what happened to me? I am having trouble putting the pieces together. It might help me to remember something."

"Are you sure?"

"Absolutely!"

"Okay... but let me know if you want me to stop."

"I will."

"Let me think... It was pouring rain, but I needed to take Maestro out for his walk. I had no sooner stepped out onto the sidewalk when all the commotion started. There was the sound of a motor revving so hard that it seemed like it might just explode. Then the sound of the spinning tires on the wet pavement. That was followed by the sound of someone screaming, and then a loud crash. I don't know if you can imagine this, Bobby, but when you can't see, let me tell you, it scared the hell out of me."

"Yes, I guess it would! Go on, please."

"Needless to say, I had no clue what was going on. Then suddenly, the motor revved again, followed by the spinning tires, and then the sound faded out into the distance. Maestro froze in his tracks, and just kept whining. I didn't know what to do. I tried to call out, but nobody answered. I tried to calm Maestro down a bit and then asked him to lead the way. I followed him across, to the other side of the street. I was very stressed, because I didn't know what to expect, and I didn't know if I was maybe in some kind of danger myself. Maestro finally stopped, sat down, and started whining again. I called out once more, and still nobody answered. At this point, all I could hear was the pounding of the rain and Maestro, who just wouldn't stop whining"

"Oh... my... God! You were so brave. I don't think I could have gone there."

A tear rolled down my cheek.

"Are you okay, Bobby? Your voice is trembling?"

"I'm good, just a little emotional. Please keep going."

"Well, since nobody else seemed to be out there, I decided to bend down and start feeling around to see what I could find. My hand touched something. It was very wet, but then everything was soaked from the rain. I realized that it was a shoe, and my heart started racing. It suddenly dawned on me that the speeding vehicle that I heard before had hit someone. Then I recalled the screaming and put it all together.

"I tried to stay calm, but I was not very successful. I kept yelling for help but still no one came. The sound of my voice was probably drowned out by the pouring rain.

"I knew that I had to do something, so I started to work my hand up your leg. It was badly mangled. I remember putting my hand on something hard, and almost throwing up when I realized that it was a bone. I remember that everything was so wet, but it wasn't a cool wet. It was a warm wet, and I knew it was blood, but it was too much blood at least as far as I could tell.

"I had no clue what I was doing, and without my sight, I wasn't very confident. I kept feeling around and found your hand. There was a pulse, though it was very weak. I needed to do something, but I needed help. I called out again and nobody came. I was feeling desperate.

"I had to stop the bleeding. I didn't know if you were bleeding anywhere else, but I knew the leg was bad. Maestro, still whining, started licking my face. I put my arms around his neck and noticed that he was wearing his scarf. I removed it and tied it around your thigh above the lacerations. I then told him to speak and he started barking. I told him to go find someone and he went barking down the street. I didn't know where he was going but I hoped that someone would hear him barking and come and help.

"I kept talking to you, Bobby, and I hoped that you would answer, but you didn't. I thought you were regaining consciousness a few times because you moaned a little, but you never spoke or moved."

"Oh my God. I remember someone touching me and I recall hearing voices that seemed really far off in the distance and I was terrified. I didn't know what was happening to me and then everything faded out."

"That was me, Bobby, trying desperately to help you."

A tear rolled down my cheek, and I got weepy again. Thomas pulled a tissue out of his pocket.

"I guess you managed, Thomas, because I am still here today to talk about it. I owe you my life. What happened to Maestro; where did he go?"

"He came running back a few minutes later with someone. The man called 911 and he proceeded to try to help you. I didn't leave your side, and neither did Maestro. The ambulance arrived not long after that, and well, here we are."

I took his hand, pulled him closer, and gave him another hug.

"You are a very brave man, and I will always be grateful."

Maestro barked.

"You too, Maestro; you are such a good dog."

At that moment, my stomach started growling.

Thomas laughed and said, "Somebody's hungry here."

I was so wrapped up in my conversation with Thomas that I had forgotten about everyone else. Carla, Tyler, and Detective Collins had sat down at the table where Thomas had been seated while he waited for me. Tyler got up and came over to me.

"Nice to see you guys hitting it off so well."

Maestro let out a loud bark.

"You too, boy. I think you have a new friend, there, Bobby. Maestro has really taken a liking to you. Mr. Fletcher, we didn't get a chance to meet. I'm Tyler Murphy, Bobby's friend."

Tyler reached out and took Mr. Fletcher's hand.

"I am happy to finally meet you. I can't thank you enough for what you did. You are a hero indeed."

Maestro barked again.

"You too, Maestro. That is one smart dog. He seems to understand everything we say. You are such a good dog."

Tyler bent down and patted Maestro around the neck. Carla also got up and introduced herself to Thomas, and then to Maestro, who was very happy to be getting all this attention. Detective Collins helped Thomas back to his seat at the table. My stomach growled again.

"I'm going to go and see what is going on with our lunch," Carla said as she turned and headed back toward the hospital entrance. She hadn't quite made it to the doors when I saw them open.

"You didn't start the party without me, did you?"

It was Lou. He was pushing a large cart with a lot of trays on it.

"Anyone hungry?"

Lou laughed as he came over and gave me a big hug. "What's new," he whispered, "and how's my best girl today? I see they got you out of that room of yours okay."

"I am great," I said. "What a wonderful surprise, lunch out on the terrace."

It was a beautiful day, indeed. The sun was shining and there was a small breeze spreading around the aroma of the fresh spring flowers. The relaxing sound of the water trickling from the fountain just made everything seem perfect.

I was out of my room and surrounded by my friends, old and new. Who could ask for anything more? Carla and I horsed around like we usually did, and everyone laughed along. We had a wonderful lunch that Lou prepared and enjoyed with us. Chicken Cordon Bleu, he called it, with steamed asparagus, a small Caesar salad, and dessert. He really outdid himself again. The food was great, definitely not your typical hospital menu. When I finished eating, I lay back and looked around at all my friends as they laughed and chatted together, and I realized how blessed I was. Detective Collins was also laughing and carrying on. It was nice to see a less serious side of him. For a cop, he seemed like a really great guy. I probably shouldn't have judged; it was a very important job, after all.

As I watched and listened, my eyes started to feel a little heavy. I guess all the excitement and fresh air was tiring me a bit. I leaned back and closed my eyes for a few minutes. I listened to their conversations as much as I could, but my mind kept trying to focus on the trickling water. It kept getting louder and louder. That, with the sound of the birds chirping and the wind whistling through the trees, reminded me of my safe place.

I was lying on my back on the log that crossed the river. The sun was peeking through the trees, but the wind was getting stronger. The breeze was cool. The birds started to fly around, wild and low. Something was coming for sure. I could hear what I thought was thunder far off in the distance. It was hard to tell, though, with the sound of the water rushing underneath me. I sat up and looked around. The sky was starting to cloud over.

No, please don't, I thought to myself. *I haven't been here in a long time. Let me enjoy this moment, please.*

The sky kept getting darker and the wind kept getting stronger. Lightning streaked across the horizon. I was starting to worry. I didn't know where I should go or what I should do. Suddenly I heard a rumbling noise off in the distance. It sounded like it was getting closer. It wasn't thunder. It was not the same sound as before. It was getting closer still. What could it be? I was very confused. My chest tightened up and I started to hyperventilate. I couldn't tell where the sound was coming from. I slowly turned around. I saw a bright light coming toward me. I heard a big bang and I started to scream.

Suddenly, I opened my eyes. Everyone was yelling and running around. Tyler threw himself on top of me. Everyone else seemed to be running for cover. Detective Collins was yelling for everyone to get down. The guards were scrambling around, guns held high. I was terrified and started to cry. Tyler held me tight.

"It's okay, baby; I'll protect you. Just try to stay calm."

I held onto him with all my might. I couldn't figure out what was going on. I remembered screaming, but that was all. No, not true, I also remembered a loud noise and a bright light. It seemed very similar to my accident. I think I might have been reliving it. But why all the commotion out here? I was really puzzled now.

"Is everyone okay?" Detective Collins asked. The guards were still running around. Thomas was on the ground on his hands and knees. Maestro was very excited. Thomas looked like he was having a hard time controlling him. Detective Collins went over to give him a hand. He did his best to calm Maestro down then he took off with the guards. I watched as Carla got up and walked towards me, slightly bent over. She looked scared to death.

"You okay, Bobby?" she whispered. "You're not hurt, are you?"

"I'm not sure; what in the hell is going on out here?" I said as I gasped for air.

Tyler stood up. "I'm sorry, honey; I got scared. I thought somebody took a shot. Did I hurt you, honey?"

"I don't know. I think my medication might be wearing off. I'm confused. I kind of dozed off and I think I was dreaming. I heard a big bang, but I thought it was in my dream."

I could see Tyler's eyes filling with tears.

"There was a noise," he said. "It sounded like a gunshot… Then you screamed… Then I thought… Oh my God, I thought you…"

He closed his eyes and a tear escaped and trickled down his cheek. He bent over again and gently put his arms around me. His heart was pounding, and he was trembling all over. I held onto him with my good arm. I saw Detective Collins walking toward us and waving his arms.

"It's okay, everyone. We think it might have been a car that backfired; we don't see anything out of the ordinary."

Actually, when I really thought about it, he didn't sound very convinced.

The guards slowly walked back, still turning and looking around them. Detective Collins went over and helped Thomas back to his chair. Maestro was still very excited.

"Come here, Maestro," I said. I no sooner got the words out of my mouth and he had jumped up on the side of my chair again. Tyler got off of me just in time or he would have jumped on top of him.

"You're a good dog," I said.

Thomas did not sit back down. Instead, he stood there and talked to the detective. It wasn't long before they both turned and headed my way. Maestro got down from my lap and went and joined his master.

"Well, Bobby," Thomas said, "I guess we are going to head home. I think that we have had quite enough excitement for one day. It has been a real pleasure. I am glad to see that you are on the road to recovery, and thank you for the kerchief, it was very nice of you to save it for Maestro."

"The pleasure was all mine, Thomas. I owe you my life. If there is ever anything that I can ever do for you, don't be shy to ask. There is just one more thing you can do for me, though."

"What's that?" he asked.

"Come back and see me again, please, and bring Maestro. I really enjoyed your company today. I hope all this excitement won't keep you away. I'm sure that it won't always be like this."

"Don't worry, Bobby. I'll be back. A little excitement never hurt anyone."

Maestro barked.

"I guess it's okay with him too."

I took his hand in mine. He smiled and said goodbye and waved to the others. Thomas knelt and put Maestro's vest back on and that calmed him right down. He was all business now. I watched as they turned down the path and walked away.

That is one smart dog, I thought to myself. *One really smart dog.*

Carla, Lou, Tyler, and Detective Collins were standing together talking. Carla, seeing that I was looking a little teary, started to walk toward me.

"Well, Bobby. That last bit of excitement wasn't part of our plans, I swear, but did you enjoy your surprise?"

"Oh man, are you kidding? I had a really great afternoon. There is nothing that I would have enjoyed more than being surrounded by my old friends and my new ones. Thomas and Maestro are really nice, don't you find? He said that they would come back and see me again. I am so happy. I feel like I owe them so much."

"I don't think that Thomas thinks you owe him anything. He is a wonderful man. Maestro really took a liking to you too. He never left your side for very long."

I heard some footsteps coming toward us and I turned and looked to see who it was.

"How's my favorite patient today?"

It was Dr. Blake. He began examining my limbs immediately.

"I heard that there was quite a commotion out here before. Are you okay?"

I told him that I was in a little pain, but I was fine and that I had a really wonderful afternoon despite that last little bit of excitement. He suggested that we head back to my room. He wanted to check my vitals and he said that he had something he wanted to talk to me about. We all obeyed the doctor's orders and headed back with Detective Collins in the lead and the guards following behind.

When we got to my room, one of the guards took his place outside my door, and everyone else followed me in. Detective Collins told me that he had wanted to talk to me today about my case, but he decided to wait till tomorrow. He said that I had had plenty enough excitement for one day. He said goodbye to everyone and left, followed by the extra guards that watched over us all afternoon. I thanked them as they left the room.

A few seconds later, the nurse and the same two orderlies that had helped to put me into this chair were back to help get me out of it. It went very well. Meanwhile, Tyler, Carla, and the doc were huddled together talking quietly.

"Are you talking about me?" I said as I got settled back into my bed. "If you wanted to talk to me about something, Dr. Blake, I think you are going to have to make it fast. After all that commotion, mixed with a whole afternoon full of fresh air, I feel like I am going to crash out any time now."

"You know what? If you are really tired, then I think you should rest. I can come back a little later. Actually, it can wait till tomorrow. Now, everyone out, doctor's orders, the lady needs her beauty rest."

Chapter 25

I opened my eyes suddenly. It was dark. I could hear the rain beating down hard on the old tin roof. The sound was deafening. The brilliant flashes of lightning lit up my whole room. Everything seemed to be in its place. I was sure that my room had been trashed by that old, ugly man. Oh God, I did not want to think about him right now. I closed my eyes again and tried to concentrate on something wonderful to try to get him out of my mind. A loud crack of thunder brought me back… and fast. I let out a scream and jumped about a foot off my bed. I looked around the room again with the glare provided by the recurring lightning. Everything looked fine. I needed to get back to sleep, but the rain was pounding so hard on the roof still. My room lit up again, only this time the light was coming from the hallway. My door was open a little bit and someone had turned on the light beyond it. I pulled the blankets up around my neck and tried to stay calm. I had woken up the devil when I screamed, and he was on his way up to my room. I knew that I was in trouble now. I closed my eyes to try to pretend that I was sleeping, but the only trouble was I couldn't tell if he was in my room yet, or if he saw me and thought

I was sleeping and decided to turn around and go back to bed. I couldn't hear a damn thing except for that rain, and there was no way in hell that I was going to open my eyes in case he was there. Then he would see that I was awake. I just stayed there immobile for the longest time.

Eventually the rain started to subside, and I didn't hear anything except this beeping noise, so I opened my eyes slowly. The rays of the morning sun were streaming through my window. I was very puzzled. The storm was over? At this point, I didn't even know if it was real or not. I must have dreamed it. Of course, I had dreampt it. I wasn't in my hospital room during the storm in my dream. I was somewhere else. I tried hard, but I couldn't figure out where. It was a really weird dream, but at the same time, it seemed vaguely familiar. I think possibly, that I had dreamed it before, only I believe it didn't end as well the first time. This time, at least, I woke up before the shit hit the fan, thank you very much.

I looked over at the clock-radio on my bureau to see what time it was. I found it strange that it was broad daylight and I hadn't seen a nurse yet. They are usually in at the crack of dawn, whether you are awake or not, to check your vitals and give you your meds.

Strangely enough, the numbers on the clock were blinking on and off, as if the power had gone out. I didn't think that a power failure was possible in a hospital, on account of the generator that kicks in right away to keep all the lifesaving equipment running. Okay, maybe I was wrong about that, but where were the nurses?

I watched the numbers as they kept on blinking. On and off… On and off… On and off… On and off… I had to turn away. It agitated me. I was starting to get nervous.

I reached out and pressed the emergency button that was wrapped around the guardrail of my bed. I waited for a few minutes, well maybe it was only a few seconds, but my patience was wearing thin, so I buzzed again. I was starting to feel panicky. A little claustrophobic maybe. It's not like I could just get up and walk out of here. I couldn't go anywhere or do anything with this cast on my arm and my leg propped up in that sling with all those pins stabbing into my bones. Oh my God, I didn't want to even think of that. It made me feel a little nauseous every time I did. I couldn't even look at them without feeling a little sick.

No matter how many times I buzzed, still nobody came. I couldn't imagine what was going on, and then I remembered about the guard that was keeping watch outside my door. I called out to him and waited. I guess he didn't hear me. I called out again, even louder, a few minutes later. Okay, okay, maybe it was only a few seconds, but I was getting really scared. There was still no answer.

Well, I decided that when everything else fails, scream your head off. There is nothing like a good scream to get everyone's attention. I took a deep breath and gave it all I had. If that didn't get his attention, nothing would. Last time when I had a nightmare, he came running in, guns a-blazin', and just about gave Tyler and me a heart attack. I waited… I waited very impatiently… I waited… still nothing.

Okay, something was wrong. My gut knew it. I was trying to be optimistic, but my gut knew it right from square one.

"Where is everyone, damn it? Would someone please help me? What is going on?"

I reached for the buzzer again and just kept pushing it. I didn't know what else to do.

I looked for the phone and saw it was on the bureau just beyond the clock radio. It was a little out of reach, so I tried to slide myself over a bit. Pain stabbed through my leg. I let out a yell. Tears started rolling down my cheeks, uncontrollably. There was no way I was going to be able to reach the phone. I didn't know what else I could do, so I just lay there and cried for what felt like the longest time. I still didn't know what time it was or how much time had gone by since I woke up.

At first, I thought it was my imagination, but the sound kept getting closer and closer. It sounded like something on wheels being pushed down the hallway. Suddenly the door swung open. It scared the shit right out of me.

"Thank God you are here! What in the hell is going on? Where is everyone? I've been yelling and buzzing forever here."

A janitor was in the doorway with his back to me. He didn't say a word. He came in, walking backward, with the mop and bucket. I asked him again and he still didn't answer me. He started to whistle. I started to scream at him. As he washed the floor, he kept backing up in my direction. I was starting to lose it. I was confined to that bed and there was nothing I could do. I kept pleading for him to answer me. He stopped mopping as he reached my bed.

I watched nervously as he started to turn around. Suddenly, I couldn't breathe, and I couldn't move. I tried to scream but nothing would come out. His eyes were big and bloodshot. His hair was tucked up under his hat. He had this terrifying grin on his face that showed his dirty, yellowed teeth. He brought his face up close to mine. I could feel the warmth of his breath on my cheek. It reeked of death, or at least that was the first impression that came to my mind at the time. It almost made me gag. My mind went numb. I had no idea what was going to happen to me.

"You have nine lives, Bobby dear," David whispered. "And I have all the time in the world. I am going to take down every one of them. You are mine now, and there isn't anything anyone can do about it. I have been waiting for this moment for a very long time and now I'm going to savor it." His arm started to come up over the side of the bed. There was a blinding flash of light. I closed my eyes for a second and then opened them. The morning sun was reflecting off a large switchblade that he was holding in front of my face. He was playfully blinding me over and over again with the reflection. It took me a few seconds to adjust my vision. My eyes started to blur over from the tears building up inside of them. The reflection wasn't as blinding anymore. It slowly disappeared, and darkness took over…

"Miss Hansen? Are you okay, Miss Hansen?"

The sound of her voice startled me. I wiped my eyes with my good hand. It was Nurse Bailey. She was leaning over me. She looked very concerned.

"Why are you crying, Miss Hansen?"

"This is not happening; where is David? He was here a minute ago. You didn't let him get away, did you? Oh my God! Where is the guard? Did he not see him?"

"Calm down, Miss Hansen; you must stay calm."

"Calm, you want me to stay calm?" I screamed. "He was here a minute ago and he had a knife. He was going to kill me; I know he was. I can't believe you let him walk right out of here!"

The door burst open. It was the guard.

"Did you see him? He was just here! He had a knife! He was going to kill me!"

"Miss Hansen, I'm sorry, but nobody has come through this door except the nurse. I have been out here all night."

"What are you talking about? He was just here! He was... Oh my God, he was wearing his old uniform! He came in with a mop and bucket! He was washing the floor! Then he held a knife in front of me! He was going to kill me, I tell you! You need to find him before he gets away!"

The guard didn't move. He just stood there looking at me.

"What are you doing?" I screamed. "Don't just stand there. Go find him before he gets away."

I was struggling to get up, but the nurse was holding me down.

"Miss Hansen, you must calm down. Guard, hurry and get Dr. Blake."

The guard left the room running. I kept yelling and she kept trying to calm me down. I was growing weak and finally stopped fighting her. I was crying though. I was crying so intensely that I could hardly breathe. I heard Dr. Blake, but I couldn't see anything because of the waterworks. I tried to speak but I was so out of breath that the words wouldn't form. I didn't hear a sound from the doc; I just felt a little prick and it was over, back to la la land.

Chapter 26

Without even opening my eyes I could tell it was going to be another beautiful morning. I felt the heat from the sunshine warming up my room. I couldn't feel any motion from the waves, and I could hear the seagulls singing their morning song. I yawned and stretched and slowly opened my eyes. The sun was very bright and beaming through the porthole. I guess I forgot to close the blinds. It didn't matter, though; who needs blinds when you are alone at sea. I was feeling very lazy, but the scent of freshly brewed coffee urged me on as I got up and headed into the Galley. It was six a.m. on the dot and I was exhausted from a late night in front of my computer.

My writing went very well last night, and I couldn't tear myself away from it. Some sessions go well, where the words just flow so easily from my mind to my computer, and other times are a total disaster, where I can't see my screen for the waterworks. Well, all in all, between the nightmares, the tears, and the fond memories, and there were some, strangely enough, it was going well. Scary as hell sometimes but in general, I'd say I was making progress.

I fixed myself a cup of coffee and put a slice of bread in the toaster. I was a little hungry and I wasn't going to last till I came back up from my dive and made a proper breakfast. I took my coffee and toast and went up on deck. I had barely got myself settled down when I heard a big splash.

"Not now, Fred," I said, "let me wake up a little first."

My buddy, Fred Astaire, was always out there, waiting for me to join him in a little dance, first thing in the morning. I had become very fond of him and I didn't know what I would do without him. Every morning, unless the weather was not cooperating, we would spend quality time together. Others have come and gone, but he was always here for me. I think that somehow, he knew that I needed him. I think, for some strange reason, he needed me too.

Maybe he was watching over me and keeping me safe. I kept remembering that dream that I had about my mother and the words she said to me.

"I will watch over you."

It was silly of me to believe that a dolphin was watching over me, but hey, crazier things have happened in my life. Wow, I had thought of my mom without shedding a tear. Well, maybe I was on the way to recovery.

I was a little skeptical when my doctors told me that I had to dive right into my past in order to heal, instead of pushing the past away. I was terrified and did not want to relive all those horrible things that happened to me, but I came to realize that the more I thought and wrote about them, the easier it became. There were still new flashbacks from time to time, and the nightmares hadn't disappeared, but they were less frequent.

Suddenly, I let out a shriek…

"Fred… you little bugger! The water's cold!"

I wiped the water off my face, and he jumped again, up into the air, and came down with another big splash.

I moved swiftly away from the side and the water missed me. I quickly finished my toast and coffee and got suited up. I had kept him waiting long enough.

What a spectacular day it was. I no sooner got in the water and we were off exploring. Some of the usual gang followed along. Up and down, round and round. What a time we were having. Fred was the leader as usual. I always felt safe with him in charge. We strayed a little farther than usual this time. We normally stayed pretty close to my boat. I was okay with this because Fred had never steered me wrong.

It was almost like he was on a mission today. He kept moving forward and I followed along with the other dolphins. He made his way to the bottom. There were a few patches of coral here and there, but other than that it was just sand.

Fred stopped and waited for me next to a formation of coral. I caught up with him and started to look around it. It was amazing. There were beautiful almost flower-like tentacles all over it. I disturbed a few creatures as I got closer. It always made me feel guilty. I hated that. I turned and looked at Fred and it seemed like he wanted me to stay there and keep looking. Was there something I was missing?

I turned back to look closely at and around the coral again and something caught my eye. It was sticking out of the sand a bit. Was that what this adventure was all about: a treasure hunt? Wow, how fun was that.

I didn't want to disturb the coral, so I dug my way through the sand to get closer to whatever it was that was hidden there. With the tip of my fingers I caught the end of it. Slowly, I began to pull it towards me. It was a little heavy. I was very anxious to see what it was. It took a little work, but I managed to retrieve it from its hiding place.

Wow… it was a sword. Not like anything I'd ever seen — mind you, I have never really seen a sword in person. It was not like "The Three Musketeers" kind; it was more like a large dagger. It was going to need a good cleaning if I wanted to examine it more carefully. Who knew I would be treasure hunting in my spare time? I looked at Fred and he seemed to be content and ready to head back. I nodded, and off we went.

It didn't take long to get back to the boat. I said goodbye to my friends and prepared to climb on board. It was a little difficult carrying a dagger and my gear up the ladder. Stabbing myself would not be a good idea while I was alone out here.

Well, I made it up okay with Fred watching over me every step of the way. I waved and gave him the thumbs up and off he went.

I had an amazing morning. I carefully cleaned off the dagger and realized that it was no ordinary weapon. It had what seemed to be precious stones around the handle. I didn't know much about jewels, so I had no clue if they were real or not. Oh well, it was very beautiful though, so I decided I would just hang it up somewhere as a souvenir of my dive. I had a late breakfast, did a little more writing, and before I knew it, the day was winding down. Another beautiful sunset.

Chapter 27

Beep… beep… beep… from far off in the distance I could hear it. It kept getting louder and louder. I tried to open my eyes, but I couldn't. There was nothing but darkness in front of me, a terrifying endless nothing. I searched for signs of anything, but there weren't any. Beep… beep… beep… was all there was. It was the only sound I could hear, echoing in this vast blackness.

Stay calm, I thought, *concentrate, and take a deep breath.* Oh good, I could hear my breath, I can feel my chest rise. I was really here, wherever here was. I felt pressure on my back. It felt like I was lying down. Okay, that was something, what else. I focused on my hands and tried to move them, without success. It felt like my legs were there; well, I mean, of course they were there, but they also remained immobile. My mouth felt very dry and I couldn't pry it open.

Beep… beep…beep… it was getting a little fainter, as if it was leaving my side. Leaving me in my big empty nothingness, alone and frightened.

No, I thought to myself, *don't leave me, I beg of you.* Why I thought that, I don't know. I didn't know what in the hell it was. I could hardly hear it anymore and I felt like I could cry, but of course my emotions were not quite in working order either. My mind, though, it was working. It was working freaking overtime. I was imagining every damn scenario possible for what was happening to me. I tried to stop thinking about it, but it is pretty hard… when there is nothing to take your mind off it. Sing… that is what I thought I should do. Sing? Well, of course I couldn't sing… my mouth wasn't moving… but I started singing in my mind.

Okay, here we go, I really am going crazy… Ninety-nine bottles of beer on the wall, ninety-nine bottles of beer…

Oh my God, somebody, shoot me now. Could somebody please put me out of my misery?

"Bobby… Bobby, honey… are you okay?"

Twenty-four bottles of beer on the wall… twenty-four… Oh, what's that, I think I hear a voice?

Okay there, who is it? Speak up again, come on. Oh gosh, I can hear the beeping again. Ah man, what's up with this. Come on, speak. Is it my imagination?

Beep… beep… beep… there it was again. Getting louder and louder.

"Bobby… wake up, Bobby. You're dreaming. Come on, honey."

My eyes opened suddenly, and it felt like they had been glued shut. Tyler was hovering over me. I was scared, like I wasn't sure if I was still dreaming or not. He watched me for a moment with a puzzled look on his face, then he spoke.

"Bobby, honey, you were dreaming. Are you okay?"

I didn't move, and I didn't speak; I wasn't sure if I could. I stared at him for a bit, and he started to get nervous.

"I'll get the nurse," he said. "Don't move; I will be right back."

Don't move? Was he kidding? I stared at the ceiling. The light was bright. I couldn't move. I couldn't understand what was happening to me. I didn't feel anything. Was I dead? I couldn't be because Tyler spoke to me. He went to get someone. It seemed like a long time had passed before he came back.

"Dr. Blake..."

I tried to speak but nothing came out. He was talking to me, but it was like I wasn't there. I could hear him, but I couldn't respond. What was happening to me? I looked at Tyler then back at the doc, then I looked at Tyler again, and then back to the doc. My eyes kept going back and forth from one to the other. I was freaking out. I felt like I was going to explode.

"I think she's in shock. She is not responding. She looks scared to death. She has been through so much. This last episode about David being in the room with her, and everything else that has been happening, I don't even know how she has managed to cope with all these things as long as she has. I will give her another sedative and see if she will sleep it off. I am just hoping that she doesn't shut down completely. She will need her friends more than ever, now."

He pressed my buzzer so the nurse would come in. He wrote something down on a piece of paper and handed it to her. He asked her to take care of it right away.

He put his hand on my head and smiled.

"We are not giving up on you. Hang in there; you need to get some rest."

He told Tyler that he should say his goodbyes, and that I would be asleep for most of the day. Tyler bent down and kissed me on the forehead and they both left the room as the nurse came back in. Back to la la land again for me.

Chapter 28

"Roberta, it's time to get up."

I was already awake. I hadn't slept very well. I was not looking forward to that day. I understood that Mrs. Crawford was an older woman, but why wouldn't they let her keep me? She was really nice to me and Mommy liked her a lot. I missed Mommy. Why did she have to go? Now Mrs. Crawford was leaving me too. Why did everyone leave me? Social Services had found a home for me, she said. I had a home. I didn't want to go away. I wanted to stay there with Mrs. Crawford. I started to cry. I wrapped myself in my blankets, hugged my pillow, and sobbed.

I heard a tap on my door.

"Roberta, are you okay in there?

She opened the door. I was completely buried under my blankets. She came over and sat on the side of my bed.

"Roberta, honey, I know this is hard. I feel very badly about it. I wish I could keep you too, dear, but maybe they are right. Maybe you would be better off with younger people taking care of you. Maybe with some other children to play with."

I took my head out from under the blankets and wiped the tears from my eyes.

"Do you think they will have other children?" I asked.

"I'm not sure. They haven't really told me much about them. I sure hope they do. It will be much better for you. You do know that I love you, my dear, and I am so sorry about everything that is happening. I wish I could fix it and bring your mom back and make everything go back to the way it used to be, but it is not possible. What's done is done. There is no going back. I wish there was."

Mrs. Crawford began to pet my hair and looked at me sadly.

Tears collected in her eyes and I started to cry again. She took me in her arms and held me tight. She held me for the longest time. I didn't want her to let me go. I closed my eyes and remembered how Mommy used to hold me and how she told me that she would love me forever.

Chapter 29

That same old beeping… At least I know where I am. Oh, unless it's another nightmare in my hospital room; that wouldn't be good. Na… I am feeling too relaxed. Too drugged probably. I'm good with that, though. I'm tired of freaking out and being stressed all the time. Numb is good. It's actually very good.

Oh, I hear a noise, no stress, doesn't matter. I am not going to worry about it. This is good. Somebody is talking to me. Okay, not scared, just curious. I don't recognize the voice. It's a woman. She has a very nice, calm voice. I think she is reading aloud, because she just keeps talking away all by herself. I don't hear anyone responding. I tried to open my eyes. Nothing happened. *It's okay… I will just listen. Drugs are good, oh yeah.*

"Miss Hansen, are you awake? Your eyes are reacting. It's okay, you are heavily medicated. Don't try to force anything. Just relax. I don't know if you can hear me; I am hoping that you can. My name is Dr. Ashley Carter. I was approached a week ago by Dr. Blake. He asked me if I could look in on you. I was very happy to do so. You are quite the celebrity around here. You are all that anybody is talking about. I don't know how that makes you feel, but it is a good thing. Everybody is on the alert and trying to protect you. You still have a guard at the door, just so you know, and a steady stream of visitors. I have met most of them. They have filled me in on a lot of things.

"I hope you don't mind if I call you Bobby? I would like to get to know you, and help you, too. Everyone tells me how wonderful a person you are. I would really like to see that for myself one day. I don't blame you for turning yourself off to the world, you have been through so much, but you will have to return to us soon if you want to build your strength back up, heal your wounds, and lead a normal life again.

"Yes, you needed a break from reality. That's okay, but it has been two weeks now and your friends are very worried. I really hope you can hear me. I have been in here with you for a couple of hours a day for the past week. This is the first time I've seen a reaction from you. I hope it is a good sign. I won't tell anyone and get their hopes up, just in case. I'll wait and see if it happens again.

"Oh? Somebody is knocking, please excuse me."

I could hear her footsteps as she headed for the door. Then, nothing. She must have left the room.

That was it… she was gone. I really hoped she was real; she sounded very nice…

Chapter 30

"Roberta, wake up; we are here."

I must have cried myself to sleep. It was the strange man, Mr. Frazer, who was taking me to my new home.

"Come on, move it, we don't have all day. They are expecting us."

I got out of the car and he took me by the hand. Before us was a big old farmhouse, surrounded by big old trees. There was a very big lawn, bigger than the one that Mommy had. I tried to look around, but he kept pulling me forward. We came to an old wooden doorway that had no door. We entered and walked through a shed that was piled sky-high with wood. Then we came to another doorway. The man knocked. Someone came to the door. A small woman. Not as old as Mrs. Crawford, but not very young either.

"Hi," she said. "My name is Emma; you must be Roberta."

She smiled and asked us to come in. She offered me cookies and milk. I was a little hungry. She and Mr. Frazer talked while I ate my cookies. I looked around the room. Everything was pretty old. Mr. Frazer got up to leave the room and I ran after him.

"No Roberta, stay put; I'm just going to the car," he said as he walked out the door. "I'll be right back."

I looked at the woman and asked, "Do you have kids?"

"No," she said with a smile, "but we have animals. You will love the farm."

I drank the rest of my milk and sat there till Mr. Frazer came back. When he came in, he had my suitcases in his hands. It was pretty sad to see that all my life could fit in two little bags. I started to get a lump in my throat, and I felt very nervous. They were whispering, and I couldn't hear what they were saying. My eyes were starting to swell with tears. They shook hands and he headed for the door. I got up and ran toward him.

"Wait for me," I cried… "Please… wait for me!"

Chapter 31

Here I go again, I thought, *on my endless rollercoaster ride. Nothing surprises me anymore. I never know where I am going to end up. It might be scarier than hell, or it might be beautiful. I'm just a passenger and I have no control over what is going to happen next. I just need to sit back and hope for the best.*

I seem to be at a standstill, now. I have arrived at my destination. It is still very dark; there's not a glimmer of light anywhere I look. "Where am I?" I whispered to myself.

I listened hard. I could hear something; it was very faint. I focused on it. I finally recognized the beeping sound of my monitors. I was back, well maybe not quite. Maybe just my mind. *Maybe this is all a dream.* I wondered if that Dr. Carter would be around again; she seemed very nice. I listened hard, but I didn't hear a thing.

I heard a knock at the door.

"Come in," I heard her say.

It was Dr. Carter. She was here with me. I was so happy to hear her voice. I was starting to worry.

"Tyler… how are you?" she said. "It's nice to see you again."

"Are you finished? I'd like to be with my girlfriend."

It was Tyler. A feeling of joy came over me, but only for a moment. Then came the confusion, as I became aware of his tone. That sounded rude. He didn't seem very friendly toward her.

"She's all yours," she replied. "I'll see you again tomorrow, Bobby."

She put her hand on my arm. Then she squeezed it gently and I heard her chair slide as she got up and walked to the door.

"Bye now," she said and left the room.

It got very quiet. I couldn't understand what was going on. Why wasn't he talking to me? I missed him so. I tried hard to speak, but of course, nothing was happening.

Please talk to me, Tyler, I pleaded, but of course, only I could hear those words; nothing was coming out of my mouth.

"I miss you. I want to come back to you. Please, just say something, anything."

Okay, that's good, I thought. *He is gently touching my face with his hand. I can feel the warmth building up inside of me. I do miss him. I wish so much that I could tell him that.*

Oh, please don't stop, I thought, as he slowly passed his fingers through my hair. It felt wonderful and I was getting so relaxed.

Suddenly he stopped. He quickly stood up and started pacing the floor. I could hear him walking from one side of the bed to the other. Back and forth and back and forth.

I couldn't figure out what was happening. I wished that he would just say something, but he didn't. He just kept pacing around the bed.

I was getting nervous and I started to think about how rude he was to Dr. Carter. She seemed like such a wonderful person.

Finally, he stopped pacing and sat back down beside me. He took me by the hand.

"What am I going to do with you?" he said. "You need to come back to me; I can't bear to lose you again. I can take care of you; you know I can. You need to get better, so I can take you away from this place and all these people who are meddling in our lives. They don't know you like I do. I know what's best for you, even better than you do. We will get through this mess and then I will take you away. You will be mine forever. All we need is each other. Everyone else can just go straight to hell, for all I care. They think they know what you need. They don't know anything about you. I know you, and I know that we belong together. I won't let anyone come between us. They don't know who they are dealing with."

Suddenly, Tyler let go of my hand. He stood up so quickly that the chair he was sitting on tipped over and hit the floor with a loud bang. It scared the crap out of me. I wasn't the only one, though, because I heard the guard run in.

"Is everything okay?" he said.

"No, it's not!" Tyler yelled, and he stormed out of the room.

I heard the door close.

I felt numb and didn't know what to think. That was not the Tyler that I thought I was falling in love with. I couldn't figure out what was happening. He sounded, well… obsessed.

I replayed over and over again what he had said. No matter how many times I rolled it around in my head, it didn't make any sense. What in the hell was happening?

Suddenly I felt so alone. I seemed to be a prisoner in this dark place, with no sign of escape. Tears started to flow.

I heard something, voices. They were coming from the corridor. The door opened, and I heard footsteps.

"Bobby, it's Dr. Carter. The guard came and asked me to check in on you. I hear that your visit didn't go very well. I'm so sorry about that. Tyler seems very tired lately; he's very worried about you. I will try to talk to him."

She picked up the chair, sat down next to me, and took my hand.

"We are all worried about you. You need to come back to us. I am very anxious to have a two-sided conversation with you. I know you are in there somewhere, and I really hope you can hear me when I say that everyone is pulling for you."

She put her hand on my forehead and moved my hair from the side of my face.

"I will be here for you, when you wake up."

Something was happening; I felt like I was moving again. "Goodbye Dr. Carter," I whispered to myself. "I'll come back soon."

Chapter 32

It is dark as hell again, I thought. *It is weird, though; I'm not scared. It seems my life is unrolling before me. Time travel… I don't know… maybe. I guess there is such a thing, at least to go back and visit your past life. Or maybe this is just all a big series of dreams induced by the drugs I am on. I am dreaming up a past that is a mystery to me. I know that there were a lot of bad things that happened, and I guess, in trying to figure them out, my mind is just wandering around in a daze, just dreaming up anything at all… Or not…*

Okay… here we go…

I think I see something, might be light, way off in the distance. Alright, just as I thought, moving forward now, the wheels are in motion. I don't know what to expect, but hey… there is nothing I can do, so bring it on…

I'm getting closer and closer to the very bright light. I could use my sunglasses right about now… there is movement, but I can't tell what it is. Not close enough yet. Patience… hey, I've got plenty of that. Oh, here we go, I hear something… a voice. It's calling out me.

"Roberta!"

It was a soft beautiful voice. She was back. I knew it was her.

"Mom!" I cried. "You are back, Mom; I missed you so much."

There she was, right in front of me, her arms extended as if she was going to hold me. Oh no… the waterworks again. I did not want to cry. I wanted to be happy. I could feel the love radiating from her beautiful eyes and a welcoming smile. I wanted to get closer, but it was not happening. Something was holding me back.

"My darling Roberta, I know you are having a really rough time lately, but you are strong, and you will get through it. I am watching over you every step of the way. You can't keep hiding from your life. You need to get back to reality. It is not time for you to be with me. You have your whole life ahead of you. Go back now; you have good people taking care of you. Someone new has shown an interest; she can be trusted. Let her in. Accept her help and work hard to heal yourself and get back in shape. In time, things will work out, but always remember that I will never be very far. I love you, my darling… be strong."

With that, she was gone. She disappeared so fast that I didn't even have time to say anything to her.

"I love you, Mama," I whispered. "I love you."

Chapter 33

That familiar noise again. I was back. I was still in the dark though. I focused on the sounds. There was the endless beeping of the monitors and some sounds coming from outside my door, probably someone talking to the guard or something. Someone must have opened the door because the voices suddenly got louder. I heard footsteps now, coming towards me. No stress… I felt nothing.

"Hello, Bobby, it's Dr. Carter. I hope you are in there somewhere and I am not just talking to myself. I would like to believe that when someone is in a coma or they have retreated inside themselves that they can hear what is going on around them. I want you to know, though, this is probably about the hundredth time I have repeated it, that I will be here for you, along with everyone else around here who cares a great deal about you."

There was a gentle knock at the door. More footsteps.

"Hi Tyler," Dr. Carter whispered, "It's great to see you again. I was wondering if we could get together and talk, if you don't mind. Dr. Blake mentioned an issue you might be having with my involvement in this case. I would really appreciate it if you could come to my office after your visit and maybe we could work things out?"

She got up and headed for the door. I listened closely but Tyler didn't say anything to her. As soon as she closed the door, Tyler spoke. Very softly at first, but I could understand him.

"She has no business sticking her nose in all of this. I don't want her poking around and digging up things from your past. It's none of her business. I'm the one who is going to take care of this. Dr. Blake says that her expertise is PTSD and she is very good at her job. He thinks she can be a great help to you. I think she needs to mind her own business. I don't want her poking around in your past. She needs to keep her distance, damn it. We don't need to be dragging more people into this mess."

I listened carefully but he stopped talking. He took my hand in his. He squeezed it quite hard. I couldn't move or say or do anything. He lay his head down on me. I could feel his heart racing and hear his rapid breathing. There was silence for the longest time. I couldn't understand what was going on. Why did he dislike Dr. Carter so much? He seemed so worried that she might find out something about me. I was very confused and started to feel a little uneasy.

"I'm so sorry for all of this mess; I really am," he was whispering now.

"I wish we could just start all over again. Turn back time and make all this mess go away. You need to come back to me. I will take care of you; I promise. I love you, you know? I always have."

I could hear the emotion, the trembling in his voice. It made me feel sad, but I couldn't help feeling afraid at the same time. He got up and headed for the bathroom. I could hear him crying softly. A few minutes passed and out the door he went: no goodbye, no kiss, no nothing.

His words kept rolling around in my mind. He didn't sound like himself. Why was he so negative about someone else trying to help me out? It didn't make any sense. I didn't know the woman, but from what I had heard in the few times that I had been conscious, well, semi-conscious I guess, she seemed like a really nice person and very interested in trying to help me work through all of this. Strange…

Chapter 34

I awoke, rolled over, and then heard a thumping noise. Whatever had fallen off my bed had scurried away. I was scared. It was so dark, and I didn't know what was going on. I didn't know where I was. I started to cry.

"Mommy… I want my mommy."

For a while… no one came to my rescue, and then I saw some light coming from behind the door. I realized that I was in my bedroom, well, the room that these people said was mine. It was nothing like the one I had with Mommy.

My old bedroom had nice painted walls with pictures on them. I had a toy box filled with toys and games. They weren't new… but they were lots of fun. I had pretty pink curtains and a bedspread to match. My shelves were filled with stuffed animals. I felt like a princess there, with my mommy.

I wished I had been in the car with her that day. I was forced to live in that crappy old house, with those strange people, in my very dirty, messy, freezing cold bedroom. There was old plaster falling from the unpainted ceiling and the walls were all cracked and yellowed from the buildup of ice in the cold winter months. There was dusty old antique furniture, and old books and clothing stacked all over the place. My bed was stuck in the middle of all that mess. I was terrified at night. There were all kinds of noises that I couldn't identify.

I heard someone coming up the stairs. I was still frightened and crying. The door opened. I had the blankets up around my neck.

"Roberta, honey, are you okay?" he whispered.

It was Harold, Emma's husband. He was a giant. I don't think I ever saw anyone so big. He towered over me, and even Emma, because she was very small.

"What happened; why aren't you asleep?"

"Something was on my bed!" I cried, "I heard it fall to the floor and run away. I don't know what it was; I'm scared!"

He started to laugh.

"It was just a mouse, silly. Are you afraid of a little thing like that? You are much bigger than they are."

He sat down on the edge of my bed. His breath smelled really strong. He pulled the blankets down a bit and caressed my hair and face. I shuddered away from his touch.

"Don't you worry, my dear; I will take really good care of you."

I didn't know what to do. I just lay there quietly and didn't say anything as he continued to pet my face.

Chapter 35

"Good afternoon, Bobby; how are you doing?"

It was Dr. Carter. Thank goodness, I didn't know where that was going. *Strange how these things I am dreaming about seem vaguely familiar. Is this my life playing back to me from the start? No… that is not possible. What is happening to me?* I thought. *Am I in a coma? Am I going to live the rest of my life in this dream world? Oh no, I am feeling stress again. I've got to stop thinking.*

The shrink, yes, concentrate on her. She is there, she is real. At least I think so. Okay, I can hear her talking. Funny how she seems to bring me into this semi-conscious state.

"Just so you know, you are looking better every day. The bruising and cuts on your face are healing very well. Also, in case you were not aware, you were brought down to x-ray this morning. The news is good. The arm and ribs are healing well. The leg looks good too, but it will take a lot more time to heal. One good thing about the state you are in, Bobby, is that you are not moving, and that is giving your bones a chance to set. The bad thing is that the longer you are immobile, the weaker you will get."

Oh, this is great news. I am glad to hear that I don't look like Frankenstein anymore, I thought. *I don't know how long I have been like this. It's not like I can ask. Oh well, it is probably better that I don't know. I might get discouraged.*

"By the way, Bobby, I'm not even sure you can hear me, but I feel like I need to tell you this. It hasn't gone well with Tyler. He is completely opposed to me being here. I don't like this at all. I wish we could all work together and try to get through to you. I don't like conflict. Dr. Blake does not want me to back down. Neither do Carla and Lou. I don't know if I have done anything to Tyler to offend him, but he won't talk to me at all.

"I will keep coming here to visit you. I enjoy your company very much, though I am sure you are a lot more fun when you are awake. Sincerely, I think I can be a big help to you if you give me a chance. If you come back to us, no, sorry, I mean when you come back, if you decide you don't want me here anymore, I will honor your wishes."

I was enjoying her company very much and I wasn't going to tell her to leave even if I could. Frankly, she seemed to be my only connection to reality. She seemed to be the only person that could bring me back to semi-consciousness. I was definitely going to keep her around.

"It was a beautiful day yesterday," she started, "and I was out on the terrace taking a walk and enjoying the aroma of the beautiful gardens. It was a busy place. I ran into Carla. She was having a bad day. One of her patients died and she was taking it badly. I talked with her for quite a while. She told me about the day she met you, when she had also lost a patient and went to the kitchen looking for Lou. She said that you were a big help to her. She also told me that you two have been inseparable ever since. She had some great stories to tell me about your friendship. I hope you don't mind, but this is helping me to get to know you better. We talked about the breakup of her relationship, and the loss of her mother, and how you were there to help her pick up the pieces. She said that she didn't know how she would have gotten through it without you. She said how, when she first met you, you were very nervous about getting too close to anyone, and pretty much kept to yourself. She had to almost drag you out to dinner, or drinks, but it didn't take that long before you started to be more relaxed around her, and you learned to trust and open up to her. Oh yes, about the dinners," she giggled, "I'm sorry, but we had a good laugh at your expense; I hope you don't mind. So, I hear you have a hollow leg. I don't think I've ever seen one before. You'll have to show me that. Oh, and your stomach is always asking for food. Let's see now… you love just about any kind of food, Italian is right up there at the top of the list, especially lasagna. Does cherry cheesecake sound familiar? She said that you had the biggest sweet tooth. I've got to say, though, you can't get much better than that. I kind of have my own sweet tooth problem, and I wouldn't say no to cherry cheesecake. What else was there… oh yes, blueberry pancakes. Who doesn't like blueberry pancakes? When she mentioned that, I told her a story about when I was a child and my mother would make them for me. She would let me help, of course. I would clean the blueberries while she put together the pancake batter. She would let me put in as many blueberries as I wanted. Sometimes there were more blueberries than batter, and the pancakes wouldn't hold together very well. I remember her telling that story to everyone. Oh, I'm so sorry, Bobby, here I am talking about food, and you haven't had any for such a long time. I hope you're not too upset with me. I haven't heard your stomach growl, so I guess the IV is keeping you nourished. Promise me, when you come back to us, that we will have a blueberry pancake breakfast together.

"Oh, by the way, while we were there, sitting in the gardens, I could hear the distant sound of the water fountain trickling away. It was very relaxing. She told me the stories about how the sound of trickling water took you away to some amazing places. I found that very interesting. We didn't really get a chance to talk that much more about it because she had to get back to work. We plan to get together again soon so she can tell me more about that. It might be important. Well, it was really great talking with her. You have a wonderful friend."

She held my hand and said that she would be back again soon. I heard her footsteps as she headed out the door. I was actually glad that she and Carla were talking.

Oh… Whitey… I miss you so much. I wish I could just hold you in my arms or listen to your angelic voice as you sing to me.

Chapter 36

I felt a calmness come over me. I was feeling warm all over and relaxed. In the distance, I could hear the sound of trickling water. It seemed to be getting closer. I tried to open my eyes a bit, but the light was really bright. I closed them again. Funny, no beeping sounds, that only meant one thing: I wasn't in the hospital. The trickling was getting louder. The brightness was coming through my eyelids. I put my hand in front of my face to stop the glare. It worked. I slowly tried to open them again. My hand was blocking out the sun that was beating down on what looked like a glorious day. All around my hand I could see tree branches, and beyond that, the sky. Déjà vu… I was in my safe place. That was just wonderful; nothing could make me happier.

Okay, I knew it was all in my mind, but hey, this place made me so happy. I reached my hand down behind me to see if I could touch the water. A beautiful symphony filled the air. I could feel the coolness as it flowed through my fingertips. I wanted to just roll over and fall in. I turned my head to look down at the water and I heard a whinny. Where did it come from? I sat up and looked around. Wow, what a sight for sore eyes. There she was: Dancer, my horse. Oh my God, that was my horse, I remember her. I used to ride her everywhere. She was my best friend. I got up and went over to her. She gave me a welcoming nudge. I patted her on the nose and scratched under her chin. She loved when I used to do that. She whinnied again, and then I was distracted by the sound of a motorcycle zooming off into the forest. *Where did it come from?* I wondered. Oh well, I wasn't going to worry about it. I led Dancer to the water and let her have a drink. The sun had been baking my skin, so I also knelt down to dip my hands in the water and spray some on my face. I looked down into the stream and saw my reflection. I stayed there, stunned for a moment at the beautiful young woman that was looking back up at me. I looked fifteen, like in the dream I had about Tyler and me running into the water. How was that possible? *I know this is a dream,* I thought. *I am in the hospital, hooked up to all those machines. It is like I am in the past, and the present, all at the same time.* Suddenly, Dancer raised her head and started whinnying and moving around wildly. Something spooked her. I tried to grab the reins, but I wasn't fast enough. She turned and tried to get away, but it was too late; someone had already caught her.

"Whoa," he said, pulling on the reins. "You stupid fucking bitch of a horse. How dare you try to get away from me?"

He took hold of the riding crop and raised it in the air. With his hand still holding the reins, he whipped her across the face with it several times. She jumped and pulled and fought to try to get away, but the more she fought, the more he whipped.

"Stop it!" I cried. "You are hurting her. She's bleeding; leave her alone!"

He stopped the whipping and Dancer stopped pulling. She put her head down and stood there, trembling.

"Why did you do that? She didn't do anything to you," I screamed.

He tied the reins around the branch of a tree and turned toward me. I could see the evil in his eyes as he took a step in my direction.

"No, this can't be happening! It is not real. I don't want to stay here anymore; let me go back. Dr. Carter… please talk to me and bring me back!"

Nothing was happening; I wasn't being rescued. I looked at the crazy old man, and he was still coming at me, yelling and swearing.

"You stupid fucking bitch. Do you think I'm blind? It is your fault that your horse just got a beating, and it is your fault that you are going to get a beating too. It will also be your fault when I kill your stupid fucking boyfriend. Did you really think I didn't know that you two were sneaking around in the woods to be together? Don't deny it because I just saw him ride off on his motorcycle. I told you that nobody else can have you. You are mine, you little slut. I take care of you; I own you!"

I was so stunned that I just stood there. I couldn't bring myself to believe what was happening. I was going to wake up any minute, I was sure.

Didn't happen. I was still there, and he was still yelling. I got down on my knees and begged for forgiveness. The tears were pouring down my face.

"I won't do it again," I cried. "I promise!"

He didn't stop. He grabbed me by the arm and dragged me over a stump. He started whipping my backside with the crop. Time, after time, after time. The pain was unbearable. The burning… I felt like I was on fire. I was screaming in agony. My head was spinning, and I was becoming completely disoriented. Everything was a blur. With my last breath, I called for Dr. Carter.

Chapter 37

It was dark, and I was very glad to hear the monitors beeping away. I knew I was safe, and away from that monster. Oh my God, how crazy was that. So much for my safe place. I guess it was too good to be true, after all. *That old ugly man, he was my foster dad, I'm sure of it. Oh no… please tell me I didn't…*

"Bobby, it's Dr. Carter. Are you okay, Bobby?"

The sound of her voice startled me.

"Bobby, you whispered something. Can you speak? Are you there?"

I was so glad to be back and find that she was here with me. I tried to speak, but nothing was happening.

"You're safe, Bobby; I'm here with you."

I tried again, "Dr. Carter…" but only managed a whisper.

"Oh my God, you can hear me! Just relax, Bobby; everything is going to be okay. Don't open your eyes; I will close the lights, so it's not too bright."

I could hear her footsteps moving around the room. Was I actually back, or was I dreaming? I spoke, and she heard me; I knew that I was back. I tried to speak again, but nothing came out. My throat was very dry, and I could hardly swallow. She took me by the hand.

"Don't try to speak. I have a little sponge here with cool water; I am going to put some on your lips. Try to part them a bit."

I could feel the wonderful wetness of the water; I was definitely back. I sighed. She wet the sponge again. I was so used to lying there in the dark that I didn't even think to open my eyes.

"That feels good, doesn't it? I knew you would come around. I could see little reactions when I talked to you. Can you still hear me? Don't leave me now."

I tried to clear my throat. It was difficult, but I got out a little sound. It took everything I had, and she heard me once again.

"Thank you," I whispered.

That was all I could manage. My eyes seemed to be glued shut and my body seemed, well, non-existent.

"Don't tire yourself out. It's okay. I will stay with you… rest."

Her voice was fading… into the darkness I went again.

Chapter 38

It was still dark, and everything was quiet. There was no safe place and no hell. I wondered sometimes if they might even be the same place.

I could hear something in the distance. It was barely audible, but there was something. I listened hard. It sounded like it was getting closer. It was terrifying, because I never knew where I was going to end up next. It was becoming clearer now. I breathed a sigh of relief; it sounded like birds. I felt a stabbing pain through the back of my neck and shoulders along with soreness throughout my body.

"Seriously?" I said, as I slowly opened my eyes and realized that I was face down on my keyboard. I had fallen asleep while I was writing. There were nights when I was so inspired that the memories would just keep flowing out of my mind. It didn't happen very often, though, so when it did, I just kept on writing until I couldn't hold myself up anymore. This was the first time that I actually woke up, lying on my keyboard, and I was feeling the consequences.

I tried to ease myself out of the awkward position that I found myself in, stood straight for a moment, then stretched. I didn't know what time I had fallen asleep, but it was early morning. I could hear the coffee machine brewing in the galley, timer set for six a.m. *Home sweet home.*

I was very pleased about my evening and the progress that I was making. My goal somehow didn't seem so unreachable. I was sure that my friends, and doctor, would be very proud of me.

I fixed myself a cup of coffee and then went to the refrigerator to see what kind of breakfast I could put together. I was starving. All that hard work I did last night gave me an appetite. A good look inside my refrigerator made me realize that my supplies were dwindling down. I was going to be okay for a few days, but I would need to take inventory and make a list of what I needed. I decided to take a break from my writing and do so.

My stomach growled, and I laughed at myself.

"First things first," I said, so I put the inventory idea aside and prepared my breakfast. *Two boiled eggs, cheese, toast with jam, and coffee… yum.* When I was done, I placed everything on a serving tray and headed up to the deck. I set it down and looked around. The birds were flying low and the sky was mostly cloudy, but the ocean was very still. I sat down and enjoyed my breakfast. I hoped that the skies would clear and the sun would come out, but it didn't look promising. It didn't really bother me though, because I knew that it couldn't be sunny and beautiful every day. Rain was also necessary. It wasn't going to be so painful to do my inventory after all.

I finished my breakfast and sat down and relaxed for a bit. Even on a cloudy day, I was very happy to be out here. I got up and tapped on the side of my boat.

"Funny," I said.

There was no sign of Fred Astaire this morning. The tapping would have usually brought him right to the surface, if he hadn't already shown up.

Oh well, I thought. *Maybe he is looking for more treasures so he can take me out and lead me to them on our next dive.*

I knocked a few more times, and nothing, so I grabbed my tray and went back down into the galley. It was time to get to work. I went through my refrigerator and cupboards. It didn't take me very long to complete my task. I was getting low on just about everything and had compiled quite a list. It was time to call the marina and have them prepare my supplies.

I heard a big splash outside and a smile came across my face. I knew it had to be Fred, so I went up on deck to greet him. Sure enough, it was him, but he seemed very excited about something. He kept jumping in and out of the water, non-stop. His sounds were not of laughter, but of fear.

I started to stress, and quickly looked around me. Way off in the distance, I saw some lightning streaking across the sky, and I heard the faint sound of thunder. I hadn't checked the weather report yet, so off I went back down to the galley to do so.

As I reached the last step, my phone rang, and it startled me. I hadn't communicated with anyone in more than two weeks. I looked at the display and smiled when I saw Ashley's name.

"Hi Ash, how are you doing?" I said. "What's up?"

"Bobby, are you okay?" she replied. "Have you been watching the weather? There is a big storm heading your way."

Ashley sounded very concerned.

"I was just about to. I saw lightning off in the distance, but the ocean is very calm," I said.

"Probably the calm before the storm," Ashley replied. "You need to lift anchor and head to shore. It's moving very fast."

I was still worried about being out in public.

"You know I can't go to shore; I'm not ready yet. I need to keep working. This is the safest place for me. Nobody knows I'm out here, right?"

Ashley was getting a little frustrated with me.

"Of course not, Bobby; I haven't told anyone where you are. You do know, though, that you have nothing to fear anymore, right?"

"I have told you before and I will tell you again that I will always be afraid until my mind releases all these memories that it has been protecting me from for all these years. Actually, you would be very proud of the progress I have been making. I have..."

"Bobby!" she yelled.

At this point, Ashley was starting to lose it.

"Bobby, could you just shut up and listen to me for a second. There is a severe storm coming your way, and you need to get yourself out of there. You need to go to shore!"

"Okay, okay, I hear you. I'll check my radar and get back to you. Later then."

"But Bobby, you…"

I shut off the phone and went to check the radar. Sure enough, there it was: large as life and heading my way. The storm looked to be about five nautical miles to the southeast of my position, and heading northwest, toward the coast, putting me pretty much smack dab in the middle of it.

The boat started to rock, ever so slightly, and I knew that the calm would soon be over. I grabbed my rain gear, went back up on deck, and secured the hatch. Fred was very persistently trying to get my attention. He would jump in and out of the water, heading in the direction of the storm, and then dive under and come back to the boat with a splash, and then start all over again.

I was puzzled for a moment and couldn't figure out what he was doing. Surely, he didn't want me to sail into it; that would be crazy. I stood there in a daze. Ashley wanted me to head to shore, and Fred wanted me to go toward the storm. I felt torn and didn't know what to do. I knew that Ashley meant well, but neither of us had enough experience to know how to tackle a storm of this magnitude, especially alone.

Suddenly there was a big splash, bringing me back to reality. It was Fred again, and he was getting frantic. He wanted me to follow him, and that is what I finally decided to do. He had always taken good care of me, brought me on amazing adventures, and got me back to my boat safely. There was no reason I could think of as to why I wouldn't trust him now.

I knew I had to move fast, so I took a moment to focus on what needed to be done. I lifted anchor, raised the sail, got behind the wheel, and braced myself for what looked like might be the wildest ride that Fred and I would ever take together.

He led the way, on the starboard side of the boat, and I followed. It was slow going at first because there still wasn't very much wind to speak of and my motor wasn't very powerful.

Up ahead, though, and it seemed very close now, I could see the waves rising, and the lightning, which seemed to be streaking wildly across the sky in every direction. The thunder was getting louder.

"What in the hell am I doing?" I yelled. "I am sailing into a tropical storm!"

Fear took over and I started to question my decision. I looked behind me, and I couldn't even see the shoreline anymore. It seemed totally out of reach. I looked ahead again, and the storm was getting really close. *Even if I had headed for shore,* I thought, *it would probably have caught up with me long before I got there.* I thought of Ashley and remembered that I told her I would get back to her. That call was going to have to wait. I looked in the water, and Fred was still there, leading the way. I knew right then and there that I had made the right decision to follow my friend.

"My life is in your hands!" I yelled out to him.

The waves started getting larger, the wind was getting stronger, and the sails were filled to capacity. The boat started making good speed which gave me a little more encouragement... which was good. At the same time, though, where I was heading was not very comforting, and I was just going to get there a lot faster.

The stress was getting to me and my mind started to scramble. All the craziness in my life started swirling around inside my head. I thought of Tyler, then shook it off, then Carla, and then right back to Tyler. I shook my head, trying desperately to stay in control. Then I thought of Thomas and how he saved my life, and of course Maestro.

This needed to stop. I couldn't figure out what was happening. It was really not a good time for my mind to start playing tricks on me again. I needed to concentrate and stay in the present. I had more important things to think about right now, like trying to stay alive by trying to keep my boat from capsizing in these turbulent waters.

I tried to relax and breathed deeply. Then I thought of my mom. I could see her radiant beauty and hear her calm, gentle voice…

"Roberta, my love, don't worry; you are doing very well. You will get through this just as you have gotten through all your other obstacles. Don't give up, and trust your friends. They, as I, are watching over you."

For those few seconds, I was out of danger. I felt safe and I felt loved, and I knew that I had to get through this. I knew now that my mom was out there helping me, and I had to hang on just a little longer.

Mom disappeared, and everything went back into focus. The storm was right on my doorstep. I was getting showered by the violent waves smashing up against the side of my boat. I took a quick glance overboard and looked for Fred. I couldn't figure out how, but he was still there, leading the way. I had picked up a lot of speed, and I didn't really know how fast dolphins could swim, but Fred was flying in and out of the water at an unimaginable speed.

He made a slight starboard turn, which meant that we were heading more toward the south now. *That is a good thing*, I thought for a moment, then I pushed that thought aside. It was not the time to try to analyze the situation; I was content in just following the leader.

The rain had started pouring down now, and I could barely see Fred anymore as he plowed in and out of the now very large waves. I was worried about him and didn't know how much longer he was going to be able to keep up this pace. We weren't out of danger yet.

I took a moment to assess the condition of my sails. They were stretched to their limit and I feared they wouldn't hold. Fred made another slight starboard turn and we were riding the southern edge of the storm. *Brilliant*, I thought, *it finally came to me*. He steered me into the storm so I could ride the winds and pick up the speed I needed to head south, maneuver around it, and get the hell out of there. Thinking back, I knew myself, from the lessons I took and the little experience that I had, that I would have never been able to outrun it to shore. I had made a good call.

Fred knew exactly what to do. I felt a little bit of relief, and I could see that there was hope. The blackest, darkest clouds were behind us, and even though I was still in a situation that was far beyond my capability as a sailor maneuvering in this storm alone out here, I felt confident that I was going to make it.

The rain was still really pelting down hard on me and the winds were savagely ripping at my sails. I suddenly realized that I couldn't see Fred anymore and started to panic and look around, briefly taking my attention away from the situation at hand. I couldn't leave the wheel; it was taking everything I had to hold it in place so I could stay on course. I called out to him over and over again, but from where I sat, he was nowhere in sight. I was frantic, but I was sure he was okay, and there was nothing I could to help him at this time anyway, even if I could. I knew by now what he wanted me to do, and that was to stay on a southerly course and get to safety.

I wasn't out of the woods yet, though, and I was on my own, fighting to get out of the way of this massive storm. Even if I knew exactly what needed to be done, I felt so alone, so insecure. I was getting tired, and the waves were really wearing me down. My heart was racing, and I could barely hang on to the wheel anymore. Exhaustion was taking over my body and soul and I was losing my grip.

A huge wave hit the side of my boat and I got thrown onto the deck. There was a loud crack, and I saw my sail get ripped away. I crawled back to the wheel and tried to regain control. Things were not looking good; without the sail, I didn't know where I would end up. I needed to hang on a little bit longer and try to keep steering toward the south. Way off in the distance I could see clearing skies; I just had to keep going.

In all the excitement, I had almost forgotten about Fred. I started calling out his name over and over again. I looked around and there was still no sign of him. I was really worried now. I started yelling at the top of my lungs and banging on the side of my boat… still nothing. I didn't know what else to do. He was my only true lifeline out here, and even though I still had a lot of work to do to get clear of this storm, I didn't think I would have gotten this far without him. *Maybe he just needs to take a break,* I thought. *Well, I really hope that's all it is.*

I was distracted by my thoughts when another huge wave slammed into me. The water splashed up and over the side of my boat. I was almost washed away. It took everything I had to keep my hold on the wheel. I turned around to get back into position just in time to see another huge wave coming toward me. There was no time to react; I had barely recovered from the first one. There was nothing I could do. I lost my grip and went flying across the deck... everything went black.

Chapter 39

Beep… beep… beep… There it was, the unmistakable sound of the monitors. I was back, I think, back in my hospital bed. It was still dark, though. What was going on? I had woken up last time when Dr. Carter was talking to me; had I dreamed that? I tried not to worry about it, so I focused on the sounds. The monitors, yes, I could hear them, but not much of anything else. It was very strange because I didn't feel like I was really there; I didn't feel like I was lying in bed. It almost felt like I was floating. I started to get nervous. I wished that I could see something, anything. I couldn't imagine what was going on.

I heard another noise. I was not quite sure, but it sounded like paper… yes, someone turning a page. *Dr. Carter, yes, I'm sure that it's her.* I tried to call out her name but nothing. I couldn't see, I couldn't speak, what in the hell?

"Hey, Bobby, I'm sorry about my choice of reading material; it's just that I found an article I wanted to read. Even though I was sure that it wouldn't be of any interest to you, I figured as long as you can hear my voice, it might help you come back to me. I wish you hadn't retreated again; I hope it wasn't something I said. I would really like it if you would come back and we could talk about it."

"But I'm here, Doctor; I'm here."

Nothing, she couldn't hear me; I didn't understand.

There was a knock at the door. Dr. Carter said to come in. It was the security guard. He informed her that Tyler was in the hallway and wanted to come in. That was very strange. Why would he need to ask permission to see me?

"Yes, sure," she said. "I will leave and give him a chance to visit."

I heard her footsteps leaving my bedside.

"Who in the hell do you think you are?" Tyler yelled. "I have to ask permission to visit my own girlfriend?"

"Tyler, calm down," Dr. Carter commanded, "for Bobby's sake. We don't want to stress her out. She might be hearing all of this; you never know."

"I don't give a shit what she hears; you have no business keeping me out!"

"Tyler, if you don't calm down, I will have to escort you out of here," the guard said in a very serious tone.

"No, it's okay," Dr. Carter said. "I've got this."

"Let me know if you need me."

The door closed; I guess the security guard went back out into the hallway.

I didn't understand what was happening. I wish I could see. What was Tyler so upset about? I had never seen him this way or even heard him speak like that. I was taken aback. I listened some more.

"What gives you the right to make the rules about who can and who cannot visit Robbie?"

"Robbie?"

"I mean Bobby, you know what I mean."

"This gives me the right. You have been acting really strangely these days. You are bad-mouthing me to everyone on this case and you refuse to talk to me about your relationship with Bobby. I don't know what to think. I'm just trying to help.

"You should be pleased that so many people are trying to help her, but you seem to want everyone to back off. You disappear for days on end without telling anybody where you can be reached. Everyone is worried about you, but you won't talk to anyone. You keep pushing all of us away. You don't seem to want us to help Bobby, yet you are not there for her yourself. Do you actually want her to regain consciousness? Because sometimes it doesn't seem that way."

Oh my… that didn't sound like Tyler. What on Earth? I couldn't believe my ears. He called me Robbie! *Where do I remember that from? Maybe one of my dreams; oh, this is so frustrating. I wish I could wake up,* I thought. *I don't like just lying hear listening to this without being able to respond. Why can't I wake up?*

I felt something, oh it was my hand. Someone was holding it, not quite sure who. The room got so quiet.

Dr. Carter broke the silence, "I'm sorry Tyler, that it has to be this way. I really wish we could all work together. Bobby needs all of us; we need to be cooperating with each other to find ways to help her. I know she is in there somewhere, and I am optimistic that she will come back. We need to be patient and give her the time she needs to heal."

I heard footsteps again and the door opened.

"I will leave you two alone for a while. If you want to sit down with me later and talk reasonably, Tyler, my door is always open. I have no appointments for the rest of the day. Bobby, I will come back later and read to you again."

He didn't say a word; he was too damn quiet. I really didn't want Dr. Carter to leave. I didn't know what to think about him. He didn't seem in his right mind. Why did I have to hear all of that? I was so confused.

I miss Carla, I thought. *I would feel so much better if she was here with me. I want to hear her sing to me. That would calm me down. That beautiful voice of hers, I miss it.*

Tyler was still so quiet. Why didn't he talk to me? I felt so alone. I could hear him breathing. It was quite rapid as if he was nervous about something. He kept fidgeting with my hand too, softly at first, but then he squeezed it really hard. I felt the pain but there was nothing I could do.

"What am I going to do with you?" he said.

He let go of my hand and got up. I could hear him pacing the floor. He went from one side of my bed to the other, over and over again. I wished he would stop, because even though I couldn't see him, I was so concentrated on his every step that it was making me dizzy. I was terrified. I felt so vulnerable. I couldn't move and couldn't speak, anything could happen, and it was completely out of my control. The security guard couldn't even help me because I wasn't able to call out to him.

"I need to take care of this mess before it ruins my life again."

What? I didn't like the sound of that. Now I was getting very nervous. What did he mean by this mess?

Okay, this is not right, it is not happening, I thought. *My mind is playing tricks on me for sure. What in the hell is going on in my head? Tyler is a good friend. All these visions and flashbacks are making me paranoid. I feel like I want to scream…*

Chapter 40

I opened my eyes suddenly. It was dark, but I knew exactly where I was, with that familiar sound of mice scurrying around in the attic. *Oh no, not again,* I thought. I really didn't want to be there. Emma and Harold were going at it, as usual. They seemed to be fighting about one thing or another, day in and day out. I don't think they ever said a nice word to each other the whole time I lived there, which was going on ten years. I listened for a while, but it was the usual night-time argument: he was drunk again. The problem was when he got drunk, he wanted sex. I don't think she ever gave him any. I don't know why they were together because for as long as I can remember, they have had separate bedrooms. Things were not looking good for me.

I tried not to think about them, to block them out of my mind, but the yelling got louder. That meant that he was leaving the kitchen and getting closer to the staircase. His bedroom was at the bottom of the stairs and there was always hope that he would go to his room, pass out, and sleep it off. Well, luck wasn't on my side tonight. The hall light came on and shone through my slightly open door. I braced myself for the storm.

One… two… three… four… I counted the steps as they creaked beneath his weight.

Twelve… Thirteen… Fourteen…

My heart was pounding. *Stay calm, pretend you are asleep, eyes closed, and breathe,* I thought.

The door squeaked as it opened ever so slowly, prolonging the noise. I tried not to move but I could feel myself trembling under the blankets. I was hoping it didn't show.

"Sweetheart," he whispered. "Sweetheart, are you awake? I have brought you something. Come on there, I know you're not sleeping."

His voice was getting louder.

"I brought you some scotch. We can share a drink together."

My bedroom light came on and it startled me.

"There you go. How's my special girl tonight?"

I didn't answer; I just lay there looking up at him. He started to stagger over to my bed.

"Please, not tonight, I beg of you. I am really tired and would like to go to sleep."

"I just wanted to celebrate. I haven't caught you slutting around with that asshole lately. I presume you did as you were told."

He collapsed on the edge of my bed. I managed to move out of the way just in time. He wasn't moving, and I thought I might be in the clear, but no such luck.

He groaned, lifted his head, and asked, "What did you tell him?" Then he passed out again.

I started to cry. I had lost my best friend. I had to tell him that I didn't want to see him anymore, that I was losing interest and wanted out. The memory was still fresh in my mind.

He didn't believe me and tried to hold me. I had to fight with him to get him away. I had told him to leave me alone and get out of my life. He wouldn't listen. He had grabbed me and pinned me up against a tree. He had his hand around my throat and I could hardly breathe. I couldn't understand what was happening.

"You can't leave me; I won't let you!" he had yelled. "Nobody leaves me, you hear? It's that drunken asshole that put you up to this, isn't it? Do you like fucking him more than me? I will kill him, and that's a promise. Nobody takes a shot at me and gets away with it."

I suddenly went cold. I had tried to put that day out of my mind. I couldn't believe what had happened. It was the only way to save him. Harold had threatened to kill him, and I didn't want him to get hurt. Was I completely surrounded by assholes? Now, here I was, left lying here with the biggest one of all.

I was miserable, I mean, how much could one person take? I tried to wiggle my way out from underneath the blankets, but he was on top of them and it was very difficult.

Well, there was nothing left to do so I stopped struggling. I was also worried that I might wake him up. He was still passed out and starting to snore. It was going to be a long night.

I looked down next to him and spotted the bottle of scotch. I thought for a moment and decided that I would not let it go to waste. He was going to share it, after all. I reached down and tried to get hold of it. A little farther… almost there… crash! I knocked it on the floor. It made a loud noise that scared the crap out of me and woke up the devil.

He looked around the room and asked, "What in the hell happened?"

"You passed out and the bottle fell on the floor."

"Were you trying to take the bottle from me? Don't lie to me, you little slut. You know I hate when you do that."

He reached down, picked it up, and started to twist the cap off. He managed to sit up, put the bottle up to his mouth, and take a sip. He turned to me with an absurd little grin on his face. He held up the bottle in front of me.

"So, what are you waiting for, isn't this what you wanted? Come on, take a swig. Let's do that celebrating I was talking about."

"I don't want any. I would like to get some rest. Leave me alone and let me sleep."

"What in the hell do you think you are doing, mouthing off to me like that? I am not leaving till this party is over."

He leaned over, put his hand on my throat, and held the bottle over my mouth. He started to pour it on me. It went in my mouth, up my nose, and pretty much all over my face. I was choking, and it was burning my eyes and my throat. The more I struggled, the more he poured. I couldn't breathe and my lungs were on fire. I didn't think I could last much longer; I felt like I was drowning.

He stopped pouring it on me and took a sip.

"This is a waste of a good bottle of scotch; what was I thinking? You just really piss me off sometimes. Look at you; you are a fucking mess. Emma is not going to be very happy about the sheets. She might even take the yardstick to your ass again when she sees this. She sure likes that thing. Makes her feel like she has some authority around here."

He took another sip and loosened his grip on my neck. I was still struggling to breathe.

"Stop your fucking whimpering," he yelled, and he brought the bottle up to my face again.

I gave it all I had left and started to scream.

Chapter 41

It's dark again, I realized. *I never thought I would be so happy to be here. Sometimes I wish I could just stay here in limbo. I can't hear anything, and I can't see anything. I feel no pain; hey, what could be better?* I was sure though, that it wasn't going to last; it never does.

Oh... here we go, something is happening, I hear something way off in the distance. It doesn't sound threatening, kind of like whispers. Okay, I am getting closer and it is getting louder. Oh my, I know what it is: it's singing, and it sounds like Carla. Oh please, what I wouldn't give to hold her in my arms. I miss her so. I wanted to talk and laugh with her like we used to, but it wasn't going to happen. My body felt like it came to a stop, like that was the farthest I was going to go. I could hear her beautiful voice though, that I missed so much, but it seemed like that was all I was going to get for this time.

As I listened to her voice, I thought of all the good times we spent together before all this shit happened. We were so happy. I think that the few years I spent with her were some of the happiest years of my life, at least the life that I remembered.

Suddenly, she stopped singing.

"You can't go in there like this, Tyler!" the guard yelled.

"I need to talk to Carla; mind your own fucking business!"

"This is my..."

"It's okay," Carla cut in.

"If you say so."

"I do, no worries. Hi Tyler, where have you been?"

"None of your god-damned business. I would really like to know what is going on with you. I thought you were my friend, but you won't even side with me. I think there are just too many people sticking their noses in this mess. I can handle Bobby. I don't need anybody else's help. She is mine; don't you think I can take care of her?"

I couldn't believe what I was hearing. He sounded possessive, as he had sounded in the woods when I told him I didn't want to see him anymore. Oh shit, please tell me that this wasn't real.

Carla spoke up, "What do you mean, she is yours? She is also my best friend. I think I know what is best for her too, and I think that the more people who are looking out for her, the better."

"You stupid bitch; what the hell do you know, anyway? You are just a servant's daughter. You are worth nothing. I don't know why I ever had anything to do with you."

It got very quiet. I heard her sniffle. My heart ached; I couldn't believe what I was hearing. She was a wonderful person and why he was talking to her like that, I couldn't imagine.

She spoke up, "Why are you doing this? You are pushing everyone away, even me."

I knew she was crying; I could hear the trembling in her voice.

"We are all just trying to do what is best for Bobby. You? I'm not so sure. You have been in here for a few minutes now, and you haven't even looked at her or asked how she is. I don't get it. I hate to think this, but this kind of reminds me of the time, years back, when your grandparents brought you back to the city and told your parents that they couldn't handle you anymore. They didn't know what was happening to you and they thought you needed help."

"What do you know about that? It was none of your business. Oh yes, your fucking big-mouth mother probably told you that; well, it was none of her god-damned business either. She was a useless human being who made her living slaving after others."

"How dare you talk about my mother that way? She took care of you as if you were her own, in that loveless mansion. Your mom never lifted a finger when it came to you. She didn't want anything to do with you. You were lucky to have my mom."

"You stupid bitch, I knew you were going to be a problem."

There was a little commotion and I heard what sounded like a slap.

"What in the hell, are you out of your mind? Guard!" she yelled.

I heard the door open.

"Never mind… I'm leaving, but mark my words, Carla White, you will not get in my way!"

"That sounded like a threat," said the guard.

"Oh, fuck off!"

I couldn't believe my ears. What in the hell was happening? Poor Carla. I felt so bad for her.

"Miss White, are you okay?"

"Yes, I think so."

"You're bleeding!"

"I'll be okay, but just don't let him back in here. Bar him off the visitors' list or do whatever it is you have to do. I don't think that it would be in Bobby's best interest if she saw him this way."

"I will put it in my report, and I will inform my replacement for the evening."

"I will call the detective tomorrow and let him know what has been going on," Carla said. "Thanks."

I felt something touch my hand; it was Carla. I could hear her crying. I felt so bad for her. She put her head down on me. I could feel her warmth, like when she used to hold me in her arms after my nightmares. It felt so good to have her back. It looked like she needed the hug today. If only I could...

Oh… I think I moved my fingers; no, it couldn't be.

She lifted her head and asked, "Bobby, are you there? Oh Bobby, please come back to me. I miss you so; my life is not the same without you. Please come back!" She put her head down and cried again. I felt so bad for her. She needed me, and here I was, locked away inside this lifeless body. I wanted out. I was ready. I needed to know what was going on. This was crazy. I was so frustrated that I felt like screaming. It was building up inside of me like a volcano that was about to erupt.

My fingers! I think they moved again. Come on, I can do this.

The door opened again.

"Carla, are you okay? The guard told me what happened. What is going on with that guy?" It was Dr. Carter.

Carla broke down again. "I don't know," she cried. "I can't deal with this right now. I want my best friend back. That is what is important to me right now. I wish I had never run into him that day. It's my fault; I'm the one that got him involved with this in the first place. I thought he would be able to help her but now he is acting like a complete jack-ass!"

"It's not your fault; you are not to blame. You were just trying to help."

She squeezed my hand. *Yes,* I thought, *I can do that too. I moved them before; I know I did. Okay, concentrate hard, come on, I need to…*

"She moved! I felt her fingers move! Come on, Bobby," Carla cried, "come back to us. You can do this."

I tried to move my lips, but they seemed to be glued together. My eyes, too, for that matter. There was light coming through my eyelids.

"Carla, pass me the cup that is on the table behind you; her lips are so dry. I will wet them a bit. You need to keep squeezing her hand. She needs to know we are here for her."

The water felt so good. Some of it seeped in between my lips and made me thirst for more. I tried to part them a little. I managed a sigh, just a tiny little sound, but enough to get both of them very excited. My other hand felt pressure as Dr. Carter must have also squeezed it.

"Oh Bobby, I have missed you so. Come back to me, please."

"Carla…" It was hard to speak because my throat felt so dry. "I love you."

"I love you too, oh my God, I am so happy to hear your voice. You have been gone for so long. Are you okay? Can you open your eyes?"

"It's too bright."

"I'll hit the light."

Dr. Carter let go of my hand, got up, and walked to the door. The darkness returned.

For a moment, I feared that I was gone again but I could still feel Carla's hand holding mine.

"Thank you, Ashley," Carla said.

"No worries, Carla; we need to keep her comfortable."

I felt the doctor's hand take mine again. As my eyes adjusted to the change, I noticed that there was a little bit of light coming through the window. It wasn't bright enough to be a bother.

I focused hard on my eyelids. I felt them twitch, but nothing happened. I was thinking that maybe they were glued shut from being closed all this time.

I moved my fingers again; it was a little easier this time. I felt like I was slowly regaining feeling in the other hand.

Dr. Carter let go of my hand again and said, "I'll be right back."

"Oh Bobby, please stay with me; I have been so worried about you. I don't want to lose you again."

My body started to feel strange, oh no… I didn't want to leave. It was different, though. My whole body was tingling, like that feeling you get when your foot is asleep.

"My body is tingling; I don't feel right," I whispered.

I heard footsteps coming back and I felt something cold on my face. It startled me at first, but it felt so good.

"Here you go; this should be refreshing. It's just a cool facecloth."

"My body is still buzzing."

"Maybe we should get Dr. Blake," Carla said.

"I'll go; you stay here and try to keep her talking."

Dr. Carter left the room. Carla and I were together again. I felt a tear roll down my cheek, and then another. I heard Carla sniffle.

"Looks like we are both crybabies, Whitey," I whispered.

"Is that how it's going to be, Looney Tunes, back to your old self again? I'm so happy to hear your voice. You still have that sense of humor, I see. How you manage that, I have no idea. I've missed you so much; you can't imagine. Where have you been all this time?"

I heard someone talking in the corridor. It was Dr. Blake.

There was a knock on the door, and then footsteps.

"I heard that our sleeping beauty finally woke up."

"Right, you mean sleeping Frankenstein?"

"Sarcasm… I like the sound of that. It leads me to believe that you are definitely back. For your information, we have been taking very good care of you while you were away on vacation. Give us a little credit."

There was a knock at the door again.

"Can I come back in, Doc?"

It was Dr. Carter.

"Yes," I said. "Come and join the party."

Dr. Blake removed the facecloth that she had left on my forehead.

"This shouldn't hurt at all." He pulled up my eyelid and shone his little flashlight in my eye. "Okay, your eyes are responding appropriately."

It was all I needed to be able to open them.

"Oh Carla, you look as beautiful as ever. I have missed you so much."

I started to cough a little. My throat felt raw.

"Get her some water; she hasn't spoken for so long, her throat must be very dry. You shouldn't force your voice too much, Bobby. Give it some time to adjust."

I watched Dr. Carter as she spoke. She was very beautiful, and except for her red hair, she reminded me a little of my mom that Christmas morning so many years ago. The resemblance was even in the way she smiled and gazed at me with those same deep blue eyes.

"I remember you, Dr. Carter," I whispered, "your voice and your kindness. I heard you reading to me and talking as if maybe I was right there with you. It was very comforting to hear your voice through all that darkness. I feel very close to you."

"That is very nice of you to say, Bobby. I was drawn to you from the very first day I came to see you. I have learned so much about you from Carla that I feel like we are best friends."

Carla came back with some water and lifted my head a bit so I could drink some.

"I knew you were the right person for the job when I first talked to you about Bobby," Dr. Blake said. "This was right in your field of study, your expertise. You seemed so passionate about your work. I made the right decision. Well, I'd love to stay and chit-chat, but I have other patients to see, so let's get on with this."

I explained to him about the strange feeling of numbness and he told me that I needed to start moving a bit; I had been immobile for too long. He promised to send someone in to massage my muscles. He checked my vitals and took a few notes.

"Glad to have you back with us. Well, as I said, I need to get back to my other patients. I'll check in on you tomorrow. Get some rest, but uh… don't forget to come back."

He said goodnight to us all and headed for the door.

Before leaving the room, he turned, smiled, and said, "Get this girl a mirror."

Chapter 42

I awoke with a start, practically jumping out of my skin. I gasped for air and started coughing. I tried to lay still for a moment and calm myself. I opened my eyes; they were burning. The sun was very bright and warm and shining down on me. I was soaked to the bone. My head hurt, and I felt dizzy and a little disoriented. I seemed to be swaying, and it was making me feel nauseous. I heard a sound, and then water splashed up onto me. It was all coming back. I smiled, then I heard that sweet sound of laughter and knew for sure that it was Fred, and he was okay. Surprisingly, we had both survived the storm.

I turned over onto my side to try to get up. I felt the nausea still building up inside of me. My stomach heaved, and I threw up what seemed to be an endless supply of seawater. I had probably swallowed a lot of it while I was unconscious. My lungs and throat were on fire.

I slowly sat up and tried to adjust my eyes. They were also burning from the salt water. I looked up at the sky. From where the sun was, it seemed to be about midday, but which day, I was not quite sure of. I had no clue how long I had been out for. I glanced in sadness at my sail-less mast and couldn't figure out how I had gotten to safety without it, wherever safety was.

Fred was chatting up a storm out there and jumping around in the water. I needed to try to get up and see what all the commotion was about. I called out to him, and he jumped up into the air again and came down with a big splash. It took a lot of effort, but I managed to get to my knees. I was still feeling nauseous and had to move slowly. I managed to lift myself high enough now to peer over the side. I saw Fred jumping around erratically. I called out to him, and he got even more excited. With my blurry salt-soaked eyes, I tried to look past him and into the distance. I was having trouble focusing. I wasn't sure, but I thought I could see a shoreline. Then I heard something but couldn't quite make out what it was. It started out very faint, and then kept getting louder. I finally realized that it was a motor. I rubbed my eyes, trying to get a better look. Yes, it was definitely a boat, and it was coming right for me.

I suddenly feared for my life. I wanted to hide as much as I wanted to be rescued. All those years of living in fear still played hard on my mind. I always imagined the worst. Well, I had no choice now but to sit and wait and see what was going to happen. There was nowhere to run.

Over the roaring of the motor, I thought I could hear someone yelling. I couldn't quite make it out, so I focused hard on the sound. Finally, I could hear it clearly.

"Bobby!"

Someone was calling out my name. They were coming to rescue me. I felt reassured. Overcome with exhaustion, I lay back down. Help was on the way.

I stayed there quietly for just a few minutes till I heard their boat pull up alongside of mine.

"Bobby… Bobby, are you okay?" It was Ashley.

She climbed on board and ran over and put her arms around me.

"Oh my God, Bobby, are you okay?" she cried. "You have blood on your… oh, and there is vomit everywhere. What in the hell happened? I was so worried about you. How did you get out of that storm? I can't believe you made it."

"I lost my sail," I whispered.

Ashley shook her head as she brushed the hair out of my face.

"You are lucky that is all you lost."

"It's okay, Ash," I said. "I had Fred to help me get through it. He led the way, and I followed him, and here we are, safe and sound."

"Who's Fred?" Ashley said. She looked very puzzled.

I told her to tap the side of the boat and call him.

"Don't be silly, Bobby," Ashley said. "We need to get you to a doctor. I think you might have hit your head a little too hard."

"Seriously, Ash," I replied, and knocked on the deck floor. "Fred," I called out.

Suddenly there was a big splash. Ashley looked around in disbelief.

"What did I tell you?" I said.

Ashley couldn't believe her eyes. "Holy shit!" she yelled. "Fred is a dolphin? Have you been training dolphins in your spare time?"

I giggled. "Not really," I said, "I think that he has been training me. He is my best friend out here and he has been taking very good care of me."

Ashley watched Fred as he danced around in the water.

"I can't believe it," she said. "Incredible. It's very nice to meet you, Fred."

Fred was so pleased with himself that he dove down again. Seconds later, he came flying up into the air, flipping and turning, and then he splashed down right in front of Ashley, showering her from head to toe.

Ashley screamed, and I started to laugh.

"I already had my shower today, Fred; but hey, thanks anyway."

Fred let out his joyful sounds of laughter. He was such a character, it was like he understood everything anyone said to him.

Ashley turned and gave me a look. "Okay, that's enough fooling around," she said. "We need to get you to shore. Where's your first aid kit, so I can try to clean you up a bit?"

"No clue, Ash," I replied. "I haven't been in the galley since the storm hit. I woke up here just a little while ago. I got knocked unconscious. I don't even know how long I was out. I'm sure that everything is all over the place down there. Go ahead and take a look."

"Is there anything I can do to help?" someone called out from the other boat.

"It's okay," Ashley responded. "I've got this. Just stay put; we will need a tow."

Ashley disappeared below deck. I closed my eyes for a moment and wondered how I got out of the way of the storm with no sail and being down for the count. I remembered my mom and had a feeling that maybe she had a lot to do with it. It sounded silly, but the thought comforted me.

Ashley came back up on deck.

"It's actually not too bad down below. There are a few things scattered around here and there, and there's some water, but not too much. It could have been a lot worse. Oh, and I found your kit and your backpack. I hope your laptop didn't get wet."

"The pack is supposed to be waterproof; I hope I didn't lose all my notes. I was making a lot of progress, you know; things are coming back to me," I said. "I need to keep it up a little longer. I will tell you all about it; I promise."

Ashley knelt next to me and a tear rolled down her cheek. She took my head in her hands.

"I was worried sick; I thought I had lost you. Do you really have to do this alone?" she cried.

Ashley opened the kit and looked through it. She found what she needed and started to temporarily clean up my head wound.

I watched her as she did so and thought about how lucky I was. If it hadn't been for her, and all the help she gave me in trying to sort out my life, I probably wouldn't be around to talk about it. *Despite all the craziness and danger in my life, Ashley believes in me*, I thought, *and I am very grateful for that.*

When she was done, she bent down and kissed me on the forehead.

"We need to tow you to shore and have the boat checked over for damage, and you need to see Dr. Blake, and be checked for damage too," she winked. "I won't take no for an answer," she said.

I didn't protest. We said our goodbyes to Fred, and I told him that I would return soon.

The trip back to reality was a necessary evil. I was still very nervous about being in public though and hoped that nobody would recognize me. I had gotten really tired of being in the spotlight after my whole sordid life had gotten plastered all over the news headlines. I really didn't like being the center of attention and wanted to have some privacy.

"Nobody knows that I'm here, right?" I asked Ashley as we were being towed to shore.

"Quit being so paranoid; you are old news now," Ashley winked again and smiled. "Don't worry, I'll take good care of you."

I smiled back at her. "How did you find me?" I asked.

"Your phone, silly," she replied. "Oh, I almost forgot, I found it when I went looking for the first aid kit. It doesn't look damaged."

Ashley pulled it out of her back pocket and handed it to me.

"When you didn't call me back," she said, "I got in my car and headed for the coast. I followed your phone… technology… love it."

"Oh wonderful!" I replied. "Does that mean anyone can find me?"

Ashley shook her head and looked toward shore. We were almost there. She had called an ambulance and we could see the paramedics waiting for us on the dock.

When we arrived, I started to get nervous as I watched them come on board. They wanted to put me on a stretcher, but I was stubborn and insisted on walking. Ashley took me by the arm and we followed the paramedics to the ambulance. I found it strange to be on solid ground. One of the technicians did an examination of my head wound, cleaned and dressed it, and then checked for other injuries. He gave me the okay to go home, but with a promise to see my doctor as soon as possible.

While I was being treated, Ashley removed my personal belongings and my laptop from the boat and went to the marina office to explain the situation. She came back for me and helped me to the car.

Ashley had driven the five-hour trip here to try to find me, and now she was too tired to drive back, so we decided to rent a room for the night. I barely made it to the hotel myself without starting to nod off. I was really exhausted from my adventure. I dragged myself out of the car and into the room. Just as I was about to flop myself onto the bed, I got intercepted.

"I don't think so," Ashley said. "You need to clean up first."

I didn't protest; I knew Ashley was right. I made my way to the bathroom and looked in the mirror. A dirty drowned rat is what I saw looking back at me.

"Oh my," I said. "I guess it's a good thing we didn't take that ride home."

I turned to Ashley and we both started to laugh.

Chapter 43

It was morning and I didn't even remember my head hitting the pillow. I had a very good night's sleep. No nightmares, no flashbacks, nothing… it was a total blank. I woke refreshed and ready to make the trip home. Ashley, not so much. She had worried so much about me and it still weighed heavily on her mind. We loaded the car, grabbed a quick breakfast, and then we hit the road. I was still nervous about being in public, but Ashley reassured me that everything was going to be okay. We were going home, to our beautiful country estate, nestled in the mountains, with nobody around.

We had bought the place about six months earlier, a few months after Dr. Blake had given us the news that he was moving back home to Charlotte, North Carolina to be closer to his family. He had already gotten hired by the hospital there. I didn't really want to lose him as a doctor, and we had become more than that. With everything that happened, we had become very close, more like friends.

After the case got blown open, both Ashley and I thought it might be a good idea to move away and start a new life together somewhere else. Dr. Blake told us about his home town and it piqued our interest. We went to visit him a couple of weeks after he moved, and sure enough, we fell in love with the area. We looked around a bit, and found our beautiful little country house on a riverbank in the mountains. The neighbors were few and far between. It was perfect.

Not too long after that, I decided to buy a sailboat to have some time alone to rest and enjoy my new life, and at the same time try to put the missing pieces of my previous life back in place. Parts of it were still a mystery to me. I needed to do a lot more work on it. Ashley was against the idea at first, but she understood how important this was to me. She helped me choose the perfect sailboat and we even took the sailing and diving lessons together. We became inseparable.

When the time came that I was ready to set sail, it was a very difficult day for both of us. I got so used to having Ashley around, day in and day out, that I wasn't even sure about my decision anymore. I didn't know how I was going to deal with being alone. Ashley couldn't come with me anyway, because she was opening a clinic in a little town close by and was starting the following week. It was probably a good thing, though, because I had originally planned to do this alone and I needed to follow it through. I wanted to do as much writing as possible, and with someone else around, it would be more difficult to concentrate.

"Are you okay, Bobby?" Ashley asked.

I was so deep in thought that I barely heard her.

"I'm sorry; I was on another planet. Actually, I am a little nervous. It feels weird to be going home. I feel like I am not finished what I set out to do. I will need to go back."

Ashley turned and looked at me.

"Don't get me wrong, Ash," I said. "I am really grateful that you came and rescued me; you know that, right?"

"I understand that you need to do this, Bobby, it's just that I miss you so much, and I worry about you out there all alone. You were very lucky this time, you know; you could have been swallowed up by that storm."

"What are you talking about?" I replied. "I had Fred on my side."

Ashley gave me that look again.

"Just kidding, Ash. I know; you're right."

"So, tell me about Fred," she said, "and who names a dolphin Fred?"

We both laughed, then I started to tell her the story.

"I don't know what to say; he showed up a couple of days after I set sail. There were quite a few of them actually, but he stood out from the pod. He wanted all the attention. He performed spectacular acrobatic shows for me. I was amazed at how talented he was. The following day, he was still there, along with his friends, and I decided to join them. I put on my diving gear, jumped in, and we got acquainted. It was love at first sight."

I paused and glanced over at Ashley, who had a big smile on her face. She was very beautiful.

"Don't stop now;" she said, "I want to hear more about this love affair."

I giggled. "Love affair? Very funny. Well, I was a little nervous at first about jumping into the water with them, but I soon got very comfortable with my new friends. Fred was always by my side. He loved to dance with me. I would hang onto his fin and he would spin and flip me all around. That's where I got the name Fred, Fred Astaire. Other dolphins came and went but he was always there, taking me on some wonderful diving adventures."

"Wow," Ashley said. "That's amazing. I knew that dolphins were friendly, but to stick around every day to spend time with you, well, that's incredible. I don't know what to make of that."

I threw my arms in the air.

"I don't either," I said, "but I was very happy to have him around. Seriously, he is the one that led me out of that storm. I don't know how he did it, but he did, and I am still around to talk about it. I will miss him, though; I hope he finds me again when I go back."

"Wow, I have chills, Bobby. You have a guardian angel."

I reached over, took her by the hand, and lay my head back on the seat.

"And I thought I was crazy," I said, "but I was thinking the same thing."

Chapter 44

I heard a drumming sound in the distance, no... not sure what it was, it was too steady to be drums. It was very faint at first, but it was getting louder. I was very drowsy and not sure if I was dreaming or not. Still getting louder. I was feeling nervous and claustrophobic. I was starting to gasp for air; I wanted to scream. At this point, I felt like my eardrums were going to explode. It sounded like a jackhammer pounding inside my head. I could hardly stand it. I opened my eyes suddenly. I didn't know where I was, and I couldn't move. I started to scream. The noise stopped and whatever I was laying on started to move.

"Miss Hansen, are you okay?" I felt someone touch my leg.

"Miss Hansen?"

I slowly moved out of the tunnel I was lying in.

"Oh man, I'm sorry; I must have dozed off. When I woke up, I didn't know where in the hell I was; forgive me."

"It's okay, Miss Hansen; we were pretty well done here, anyway. I'll have the orderly take you back to your room. He'll bring you back again later this afternoon for just one more test. I'll see you then."

More tests… always more tests. I guess that all that time I spend locked inside of myself had a lot of people worried. The good doctor says that my body must have decided all on its own to shut down so I could heal, I thought. So far everything seemed to be normal; well, as normal as it could be after an accident like mine.

Off to my room we went, with the guard leading the way. He took his place outside my door. The investigation was still ongoing. I hadn't seen Detective Collins in a few days. He came to see me after I came back to reality. He had some question that he had never gotten to ask me.

They were questions about David, of course. Detective Collins had been to the diner and shown David's picture around. He found out from the staff that David had often come in with a friend. Detective Collins asked me about that, but I couldn't for the life of me remember his name, or if David had even introduced him to me. He asked other questions too, but I wasn't much help there either. All I remembered from those encounters was how nervous David made me feel, and Carla too, and how we got away from him as fast as we could.

The guard opened the door once again and announced that Detective Collins was here. I waved him in.

"Speak of the devil," I said. "I was just thinking about you."

"I'm sorry to disturb you, but this can't wait. I came by earlier and the nurse told me you were gone for an MRI. Is everything okay?"

"I think so, but they are just trying to figure out why I slipped into a coma."

"I tried to reach the doctor, but he is not available. Is there anyone you can call, like Miss White, maybe? Is she working today? I have something to say that might be a little disturbing and I prefer that someone was here with you."

"I don't like the sound of that. You are starting to worry me."

"Actually, if she is here, I would like to inform her too."

I dialed her extension number and she answered right away.

"Carla," I said, "Detective Collins is here, and he would like to talk to both of us."

She paused for a moment and I heard her talk to someone. She came back on and said that she would be down in five minutes.

I told the detective, and he continued to shuffle through his papers. I couldn't imagine what it was that he needed from Carla and me.

Of course, my mind at this point started to dream up all kinds of scenarios. I tried not to think, to turn it off, but all those crazy ideas were…

"Carla, thank goodness you are here."

She had just walked through the door. The suspense was killing me.

"Easy there, Looney Tunes. What's up, Detective? I can't stay long; I have a patient coming out of the OR soon and I need to be there."

"This won't take long at all," he said. He continued, "Do you remember, Miss Hansen, last time I was here, and I asked you about David's friend, the one you saw with him in the diner?"

"Yes, I told you that I didn't remember his name."

"Well, we managed to spot him, and David actually, on a video surveillance camera in front of a bank on the morning that you said you saw them together. The cam got a clear shot of David's friend. Fortunately for us, he didn't cover his tracks as well as David."

"So, you found him?"

"Well, I put his photo in the system to see what it would come up with. We got lucky and even had an address to go with it."

"Did you go see him? Did he tell you where David is? Did you find him?"

"Hold on; you are moving a little too fast. Let me finish."

Carla took me by the hand. She looked very anxious too.

"Okay, go on," she said.

"Well, we went to his apartment. We knocked on the door and identified ourselves, and nobody answered. We tried to turn the door handle and it was unlocked. We went in, still calling out to him, and still no response. Nothing was disturbed, so we figured that nobody was home. We searched the rest of the apartment and ended up in the bedroom. It looked like there was someone in bed. Again, we called his name and then pulled the blankets back."

"I don't understand," I said. I was getting a little freaked out.

"He was lying there as if he was asleep. It looked like he had been suffocated to death. There didn't seem to be any sign of struggle."

"He's dead? You're kidding! Things just keep getting better, don't they!"

"Just to be sure it is him that you saw with David, I would like you, if you could, to look at this picture."

I felt a lump in my throat. I glanced at Carla, she nodded, and then we looked at it. It was definitely him. He really did look like he was sleeping. A tear slid out of the corner of my eye.

"Who is he?" I asked.

"His name was Frank Johnson. We are still trying to find out how David and he were connected. There are old pictures in his apartment of the two of them together, and they look much younger."

"Who do you think did this?" I paused. "It's David, I'm sure of it, and he'll be coming after me next!"

"We don't know what happened there. We are still investigating. Judging by the pictures I saw, though, they looked very close."

"I know it's him; I can feel it! What's going to happen to me?"

"Listen, it's a lot to ask, but please don't get all worked up about this. I will take good care of you. You have never been without a guard, not even when you were in a coma. This case is still ongoing, and I won't rest till I bring him to justice. You have my word."

"Bobby, you know we are all looking out for you. He's right; there has always been a guard, and they are good… even I have trouble getting in sometimes." Carla smiled and squeezed my hand.

"Well, I need to get out of here," Detective Collins said. "I will go back to that apartment and see if they have found anything else, that I can work with. You might want to let your friend Dr. Murphy know what is going on. He keeps calling me to see how I am doing with the investigation. He is very persistent. He's really looking out for you. You are a lucky girl."

"Lucky, my ass!" Carla put her hand over her mouth. "Did I say that aloud?" She was slightly embarrassed. "Oh shit, my patient! Sorry, folks, but I need to get back to work too."

She gave me a hug and off she went.

"Did I miss something?" Detective Collins had this strange look on his face.

"It seems that lately, even before I came out of the coma, Tyler has been acting strangely. I haven't even seen him since I came to. Carla told me that nobody knows where he is half of the time, and he disappears for days on end and doesn't tell anyone how he can be reached. He is not getting along with anyone who is trying to help me with my recovery. While I was still in the coma, but semi-conscious, I heard them arguing. I'm sure that he slapped Carla across the face. I don't think I want to see him right now, anyway. Carla is my best friend and I won't put up with anyone who hurts her."

"Oh yes, my bad, where was my head, the guard did tell me there was an incident, but I didn't know how serious it was. I'll call him today and try to find out what's going on. Maybe he will open up to me. In the meantime, concentrate on getting well. I'll keep you posted."

Chapter 45

It was a beautiful sunny day, and Dancer and I were out for a morning ride. The snow was almost all gone, except for a few patches here and there. Dancer was feeling a little frisky after a long winter cooped up inside the barn. It was going to be good for him, and me, to get out for some fresh air and exercise.

School was very tough this year for some reason. As my fellow students got older, they became even more hateful toward me, being the outsider and a foster child who didn't fit in. It made my life very difficult. Even the teachers were still so narrow-minded that they could not accept this outsider being in their classroom. I was miserable. I felt so alone. Last fall, I had told Tyler, my only friend in the world, that I couldn't see him anymore. I couldn't take the risk that old Harold would hold true to the threats he made. I cared a lot for Tyler, but I didn't want him to get hurt, and knowing what Harold was capable of, I didn't want to take any chances.

The forest was peaceful; there was hardly any wind to speak of. I stopped at the riverbank so Dancer could take a drink. My log was still coated with snow and had icicles dripping off it into the river. I stood still and didn't move. It was so quiet, a kind of quiet that you wish would last forever, with no yelling and no fighting. I looked around me and there was nothing but nature's beauty and me and my friend Dancer who was really enjoying the fresh spring water. Times like these I cherished immensely. It was the part of my life that gave me the most peace.

Dancer pulled his head up and whinnied. He had very keen senses; he could hear something. I went over to him and grabbed his reins. I still didn't know what the commotion was. I listened hard and looked around, but I didn't hear anything. I decided that maybe it was time to head back, though I didn't really want to leave this place.

I put my foot in the stirrup, and was just about to mount, when I heard something in the distance.

"Whoa, Dancer!" I said. "Whoa!"

He got very excited and I had to pull on the reins to quiet him down.

"Take it easy, boy, whoa!" I patted his forehead; that always seemed to calm him down.

The sound was getting a bit louder. It was coming from the Murphy farm. As it got closer, I could hear the sound of a motorcycle, and I knew right away that it was Tyler. I needed to get out of there and fast. I didn't want to have to confront him again. I missed him so much, but I had to keep my distance from him for his own safety. I jumped into the saddle and squeezed my heels into Dancer's sides, and off we went, trotting at first but then into a full gallop. I loved when Dancer let himself loose, and so did he. It was such a feeling of freedom; I couldn't get enough of it.

It wasn't long though before the motorcycle was on our tail, and I decided that we had better stop and see what he wanted.

I pulled down on the reins and brought Dancer to a halt. Tyler continued past us, and then he turned around. He came back toward us, and went past us again, and then turned around again. He kept doing this and Dancer was getting very excited. I had trouble holding onto him.

As Tyler came close to me again, I yelled, "Stop that; you're scaring Dancer!"

He kept going and didn't listen to me at all. I couldn't understand what was happening. I couldn't hang on to Dancer anymore; he was frantic. I decided that the best thing to do was to dismount and let him go. I didn't want him to get hurt, or myself. He never liked that motorcycle. I let go of the reins and off he went, at a full gallop.

Suddenly, I felt very alone. I needed to deal with Tyler, who seemed to be totally out of his mind. What in the hell was he thinking? I was just trying to protect him, and now he was trying to scare the hell out of me.

As he came around for another pass, I yelled, "Tyler! Stop!"

He eased up on the gas, turned around slowly, and came back toward me. He came to a stop about twenty feet in front of me and revved the motor.

I was scared and confused. I was alone out here, on foot, and I was going to have to deal with this. I stood my ground, put my hands on my hips, and stared him down.

He started to inch his way forward, without taking his eyes off me. I held my own; I didn't move. What else was I supposed to do? I couldn't outrun him and his damned bike.

"Tyler!" I yelled. "Could you please stop? What in the hell are you doing?"

"Am I scaring you, Robbie? Do I scare you as much as your old man does?"

"Stop it, Tyler! Yes, you are scaring me. Why are you doing this? I told you that I couldn't see you anymore. I meant it!"

"I don't believe you! You can't love him more than you love me. It isn't possible. He is an old, ugly rapist bastard. All he has ever done to you is hurt you. You have always come crying to me, whenever he has beaten or raped you. I love you, and I want you all to myself. I can take you away from him. You are mine, damn it! Don't you understand? I won't ever let you go!"

"Tyler stop, that is nonsense. I do not love him. Yes, he has been abusing me, ever since I was placed in their care, but I have nowhere else to go. He will hurt anyone who gets close to me. He threatens me with that all the time. There is nothing I can do. He will kill you; he told me so. He shot at you once already; he will do it again."

"I will kill him first. You are mine and there is nothing he can do about it."

"Please stop this; you are out of control. I don't like your tone. He thinks he owns me because I live under his roof. That won't be forever. As soon as I can legally get out of there, I will. But you don't own me either. I am nobody's possession. Please don't speak to me like that. I can do whatever I want. Once I leave this place, nobody will ever force me to do anything I don't want to do, again."

He revved his motor very loudly.

"I always get what I want, Robbie, and what I want is you. You will see he is a dead man, and when that happens, I am coming back for you. You will thank me in the end. I will give you everything you want, but you will be mine, forever."

My eyes filled, and I could barely see him standing there in front of me. I couldn't believe what I was hearing; it couldn't be true. Tyler was always there for me; I loved him. Why was this happening?

I wiped the tears from my eyes and stood there, paralyzed. I couldn't move; I was very much in shock. He got back on his bike, turned it around, and I watched as he sped away.

I came to my senses and decided to turn back and head home. I was very rattled, and I wished that Dancer hadn't gotten spooked. I looked around and called out his name. Just as I did, I heard that motorcycle again. I turned and looked and saw him heading straight for me.

I wanted to run, but there was no use. I stood there and watched him till he came to a stop.

He got off and came and stood in front of me. I could smell liquor on his breath and knew that he was wasted. His eyes were watery as if he had been crying. I knew where this was going, and I really didn't want to be there.

"Robbie, my love, I am so sorry. You know I love you, and I would do anything for you. You can't just stop seeing me. I can't deal well, being without you. I know you are worried about what that bastard will do, but you shouldn't be. I'll take care of him; I promise. Give me a little time to figure things out and I will put an end to his hold on you. He will never hurt you again."

I just stood there, stunned. What in the hell was he thinking?

"Stop this nonsense, Tyler. You are talking crazy. I have about one year left before I can leave this hellhole; I need to just stay quiet and try not to get into too much trouble with him. One more year, and I will be free."

He grabbed me by the arms. "Robbie, I am not going to lose you. You will come with me and we will start our life together. You will see; it will be great. It'll be just you and me. I will take care of you."

"But Tyler, I don't want to be taken care of. I want to be my own person and make my own decisions. I want to…"

He grabbed me by the head, pulled my face close to his, and started kissing me. I tried to push him away.

"Stop it!" I yelled, freeing myself a bit from his hold.

He continued to try to kiss me and I kept pulling away.

"Stop pushing me away, Robbie; you know you like it. Maybe you like it a little rougher, is that it? Like that bastard does, you know, beat you first and rape you later, when you are too tired and sore to fight back. Maybe that's the trick."

He grabbed me by my ponytail and pulled down hard on it, exposing my neck. He started kissing it. I smacked him on the side of the head. He let go.

"Wow, aren't you the feisty one? I can see how this turns him on."

"Stop it, Tyler; you are drunk. Don't do this; it isn't funny!"

He grabbed me by the front of my jacket and pulled me in close again. He forced his lips to mine. I tried to turn my head, but he had such a tight hold on it. I kept pushing on his shoulders to get him away from me, but he was too strong. As a last resort, I kicked him in the groin. He backed away from me with a painful groan, and then I saw the anger in his eyes. He raised his fist, and with all his strength he plowed it into my face. I heard the crush as I flew backward and landed on the ground. In seconds, he was on top of me. I tried to get out from under him, but I couldn't; I didn't have the strength.

"Is this how he does it to you, baby? Come on, I've seen the cuts and bruises. You come and cry to me, and then you go back for more."

"Please, Tyler, it doesn't have to be this way! I thought you were my friend. I care about you; I do!"

"I love you, and I don't want to be just a friend. We had plans and we will keep them, whether you like it or not."

I managed to push him off, but he rolled right back on top.

"Come on, baby; you know you like it."

He put his hand around my throat. I could hardly breathe.

I started to struggle for air. My hand touched something on the ground next to me, a branch, no, a rock, I wasn't sure. I tried to focus and managed to grab hold of it; it was a rock. I mustered up all the strength I had left and hit him on the side of the head with it. He keeled over sideways, and I made my getaway. I didn't look back; I just kept running. As I was about to reach the property line fence, I heard him; he had caught up with me. He was right on my tail. I started to scream, and he plowed into me. I went flying into the fence, head first. The side of my neck slid across one of the barbed wires. The pain was excruciating. I put my hand to my neck; there was so much blood. I came to my senses and looked back at Tyler, who was just standing there looking at me.

"I'm so sorry, Robbie," he said. "I didn't mean for that to happen."

He started to come toward me… and I started to scream.

Chapter 46

"Good morning, Bobby," Dr. Carter said as she walked into the room.

I wiped the tears from my face. She reached over and handed me the box of tissues.

"Good morning," I replied, through my tears.

"What's going on, Bobby?" she asked.

"I don't know, I mean, I'm just tired of all of this. My mind is mush. I don't know what's real and what's not anymore. There is so much craziness. I would really like it to stop."

"What happened?"

"I had a bad dream."

"Oh no, I'm so sorry."

"It's times like these I really miss Carla. I know she will stop in to see me before going upstairs to the pediatric ward, but it was so nice having her next door to my apartment. She would always come and rescue me from my dreams. She knew exactly what to do and say to make me feel better."

"She's a great friend. Was your dream that bad?"

"Yes, well, not really; it was more confusing, than anything else. I'm so mixed up. I don't know who my friends are anymore. I don't even know who I can trust."

"You are talking about Tyler, right? Did you dream about him?"

"Yes. That's crazy, right? I haven't even known him for very long, yet I'm having these crazy dreams about him, and they make no sense at all. They scare me. In these dreams, we are both very young. Sometimes we are madly in love with each other and then sometimes, well... What in the hell is happening to me?"

"I don't know, Bobby, but you need to talk about this. It is nice that Carla has been there for you to console you when you needed it. You are lucky to have her. This is serious, though, and your past seems to be the key to the problems that you are having now. I am here for you; you know that, right? We have talked a bit about what is going on now, but I wish you would talk to me about your past, about these dreams that you've been having. I can help you sort them out. You can trust me, Bobby."

Tears started rolling down my face, uncontrollably.

"I'm so sorry, Bobby; I didn't mean to get you going like this."

She grabbed some tissues and gently wiped the tears from my face.

"I don't know why my mom had to die and leave me in all this mess. I miss her so much."

"Can you tell me about her?" Dr. Carter asked. "Do you remember your mother?"

I hesitated and tried to gather my thoughts. I must have smiled, because Dr. Carter smiled back at me.

"I didn't until the accident," I said. "I dreamed, well, I don't even know what to call it. Was it a memory? Was it a dream? I can't even tell the difference anymore, but it was beautiful."

"Well, it doesn't sound like a nightmare; you are smiling. Do you feel like telling me more about it?" She gazed at me and said, "You know, you are very beautiful when you smile."

"Thanks, Dr. Carter, that's sweet. I still feel like I'm a mess though."

She started to say something, and I cut her off.

"I know, I know, I'm just kidding. I guess I just don't know how to take a compliment. I was always an outcast. It's hard to get past that."

She never took her eyes off me as I started to tell her about my dream. That beautiful Christmas morning where I watched myself as a child and my mom spend the morning together, in front of a big beautiful Christmas tree, unwrapping presents. I told her how real it seemed, and how I could almost feel the love radiating from them.

"Wow, I have goosebumps," she said. "It sounds like a beautiful memory to me."

"It was a memory, though, because I have the locket to prove it."

I reached up to my neck to show it to her, but it wasn't there.

"Oh my God, my locket; it's gone."

I started rummaging around in my bed while Dr. Carter tried to calm me down.

"Bobby, I've seen it on you, but we've just never talked about it. I figured that it was a present from Carla or something."

"It's all I've got from my mom," I cried. "I can't lose it."

Dr. Carter started searching the room.

"I'll be right back," she said. "Just stay calm."

She left the room. I couldn't imagine what might have happened to it. I couldn't bear to lose it.

Moments later, she came back in with the nurse following behind her.

"I'm so sorry, Bobby," the nurse said. "I put it in the back of this drawer for safe-keeping. I know how important it is to you. It had to be removed before having the MRI yesterday, and then, after that, the detective came to see you, and then, well, I guess I got too busy and forgot to get it back to you."

She reached into the drawer and pulled out a tissue.

"I wrapped it in here so it wouldn't get tangled."

I watched her as she pulled it out.

"What a relief," I said. "Funny, I don't remember anything about that."

"Well, it was really early in the morning and you were a little groggy. Also, you had been sedated so you wouldn't move during the MRI. Would you like me to put it back on you?"

"Yes please," I said. "No wait, it's okay. I'll take care of it, thanks."

She handed it to me, then said goodbye and headed toward the door. Dr. Carter thanked her.

"Well, that's one mystery solved," she said and smiled.

"This is the locket that I saw my mom give me in that dream. They gave it back to me when I was released from prison. It was the only possession I had. There were no pictures in it and the chain was broken. I had no clue where it came from. I'm not quite sure why I kept it, but I'm glad I did. Tyler found it when we were cleaning up my apartment after it got vandalized."

"May I?" Dr. Carter said as she reached out her hand.

I gave it to her… and she examined it.

"It's very beautiful."

"Actually," I said, "you could do me a favor. You could open it up and remove the picture."

Dr. Carter looked inside and then glanced back at me.

"It's a picture of you and Tyler?"

"Yes, he put it there and had the chain repaired."

"You want me to remove it?"

"Yes. He does not belong in that heart with me. Not after the stupid things he's been doing lately. I am not his wife, and I will never be his wife, ever."

"Okay, I think I missed something somewhere along the way. What are you talking about?"

"I don't know; he seems very possessive when it comes to me."

"That's an understatement," she said and winked.

"Seriously, I feel like he thinks he owns me, and then, there are my dreams."

"What happens in your dreams, Bobby?"

I watched her as she fiddled with the locket.

"When the dreams first started, I only saw a young couple who were very much in love. I never seemed to be close enough to see who they were, just that they looked so happy. Oh, and it was very confusing, because they were in my safe place."

"Your safe place, the one Carla told me about?"

"Yes. They were there. Sometimes on my log I used to lay on, and sometimes I would see them running into a lake together. I was upset that they had invaded my place, but they looked so happy. So, I was happy for them."

"When did you realize who they were?"

"In another dream, where I got a close look at them."

"What did you think about that?"

"Well, Tyler and I were getting really friendly at that point, and I just figured that I was dreaming about us being in a beautiful relationship. At the time I didn't know that it wasn't going to last."

"What happened, Bobby?"

"As the dreams progressed, he became very possessive. Like the drunk old man, he didn't want me to be with anyone else, but him."

"What?"

"Oh, I'm going on and on, sorry. My nightmares started with an old drunk…"

We heard a knock on the door.

"May I interrupt. The guard told me that you were in here, Dr. Carter, but I really don't have a lot of time."

"It's okay, Dr. Blake; I can come back later."

"That won't be necessary; I will only take a minute. Is that okay with you, Bobby?"

"It's fine with me. What's up, Doc?" I looked up at him and burst out laughing.

Dr. Carter started to giggle too.

"You're a real comedian, aren't you?" he said with a smile. "Glad to see you have been able to keep that sense of humor of yours through all of this. It's probably what keeps you going."

"Maybe I'm just crazy… period."

"Crazy in a good way," Dr. Carter added. "I think I will leave you two alone. I have a few things I need to take care of, but I'll be back, and we will continue the conversation."

She smiled, nodded at Dr. Blake, and left the room.

"It's nice to see the two of you hitting it off. Is she able to help you with your memories?"

"She's great," I said. "She is easy to talk to and I feel very comfortable with her."

"I'm glad to hear that. I am a little worried, though."

"Is it the test results? Is something wrong?"

"No, nothing like that; everything came back normal. The nurses are telling me, actually even the guard, that you are not getting much sleep, that you wake up screaming."

As the words left his mouth, I yawned hugely.

"That's what I'm talking about. I am going to give you something to help you sleep, nothing too strong, but something to make you relax. You will start taking them tonight and we'll see how that goes. In the meantime…"

I yawned again.

"I guess that's my cue; I'll stop in later."

I closed my eyes and started to fade off.

Chapter 47

I heard the door open. I looked over and it was Dr. Blake.
"Back already?" I said. "Did you forget something?"
He didn't say anything and just walked over to my closet. Strange… he was carrying a suitcase.
"What are you doing, Doc?" I watched as he started packing my things. "Dr. Blake, please answer me."

He slowly turned around… I froze. It was Tyler, and he had evil written all over his face.

"Tyler, no…"

He turned and walked toward me. I was terrified and was about to scream, when he reached over and put his hand over my mouth.

"You can't fight me; you are not strong enough. Nobody is. They will not come between us; I will kill them all."

His eyes were bloodshot, and they stared me down. I needed to do something; I could hardly breathe. I did the only thing I could think of and bit him as hard as I could. He released me and I started to scream.

Chapter 48

"Bobby, Bobby… wake up," Ashley said. "You are having a bad dream."

I woke with a gasp, trying hard to catch my breath. I was disoriented, and my heart nearly pounded out of my chest.

"It's okay, Bobby; I'm here. Nobody is going to hurt you," Ashley said, trying to comfort me.

I looked around wildly in fear that Tyler might still be there. Ashley tried desperately to calm me down. She put her arms around me and spoke gently.

"Bobby, everything is okay. Try to calm down. Take a good look around you; we are still in the car. Breathe, Bobby, come on, I've got you, everything is going to be alright."

I took a deep breath and tried to relax. It felt soothing to be wrapped in Ashley's arms.

"You fell asleep, honey, are you okay? Are the nightmares still this severe?" she asked.

"Yes, I mean no, I mean, they come, and they go."

I was still a little confused.

"A lot of things are coming back to me," I said. "They are getting easier though, well, most of the time. This was a bad one. I don't understand some of my dreams, like this one. It doesn't seem real. It doesn't make sense to me at all."

"It was about Tyler?" Ashley said softly. "I thought I heard you mention his name."

I shook my head and snuggled up against her.

"Yes, you're right," I said, and a tear rolled down my cheek. "I really don't want to talk about it."

Ashley moved me over a bit and turned me around, so she could look in my eyes.

"Bobby," she said, "you need to get past him, and it won't happen if you keep pushing your memories of him away. You need to face this."

"I know I do!" I cried, "but it's just too crazy. I can't understand how I didn't recognize him! I let him into my life, all over again, without remembering what he had put me through. It was my own doing. He was very sympathetic to the problems I was having, and it seemed like he really wanted to help me. I really thought I was falling in love with him. Little did I know. How stupid am I?"

"You are not stupid, and I don't ever want to hear you say that again. You needed help and he skillfully worked his way back into your life. He fooled everyone, not only you; he was just that good. You did nothing wrong, and you can't keep blaming yourself. Come here."

She pulled me back into her arms, held me close, and stroked my hair. We stayed there in each other's arms until I stopped crying. I shifted a bit and turned to look at her again.

"Thanks, Ash," I said, "I don't know what I would have done without you. Despite the danger, you stayed by my side."

Ashley smiled back at me. "I wasn't going anywhere. You needed my help, and I chose to stay. I have no regrets."

My stomach growled, and we both laughed at the interruption.

"Come on, let's go inside. Your stomach has spoken," Ashley said. "I will see what I can put together for lunch. It's been a long drive, and I'm hungry too."

We got out of the car. With my mind still on Tyler and that dream, I reached up and touched the scar on the side of my neck.

"Bastard!" I said, then I caught up to Ashley.

We were halfway to the porch when I stopped and looked around me.

"Wow... look at this place. I forgot how beautiful it is. You have been taking really good care of it."

"Come on, slowpoke," Ashley said.

We prepared a beautiful lunch of leftover chicken stew and salad. Ashley opened a bottle of wine, and then we went out on the porch and talked about everything I had missed while I was away.

"Remember last time we talked, and I told you about Thomas?" Ashley asked.

"Oh yes, damn, I almost forgot about that," I replied. "How is he?"

Ashley explained that he had had a mild heart attack, and that he was okay, but he needed to be very careful. She also told me that Thomas had a sister, and he had moved in with her. His sister had recently lost her husband and was now living alone, and so she offered to take him in. Thomas was always very close to her and seemed happy about that.

"Thomas calls every once in a while to check up on you," she said. "He is a very nice man. You were lucky to meet him."

"Yes, I am very lucky," I replied. "He is so sweet. I will call him while I am home."

Ashley's phone rang, and she went into the house to answer it. I sat there quietly and enjoyed the view. Our porch looked out toward the mountains, and we could hear the beautiful sound of water trickling down the river that ran alongside our property.

Ashley came back out, sat down next to me, and took me by the hand.

"I have a surprise for you," she said.

I looked at her and smiled. "Ah, that's so sweet, you shouldn't have."

I sat there, waiting patiently for Ashley to speak up about it.

"So?" I said.

Ashley laughed.

"That was Dr. Blake," she said. "He knew that I was leaving yesterday to try to find you, and he called to see if we made it back okay. He is really looking forward to seeing you, so I invited him to supper. I hope that is okay with you."

"Are you kidding?" I replied. "Nothing would make me happier."

I gave Ashley a hug. It lingered longer than expected and felt wonderful. I realized at that moment how much I missed her.

We went back into the house and started a grocery list.

"I shouldn't be too long," Ashley said. "It's about a fifteen-minute drive to town, so I should be back in about an hour."

"No," I replied, "I mean, I'm coming with you."

"Really! I didn't think you wanted to be out in public."

"You're right, Ash; but I really don't feel like being alone either."

"Okay," Ashley said, "I will try to make it as painless as possible. I will have a few stops to make, though."

"I know, but as long as I'm with you, I should be okay. Where do we have to go?"

"I'll explain on the way. We'd better get a move on if we want to get back. Maybe I'll have time to do a quick drive by and show you where my new office is."

"Cool," I said, and off we went.

We drove for about ten minutes, and Ashley slowed in front of a small commercial building.

"There it is," she said, with a big smile on her face. "My new office."

I gazed out the window, then turned back to her.

"I'm so happy for you, Ash." I reached over and took her hand.

We continued on our way.

"So, what next?" I asked.

"Well, we need to go to the butcher shop, and get something to cook on the barbecue, then we'll stop at the fruit and vegetable stand. Oh, and if you don't mind, we can make one more stop at the Sweetie-Pie pastry shop.

"Mmm… dessert," I said, and licked my lips.

Ashley laughed. "I had a feeling that you wouldn't say no to that."

Ashley was very efficient. She knew exactly what she wanted and where to find it. It wasn't long before we were on our way home.

I sat there daydreaming for a bit. My mind started wandering into places I did not want it to go. I tried to suppress it.

"I'm sorry, honey," Ashley said. "I know this was hard on you; I tried to go as fast as I could."

She reached over and brushed my hair out of my face.

I was staring into the side view mirror. I was starting to get very nervous. Ashley reached down and took my hand.

"Are you okay, Bobby?"

I didn't answer. My eyes were glued to the side view mirror of the car, and I was expecting something to race up behind us at any moment.

"Bobby, honey, what's wrong?"

I took my eyes off the mirror, just for a moment, and looked at her.

"I don't know; I am just feeling really exposed right now, like someone is out there watching me. I know that I am not in danger anymore. Nobody knows me here. I'm just tired, I guess. I think that maybe the storm got the better of me."

"I can call Dr. Blake and cancel our dinner, if it's too much for you," Ashley replied. "We can do it another time."

"No, it's okay; I'm happy that he's coming over. I will try to take a nap when we get home."

Chapter 49

"Good morning, Bobby; sorry to have to wake you up. It's a big day today. We are removing your leg brace, and the doctor will be in early."

It was Nurse Bailey, or Helen, as she insisted that I call her now. We became very friendly during my stay at the hospital. She was always on the day shift, and that was when most of the action took place. When you are immobile, you depend on your nurse to take care of your every need — and that means everything. Seriously, after a while, you have no dignity left. She wiped and cleaned my ass more often than I choose to admit. You can't get any more personal than that.

She was very patient.

She'd always say, *"It's part of my job, taking care of you when you can't."*

I really appreciated all that she did for me.

"Oh my… they are taking it off?"

"Yes, the doctor will be in shortly to explain the process."

Suddenly I felt very nervous. I didn't know what to expect.

"Don't worry, Bobby; you know you are in very good hands."

Lou showed up to pay me an early morning visit. He was, as usual, very cheerful. I guess he knew what was going to happen today and he just wanted to come by and see if I was alright.

"I hear that it's a very big day for you," he said. "Are you okay?"

"I don't know; I'm a little scared. I have no clue what is going to happen yet. I guess I'll find out soon enough. The doctor is supposed to come and see me soon."

It was a very busy morning. The doctor came in, checked my vitals, wrote some notes in my file, explained the procedure, gave me a shot of I don't know what to keep me calm, I guess, and off I went, to the OR.

Chapter 50

I awoke with this kind of buzzing sound in my head. My eyelids were very heavy; I could see some light coming through them. I tried to force them open. I could feel someone holding my hand. I tried to speak, but nothing was happening.

"Bobby, are you awake?"

"Yes," I managed, just a whisper. I barely heard it myself.

"Bobby, it's Dr. Carter. It's okay; everything went well. You are out of surgery. Are you in any pain?"

My eyes came into focus, and I finally saw her smiling face. She was very beautiful.

"I don't know; I'm feeling a little groggy. Is my leg okay?"

"Well, as far as I can tell it's still there," she winked.

"Oh, so you're a comedian in your spare time," I whispered, and smiled back at her. "Maybe I'll race you down the hallway tomorrow."

Dr. Carter started to laugh.

"Seriously, I don't really know anything," she said, "just that there were no complications."

"That's good," I said.

"I was told that the doctor should be in soon to see you."

"Will you stay with me, Dr. Carter?"

She smiled and squeezed my hand.

I faded off…

* * * * *

"Bobby, it's Dr. Blake."

I opened my eyes. Sure enough, there he was. I was feeling so stoned.

"I need some water."

Dr. Carter was still there and started to sponge my lips with that nice, cool ice water.

I watched as the doctor wrote notes in my file.

"Is that all you ever do… write notes in people's files?"

"It's nice to see that you are back to your old self, Bobby. For your information, I was doing the surgery, and you were sleeping on the job. No worries, though; I didn't need your help. I was just fine on my own."

I loved that he had a great sense of humor. It made things much easier to deal with.

"So, how is my leg?"

"Everything looks good, but it will be hard to tell until you start to try to use it. The rest of the work will be up to you. There will be more therapy and hard work on your end. But hey, you've come this far; I'm sure you will make it okay."

Suddenly, there was a commotion outside my door.

"Excuse me a moment," he said.

He headed for the door and closed it behind him.

Moments later, Helen came in.

"Hi again. I hear everything went well. I need to check your vitals. Dr. Carter, can you stay?"

She did the usual temperature and blood pressure checks, and then she pulled out a syringe.

"Here we go again," I said.

"You need to stay calm, and this should help if you are feeling any pain, just for a couple of days. After that well, we will see. Training will be hard. You can do it, though; we have seen what you are capable of."

"What's going on out there?" I asked.

"Dr. Blake will be right back," she replied, making eye contact.

That was weird; she didn't really answer the question. I kept looking at the door waiting for him to come back in. Something was up; I could feel it. Helen gave me a shot to stay calm; well, it was not going to have enough time to work.

"Something is up, Helen. I know you too well; you are hiding something."

I no sooner got the words out of my mouth when Dr. Blake came back in, followed by Detective Collins.

I just stared; I didn't know what to think. *Stay calm*, I thought, *stay calm*.

Dr. Carter held my hand and stroked my hair. I was happy that she stayed with me.

Dr. Blake came to my bedside and spoke up first.

"Detective Collins has some questions for you, and I don't want you to get too excited. There is probably a logical explanation."

Logical explanation for what? I thought. *Don't get excited? Right...*

"Good afternoon, Miss Hansen. I know that you just got out of surgery and I didn't want to bother you, but I am trying to locate Miss White. She left me what seemed to be an urgent message last night and by the time I got it, I figured it was too late to call her."

"That's easy; she told me yesterday that she was working the early shift this morning. Her shift isn't over yet; she should still be up in the pediatric ward."

"But she isn't; that's the problem."

"What do you mean, she isn't? She told me she would be in early today."

"I went up there this morning. The other nurses said that she never showed up, and she didn't even call in."

"That's not possible; she wouldn't do that!"

Dr. Blake put his hand on my shoulder and said, "I made a call, Bobby. She didn't come in, and nobody has heard from her. They had to get someone last minute to take her place. Detective Collins needs your help to try to locate her."

Detective Collins pulled out his notebook and started with the questions.

"I know that you and Miss White are very close," he said. "Do you know her family too? Can I have their contact information?"

"She doesn't have any family left. It was just Carla and her mother, and her mother passed away not very long after we became friends."

"What about a boyfriend, other friends?"

"No, I don't think so. She's friends with a lot of people, but she doesn't really hang out with anyone that I know of. Of course, I have been stuck in here for a while, so I can't really be sure. She used to have a boyfriend, but he left her a while back. He was very abusive but I don't think she has heard from him in a long time; she would have said something, I am sure. What did she call you about? What was in her message?"

"She didn't really say, but she sounded really nervous, maybe scared, and she mentioned Tyler. She wanted to talk to me about him."

"You know that they have been fighting, right? Remember, I told you that I thought he had slapped her when they were arguing in my room? He has been acting very strangely. He was even making me nervous when I was lying in my coma and he was alone with me. He seemed confused, angry, and very agitated… you don't think… oh my God… this is not happening! Did you check her apartment?"

"Of course I did, Miss Hansen. That's why I'm here. I don't know where else to look! Something was odd, though: her door was closed but not locked. I looked inside and called her name, but nobody answered. I thought maybe she just forgot to lock it."

"She would never do that, and on top of it all, she is not at work! That means something is very wrong! I know it!" I practically yelled at the detective.

"Well, I think that this is quite enough for now, Bobby," Dr. Blake ordered. "You need to try to rest, and Detective, I'm going to have to ask you to leave. I don't think that Bobby can tell you any more than she already has."

"One more thing, please, Miss Hansen. I need to find Tyler to ask him if he knows anything about her whereabouts."

I told him quickly everything I knew about Tyler. Where he lived, his office, and his grandparents' farm. His parents, well, I had never met them. Dr. Blake was losing his patience and escorted the detective out of my room. "I'll come back later and check on you," he said as he closed the door behind him. Dr. Carter stayed with me for a while.

I was very worried about Carla. *She would never take off like that and not tell anyone, and missing work without calling in? Never!*

Dr. Carter tried to calm me down. All these crazy, scenarios were going through my mind. I didn't want to believe that Tyler would do anything to hurt Carla. It didn't seem possible. Yes, he had been acting really strangely lately, but was he crazy enough to harm her in any way?

"I'm really worried, Dr. Carter. Carla would never go somewhere without telling anyone. She's more responsible than that. Something is very wrong."

"I know, Bobby, but you need to let the detective do his job. There is nothing you can do."

"But Dr. Carter, she's my best friend, and my life is a mess, and I have unintentionally dragged her into it, and now, something has happened to her and it is probably my fault."

"Bobby, stop please. This is not good for you right now. You need to concentrate on your recovery. Everyone is working hard to try to solve this. Give them a chance."

"I know, Dr. Carter, but it is hard to just lay here and…"

"Bobby, listen to me. I will try to stay informed about everything that is going on, if you want me to, and I will keep you posted. Now, I have a favor to ask of you. I am here for you, and I feel like our relationship has become more than just doctor-patient. I enjoy your company and I want to stay around and help you get through all of this."

"I really enjoy your company too, Dr. Carter. You are the highlight of my day, but I don't know what I could possibly do for you right now."

"It's easy; you can stop calling me Dr. Carter. My name is Ashley."

"That's a beautiful name, Ashley. Thanks, I could really use a friend right now."

Tears started to roll down my cheeks and she took me in her arms. She told me to stay positive and that everything would work itself out. Still I cried.

Chapter 51

I heard a tap on the door, and then it opened. I wiped my tear-soaked eyes.

"Oh Bobby, honey, are you okay? Did you have a bad dream?"

"Oh Ash, remember when Detective Collins came to see me at the hospital, looking for Carla?"

I saw her eyes fill with tears. "Yes, I do. I still can't believe it myself."

She took me in her arms and asked, "Are you going to be alright? Come on, honey. Why don't you go in the washroom and freshen up, then we can go out on the porch and wait for Dr. Blake to arrive; supper is almost ready."

I cleaned up a bit, then joined her in the kitchen. She poured us each a glass of wine, and then off we went to the porch.

I sat down, took a deep breath, and looked around. It was so peaceful and beautiful out here.

I smiled and took her by the hand.

"Hey Ash… did I thank you for rescuing me yesterday?"

"Shush and drink your wine." She winked.

Off in the distance, I could see dust rising from the dirt road. I watched with anticipation as the car approached.

"Close your eyes, Bobby; I have a surprise for you."

"What are you talking about, you told me that you invited Dr. Blake for supper, wasn't that it?"

"No, there's something else. Close your eyes, please, and don't peek. I am going to meet him at the car."

I put my hands over my eyes but was trying to see between my fingers, and Ashley saw me.

"Come on, Bobby; promise you won't look?"

"Okay… okay, cross my heart."

I listened hard. First, I heard her footsteps as she headed toward the driveway, and then I heard the sound of the car coming to a stop.

I heard them talking but I couldn't make out what they were saying. Suddenly there was a rustling sound in the grass, and it seemed to be getting closer. Then there was a loud bark, and I recognized it right away.

"Maestro!" I yelled, and I opened my eyes just in time to see him jump up into the air and pounce on me.

I screamed with laughter as I fell backward onto the porch.

Ashley came running. "Oh no! Are you okay? Maestro, no! Sit!"

Maestro sat down alright, right on top of me. He kept licking me and nudging me to pet him.

"Okay boy… calm down. Let me up."

Ashley took hold of him. Dr. Blake was laughing at us. He reached out his hand and pulled me up.

"Aren't you a sight for sore eyes. You are looking very well."

I gave him a big hug. It was really great to see him again.

"What are you doing with Maestro? Where's Thomas?"

I knelt down and started rubbing Maestro around the neck. He still proudly wore that embroidered kerchief.

"I started telling you before that Thomas was living with his sister; well, it turns out she is very allergic to dogs, and they needed to find a new home for him."

"He is a sight dog. Shouldn't they find someone who needs one?"

"It would be too hard to retrain him, at his age, to take care of someone new, so he is your surprise. Thomas wanted you to have him. He knew that you would take good care of him. I hope you are happy, because I accepted him on your behalf."

"Are you kidding, Ash? Of course I am happy. I will gladly take care of him. He saved my life. I owe him; right, Maestro? You saved my life; I will gladly take care of you."

He barked in approval.

"Come on, boy." Ash went in the house to check on supper and brought Maestro in with her. I guess it was his supper time too.

Dr. Blake and I sat down. He saw the gash on the side on my head.

"Nice, what happened? Is that why you have an appointment with me tomorrow?"

"Well kind of," I replied. "Ashley thought it would be good to get a full check-up. Of course, the paramedics made me promise to see a doctor about it as soon as I got home. I'm fine, really. It happened during the storm; I fell back and bashed my head on something. I was knocked out for quite some time, not really sure how long. By the time I came to, the storm was over."

He listened attentively as I told him about my adventure. Like Ashley, he was amazed when I recounted how I managed to escape the storm with the help of my good buddy, Fred, who led me to safety. I told him about how we went scuba diving every morning, and danced and flew through the air together, and how he took me on amazing adventures. He sat there, mesmerized.

"That is an amazing story," he said. "I don't know, but I think that you've had too many bumps on the head." He winked.

Ashley came out the door with an extra glass of wine for Dr. Blake, and Maestro following at her heels.

"It's true; I met Fred when I found her. She called his name and he jumped into the air with a splash. I wouldn't have believed it myself."

"I'm only teasing; I believe you. Nothing surprises me when it comes to you." He winked again.

Maestro came and sat down next to me. I patted him and asked, "How long has he been here?"

"About a week; he is starting to get used to the place. The good doctor was dog-sitting while I went to search for you. I didn't want to leave him with someone he didn't know."

Maestro barked, and we all laughed.

Ashley had really outdone herself, and the meal was amazing. After supper, we had front row seats to an amazing sunset.

I told more stories about my time on the sailboat. Dr. Blake started to laugh, and we joined in, when the frogs from the riverbank started serenading us, almost drowning me out. We stopped talking and just listened and relaxed for a while.

The sky was clear, revealing the full moon and the gazillion stars that sparkled like diamonds. *Almost as peaceful as on the ocean,* I thought, *except I am sharing this view with two very special people and a very good friend.*

It was getting late, so we said our goodbyes until tomorrow. I watched as Dr. Blake drove down the road. Ashley went back into the house. With Maestro by my side, I lay down on the grass and looked up at the stars.

"The same stars I used to watch from my boat," I said to Maestro.

He barked.

I thought about Fred and smiled.

"I will be back soon, Fred, and I hope you will join me again," I whispered to myself.

Maestro was quiet as he lay down next to me. I scratched behind his ears, something he really seemed to enjoy. I was very happy to have him. I was going to have to call Thomas and thank him.

I was lost in my thoughts when I was suddenly distracted by a noise in the bushes. Maestro got up and started barking, and I grabbed onto him. "It's okay, boy," I said, and I sat up and looked around. It was hard to see anything with only the light from the moon. Maestro wouldn't stop barking. I could feel my chest start to tighten and that same feeling that I had had in the car earlier that day flooded over me again. I tried hard to shake it off.

Ashley heard the commotion and came outside. "You guys okay out there?" she yelled.

"We heard a noise in the bushes," I replied. "We're coming inside."

Ashley turned the yard light on.

"We are out in the wild here; there are animals that roam around at night. I'm sure that is all it was."

"I'm okay, Ash, honestly. I have Maestro to take care of me now." I bent over and gave him another rubdown. "You're such a good boy, aren't you?"

Chapter 52

It was early morning; I could see the sun coming up through my window. The nurse hadn't been in to see me yet. I sat up. I knew that I was starting physiotherapy this morning. I wasn't in the mood. I hadn't slept very well because I couldn't stop thinking about Carla. It had been a couple of days now, and no word. Where could she be? Where was Tyler? How was he mixed up in all this mess? I thought he was my friend. All these questions were making me dizzy. They were going around in my head, over and over again. It needed to stop; it was making me crazy.

"Carla, I need you," I whispered. "I love you."

The tears came; there was no controlling them.

I reached for the Kleenex box and accidently knocked the phone off the nightstand.

The door flew open and in came the guard, gun in hand.

He scared the crap out of me.

He ran through the room, checking everywhere.

"I'm sorry; I knocked the phone off the nightstand."

"Are you okay?" he asked.

"I just told you; I dropped the phone."

He picked it up and looked around the room again and headed back to the door.

"Okay…" I said out loud.

That was intense. He obviously had too much coffee.

Not long after, Helen came in. She looked upset. She went about her job, checking my vitals, and didn't say very much. I watched her. She barely made eye contact, and then she pulled out that syringe of hers.

"Helen, you don't look right; what's wrong? Why are you giving me that? Don't I have therapy this morning?"

"Sorry, but therapy has been canceled today. The doctor has asked me to give you this so you can relax."

Before I could protest, I felt a prick.

"But why? I am feeling fine, I think."

"He will be in to see you shortly!" Then, still without making eye contact, off she went, no bye, no see you later, no nothing. The door closed behind her.

Okay, if I wasn't nervous before, I was now. Something was up. Helen was usually very cheerful and always had something to joke around about.

I closed my eyes, trying to forget what had just happened. I thought about Carla, I thought about Tyler, what else was I supposed to do? Nobody would tell me what was going on.

I started to feel lightheaded. That was the only thing that felt light, though; the rest of me weighed a ton. I tried to force my eyes open. Even they were heavy. I didn't know what Helen gave me, but it was powerful stuff.

There was a knock at the door, and I watched as it opened very slowly. It was Dr. Blake. I managed a smile, I think, though I was not even very sure of that. He came to my bedside.

"How are you doing, Bobby? I am so sorry I had to do that. I need you to stay calm. Detective Collins is here to see you."

"I don't understand. I am so drowsy... Detective Collins?"

"Yes, he is here and wants to talk to you."

The door opened and I saw Ashley followed by the detective. They seemed to be moving very slowly.

Ashley finally made it to my side. She gave me a hug.

I looked up at her. She was saying something, and I realized that I was staring. Well, it seemed like I was, and for a very long time. Well, maybe not as long as I thought. She looked funny, well not a laughing funny, but just like umm… she was not well, or uncomfortable, that is what it was. Yes, she looked uncomfortable.

"What's wrong, Ashley? Geez, you're talking in slow motion. Are you okay?"

"Miss Hansen, I have some news I need to share with you."

"Could you stop with the Miss Hansen, Detective? We have known each other for quite a while now."

Ashley took me by the hand, "Bobby, this is serious. Try to stay focused."

"Okay, Bobby," he said, "It's about Miss White. I want to start off by saying…"

He sounded like he was giving a speech. *Oops,* I remembered, *Ashley said that I need to focus. Why am I talking to myself?*

"You were a big help to me the other day. I went back to Miss White's apartment, and things didn't look right. The door was still unlocked, and her keys and purse were left behind. There was no sign of her."

"I told you that she would never leave her door unlocked… So, where is she? This is taking so long. Come on, just find her and bring her back to me; I miss her so much."

I closed my eyes for a moment.

Detective Collins spoke again, "Is it okay if I continue, Dr. Blake?"

"Go ahead; she is just a little drowsy."

I opened my eyes again and said, "I can hear you."

"Good, I won't be too much longer. Do you remember the other day, when I asked you where I could find Tyler?"

"Umm, yes, I think so. Something about his job and his farm?"

"Yes, we followed up on the information you gave us. After lots of research, we found the farm."

"It's really nice; did you go to the lake? I used to go there all the time. Umm…" I hesitated for a moment, "I don't know, well, I'm not really sure right now… umm."

"Bobby, focus," Ashley said as she squeezed my hand.

"We searched the house. It looked like there might have been someone living there, but they were gone. I had a crew searching the ground. They went inside an old abandoned shed."

"Bobby," Dr. Blake leaned over and looked into my eyes. "Are you okay?"

I didn't answer. I was totally zoned out. I could see them talking, but it was like I knew exactly where they were going with this, even though I couldn't hear them. I was in no pain. I didn't like what was happening. I didn't want to slip away again. My eyes were getting blurry. I blinked a few times to try to clear them. I could feel a drop roll down the side of my face. I had to keep my emotions intact. I needed to speak. I felt like I was going to explode. It kept building up and building up; I just couldn't hold it in any longer.

"She's dead; is that what you are trying to tell me?" I whispered. I couldn't control it; the dams opened full blast. I wasn't even crying, really; it was just an uncontrollable flow of tears.

"I'm truly sorry, Bobby."

"Where did you find her?" My voice was steadier this time.

"We found her in one of the old sheds."

"Oh no." Suddenly I felt so alone. I stared into space for a moment and couldn't quite grasp what was happening.

"Poor Carla," I said hoarsely. "She was always there for me. She wouldn't hurt a fly. Why would someone do this to her? Somebody is after me, not her. I don't know what I have done to these people; I wish I could remember."

This had to do with my past; I was sure of it.

"What about Tyler?"

"Nowhere to be found," Detective Collins replied. "I have forensic specialists still out there gathering every piece of evidence they can find. There was a lot. Hopefully I will know more in a couple of days."

"What about David? Did you ever find him?" Ashley asked.

"No sign of him either. We are trying to find a connection between the two of them to understand how they might be tied in together."

"This is all my fault. They are trying to get to me, but with that guard outside my door, they are going after the people I love instead."

"I wish you wouldn't blame yourself," Detective Collins said. "I am doing my best to try to figure this thing out. I know that you tie in somehow with these men; I just haven't been able to make the connection."

"My best friend in the whole world is dead, damn it. Tyler, who I thought was on my side all this time, and whom I actually thought that I was in love with, has gone completely off the edge. I don't even know where he is and how he is involved in all this mess. My life is exploding before my eyes. Flashbacks, nightmares, hell, I don't even know what is real anymore. I'm in and out of consciousness and for all I know, I could be dreaming right now."

The doctor cut in, "Okay, I think we need to put an end to this right now. Detective Collins, this really isn't doing anyone any good. I think you need to let this go for today, and Bobby, you need to quiet down."

"I am sure you know about my past, Detective, right?" I said. "So, you must know that I am a monster. People die around me, and somehow, in the end, I am responsible."

"Yes, I read your file, but these acts of violence are not on you. You can't blame yourself. You have no…"

I cut him off… "Ashley," I looked her in the eyes, "I am begging you, please leave this room and never come back. I really don't want to have your death on my conscience too."

"I am not going anywhere, Bobby. I will be very careful, but I am sticking by you until this mess is cleared up."

"Is anyone going to listen to me?"

"Bobby, please."

"Let me finish, Doctor. Detective, I know you are not a stupid man; I am sure that you have done a background check on me. You know what I am capable of. I am cursed. Bad things happen to the people I am closest to. I appreciate all your hard work, but maybe you should just lock me up again and throw away the key."

"Don't be silly, Bobby; that is not the way I do business. Yes, I have dug up everything I could find about your life. I have read through every piece of information on record, but I don't believe everything I read. I would like to hear it from you. I will give you a day or so to rest, then I would like to spend time with you and go over what you remember. There must be something..."

He kept talking as I started to fade out...

Chapter 53

I was lying there, eyes closed, half-asleep, when I started to hear a strange sound. I rolled over and tried to zero in on it. I was always a little nervous about where I might be zoning out to. I focused on the noise. It sounded like heavy breathing and that wasn't very comforting. I opened my eyes a crack and could see the sun coming in through the blinds. Suddenly, I got slapped across the face by a big, slimy, wet tongue.

"Maestro!" I yelled. I was very excited. "You weren't a bad dream. I'm so happy to see you."

He jumped and landed with his front paws on the bed.

"Oh no you don't," Ashley said as she walked into the room. "You know you're not allowed on there."

Maestro got down.

"Good morning, sleepyhead. Are you going to stay in bed all day?"

"Oh no, you're kidding me, right? What time is it, anyway?"

"It's not so bad, it's only ten a.m. You were sleeping so soundly, I didn't have the heart to wake you up. Would you like some breakfast? Well, at this time, I think I should call it brunch."

Ashley winked and leaned over to kiss me on the forehead, then she led the way to the kitchen, Maestro at her heels.

"Come on, I'm starved; I was waiting for you."

"Something smells good," I said, as I yawned and stretched and got out of bed. "You're very cheery this morning?"

Ashley smiled. "It's a gorgeous day, sleeping beauty. I think we will have our breakfast outside and try to squeeze in a little walk before heading into town for your appointment with Dr. Blake which is later this afternoon."

It was a warm, sunny day. We had a wonderful breakfast together, and it wasn't long before we had our hiking boots on and were ready to take Maestro on a walk in the forest. It was my first time out there, and I was very happy to join them on their journey.

As we walked, I started to tell Ashley about the dream I had, or re-enactment, or whatever it was. A lot of the things I dreamed about were actually real events. Some were very scrambled and confusing nightmares, but some, I was realizing, were things that had really happened. It was like my memory needed to recall them to put them into their place in my puzzle. This one, though, was very real, and very painful.

"I remember that day," Ashley said. "I felt so bad for you. Poor Carla, I hadn't known her for very long, but I knew from the few times we chatted that she was a wonderful person. I know you cared a great deal for each other. I remember that you blamed yourself and said that everyone that got close to you ended up getting hurt."

"It did seem that way," I said, as I wiped a tear from my cheek, "but look at you, you're still around."

"Yup, you are stuck with me. Actually, at the time, I tried not to show it, but I was a little worried. Crazy things were happening all around you. Nevertheless, I wasn't going to leave your side; we were making too much progress in our sessions."

"I'm glad you hung around. I couldn't have gotten through all of it without you."

Maestro barked. I guess he wanted to say that he was by my side too.

"Yes, you too, Maestro," I said. "I am very happy that you are here too; you're such a good boy."

I knelt down and gave him a big hug.

"Yuck!" I yelled, as I got rewarded by a big, wet lick, again.

I got up and we continued walking.

"Come on, boy."

We reached the end of the field and were about to enter the woods to join onto the hiking trail when Ashley stopped and looked around her.

"What's up?" I said. "Why are we stopping?"

Ashley examined the fence and looked around again.

"I don't know," she said. "I usually keep this gate closed."

She shrugged, and brushed it off, and told me that she had probably forgotten to close it the last time she went hiking. After all, she was the only one who ever went hiking up there; the trail was on our property. She took me by the hand, and we continued on our way.

We followed a path that wound around large boulders and trees. We crossed little streams and passed by beautiful waterfalls. We soon came to the foot of a slightly more vertical trail up the mountainside, and I stopped to take a breather. Obviously, Ashley was in better shape than I was. Maestro had no trouble keeping up either.

"Whoa girl," I said, "you don't get this much exercise on a sailboat. I don't think I can make it up that hill."

"I'm sorry, Bobby," Ashley said. "I can get slightly carried away when I'm hiking. Break for a bit. We can't go very much farther, anyway, till we need to turn around and go back. You have your appointment, remember?"

We sat for a while and enjoyed the quiet, then we got ready to make the trek back home. Maestro jumped up and started barking, then just as Ashley was about to grab him by the collar, he took off running.

"No Maestro," she yelled, and ran off after him.

Suddenly, I felt very alone. There was no way I could keep up with them, so I waited. They were going to have to come back this way eventually. I sat back down and looked around me. That annoying feeling of *déjà vu* came over me again. I turned my head toward every little crack of a branch, and even the birds taking off in flight startled me. I couldn't shake the notion that someone was out there watching me. I tried my best to stay calm, but I was very quickly losing that battle.

I started calling out to them.

"Ash... Maestro... where are you?"

"Ash..."

I heard a noise behind me and quickly turned to see what it was.

"Ash," I yelled, "I was so worried. Don't ever leave me like that again, please."

I ran into Ashley's arms and held her tight.

"I am so sorry, Bobby. I was so shocked that he took off like that, I didn't even have the time to think that I was leaving you behind. I won't do it again, I promise."

She took me by the hand, and with Maestro on the leash this time, we headed back.

"Funny," Ashley said, "I have been taking him in here for walks and taking him off the leash every day since he moved here, and he has never done that. He must have heard something. I'll have to be more careful."

In no time, we were back to the house and getting ready to go to town. We left Maestro at home and were on our way.

I still had trouble shaking that uneasy feeling that came over me in the woods. I thought maybe it was because I had spent too much time alone on my boat. It felt weird to be around where there were other people in the picture. Someone even innocently looking at me from a distance, for no other reason at all except maybe seeing someone new in town that they haven't seen before, made me very uncomfortable. Spending so much time fearing for my life had really left its mark.

Into the hospital we went. It was a lot bigger than St. Mary's, and a lot newer too. Ashley knew her way around, so I followed her lead. We came to a reception area, and Ashley announced our arrival. We were told to be seated and that the doctor would be out shortly.

We had no sooner sat down when Dr. Blake came out to greet us.

"Wow," I said, "now that's what I call service."

"Don't feel so special; my last appointment was canceled." Dr. Blake winked.

Ashley came in with us; I wanted her to be included. Actually, I didn't want Ashley to leave my side. We sat down together, and Dr. Blake asked the usual series of questions that a doctor would ask a patient before a complete physical. He was being very professional about it, even though we had more than a doctor-patient relationship. We had become good friends. With everything we had gone through together, it was inevitable. He asked about my older wounds, and then he took a look at my newest bump on the head.

"Nice job," he said. "Another scar to add to your collection."

Ashley giggled. "Yup, she's starting to look like a road map."

They both had a good laugh at my expense.

He ordered some x-rays and a brain scan, in case I might have lost a few more screws, as he put it, so that meant another trip to town was going on our calendar.

The doc hadn't had any lunch yet and neither had we, so we decided to head out and have a quick bite together. There was a little diner just down the street from the hospital.

I got that feeling of *déjà vu* again, and it was a little unsettling.

The diner looked a little like the one near St. Mary's, but a lot newer. We found a booth and sat down. Dr. Blake and Ashley both could see that I was a little nervous. I kept looking around me all the time and didn't really pay much attention to their conversation.

"Bobby, honey," Ashley said, "would you prefer we go straight home? I can prepare you something there, or we can order our lunch to go and eat on the way."

Doc reached over and took me by the hand. "It's okay, Bobby; nobody can hurt you anymore."

"That's what everyone keeps saying," I replied, "but I feel like Tyler is still out there. I was okay on my boat, but now that I am in public places, I feel like he's still after me, hiding in the shadows, waiting for the perfect moment to capture me."

My eyes started to blur. I grabbed a napkin from the holder to catch my tears. I really didn't want to cry anymore. It seemed like I spent my whole life crying. The waitress came to our table and I turned away and looked out the window, so she wouldn't notice. Ashley ordered two burgers and two drinks to go, and Doc ordered his lunch.

I felt bad about ruining their lunch, but I was just too damned uncomfortable, so I didn't protest.

Ashley put her hand on my thigh. I turned, forced a smile, and then looked back out the window. They continued to talk, and I scanned the street. It was lunch hour and it was pretty busy in town. It was a beautiful day, so there were lots of people walking around. I saw a couple on the other side of the street, waiting for a bus. They were sitting next to each other, his arm around her. They looked so much in love.

I tried hard to suppress it, but it brought back memories of Tyler and me, when we were both very young, like in my dreams. When the summer holidays were over, I remembered how I would go with him to the bus stop to see him off. I remembered the sadness I felt as I watched the bus pull away.

I couldn't believe that I still had fond memories of him, after everything he did to me. He ruined my life, and I still lived in fear because of it. I had no reason to anymore though, because, according to Detective Collins, Tyler was dead. Still, I had this nagging feeling inside of me that made me think that he was still out there.

My vision cleared up just in time to see the bus pull up.

It came to a stop and some people got out, making room for the happy couple and some others. I watched as the couple sat down; again, he put his arm around her. My eyes moved behind them.

I gasped and put my hands over my mouth. I couldn't breathe. *Tyler*, I thought, *no, it couldn't be.* I was sure that I was still daydreaming.

Ashley grabbed hold of me.

"Bobby, what's wrong, Bobby?" she said. "Come on, Bobby… breathe... look at me."

She put her arms around me, and without success, tried to turn me away from the window.

"Bobby, you're okay. There's nothing out there; breathe!"

I watch as the bus pulled away. I felt the fear and anger building up inside of me. I let out my breath and started to hyperventilate.

"I saw him!" I cried. "He was on the bus. I know it was him. Oh my God, he's still after me!"

The waitress came to the table with our food. "Is everything okay?"

"I've got her," Dr. Blake said as he pulled some money out of his pocket and handed it to Ashley. "Take care of the bill, please; I'll take Bobby outside."

"Can you please wrap up my lunch to go, too?" he said to the waitress.

All this was going on, and I couldn't seem to calm down. I looked at Dr. Blake, then at Ashley, and they both seemed on edge. I couldn't stop gasping for air. Doc helped me to my feet and held me up as he tried to walk with me to the door. In my panicked state, I kept looking around me. Everywhere I turned, people were watching me. I felt like I was going to explode.

We were halfway to the door when my breathing started to slow down, but then everything else seemed to be slowing down too. The door looked like it was moving farther and farther away from us. I could see the doc's mouth moving really slowly and his voice sounded like an old warped record. Actually, all the sounds around me seemed to be in slow motion. My legs suddenly felt very weak, and I didn't think I was going to be able to hold myself up anymore. The numbness took over my body and my vision started to blur again. The buzzing in my head was getting louder.

"I saw him," I whispered. "He was..."

I looked up at Dr. Blake, then darkness overtook me.

Chapter 54

I opened my eyes; I was so afraid.

"Ashley, please. I don't want to go back there. I'm sorry. I know that we just got started again, but I am feeling a little anxious."

I could feel a tear roll down my face.

"I'm so sorry, Detective; I can't relive that again. I know it will help you, but it is just too painful."

"It won't just help me, it will help you," he said. "There has been a terrible injustice here, I am sure of that, and I am going to do everything in my power to get to the bottom of it and make things right for you."

"Is it okay, Detective, if we take a break?" Ashley asked. "This has been really tough on her. Bobby and I have been at it for a while now; it is emotionally draining."

I leaned back on the couch and closed my eyes.

"May I ask what exactly we are doing?" the detective asked.

"It's called Recovered Memory Therapy," Ashley replied. "It involves many different techniques. Hypnosis, for example, is one way of recovering repressed memories. There are relaxation techniques, and also guided imagery and visualization.

"All this to say that, little by little, we have been putting pieces of Bobby's life in their proper place. In other words, we have been working hard to recover and organizing her memories. It has been a long and painful process."

"It sounds grueling. I'm so sorry to have to put you through this, Bobby, but Ashley, you're the one who asked me to come here today, why?"

I opened my eyes again, and half-smiled.

"Because," Ashley replied, "I believe we are almost there. I am hoping that by the end of this session, you will have all the answers to your questions."

Ashley took my hand.

"Everything is going to be all right; I promise. We will get through this."

"Well," the detective said, "I have no problem with taking a break. I'll go get some lunch and come back, say around two?"

"Sure, that would be great," Ashley replied. "Is that okay with you, Bobby?"

I nodded.

He smiled and left the office. As soon as the door closed behind him, I started bawling. Ashley grabbed the tissues and came and sat down next to me. She put her arms around me.

"I'm here for you, Bobby. I'm not going anywhere."

She dialed her receptionist and asked her to order us some lunch from the deli. I didn't really feel like eating but she said that I needed to keep up my strength. I lay down on the sofa and closed my eyes. It wasn't a very good idea because my mind started to wander where I didn't want it to go. I opened them again.

Ashley looked over at me and smiled. "I know that you aren't the monster that you claim to be. We will get to the bottom of this. You will feel all that weight that you have been carrying around with you most of your life lift off your shoulders, and you will get the freedom that you deserve."

I smiled back at her. She truly believed in me, the same way that poor Carla had. I missed her so much. It pained me so to think that, because of me, her life was cut short. She had no idea that she was messing with a hornets' nest when she brought Tyler into my life. It wasn't an accident when he bumped into her in the hospital. He manipulated her the same way he manipulated everyone else in his life. My past caught up with me, and unfortunately, it also caught up with the people I loved.

There was a knock at the door.

"Looks like our lunch is here."

The receptionist put the packages on the coffee table and looked up at Ashley.

"Thanks, we'll take it from here. Detective Collins will be coming back at two; you can just send him right in, please."

We sat together and ate our sandwiches. She got up and went to a cupboard behind her desk.

"Wine, anyone? This might help to relax you a bit."

She poured us each a glass.

"So, that's where you keep your stash."

It was nice. We talked about the future and about all the things we dreamed of accomplishing. I enjoyed her company very much. She was caring, understanding, and lots of fun, especially when she wasn't in work-mode.

"How are you feeling now, Bobby? It's almost time."

I looked over at the clock. Ten minutes and counting...

"I'm okay." I looked at her and winked. "I'm ready to take on the world."

"It's not the world that I'm worried about; it's Detective Collins. Are you ready for him?"

I watched her as she became very professional, very serious. It was a good look for her; she was very beautiful. She had a gentle smile that told you everything was going to work out.

"You have nothing to worry about; I will be right here with you. You will have your eyes closed, and you won't even realize that there is anyone else in the room. We have done this together many times. You just have to relax and go with the flow."

That being said, we finished our wine and cleaned up the table.

Two o'clock came and went. I guess his lunch hour went on longer than expected. Ashley glanced at her appointment book and I just sat on the couch and watched her. I noticed that when she was deep in thought, she would pinch the end of her chin.

"Watch you don't wear it off."

She looked up at me over the top of her reading glasses and snarled.

"What's up?" I said as I saw her look up at the clock and then back down at her appointment book.

"I'm just trying to figure things out here. I wasn't counting on Detective Collins being late and our session might go on longer than expected. Give me a few minutes and I will try to clear the rest of my day."

"We can reschedule to another day if you want."

She laughed sarcastically and said, "You would like that, wouldn't you? I'm not letting you off the hook that easily. We have worked too hard for this. Let's give him a few more minutes and see what..."

Her phone rang, and she hit the speaker button.

"I have the detective on the other line; should I patch him through?"

"Yes sure, thanks." She picked up the phone.

"Detective... yes, she's still here... no worries, it's not a problem... We'll be here, see you later then."

"What's going on; he can't make it?"

She pushed the speaker button again and told the receptionist to call her patients and re-schedule their appointments for another day.

"He said that he had a work emergency, but he is on his way and should be here at three."

"I wonder if it has anything to do with me. I really wish this whole mess would come to an end. I know that he is working hard on this case, but there doesn't ever seem to be much progress."

"That is because only you hold the key to your past, and the answers to this big mystery are trapped inside your head. You need to release them to the detective so he can have something to work with."

"I am trying; you know that. Every time we get close ..."

"Stop right there; we are making great progress. We are getting closer and closer to the truth. You might not notice, but I do. It's baby steps, but we are almost there. Today is the day we get past that last hurdle. I know you are ready, or I would not have asked Detective Collins to join us."

She sat down next to me and put her arm around me again.

"Bobby, I need you to trust me when I tell you that you will never be free until you let go of all those memories that you have kept locked up for all these years."

A tear rolled down my cheek again.

There was a knock on the door, and it opened slowly, revealing Detective Collins.

"Sorry, the receptionist told me to come right in; is everything okay?" he asked.

"Absolutely, come in. Bobby and I were just relaxing, and I've been giving her a little pep talk. You saw this morning how difficult this was for her. It's not easy for anyone."

"I know, Dr. Carter, I realize that. I have all afternoon, Bobby. I want to protect you, but I desperately need your help. Take all the time you need."

He sat down on a chair to the left of me. Ashley put on some soft music, dimmed the lights, re-adjusted the recording equipment, sat down on the chair in front of me, and looked me in the eyes.

"Are you ready?"

I took a deep breath and looked over at the detective.

"As ready as I'll ever be."

I looked back at her and she smiled.

"Alright, Bobby, you know the drill. Lean back, relax, and close your eyes. You can do this."

I concentrated on her voice; it was very calm.

"Take a deep breath, Bobby, and slowly exhale... and again. Listen to your breath as it escapes your lungs. Can you hear your heart beating? Listen hard… Relax and slow it down. Feel the tension disappear from your body.

"Listen to my voice and I will guide you. Can you hear me, Bobby?"

"Yes."

"I want you to go back… back to that night in your bedroom. The night that all the screaming and fighting woke you up. Take a deep breath, Bobby, and tell me what you see. Look around the room, describe it."

"I woke up and I couldn't see very much. The room was dark. I could hear some yelling and screaming coming from downstairs. I got really nervous because it was a lot worse than their usual fighting."

I felt a tear roll down my face.

"Bobby, you are doing fine; I'm right here. What happened next?"

"The screaming stopped and there was silence. I couldn't hear anything. I don't know how much time passed but the next thing I saw was the stream of light coming from underneath my door."

"What did you do then, Bobby?"

"I remember getting up, making my bed so it would look like I hadn't been there, and then hiding in the closet."

I sat quietly for a moment and collected my thoughts; this was not going to be easy.

"Bobby?"

"Sorry, I just needed a moment. Okay, I remember looking through the cracks in my closet door. My room lit up with the light from the hallway as they slowly came in."

"Okay, Bobby, I need you to focus. I need you to take a good look at them. We need to know who they are; this is very important."

"I can't, I'm too scared. Anyway, it's too dark; they have their backs to the light."

"Try harder... focus… watch their every move. They must turn toward the light at some point."

"I'm sorry. I'm trying hard, but I just can't; they won't turn around."

"It's okay, Bobby. Go on. You are safe, and in my office; don't forget that. I'm right here."

I suddenly got the feeling that I didn't want to go down this road again. It must have been really painful… or I wouldn't have blocked it all out. I needed to put an end to this nightmare, though, so I tried to calm myself down again and continue.

"They are fighting."

"What are they fighting about?" Ashley asked.

My voice trembled, "You said that nobody was home, and we were just going to rob the place. You said that you knew where they hid their money. We were going to rob them and leave, that's all. Why did I let you talk me into this?"

"So, sue me." Suddenly my voice was deep and angry. "It was payback time for all those years of abuse. But hey, they put up quite a fight, didn't they? It was beautiful to see the look of fear on his face. Hers too; she didn't do us any favors either. She enjoyed beating us with that damned yardstick as much as he enjoyed raping us. They both got what they deserved. They can rot in hell, for all I care, after what they put us through.

"Murphy was right though, he said that we had to confront our aggressors to be able to free ourselves. I feel so liberated now; don't you? I really enjoyed this. We just have to make sure that we don't leave any evidence behind that could tie us into this mess, and that includes any witnesses. Too bad for Murphy that he didn't keep better track of his girlfriend's whereabouts. I'll take care of our little loose end right here and now. I love you, man, and I won't let anything bad happen to you, so you just need to do as I say, okay? Go downstairs and I will take care of this; nobody will ever know that we were here."

The words flowed out of me like a memorized speech; I surprised even myself.

"What…" I looked over at Ashley. "Tyler, no, it can't be. He knew about this? I can't believe…"

"Bobby… don't stop now, you are doing so well. Don't think about Tyler; we need to find out what happened here. You need to keep going," Ashley encouraged.

I sat for a moment, *how could I have been so naïve?* I thought. *How could someone that I thought I was in love with turn out to be such a monster?*

"Bobby, are you okay?" Ashley asked. "Are you able to continue, or do you want to stop and try again tomorrow?"

By now, the tears were rolling uncontrollably down my cheeks. There was no stopping them.

My visions started again. "Oh wait, the nervous one is leaving," I said as I wept. "The crazy one knows I'm here. He's looking for me. He's not going to leave until he kills me."

"You are still here, Bobby." I opened my eyes a bit and saw her nod. "He didn't kill you. Now take a deep breath. You're doing fine."

I took a moment to settle down, then I continued.

"I see him through the cracks. He is coming to the door. Oh my God, he is opening it."

"You are just thinking back, Bobby. Nobody can hurt you. You can do this," Ashley urged.

"Okay, I know, this is not real. I can do it."

I stayed quiet for a moment again. I didn't like where this was leading, but I had to go on.

"I moved to the back of the closet and braced myself. I could feel something on the floor, something metal, oh, my old curtain rod. I screamed as he reached in, grabbed me by the arm, and tried to pull me out. I took the rod in my hand, held it firmly, and with all my strength, I hit him across the face with it. He let out a yell, and it only made him angrier."

"You fucking bitch!" he growled

He backed up and put his hand to his cheek.

"Go away!" I yelled. "I won't tell anyone. I don't even know who you are!"

He took his hands away from his face. There was a good-sized gash on his cheek.

"Look what you've done!" he yelled.

I stopped and thought for a moment. Something seemed very familiar.

"Oh my God, the scar," I looked at Ashley again. "David had a scar on that side of his face. How can that be? I think it's David!"

I started breathing heavily. This was becoming a little too much.

"Okay, Bobby, that is great," she said. "We know who he is, but we need to know what happened that night. I need you to relax; can you do that? You are not there with him in that room. That happened over twenty years ago. This is not real; you must remember that. I would like you to breathe with me for a moment. Listen to my voice. Take a deep breath in, hold it a bit, and now exhale slowly. Again, deep breath in, hold, and exhale. You're doing great. Now, do you want to continue? We can stop it here if you wish, but we will have to start all over again another day. Tell me what you want to do."

"I have to go on, Ashley. I know I need to find out what happened to me that night. Just don't leave me."

"I'm not going anywhere. I'm ready when you are."

I nodded. "He reached in again, and as I kicked and screamed, he managed to grab hold of my leg. He pulled me out of the closet, through the room, and then dragged me down the stairs. I grabbed the railing, but I didn't have the strength to hang on. He pulled me through the dining room and into the kitchen. I kicked and screamed all the way there."

I had to pause for a moment; I was having trouble breathing again.

"Are you okay, Bobby? What do you see?"

I wanted to describe it to Ashley, but I was having trouble finding the words.

"The kitchen is destroyed," I cried. "I can't believe what I'm seeing. There is blood everywhere. Oh my God, I see Harold; he is barely recognizable. He has been beaten to a pulp. He is sprawled out on the floor. He looks so broken. There's a knife sticking out of his chest."

"Do you like what you see?" David asked. "It must be nice for you too; after all, they probably beat the shit out of you, like everyone else. Old Harold though, he must have really loved you. I bet he raped you every night when he got wasted. Anyway, they will never hurt anyone, ever again. Too bad you weren't away like you were supposed to be. I almost feel sorry for you, but now, you are going to have to die too."

"What are you doing? I thought you were going to take care of her."

"The voice came from behind me," I told Ashley. "It must be the other guy, he is in the kitchen. What do I do?"

"Okay, Bobby, you need to turn and look at him. We need to know who he is."

"Really? Shit, okay, I'll try. Um... I see him; he's coming toward us from across the room. I don't know, it's hard to tell, he is so young. I don't recall ever seeing him before. He is short and very thin. He's a redhead, if that helps."

"You're bleeding," he yelled at David, "and you didn't want to leave any evidence?"

"Oh, shut the fuck up and make yourself useful. Get upstairs and make sure you clean up every speck of blood that you see and get that stick she hit me with; we need to take it with us and dispose of it. Close the closet door and make sure the room looks undisturbed so they don't check around too much in there. Check the stairs on your way down; make sure they are clean. Do you think you can handle that?"

I glanced at Ashley and continued. "During his argument with his friend, I think David kind of forgot that he had me by the arm and he loosened his grip. I saw my chance and decided to take it. I leaped from the floor and tried to run for it. He was quicker than I was, though, and he grabbed me, picked me up, and threw me against the wall. I hit it hard and landed on the floor.

"A surge of pain came through my body, but I tried to turn my head to see where he was. I screamed as I came face to face with Emma. She was badly beaten too. She lay still with her bloodshot eyes wide open. The fear had not yet left them. I looked up just in time to see my baseball bat come down hard on me. I screamed again..."

"Bobby, you did it!" Ashley announced. "It's okay. There is no baseball bat, and there is no David. Nobody is hurting you. Listen to my voice. I'm going to bring you back. Bobby, breathe deeply... exhale. Breathe deeply once again... exhale. When I touch your hand, I want you to open your eyes."

I opened my eyes and broke down. Ashley came and sat next to me. She put her arms around me. I was trembling uncontrollably.

"I'm so sorry I had to put you through that," she whispered, "but it was the only way."

"Oh, my God, I didn't kill them. It wasn't me."

I cried some more.

"I am… I don't know what to say," Detective Collins declared.

I had almost forgotten that he was in the room.

"But Bobby, I don't get it," he said. "The report said that you had…"

"I know what they said, I was listening to them say it for many years, but I just didn't remember anything. Oh Ash, thank you." I started to cry again. "I remember now."

"It's okay, Bobby. I knew all along that you couldn't have done those things."

"No, I mean, I remember it all now. I woke up with a painful throbbing in my head. I tried to open my eyes but there was so much blood. I wiped them and looked around the room to see if they were gone. There was no sign of them. I checked to see if Emma was breathing but she hadn't moved, and her eyes were still wide open. I remember how those eyes seemed to bore a hole right through me. I turned my head and tried to get up. I didn't have the energy. So, I started to pull myself along the floor. I didn't think that Harold was alive, but I had to check. I got to his side and saw that his eyes were closed. I grabbed his arm to shake it a bit and called his name. Suddenly his eyes opened. I remember screaming…"

"Oh, my God, Bobby," Ashley said.

"'Help me, Roberta,' he said, as he reached for the knife that was still stuck in his chest.

"I didn't know what to do. My head was spinning; blood was dripping down my face. I could barely see. It took every bit of energy I had, but I managed to pull the knife from his chest. That's it… I must have blacked out after that."

"That is how they found you," Detective Collins added, "passed out with the knife in your hand. Your prints, your blood, and his blood all over it. I read it in your file. You have answered so many questions for me this afternoon."

Ashley piped up, "But she was badly beaten too. What in the hell did they say about that!"

"An argument gone bad? I don't know what they were thinking. Don't yell at me; I didn't do the investigation."

"I'm sorry; it's just so unbelievable."

"The report went on to say that they didn't find any evidence to prove otherwise. They also had testimony from nearby neighbors who said that they were very abusive foster parents. They mistreated the children they kept over the years. Everyone in town felt sorry for the children, but they didn't feel it was their place to speak up. They had regular visits from social workers. It was up to them to make sure the children were safe."

"Are you fucking kidding me!"

"Ash!" I was shocked. She didn't usually swear.

"I'm sorry; I can't believe that people would even admit to that."

"Bobby, I need to ask you something. Do you remember the guy that was with David in the diner?" asked Detective Collins.

"Yes, the one you found dead in his apartment?"

"Yes. I have a picture here in my file that we found in his belongings. He looks to be in his late teens, and he is with another boy. Do you mind taking a look at it?"

"Umm… I guess, if it will help."

I took the picture in my hand and started to tremble. My eyes filled, and I couldn't get the words out of my mouth.

"Bobby!" Ashley grabbed the picture and threw it on the floor. She took me in her arms again and held me tight.

I tried to speak again but only a whisper managed to escape my lips.

"It's them," I cried, pointing to the picture on the floor. "It's them." I cried some more.

Detective Collins reached down and picked it up off the floor.

"I need to ask you something else, Bobby. This won't hurt so much, I promise."

I wiped my tears, blew my nose, and then turned and looked at him.

"Sure… go ahead."

"I want to look into reopening your case. You were wrongfully imprisoned, and I would like to clear your name. With all of this new evidence, which is obviously tied to your past, we shouldn't have any problem. I need to concentrate right now on trying to find

David Allen, and your friend Tyler of course. I'm not quite sure of his involvement in this right now, but I have an APB out on both of them. In the meantime, you need to be very careful. You too, Dr. Carter. You will still have your guard outside your door, at least until I find David."

"Sure, that would be great; thanks so much for believing in me, Detective."

He got up, said his goodbyes, and Ashley saw him to the door. I watched as they chit-chatted in the doorway before he left. I didn't really pay much attention to what they were saying. I was confused and exhausted. I closed my eyes for a moment. I couldn't shake the image of Harold's and Emma's brutally beaten, lifeless bodies. I could have died with them. This was so crazy. I spent half my life in prison for killing them. How did things like that happen? Then there was Tyler. I couldn't believe that…

"Bobby, are you okay?"

"Yes, Ashley, but this is crazy. It's so unbelievable."

"It sure is; no wonder your mind blocked it all out. I'm having trouble believing it myself."

"Ashley, what about Tyler? I can't believe that he had something to do with this. I am so stupid!"

"You are not stupid; none of this is your doing. You are a victim."

"And I'm still in danger. When will this nightmare end?"

"Soon. Today was a big day. The detective has a lot to go on now; he will find them."

"Thanks, Ashley, for all your help. Really, I don't know how to thank you. All these years I thought I was a monster… I'm not a monster, Ashley; I'm not a monster…" The dams opened…

Chapter 55

I felt something cold on my forehead as I slowly opened my eyes. "Bobby… Bobby, honey… Come on, Bobby," Ashley said as she gently stroked my face.

I had to think for a moment about where I was. Ashley and Dr. Blake were leaning over me with very concerned looks. I was confused and didn't really know what was happening.

"Bobby, honey, it's okay; we are here with you."

"Where am I?" I whispered.

"You collapsed. We are still in the diner, across from the hospital. You had an appointment with the doc. Do you remember?"

Dr. Blake put his hand on my shoulder.

"Bobby, what happened?" he said. "You had a panic attack. You looked like you saw a ghost."

My eyes bolted wide open and they darted from one side of the room to the other.

"Oh my God; I saw him!" I yelled, as I started struggling to get up. "I saw him; he was on the bus!" I started to tremble uncontrollably.

Ashley pulled me into her arms and tried to console me.

"It's okay," she said. "Everything is going to be all right."

"You don't understand," I said, "I saw him. He knows where I am. I have to get out of here!"

"You need to stay calm, Bobby," Ashley said.

"I saw him, Ash; I swear!" I replied.

"You saw who, Bobby?"

I took a moment and glanced at both of them before answering, sizing them up, somehow.

"I… I guess you didn't see him?"

"What are you talking about?" Ashley said. "Tell me who you saw."

"You are going to think I'm crazy."

"I already know that," she said, and she winked. "I'm sorry, I couldn't resist, you walked right into that one."

I smiled and started to pull myself together a bit. I wanted to tell Ashley, but at the same time, I, myself, was questioning what I may or may not have seen. It was obvious to me that nobody knew what I was talking about. Well, to be fair, they weren't even looking outside the window, so they probably wouldn't have seen him even if he was there.

I thought about it and remembered how that couple reminded me of my past with Tyler, and maybe it just got my imagination going. I knew how easy it was for my mind to bounce around in and out of reality. It was playing tricks on me; surely that's what it was. I was trying very hard to convince myself of that. I wasn't completely successful, though, but I decided to keep it to myself.

"Are you feeling a little better, Bobby?" Doc asked as he removed the wet cloth from my forehead. "Can you get up?"

"I think so."

"Do you have panic attacks like this often? Do I need to be concerned?" he asked.

"I'm sorry, Dr. Blake, I swear this doesn't happen very often. I still have nightmares now and then, but as I explained to you yesterday, I am really doing well. I've been keeping track of everything in my journal and things are coming together for me. Honestly, you don't need to worry."

"Okay… Ashley, you need to keep an eye on this one, please," he winked. "I do have other patients who need me. I'd better get back to work. Oh, and Bobby, I'll see you when you come back for your other tests."

The waitress came by to see if there was anything more she could do for us. Dr. Blake thanked her and handed her the wet towel. We grabbed our lunches and headed outside. I was a little nervous and kept looking around me, just in case I wasn't imagining things, but I tried my best to stay calm. I couldn't take my eyes off the bus stop though. It all seemed so real. I knew that it was not possible, but I really thought it was him.

Dr. Blake gave us each a hug, said goodbye, and headed back to work. *So much for lunch*, I thought. Ashley took my hand, and we headed down the street to where we had parked the car.

"Hey Bobby," Ashley said. "I know you are tired, but it is such a beautiful day and there is a park just around the corner. Would you be okay with having our lunch there? I really don't feel like eating while I drive, and our food will be cold by the time we get home. We could find a bench to sit on and catch some rays while we eat."

"Sure, if you want," I replied.

I didn't really feel like it, but in the end, it was very enjoyable. It reminded me of the wonderful days I used to spend in the park with Carla. All I had now were the memories, and they are good ones. I missed her so much.

I was very thankful to have Ashley in my life now; I didn't know what I would have done without her. Ashley helped me so much. She stayed by my side through all of this. *We have a great relationship*, I realized. *Ashley understands me. She knows that I have a lot of healing to do and need to work hard at putting the scrambled pieces of my life in order. She also knows that I need my me time, to try to figure it all out. She doesn't like the fact that I want to be out on my sailboat alone, but she knows how important it is to me, so she backs down. She won't be very thrilled when I tell her that I am ready to head back out, but we will have to cross that bridge when we get to it.*

We were almost done our lunch when Ashley spoke up.

"You've been pretty quiet?"

"I was just daydreaming, you know, my usual."

"Are you sure you're okay? You really freaked out in the diner."

"I know, I'm sorry. I'm just tired."

Ashley shook her head.

"That might have worked on Dr. Blake, but you're not fooling me."

"I'm sorry, Ash, I'm just, you know… I just don't know what's real anymore."

"Come here," Ashley said, and she put her arm around me. "You know, I can see right through you. Talk to me."

Without even giving it a second thought, the words came flying out of my mouth.

"I saw Tyler!"

I started to tremble and then the tears started to flow.

"It's okay, Bobby, let it out. There is nobody here but me."

Ashley held me as I cried, stroking my hair and gently rocking me. It was very soothing, and I started to relax. I raised my head.

"Thanks, Ash," I said.

"What for?"

"For putting up with me."

"I wouldn't want to be anywhere else," Ashley replied. "Now, let's clean up and go home. We've had enough excitement for today, and Maestro must be very anxious to see us."

We hightailed it out of there, windows open, music cranked up, and singing our little hearts out. Ashley always made me feel good. She knew the right things to say and do no matter the situation. There wasn't a negative bone in her body. I loved her very much.

In no time, we were home. We walked up to the front door, no question, Maestro saw us coming. He was wagging his tail and barking like crazy.

"Brace yourself," Ashley said as she opened the door to let him out.

"Maestro!"

Oh my, he practically knocked me down again.

"Ok, boy, you have to stop doing that." I bent down and patted him.

"It's just because he is so happy to see you. He will calm down soon; he did the same to me," Ashley said.

We went back out, took him for his walk, and then decided to get out the lawn chairs and relax in the sun. Ashley put on some of my favorite blues and brought out two glasses of wine.

We had a wonderful afternoon. We talked about our future, which for me was uncertain. I didn't really know what I wanted to do with the rest of my life. I still felt like there were plenty of missing parts from my past that I needed to deal with, and until I did, I didn't feel like I could move on.

Ashley, on the other hand, knew exactly what she wanted. She had her life all figured out. I loved that about her. She kept me grounded, and at the same time she gave me the freedom to do what I thought I needed to do — even though she sometimes didn't agree, like the sailing alone part. When we first moved out here, I tried to stay home with Ashley and figure things out, but there were just too many distractions, and of course, I was still big news, and I couldn't seem to go anywhere without people looking my way and whispering. I needed to be alone, and my sailboat was the answer.

Before we knew it, the sun was starting to fade, the music had stopped, and we had polished off the bottle of wine. Maestro had snoozed next to me the whole time. When we got up from our chairs, he jumped up. We took him for another short walk then went into the house to prepare dinner.

After we finished eating, I took out my laptop. I wanted to catch up on my writing. I sat on the sofa, got comfortable, and turned it on. I read a few pages back to remember where I had left off. I read back a few more pages, but I couldn't seem to get into it. My mind started to wander. I thought about the bus, big mistake — there was no way I was going to be able to concentrate after that.

I went back into the kitchen where Ashley was still hanging out.

"What are you doing, Ash?"

"Well, I didn't want to disturb you, so I decided to figure out our meals for tomorrow and the rest of the week."

"Well, by the look of that grocery list, it seems like you've accomplished more than I have."

"Oh no, was I disturbing you?" she asked.

"No, I was just distracted," I replied. "I'm sorry about today. You know me and my imagination."

"It's okay, Bobby."

"You know, Ash? I have been doing very well with my writing. Yes, sometimes memories get a little extreme, but not like today. I am usually able to stay in control, but I think, being here with you, having Maestro by my side, seeing Dr. Blake again well, that might be just a little too much *déjà vu*."

Chapter 56

The sun was beating on me as I climbed down the ladder into the turquoise water to join Fred. He was so happy to see me again, and I, him. It seems like he had hung around and waited for me to come back. I didn't think that I would ever see him again.

We had a wonderful reunion; we slow-danced in our watery paradise for the longest time. A few of his friends joined in, some new ones and some that I had recognized from before. Funny how dolphins seem to all look alike, but really, they don't when you get to know them. I could pick out Fred even if he was surrounded by a thousand other dolphins. He was swift, and very acrobatic, maneuvering around the others, always putting on a show. He loved to be the center of attraction. He was definitely the leader of the pod. He was smart and very friendly, and radiated happiness with his joyous laughter.

I gripped his fin tightly as he pulled me through the ocean. Warm water caressed my skin as we made our way down. We weaved through the beautiful coral formations. Fred slowed down, and I let go. I wanted to explore the magnificent reef.

There was a group of seahorses following each other through the colorful coral, being ever so cautious not to get too close to any of those live tentacles. Everything was so camouflaged down here. What you thought was a piece of coral one minute, swam away the next. To my dismay, one of the seahorses got a little too close. It vanished into the reef.

I realized that I had lost track of Fred, so I turned to see where he was. To my surprise, a giant manta ray passed right by me as he took flight. I watched as he followed the ocean floor and disturbed the sand every now and then as he got too close. They were huge creatures of the sea. So graceful and so beautiful. I imagined what it would be like to take flight with something like that. What an amazing journey that could be. A school of almost transparent-looking goldfish changed direction as he glided through their path. It is so amazing to see how fast they can zig and zag all together in perfect synchronicity.

I felt a nudge on my shoulder that brought me back to reality. It was Fred of course. I guess he was feeling left out. I grabbed his fin and off we went again, zig-zagging through this breathtaking coral maze.

Something in the distance caught my eye, but then Fred turned in the other direction. No clue what it might have been, but hey, there was lots to explore down here.

We moved on a bit farther till we came to another cluster of coral. This one seemed to be on the edge of a plateau, or underwater cliff of some kind. The ocean floor dropped out of sight just past it. All I could see ahead was darkness. I wasn't going there, but then neither was Fred. He immediately turned and swam in the opposite direction, right back to where we were before.

Again, I saw something in the distance, but again, Fred had other plans, he turned slightly and moved upward a bit, about midway from where we were to the surface. The water was starting to get cloudy. I started to get a little nervous, but I knew I was safe with Fred. I just hung on tight, making sure we didn't get separated. Visibility was becoming a problem and I didn't know where in the hell I was. He turned around again, heading back to that first coral reef.

That thing that I saw before in the distance, well, it seemed to be getting closer. Fred turned again. It seemed like he needed to get out of there, but every direction we took brought us right back to here. He seemed a little nervous too, making me start to freak out. That is not a good thing when you are underwater.

That mysterious object was much closer now. Fred seemed to be trying to avoid it. He started to slowly swim straight up to the surface, taking into consideration my decompression time. The water was clouding over all around us. I was anxious to get back to my boat. There was movement in the waters above us though. *Sharks*, I thought. Oh no, they seemed to be circling which was not a good sign. Fred didn't like that option either, and he turned. We headed back to the bottom. This was bad news. I hung on tight; it was all I could do.

I took a moment to look at my regulator, and as I did, I lost my grip on Fred. Well, I had bigger problems. On top of everything else that was going wrong, I was getting low on oxygen. I needed to get to the surface and fast.

I didn't even know where I was anymore. We had changed direction so often that I was totally disoriented. I closed my eyes for a moment to try to relax. I felt another nudge on my shoulder. I smiled and thought that Fred had come back for me.

I opened my eyes and saw him swimming toward me; he was moving fast. So, it wasn't him that touched my shoulder? I started to tremble. I didn't want to, but I had to turn around to see what it was. Before I could do that, though, seaweed started coming up from the ocean floor. It was swirling around my legs and waist. I tried to pull at it, but it was too strong and growing out of control.

Fred was doing his best to try to rip the seaweed away from me, but he wasn't having any luck either. The water was getting darker. Fred was still trying to free me. I could barely see him anymore, but I could feel his movements as he frantically pulled at the weeds. The water was changing color to a crimson red. I gasped, when I realized that it was blood. It was getting very thick. I couldn't tell where it was coming from. I shuddered when I remembered about the sharks that were circling above.

Visibility was diminishing as the blood saturated the water. With my free hand, I reached down to pat Fred to show my appreciation, even though I knew that he was fighting a losing battle. Suddenly he stopped what he was doing and floated upwards. I gasped again when I saw the spear that was right through his body. The blood was pouring out of it.

I couldn't breathe. I didn't know what to do. He wasn't moving anymore; he seemed to be suspended in front of me.

Unexpectedly, another spear swished passed my head and plunged into his lifeless body. I couldn't stop myself and I turned my head to see where it came from. I froze at the gruesome sight before me: a half-decaying corpse with a spear gun in his hand.

That was not possible; the thing was dead for sure. I couldn't take my eyes off it as it floated around in the current. It would come close to me then get pulled back, close to me again, then pulled back again. I couldn't move; I was still entangled in those dreadful weeds. The body came close to me again and stayed right in front of my face. I got a good look at it this time. No, it couldn't be; that was not possible. It was Tyler. I watched in fear as his arms came up, spear gun pointing right at me, and he opened his glowing red eyes. I tried to scream but I had no oxygen left.

"You are mine, Robbie; nobody else can have you. We will be together forever."

Chapter 57

I woke up with a scream and Ashley jolted awake beside me. She immediately turned her bedside light on and took me in her arms. Maestro started barking like crazy and jumped up on the bed to join us. I was trembling so much that I couldn't speak. I just cried, a steady stream of tears flowing down my cheeks. Maestro, who wanted desperately to comfort me, was relentlessly trying to lick the tears from my face. Ashley had to practically fight him off to comfort me.

"Maestro! Get down, boy!" she yelled. "You know you are not allowed on the bed! Get down!"

While all of this was going on, I kept reliving my nightmare about Tyler with his decaying body floating in front of me. The image seemed to be burned into my mind.

"You are mine, Robbie; nobody else can have you… You are mine, Robbie; nobody else can have you… You are mine, Robbie; nobody else can have you…"

His words just kept echoing on and on…

I started to wail very loudly and had difficulty taking in a breath between each outburst. Ashley rocked me and tried her best to console me.

Maestro started barking again, but he didn't get back on the bed.

"Bobby, honey, it's okay," Ashley said. "I've got you; it was just another bad dream."

I tried to speak, but I just kept gasping for air.

"Bobby, you need to calm down; you are going to hyperventilate again. Remember what happened yesterday?" she said.

I didn't want to remember yesterday. I didn't want to think about my dream, either. I held Ashley very close to me and tried to calm myself down, but that damned image wouldn't go away.

"You are mine, Robbie; nobody else can have you..."

"It was a bad dream, Bobby. Everything will be fine. I won't let anything bad happen to you."

Ashley continued rocking me as she caressed my hair. It had a calming effect. I soon started to breathe a little easier, knowing that Ashley was there for me and that I wasn't alone.

I never closed my eyes, though, for fear that I would see Tyler's rotting corpse again.

"Ashley," I whispered, "I'm so sorry."

"Don't be ridiculous," Ashley replied. "It's not the first time you have an episode like this and it won't be the last. I signed on for this, remember?"

She winked and then smiled.

"I love you, you know that, right?" she whispered. "I won't ever let anyone hurt you again."

Ashley did sign on for this, in a way. Since the day I came out of my coma and even before that, Ashley was there by my side.

When I found out about Carla, I was totally devastated, and I didn't know if I was coming or going half the time. Sometimes I didn't even want to go on, but Ashley wouldn't let me give up.

The investigation had kicked into high gear. The detective was pulling every resource he had, and he was bound and determined to solve this case. I was still trying to heal from my accident, but the painful physio every day and the fear for my life had taken its toll. I felt like I was drowning. It seemed like no matter how hard I tried to get my life together, there was always something pulling me down, something keeping me from being happy.

Still, Ashley stayed by my side through it all, even if she was very likely putting her own life in danger too. I was the main target, but it was the people around me who were getting hurt. I had begged Ashley to stay away from me, but she wouldn't listen. She said that she was willing to take the risk. She knew that she could help me, and we were, in fact, making great progress with my therapy, so she wanted to see it through.

"Bobby, honey."

She startled me, and I jumped.

"I'm sorry, I didn't mean to scare you, but it's four thirty and I really don't think I will get back to sleep again, and you neither, I presume. Why don't we get up and I'll make some coffee, and we can relax, talk, and watch the sun come up."

I reached for a tissue, wiped the tears from my eyes, and blew my nose.

"That sounds like a great idea," I said. "I really don't want to fall back to sleep right now, anyway."

We headed out to the kitchen together, Maestro at our heels. I never left Ashley's side. She made a pot of coffee, I prepared two cups, and we went into the den, which faced directly east. The perfect spot to watch the sunrise. I brought along a box of tissues, for good measure. I figured that if Ashley wanted me to tell her about my dream, I would be armed and ready.

Well, they did come in handy; the waterworks started almost immediately after we sat down. Ashley didn't waste any time in asking me about the dream, and I couldn't hold back the tears. I really didn't want to go back there, but Ashley insisted. The dream just still felt too damned real. I remembered every little detail, just like a scary movie that you can't get out of your mind. I told Ashley about Fred, and how he tried so hard to get me out of there. I explained how I could almost feel Fred's pain as I remembered watching that second spear pierce through his lifeless body.

I took a little breather and then I told Ashley about Tyler's rotting corpse holding the spear gun in his hand and pointing it right at me, while he spoke. I started to tremble, and Ashley took me in her arms again. I whispered those words that kept echoing through my mind.

"You are mine, Robbie; nobody else can have you…"

"It was just a really bad dream; you know that, right? I wish I could do more to help you," Ashley said. "Your mind is still trying to process your past. We will get through this, I promise."

"Ever since I saw him, or rather, think I saw him on the bus, he has been on my mind. I can't seem to get rid of him, no matter how hard I try. It's like he's haunting me. I know that you think it's crazy, Ashley, or maybe I am going crazy, but I just can't shake the feeling that he is still after me."

"Oh Bobby, you know that it's not possible, right? He's dead. You are projecting. It was someone that looked a lot like him, maybe. Detective Collins told us that he was killed, remember?"

"I remember what he said; it's a little vague though. But I know what I saw, and I can't get him out of my mind. I know it sounds far-fetched, but my gut tells me that he is still out there."

The tears started again, and I curled up in Ashley's arms.

"Okay, I hear you. I know that you're not crazy, and if it will make you feel better, maybe we should give Detective Collins a call later today and see what he thinks about this."

"That sounds like a great idea," I whispered.

We put that conversation to rest for a bit and just lay there, in each other's arms. We watched the bright orange and purple sunrise. It looked like it was going to be another beautiful day.

Maestro soon became restless. He started pacing around the den. Ashley got up and put him outside on his chain, and then we went into the kitchen and prepared breakfast. It didn't take long before Maestro started barking at the door. I guess he was hungry too. We all had breakfast and then got ready to go for a walk. Maestro was very excited about that.

We headed through the pasture till we came to the entrance of the trail. The gate was open again.

"Not again" Ashley yelled. "Damn it, I'm sure I closed it last time we walked."

"You did," I replied, "I remember. You were upset that it had been left open and you made sure that you latched it when we came back through on our way home."

"It's a beautiful trail, and I don't mind if the locals use it, but at least they could ask permission, or just close the freaking gate when they see that it is usually kept closed."

"So, you think it's locals?" I asked.

"Who else would it be?"

"I don't know. I'm just paranoid; you know that."

I casually scanned the area, hoping that Ashley wouldn't notice.

"You are still worried about yesterday, I know. We'll call the detective as soon as we get back, I promise."

We had a beautiful, incident-free hike in the forest. I was a little better at keeping up this time. Ashley had turned into quite a machine, hiking these mountains every day. Maestro had no problem keeping up with her. When we reached the pasture on our way back, we made sure that the gate was latched properly before heading to the house.

We walked in the door and I went straight to the refrigerator for refreshments, while Ashley prepared to make her phone call, as promised.

"I don't imagine he will answer but I will leave a message for him to call us back," she said as she dialed. "I am going on speaker, in case you have something to add."

"Hello, this is Detective Joe Collins, how can I help you?"

"Uh… oh… hi… I'm sorry, I wasn't expecting you to answer. It's Ashley Carter. Bobby is here with me."

"Oh, Dr. Carter, Miss Hansen, it's really nice to hear from you. How are you both doing?"

"We are well, thanks," Ashley replied, "but we have some questions for you. Do you have time to talk or would you like to call us back?"

I brought our drinks into the living room and sat down next to Ashley.

"Hey Detective," I said.

"Miss Hansen… how's it going? It's been a while. Hey, last I heard, you were taking off on a sailing adventure."

"Yup, I got caught in a tropical storm and my boat took a beating but I'm okay. Now I'm back on solid ground."

"Glad to hear you are okay. So, what can I do for you? You say you have some questions? Well, I have a little time right now so, sure… what would you like to know?"

Ashley jumped in, "We don't want to take too much of your time, you must be very busy, so I guess we might as well get right to the point. It's about Tyler. Bobby thinks she might have seen him yesterday."

"No, that's not possible," he said. "Tyler Murphy is dead."

"Listen, Detective, I am doing very well these days and I am slowly sorting out my past. I am not going crazy, but I am very sure that I saw him on a bus when we went to town yesterday. He was looking right at me."

Tears started flowing down my cheeks.

"I'm sorry, Miss Hansen, and for the record, I never thought you were crazy, but there's no way… he's dead."

"You say that, but…"

Ashley got up and brought me over the box of tissues.

"Here you go, Bobby; I've got this."

I nodded, leaned back in the sofa, and wiped my tears.

"Listen, Detective, we were talking about it today, and Bobby only vaguely remembers what you said when you went to the hospital to tell her about the day you caught up with Tyler and David. I wonder if you can recount to us again what transpired."

"It's not a problem. Just give me a minute and I will get out the file. I will never forget that day, but at the same time, I just want to make sure I have all my facts straight; it's been a while."

Ashley leaned back next to me and we waited in anticipation for him to start.

"Okay, here we go. It was early January, and we still had a warrant out for both Tyler and David. Their pictures had been sent to all the media outlets. It took a while, but we got lucky. A gas station attendant called and reported that he had served a client that bore a resemblance to one of the men he had seen on the news that the police were looking for.

"I sent a couple of officers, Davies and Richardson, down there right away because I realized that it was close to Tyler's farmhouse where we found Miss White. The officers showed him the pictures and the attendant confirmed that it was David Johnson, alias David Allen, that he had served. I hightailed it out to the farmhouse. The officers were waiting for me at the end of the lane. There were a few sets of tracks in the snow. I remember thinking how lucky we were that they might be there together."

We heard the detective shuffle some papers and waited patiently for him to continue.

"I had called for back-up from the local police, but I didn't want to wait too long, so we started up the lane without them. We parked far enough away from the house so we wouldn't be spotted. We went the rest of the way on foot, hiding behind trees or whatever we could."

He hesitated again, for a moment.

"I'm sorry, I'm reading practically straight from the report. I just don't want to forget anything."

"It's okay, go on," Ashley said. "Are you okay, Bobby?"

"I'm fine with this; I want to know every detail."

"Alright then," he said. "Let's see now… I sent Davies and Richardson up the steps to the main entrance of the house and I went around the side toward the back, figuring that if they spotted the officers out front, they would run out that way. As I rounded the corner, I saw someone running. I picked up the pace and followed. I wasn't sure who it was. He had his back to me and was wearing winter attire, but I continued my pursuit. I called out to him, identifying myself, and he kept running. I heard a gunshot and I saw him go down. I went running toward him, thinking it was one of my officers that shot him. Then before I could reach him, I heard another shot, and I felt a sharp, burning pain in my arm and realized that I was also being targeted. I went down too."

"Yes, I remember you had your arm in a sling when you came to see me," Bobby said. "So, you're okay?"

"I'm fine; luckily, it was just a flesh wound. It went in one side and out the other, missed the bone completely."

"I'm really glad to hear that. So… what happened next?"

"I kept my head down, but I turned to try to see who was shooting, then another shot rang out from inside the house, then another few shots. It was frustrating, because I couldn't really tell what was going on from where I was. I looked ahead at the person lying on the ground in front of me. He was still down and didn't look like he had moved. I tried to drag myself over to him, but with all the snow, I wasn't getting very far. I remember feeling a sharp pain and almost losing consciousness."

He paused.

"Are you okay, Detective?" Ashley asked.

"Yes, Miss Carter. I'm fine. I can appreciate, though, Miss Hansen, how thinking back on traumatic events can be very painful. Just needed a moment. I'm okay.

"Let's see now, I remember hearing a voice, and it brought me back. It was Officer Davies coming to check on me. He informed me that his partner saw David Johnson shooting his gun out the back door and called him out. Mr. Johnson turned and shot at Richardson, and Richardson shot back. Richardson went down and then Officer Davies shot at Mr. Johnson and he went down too. Davies checked on his partner, who was unconscious but still had a faint pulse. He called for paramedics and then came to check on me. We heard sirens in the distance. Help was on the way."

"I didn't remember the part about the officer who got shot. I hope he's okay," I said.

"Sadly, he died before the ambulance could get to us."

"I'm so sorry."

"Thanks, Miss Hansen; he was a good man."

"So…" Ashley hesitated a moment, "was it Tyler you were chasing, who went down right after you heard the first shot?"

"Yes, all the evidence points to him. I'm getting to that."

"Oh... okay," Ashley whispered.

"Officer Davies helped me to my feet. He held onto me as we walked over to check on him. He was lying face down in the snow, a little distance from where I fell. There was so much blood on the snow all around him. I couldn't imagine that this person was still alive. We heard a cracking noise coming from under our feet. I remember looking around and noticing that we were on very flat terrain. It suddenly came to me, and I remember yelling out loud, that we were on the lake. The officer grabbed hold of me and practically dragged me back to shore. We turned around just in time to see the body fall through the ice."

"So… see? You don't know. It could have been anyone," Bobby interrupted.

"It was Tyler, Miss Hansen, we are sure. When we went back to check on Officer Richardson, to our surprise, we were greeted by Johnson. He was sitting, slouched up against a wall, completely covered in blood, and with his gun aimed right at us. I put my hands in the air and tried to talk to him. He asked us to throw our guns down, which we did. He had heard the sirens too and told us to keep them away. He allowed me to send Richardson around front to hold them off. He seemed to want to talk, so I took advantage of that. Time was running out, though, and I needed some answers. I asked him about Frank Johnson, and he started to sob.

"Johnson said, 'He was my brother and that fucking Murphy killed him. He needed to die. I hope he rots in hell.'

"He started to choke, and I moved forward a bit. He raised his gun again and told me to stay back.

"I asked if there was anything that I could do to help him, and that the paramedics were just out front, and he refused. I asked about Harold and Emma Baker.

"He said, 'A poor fucking excuse for foster parents is what they were. He worked us like slaves and raped us when he was drinking too much, which was always. She was no better; she loved to take the stick and beat us every chance she had. We lived in hell and nobody gave a shit.'

"I asked, and he admitted to killing them.

"'Payback,' he said, 'It felt fucking good.'

"I asked him what Tyler's role in all this was. He said that Tyler was his only friend while he was in foster care at the Bakers. They spent every summer hanging out together as much as they could. He confirmed that Tyler knew everything that was going on inside their house. After he and his brother ran away from there, they communicated with him from time to time.

"He said that Tyler showed up at their doorstep one day and told them about his girlfriend who was living with the Bakers and getting tortured like they did. He added that Tyler talked to him about revenge, and how he would feel so much better about himself if he acted on it. He also told them that he would give them an outrageous amount of money if they took the Bakers out of the picture. Johnson said that his brother Frank knew very little about what was going to happen, that he really didn't want to involve him, but it wasn't something he could do alone."

"Did he say who he was shooting at… who he killed on the ice?" Ashley asked.

"I asked, of course, and he said that it was Tyler. Johnson went on to say, 'He killed the only family that I had.'

"Then he started to sob again, and added, 'The girl, she was just collateral damage, she wasn't supposed to be there. Tyler said she was going to sleep over at a friend's house. I left her for dead. We hightailed it out of there before Tyler found out. We had to disappear.'

"He was getting weaker and I didn't know how much longer he would last. He said that he heard you had survived and were arrested for the murders. He knew that you had lost your memory, but he needed to be sure, so he kept track of you. He even had someone on the inside keeping him informed of your activities."

"Oh… my… God! Are you kidding me?" I yelled.

Suddenly I went numb and my mind started to wander. *Who could it have been? A doctor, one of the shrinks… no it couldn't be… or one of the crazies in the psych ward? Maybe… freaking hell, I can't…*

"Bobby, are you okay?" Ashley asked. This brought me back to reality.

"Oh… yeah… sorry, I got distracted; please continue, Detective."

"Are you sure?" he replied.

"Yes, I need to know."

Ashley took me by the hand and the detective continued.

"Alright, where was I... oh yes. David said he got the job at the hospital so he could keep track of you, and at some point, he had heard that you were having flashbacks of your past, and he knew he was going to have to finish what he had started. Then Tyler came into the picture, and that complicated things a little for him. He said that Tyler was obsessed with you, as much now as he was then, and he was ready to kill anyone who got in his way. Johnson also said to tell you that he had nothing to do with Miss White's murder. She got wise to Tyler and he killed her, the same way he killed his brother. He said he felt bad for what happened to you, that it was all Tyler's doing from the start.

"'All I wanted to do was kill those mother fuckers who tortured the hell out of me and my brother,' he said.

"Those were his last words, and with the little bit of strength he had left, he lifted the gun to his head. I turned away and the blast rang through my ears.

"The next thing I remember, I was in the hospital. I had lost a lot of blood, but I was okay.

"I gave my statement to the captain. It was very fresh in my mind.

"I'm sorry Miss Hansen, but I'm telling you... that was Tyler. Mr. Johnson shot him right in front of my eyes. He's dead; there was so much blood. There is no doubt in my mind."

"But there was no body," Bobby said. "You never found it."

"Yes, you're right. We couldn't look for him; the ice wasn't safe to walk on. We searched the shoreline till the next day, looking for any sign of someone walking off the lake. How long do you think someone with a bullet wound would last under the ice, in a frozen lake?"

"Did you search the lake after it thawed, send divers or something?"

"The local police took over from there; it happened outside of our jurisdiction. I never heard anything back from them and have no idea if they ever recovered his body. I can make a few calls if that would ease your mind."

"We would appreciate it very much," Ashley said.

"I am inclined to believe you, Miss Hansen, but I don't see how it is possible. I have learned though, since I have met you, that not everything is always as it seems. Officially, the case is closed, but unofficially, if you think you are still in danger, I will follow up on my own."

"Thank you, Detective. I have trouble believing it myself, but I have a bad feeling about this. Something doesn't feel right. Thanks for going over the report again, too. I can understand it better now than when it all happened. I was just too overwhelmed at the time."

"So, Bobby," Ashley said, "I have a question about the night your foster parents were killed; do you feel up to it?"

"I think so. I'll answer if I can. What would you like to know?"

"I'm just curious about something Joe said before. It seems that, according to David, Tyler informed him that you were not going to be there. Do you remember where you were supposed to be that night?"

"Yes, good question," Detective Collins said, "I was just wondering about that myself."

"Actually, I do remember. It came to me one night on my boat, when I was having difficulty putting my thoughts down on paper. My writing skills are not the best. I didn't get along very well in school. Being in foster care doesn't make you very popular, especially in a small town. I was an outcast. Teachers didn't like me very much, because I didn't belong, so neither did the students. I got picked on and bullied a lot by teachers as well as students.

"There was one girl, though, Darcy, who befriended me. She was a tough one. Nobody messed with her, but nobody really liked her either. She rescued me quite a few times from other bullies and we eventually became friends. I felt safe when I was with her and we became very close. I had confided in her about what was happening to me at home. She tried as often as possible to invite me to her house, so at least, on those nights, I would be safe.

"That night, though, after a full day of drinking, Harold was totally wasted and got it in his head that I was sneaking off to be with Tyler. There was nothing I could say or do to change his mind. We had a big argument, and then he beat me and sent me to my room."

"Oh Bobby," Ashley said softly as she put her arm around me and held me close. "You have told me a lot of stories about your past as the memories come back, but sometimes it seems like we haven't even scratched the surface. I feel for you, honey; I don't know how you have managed to survive all of this. You are a very strong woman."

"I second that, Miss Hansen; I've never met anyone quite like you."

"Thanks, Detective."

"Please, since everything is going to be so unofficial for the next little while, please call me Joe. I would like that."

"Thanks, Joe; it's a lot less formal."

"Well, I guess I should get back to work. No worries, though; I will try to see what I can find out and get back to you. Bye for now."

"Thanks Joe, talk to you soon."

Ashley hung up the phone. She and I had a lot to talk about.

It was way past lunchtime, so we just grabbed a little snack, two ice cold beers, and went to the porch. We spent the rest of the day mulling over all this information and trying to figure out what we should do next. It was going to be a long night.

Chapter 58

Morning came fast, and even though we hadn't slept very well, we had a very productive day. It started out with our morning hike in the forest with Maestro. After that, we headed to town for my appointment with Dr. Blake and had all the tests done that he had ordered for me. We had lunch with the doc, incident-free this time; did our errands; and made it back home just before supper. Maestro was very happy to see us again.

I tied him outside for a while and went back in to help Ashley prepare supper. We had steaks to cook out on the barbecue, potatoes to bake, and veggies for a salad, oh, and a good bottle of red wine. We were planning to have a wonderful dinner together.

It was a beautiful evening, so we decided to eat on the patio. I set the table and prepared the barbecue. There was no wind, so I decided to put out some candles and bring out my laptop to play some blues tunes while we ate.

I went inside to see how things were going and Ashley had everything under control. We went back out together, and I poured us each a glass of wine and we sat for a while and waited for the potatoes to cook.

Maestro, who was still tied out in the yard, started barking. Ashley yelled at him to stop. He didn't; he just kept barking and pulling on his chain in the direction of the woods.

"Maestro, stop," she yelled again. "It's probably just some deer or something. It's almost sunset; they tend to come out more in the evening."

She got up and went to get him. He was still pulling, and he almost got away from her, but she held on tight. Into the house he went, where she served him his supper to quiet him down.

On her way back, she brought out the steaks and started the grill. I was about to say…

"Yes, I know," she cut in, "You like your steak still mooing! Now get your butt in the house and take the potatoes out of the oven; they're ready."

Ashley started to laugh and smacked me on the behind as I walked past her.

I was on my way back out to the porch when the phone rang.

"Get that, would you, honey?" Ashley said. "I'm watching the steaks."

I put the potatoes down and went to get her phone.

"Sorry, I missed the call," I said when I came back out.

"It's okay; they'll leave a message. I'll check it later. Steaks are ready."

I went back for the salad and we sat down to eat just in time to watch the brilliantly orange sunset behind the mountains. What a spectacular view, and we had front row seats again. I watched Ashley as she gazed at the setting sun with that beautiful smile. Her eyes were glistening as she turned and looked at me.

"I really missed you, you know," she said. "I was so worried about losing you when I heard about the storm heading your way. I wish you wouldn't go back out."

"But I…"

"I'm sorry, Bobby; I didn't really want to bring that up. Let's not talk about that right now. Let's just enjoy our evening."

Ashley didn't bring it up again, and neither did I. We finished our meal and enjoyed the rest of the wine. We talked and laughed and had a marvelous time. Ashley stood up and took me by the hand. I got up too, and she took me in her arms. The music was still playing softly in the background and we started to slow-dance. It was amazing. Ashley had a way of making me feel very special. I smiled at her then lay my head on her shoulder. She combed her fingers through my hair. I had forgotten how good that felt.

My mind wandered, and it brought me back to when I was in my comatose state and Ashley was at my bedside. I remembered how her voice used to bring me into semi-consciousness. She would speak to me about all kinds of things, and it seemed like she was half-expecting me to answer her. It was almost like Ashley knew, or rather was hoping, that I was there and taking in every word that she said. She had no clue whether I could hear her or not, but she kept conversing with me just in case. Ashley had a beautiful calming voice that brought comfort to me and made me feel like I wasn't alone.

I remember laying there listening, and trying to imagine what she looked like, or even if she was real, or just another one of my dreams. I often thought that if she hadn't been there for me, I would have never woken up. Ashley was the reason that I came back; I was sure of that.

She never gave up on me, even though she was putting her own life at risk. She stuck by me through all of it. She helped me deal with all the truths that came out in the end. She was by my side throughout the court battle, and the day they cleared my name. Twenty years of my life had been stolen from me. I got very well-compensated for it, but it didn't come close to repairing the damage that I sustained. I thought, *I still feel like my life is in danger, and probably always will. I will always feel like there is someone lurking around the next corner...*

"Honey, you are a million miles away," Ashley whispered. "Are you okay?"

"Sure," I said. "I was just thinking."

"What about?"

"About you," I replied, then I kissed her.

Ashley responded, very passionately. Still dancing, she very subtly started to make her way to the door.

"Do you really think that I don't know what you're doing?" I said.

"What… I just want to let Maestro out to do his business."

"Right," I said, and I started to laugh.

Ashley opened the door to let him out... big mistake. He hightailed it out into the yard and across the field. She jumped off the porch and ran after him. I grabbed a flashlight and made my way out there too. I could hear Ashley calling for Maestro, but I couldn't see where she was. I didn't go far because I didn't know my way around in the dark very well. I was starting to get nervous, because I didn't like being out there alone either. I called out Ashley's name again and again, no answer. I heard Maestro barking, then finally, I heard Ashley. She was yelling at him. I shone the light in the direction of her voice. I finally spotted her and then ran out to help.

She had Maestro by the collar. He was barking and pulling hard to try to get away. Both of us tried to calm him down, without success. We forcefully brought him back into the house. He never relented. There was something out there that was bothering him. Whatever it was, was starting to bother me too.

"What the hell is wrong with him?" I yelled

"I don't know," Ashley replied. "He has never gone psycho like that before. Maybe we have trespassers on the property, the same ones who keep leaving the gate open. I will have to put some signs up and put a lock on the gate."

"Do you think that will stop them?"

"I don't know. Anyway, I'm not really sure what is going on."

"Should we call the police? I can't believe I just said that, but I'm scared, Ash. I keep thinking about the bus. I know that nobody thinks he is still alive, but what if?"

"I hear you, but let me just check things out tomorrow and see if there is any evidence of anyone camping out in the woods. I'll bring Maestro with me. If there is anyone out there, I'm sure he will find them. I'll even call the neighbors to see if they have seen anything out of the ordinary going on around here."

"I am going to go with you; I don't want to stay here alone."

"Of course, we have all day. Do you think you can keep up?" Ashley winked.

"Ha...ha, very funny." I threw a cushion at her.

Maestro sat there and watched as we carried on. Ashley went over to the laptop and put on some more music.

"Wine?" she asked.

"I thought we finished the bottle."

"I have one hiding in the cupboard... that I put aside for a rainy day."

"I don't think it's raining," I said, and started to laugh.

"Oh... I do."

Ashley went over and retrieved the bottle. She popped the cork and poured us each a glass. She danced her way over to me and made a toast.

"To the love of my life."

We kissed, and she handed me her glass and the bottle.

"Take these into our room, honey," she said.

"Where are you going?" I asked, as she left the room.

Ashley went into the bathroom and I heard the shower come on.

"Bobby," she said. "What did I tell you... it's raining, come and join me while the water is still hot."

I loved her silliness; I never knew what to expect from her. I brought the wine into our bedroom and went back for the candles and the laptop. I closed the door and made my way to the kitchen.

"Bobby, honey, I'm cooling down; I am going to need some major warming up here."

I quickly grabbed a treat for Maestro and headed for the washroom. Ashley opened the curtain and watched as I undressed. I took my time in doing so and threw my clothes around the room as I removed them. I could see that Ashley was getting really turned on by the whole production.

"Madam," Ashley said, as she reached out and took my hand. I stepped into the shower and Ashley pulled me close. We kissed for the longest time, the hot water trickling down between our faces and bodies. Ashley pulled away and looked into my eyes.

"I love you, Bobby. I think I did from the first day I saw you lying in that hospital bed, so helpless and so vulnerable. I promise that I will always be here for you, if you want me to be."

She grabbed the loofah sponge and squeezed some body wash onto it, never taking her eyes off me. My heart was pounding, and I was overflowing with desire. Ashley gently brushed the loofah up against my chest. I took a deep breath and closed my eyes. She slowly circled my breasts, one, and then the other. I grabbed her by the shoulders, thinking that I might lose my balance. She put her arms around me and gave my back a gentle soapy massage. I trembled with passion. Ashley was so amazing, and she knew exactly what to do. She knew where all my buttons were, and exactly when to push them. She brought her lips close to my ear.

"Are you okay?" she whispered.

I sighed, "Never been better."

"Okay… going down…"

I grabbed the towel rack to steady myself.

I felt the sponge slither down past my lower back as Ashley's tongue slid down past my navel. I could hardly breathe. I grabbed hold of the curtain and just about ripped it off the rod as I lost control and exploded in total ecstasy. Ashley stopped and grabbed hold of me so I wouldn't fall.

"Okay… I guess it is getting a little too hot in here," she said. "Let's go find that bottle and finish what we started, where you can't fall and hurt yourself."

She dried me off, just a bit, and led me to the bedroom.

Maestro wasn't very happy when we closed the door behind us.

We drank a little more wine and talked as we lay naked, in each other's arms. Inevitably, hands started roaming, and soon after, screams of passion resonated throughout our home.

Chapter 59

I opened my eyes. There was a little bit of light coming through the sides of the curtains lighting up the room just enough, so I knew that I wasn't in another one of my dreams... I was home. I rolled over to look at Ashley, but she wasn't there. I could hear some noises coming from outside the bedroom door. I couldn't quite make out what it was. I listened hard. It sounded like heavy breathing and something scratching at the door. I got nervous, sat up, and pulled the blankets up around me. I heard a voice in the distance. I focused on it, and then back to the breathing and the scratching again. The voice was getting closer. I let out a sigh of relief and started to giggle.

"Maestro… get away from the door," I heard her say. "Let Bobby sleep."

"I'm awake, Ash."

The door opened, just a crack, but he managed to push his way in. He ran over to me and jumped up and put his front paws on the edge of the bed.

"I'm sorry, Bobby; I wanted to let you sleep."

"It's okay; I was awake. Something smells good."

"Come on then, I made you breakfast. I figured that you would have probably worked up an appetite after last night."

She gave me a kiss, winked, and headed back to the kitchen.

"Oh, put some clothes on. It's a beautiful morning and I set the table on the patio."

I remembered about the hike, so I got right into my track pants and t-shirt and went and joined her in the kitchen.

"Coffee smells great, and everything else. Wow… you have been busy. Can I help?"

"No, everything is under control. Why don't you take our coffees out to the porch and I will join you, momentarily?"

"As you wish," I said and headed out.

The first thing I saw as I opened the door was a big beautiful bouquet of wildflowers sitting in the middle of the elegantly set table. I put the cups down and peeked back into the house.

"Wow, Ash, you are spoiling me. You know I could get used to this."

"Well don't!" she hollered and started to laugh. "Sorry, I'm just kidding around. It is a special day, though."

"Really? My bad, have I forgotten something? I know it's not your birthday."

"No, you're right, it's not, and this probably doesn't mean anything to you because you were kind of out of it. It is the anniversary of the first day I met you in the hospital, when Dr. Blake asked for a consult. I was looking through my files early this morning and I realized that this is the anniversary. So, I thought I would do something special."

"Are you sure you didn't know about this last night?"

We laughed.

I helped her bring the food out and we enjoyed our wonderful breakfast together. I went back in to get more coffee, and Ashley's phone rang. I grabbed it, brought it out to her, and went back in, once again, for the coffee. When I returned, she was still on the phone.

"She's here... hang on," she put her hand over the phone.

"Who is it?" I asked.

"It's the marina," she whispered, "they want to talk to you."

"Sure, put them on speaker."

"She's here; I am putting you on speaker."

"Miss Hansen?"

"Yes, speaking. How's my boat doing? I was wondering when I would hear back from you."

"Sorry, we were rather busy with the storm, as you know. Yours was not the only vessel that sustained damages. You, actually, were one of the most fortunate ones."

"That's good to hear. Sorry, I didn't want to sound like I was pressuring you; I was just curious to know how she was doing."

"That's okay. Everyone has been bombarding us with calls, but we are doing our best to see that everyone is satisfied. I called last night; did you not receive it?"

"Oops," Ashley whispered.

"Oh, I'm sorry, we must have missed that. It was raining really hard here." I winked. "So, what's the verdict?"

"She's fine. A few scratches here and there, but no structural damage. The water that was inside come from the hatch; there's no leak. We repair the mast and installed a new sail, so you are pretty well good to go."

"That's great."

"Oh, and we can store your boat for a little bit longer if you need us to, but if you could pick up your belongings, I would really appreciate it. I guess in all the excitement, you forgot it on-board. I have it in my safe, but people have seen it and are talking. I don't want to be responsible for it."

"What? I don't know what you are talking about."

"Your dagger."

"My..."

I had to think for a minute. Ashley had a strange look on her face.

"Oh yes," I replied. "That thing. I totally forgot about it."

Ashley whispered, "What in the hell?"

I shushed her and continued.

"So... you have it?"

"Yes, like I said it's in my safe, but I don't want to keep it. It looks like it's worth a pretty penny, and I wouldn't want anything to happen to it."

"Okay, I understand. Thanks for taking care of it. I will call you back this afternoon and let you know my plans."

"Great, I'll wait for your call. Later then."

Ashley hung up the phone. "What in the hell was that all about?"

"Oh my God, I totally forgot about that," I said.

"About what?"

"It's a dagger that we found diving."

"We? Who's we?"

"Oh, sorry, Fred and me... Fred the dolphin."

"Well, I gathered that; I don't know any other Freds. You never told me about that. Okay, start from the beginning."

"Fred and I used to dive every morning, weather permitting. We didn't usually stray very far. We normally just swam around and played with the other dolphins. We would also check out the reefs for anything interesting that might be going on. We just enjoyed each other's company."

"Sounds nice."

"Anyway, one day during our dive, I noticed that he seemed to want to stray a bit. I was hesitant, but I trusted that he knew my limits and wouldn't lead me into trouble, so as he circled back toward me, I grabbed his fin and off we went on our adventure."

"What happened to never stray too far from your vessel!"

"I know, Ash, but I trusted him. Let me finish."

"Okay, sorry."

"We were moving right along till he slowed down and came to a stop. I looked around us and there wasn't much of anything, except for a little clump of coral. He moved closer to it and I followed. He seemed to want me to examine it, so I moved, still a little closer to take a good look at it. That is when I saw it."

"The dagger?" Ashley asked.

"Yes. I didn't know what it was at first; there was just a little corner of it sticking out from under the coral. I gently pulled it out from its resting place. It was covered in growth from the ocean floor. I thought it was a broken sword because of the handle, and it wasn't very long."

"What happened then?" Ashley asked.

"Nothing. I brought it back to the boat, cleaned it, and hung it up in the cabin. I totally forgot about it after that."

"Where do you think it came from? Do you think it's worth anything?"

"No clue. I couldn't tell a real jewel from a fake. Anyway, it looks like we are going to have to go and get it, and you can see it for yourself."

"I guess we need to plan a road trip. We'll call him back after our hike. We'll talk about it as we walk."

"Seriously? I'm stuffed; I don't think I can move."

"Suit yourself, but you said last night that you didn't want to stay here alone."

"You're right, I did, but can we just relax a bit more first?"

"Okay, sit and digest a bit but I'm going to get my backpack ready. You have half an hour, then you need to get your lazy butt moving."

She winked, gave me a kiss, and then went into the house. I closed my eyes and listened to the birds chirping. *I could get used to this,* I thought.

It wasn't long before I heard Ashley calling me. I went inside and she and Maestro looked like they were ready to go. I got into my hiking boots and we headed out the door. Ashley held on tight as Maestro led the way. He was very excited.

There wouldn't be any stopping to smell the roses on this trip. We were on a mission: Ashley was looking for trespassers. As hard as I tried to kind of laugh this off, deep down inside of me I was terrified. Even though nobody else thought it was possible that he was alive, my gut was telling me otherwise. If he was out there, he would be coming after me. I just couldn't shake that feeling.

"Earth to Bobby, are you okay?" Ashley said.

"Sorry, I have a lot on my mind."

"You're worried, I know. Nothing is going to happen; we are just checking the forest for trespassers. We have Maestro; he will protect us."

"Right, he will lick them to death?"

"Don't underestimate him; he didn't seem very happy last night when he was barking. Anyway, I came prepared."

She pointed at what was hanging off her belt.

"What in the hell is that?" I asked.

"Bear spray," she replied.

"What?"

"Well, if it works on bears, I feel safe. Now, let's get going. I won't let anything happen to you, I promise."

She took me by the hand and off we went, Maestro in the lead.

We were moving right along. I hadn't gone this far before and had no clue where we were.

"Are we still on our property? It seems like we have been walking for hours."

"We have, silly, and the answer to your question is yes. Don't worry, I know where I'm going. We are heading to the top of that ridge."

I looked up. "Are you freaking kidding me?"

"We can see everything from up there," Ashley said. "Don't worry, I have been up there before. I know how to get there and back blindfolded."

"What? So… you have a compass stuck up your ass? Are you sure you know where you're going?"

"Ha…ha… come on, Bobby; you wanted to come, now get your butt in gear."

"I know, I know, I'm just kidding around. You're a freaking machine. Can't we just take a little break, five minutes, so I can catch my breath... anyway, I need to pee?"

"Sure, go ahead." Ashley reached into her pocket and handed me a Ziploc bag and a tissue. "You can go on the side of the trail there, just don't throw…"

"I know, the tissue goes in the bag."

I looked up and down the trail before I squatted, which was silly; we were on our own property. To be fair though, we were looking for intruders, so it wasn't really that ridiculous.

I did my business, and just as I was about to step back onto the trail, something caught my eye.

"Ash, quick, over there!"

"What?" she whispered.

"Over there, I saw something moving fast. It looked… I don't know, something white."

"Where?"

I tried to point it out to her, but I didn't see it anymore either.

"I'm sorry, I thought I saw something move; I guess I'm just a little jumpy."

"It is possible, Bobby. There is a little stream down at the bottom of this slope and wildlife often gather there to drink."

"Should we check it out?"

"Sure, if you want; it might be a good place to take a break."

"I was hoping you would say that."

"I know," Ashley winked.

The climb down was a little tricky. There was no trail, so we were just making our own way, climbing down rocks and weaving through the trees and shrubs. Ashley and Maestro had no trouble getting through. It was a little harder for me, but I made it.

"Wow, that was something!" I said.

"Yes indeed, so now you will need your rest, because we are going to have to go right back up the same way we came."

"What! There's no other way?"

"Not really; we need to follow the trail."

"Oh crap, what did I get myself into?"

Ashley shook her head and started to laugh.

Maestro headed straight for the water. I looked around me and had that old feeling of *déjà vu* again. It was beautiful. The sound of the water trickling over the rocks and the fallen tree over the stream all brought back memories of my safe place.

"It is so beautiful here," I said. "Remember the safe place I told you about? It looked very similar to this."

A tear started rolling down my face. I closed my eyes for a moment. Ashley put her arms around me and held me close.

"It's okay, honey; I'm here. It is a very beautiful place, and you were happy in your safe place too. It's everywhere else that was hell. This is your place now, all of it, and I will make sure it stays that way.

Now let's rest a bit and enjoy the view and then get back on the trail and finish what we've started."

We made our way over to the fallen tree and slid across it so we could hang our feet over the stream. Maestro lay down and rested nearby. We held hands and watched the water as it splashed over the rocks. Ashley reached into her backpack and pulled out a couple of snack bars and water bottles.

"I heard your stomach before; we don't want to keep it waiting."

"I was getting a little hungry," I replied. "Thanks."

When we were done, we got off the log and prepared to get back up that hill. As I bent down to tighten the lace on my boot, I saw a paper wrapper under the log where we were sitting.

"Hey Ash, here, I think you dropped this."

"What is it?"

"The wrapper from your snack; I still have mine."

Ashley pulled hers out of her pocket.

"I've got mine right here," she said. "Let me see that?"

She took the wrapper from me and examined it.

"Okay," she said. "Somebody has been here; this is not ours."

"Maybe you dropped it on another one of your hikes."

"No, it's not a brand that I buy," Ashley replied. "It has nuts; it's someone else's."

"It hasn't been here long; it isn't weathered at all."

"Oh no…"

"Oh yes, we have trespassers."

Maestro came over. It looked like he had picked up a scent from the wrapper. He was getting very agitated. I started to stress as I scanned the area.

We climbed back up the hill and continued on our way. Maestro was raring to go after that rest. I found the climb quite difficult, but we made it. We sat down at the edge of the cliff, relaxed, and enjoyed the view.

"Wow, this is amazing," I said. "You've been up here before?"

"Many times, yes. It's like my dessert after the hard work getting up here. Are you okay?"

"I'm good; this is great. It's very beautiful here. I don't know how I'll feel tomorrow, but I'm trying not to think about that. I've got other things on my mind."

I took Ashley's hand and asked, "So what are we going to do? Do you think that when I saw something move before that it was the intruder?"

I was trying not to say his name, but in my mind, it was him. Ashley turned and shrugged. She knew exactly what I was thinking; I could see it in her eyes.

"When we get back, we will call the local law enforcement. Then we should get back to Detective Collins to see if he has any news. He seemed like he wanted to help."

We started to head down the mountain. We took a different trail going back. We were about an hour into our descent, when Ashley stopped. She put her hand over my mouth and whispered, "Be quiet; I see something."

She pointed to the right of the trail. It looked like someone had set up camp. We looked around and didn't see anyone.

"Stay here," she said, as she headed over to inspect the area, holding Maestro close to her side.

Of course, I wasn't going to stay there by myself, so I quietly followed behind her.

"Whoever was here left in a hurry, and not that long ago," Ashley finally said.

There was scattered garbage and a log, strategically placed to sit in front of a now extinguished campfire.

"Not long ago, how do you know?" I asked.

"Watch."

Ashley picked up a branch that was blackened on one end which was lying next to the campfire. She stuck it into the center of the ashes. She pried down on it and bright red coals came to the surface.

"Oh my God," I gasped and then looked around again for fear that someone might be out there watching us.

"How did you know?" I asked.

"I felt the heat on my legs as I walked past it. Someone has been squatting out here for a little while. The terrain is very worn around the campfire, and the bastard left all his garbage behind."

"I'm not liking this at all," I said.

"Me neither… let's get out of here."

Maestro wasn't interested in going, though; he was sniffing all over the place. Ashley tugged on the leash a few times and he finally obeyed. We headed back down the mountain.

"What was that?" I said, then stopped dead in my tracks.

"I don't know," Ashley replied. "Maybe thunder?" She shrugged.

We continued on our way. Maestro still seemed to be following a scent even on the trail. That was making me very nervous. We were finally nearing the bottom when Maestro started going ballistic. It took both of us to hang onto him.

"What in the hell is wrong with him?" I yelled.

"I don't know; let's hurry!"

We ran the rest of the way till we got to the field. Then we stopped. Ashley took a good look around to make sure that the coast was clear, and we weren't in danger of running into anyone.

I was glad for the break; I was so out of breath. I turned to Ashley and saw the look on her face.

"What now?" I asked.

Ashley didn't answer. I turned to try to see what she was looking at just as she started to run.

"The house!" she yelled.

She pulled out her phone and threw it at me as she ran off, Maestro by her side, still barking his head off.

"Call 911…"

I froze as I looked toward the house and saw the smoke rising.

"Hurry!" Ashley yelled.

I fumbled with the phone a bit, called the number, gave all the details, and then tried to catch up with them. Tears blurred my vision as I reached our yard. I could hear Maestro barking, but I couldn't see him through the smoke.

Ashley wasn't anywhere in sight either. I called out to her several times, but she didn't respond. Maestro ran over to me, still barking.

I was very worried about Ashley, but I didn't know what to do, and without giving it a second thought, I ran into the house after her.

The smoke was so thick, I couldn't see anything.

"Ashley," I cried. "Where are you? Ashley..."

There was no response.

I ran into the bedroom, hoping to find her there, and called her name again, but there was no sign of her. I thought of my laptop, so I grabbed my pack and threw it over my shoulders. I left the room and headed toward the kitchen.

"Ashley, where are you?" I yelled.

I couldn't see a thing anymore. I was choking, and I didn't know how much longer I could stay in there. The heat was unbearable. I don't think that I even made it as far as the kitchen when something exploded. The blast threw me backward and onto the floor. I was stunned for a moment, then survival kicked in and I jumped to my feet to try to get out of there. I headed in the opposite direction of the explosion. I was probably about halfway through the living room when I tripped over something and fell to the floor again. I scrambled to my knees and felt around to try to find what I had tripped over. It didn't take me long to recognize the shape on the floor.

"Ashley, oh my god... Ashley!"

She was not responding. I was screaming at her, but nothing, she was unconscious. I was choking and could hardly take a breath. I didn't have the strength to get to my feet, so I grabbed Ashley by the arms and started dragging her across the floor. I was hoping that I was going the right way, but after my fall, I got totally disoriented, and with all the smoke I couldn't know for sure. I kept going, though, just out of desperation. I came to a wall. I couldn't stop, I had to keep moving. I made my way alongside of it, hoping to find the door. Ashley was getting heavier as I got weaker.

I heard the sound of sirens in the distance. I couldn't stop now; we were almost there. My mind was getting fuzzy, and the lack of oxygen was taking its toll. I started to freak out and didn't know where in the hell I was anymore, and then I heard barking.

"Maestro!" I yelled.

He gave me renewed hope. I knew that we were close. I had to hang on a bit longer. I pulled, and pulled some more, but I wasn't getting anywhere.

"Maestro!" I called again, with the little bit of energy I had left.

I felt a wet tongue lick the side of my face and knew that he had found us. Together, we tugged and pulled at Ashley to try to get her out of the fire. I had no clue how far we were from the door, but at some point, I just stopped. I was overcome with exhaustion and couldn't go any farther. I keeled over and lay my head on Ashley's chest. Ashley didn't budge, and at that point, I couldn't move anymore, myself. Maestro started barking again, non-stop. There was nothing I could do. It was over, I was fading fast…

Chapter 60

I heard a sound, not sure what it was. Maybe a soft breeze, or water flowing. I couldn't see anything, though; it was too dark. I wasn't afraid; I felt like I was in a good place.

"Hello," I said. "Is anybody out there?"

I saw something glowing off in the distance. It started out like a small dot, and slowly started to grow. I had to close my eyes for a moment so they could adjust to the light; it was so bright.

I heard a sound again, seagulls this time, I think. Yes, and children laughing. I slowly opened my eyes to a spectacular view. The sun was shining brightly in the sky over the beautiful turquoise water, and the beach was filled with people. Some were sunbathing, and others were splashing around in the water. They were having lots of fun.

I looked around me to see if I recognized the place, but I didn't. What was I doing here? I looked toward the ocean and saw sailboats in the distance. I wondered if one of them was mine, but why would I be on shore? I was confused. I took a closer look at the people on the beach, their hairstyles and bathing suits, and then I realized that they were not today's styles. I don't know what year it was, but this was not present day.

"Roberta!" I heard someone calling. "Roberta, honey, where are you?"

I turned toward the voice and then I saw her. My heart was pounding, and I felt the love radiating from her. I was so happy to see her again. She was so beautiful. Her satiny blond hair was flowing behind her as she searched…

For me? Oh my God, I was here? I don't remember this at all. I needed to help search. I scanned the people on the beach, especially where there were children playing. Suddenly all the voices got muffled. I didn't know what was happening. I focused hard. I heard something behind me. It was faint, but I could hear enough to know it was a child's laughter. I slowly turned around to see where the voice was coming from. A big smile came over my face. I couldn't believe my eyes: it was me, a really tiny me. I was so cute and so small. I couldn't have been more than three years old. I was playing in the water, fearless, letting the waves crash into me.

Mom spotted me and came running.

"Roberta, I told you not to leave my side. You can't go in the water alone. What am I going to do with you?"

She sat down next to me and they started splashing water at each other. I really wanted to join in, but I was obviously just a spectator on another one of my trips down memory lane.

"Mommy, Mommy, let's go swimming in the water."

"It's deep, Roberta, and you don't know how to swim yet."

"But I can if you hold me, please Mommy? I want to be like a fish."

"You are a fish. Just like your daddy, I'm afraid," she said, and a sadness came over her.

My jaw dropped. I had never really thought about my father. I don't remember him at all. It is like he never existed. I listened closely, hoping she would talk some more about him.

"Daddy's in the ocean, Mommy; you said he wasn't coming home. He was looking for treasures; do you think there is treasure here?"

"No, Roberta, there is no treasure here, and diving for treasure is very dangerous. Promise me you will never do that."

"But he found some, you told me."

"Yes, but jewel-covered artifacts buried on the ocean floor were more important to him than coming home to us. I'm sorry, I really don't want to talk about him anymore."

She was getting a little upset.

I started to cry, and she took me in her arms.

"I'm sorry, honey, I didn't want to yell at you. I should have never brought him up. Come with me, I will take you for a swim. I love you, Roberta, and I don't want to lose you too."

I couldn't believe my ears, diving for treasures? Tears started to flow, and my vision was blurring. I closed my eyes for a moment. I was so overcome with emotion that I couldn't breathe. I started to hyperventilate. I was gasping for air and my lungs felt like they were on fire…

Chapter 61

"Fire!" I yelled, as I opened my eyes, and struggled to get up. Something was on my face and I tried to push it away.

"Miss Hansen, please stay calm, you are going to be okay."

I looked up and there was a fireman leaning over me and many others huddled around. I felt the mask around my mouth.

I didn't know what was happening; hell, I didn't even know what was real anymore. I had just come from a beach, and now I was lying on the ground surrounded by firemen. Firemen? Fire? Oh my God!

"Ashley!" I yelled. I couldn't talk with that stupid thing on my face.

I ripped the mask off. "Ashley!" I yelled again. "Where is she?" I screamed.

"Get Dr. Carter, quickly!" someone yelled.

I needed to see her; I was sure that I had lost her.

"She's okay, Miss Hansen, she's with the paramedics," one of the firemen said.

I tried to lift my head and look around, but I didn't have the strength. I lay back down and the fireman put the oxygen mask back on me.

I tried to relax, but I needed answers. I heard something, but I couldn't quite make out what it was with all the noise around me. I listened hard and heard it again.

"Maestro!" I called out through the mask.

I heard a bark.

"Maestro? He's okay?" I said.

"He sure is," the fireman replied. "That's quite the dog you've got there. Somehow, he dragged both of you out of that burning house."

"I want to see him," I yelled.

I barely had time to finish my sentence when I saw him plowing his way through the crowd. He came to a screeching halt when he got to my side, and then he just sat down and looked at me. He probably wasn't sure what to make of the situation. The mask over my face seemed to be a little disturbing for him, I guess. I was about to take it off when…

"Bobby!"

I grabbed hold of the mask and threw it aside.

"Ash!" I yelled.

I started to sit up and Ashley came running through the crowd and threw herself on top of me.

"I was so worried about you, Bobby; I thought I lost you."

"I thought that I lost you too," I replied. "I found you on the floor."

We held each other closely.

"Okay, boys, show's over here," one of the firemen said. "We have lots of work to do. I'll check up on you girls in a bit. The paramedics are not far, if you need them."

I felt a wet tongue on my cheek. I'd been so focused on Ashley that I almost forgot about Maestro.

"Maestro, you saved us. You're such a good boy."

He was so excited that he sat right down on top of me, his front paws on top of Ashley, and let out a loud bark.

Ashley rolled over and lay down next to me. Maestro got up and started prancing around us.

"Take it easy, Maestro," Ashley said. "We love you too."

I turned on my side and pulled Ashley close to me again. I pressed my lips against hers and held her there for the longest time. I didn't ever want to let go, and I didn't care at this point who was around us. I didn't lose her, and right now, Ashley was all I had left in this world.

"Ouch, what in the hell?" I yelled.

Maestro jumped on top of us again; I guess he wanted a little attention too. We gave him a good rubdown, and the whole time we were doing that, I noticed that Ashley never took her eyes off me.

"Are you okay?" she asked. "You do realize that our house is burning down as we speak, right?"

"Oh my God, Ash, my brain is so scrambled right now that I don't know if I am coming or going. I think I am getting numb, like, oh well, just more shit happening to me, bring it on, what else can go wrong. Then other times, I do worry, and I am scared and lonely. The one thing I do know for sure right now is that I love you, Ash. I thought that you were dead when I found you on the floor in the house. I really don't give a shit about our home right now. Yes, it really sucks, but I'm just happy that you are alive. Why did you run into a burning house, anyway?"

"I thought I could try to put the fire out. I didn't want to lose our beautiful home. I headed straight for the kitchen where the fire seemed to have started but it was so hot in there and I couldn't breathe. I tried to get to the fire extinguisher, but I couldn't see what I was doing so I headed back out. I didn't get very far, and I started choking. I remember the burning in my lungs and then falling to the floor. Next thing I knew, I had an oxygen mask on my face and paramedics around me. Oh, and what do you mean you found me on the floor? Why were you in a burning house?"

"Why do you think? I was calling you from the yard and you wouldn't come out, so I ran in to look for you. I searched the house calling your name and you weren't answering. I started choking, and

I couldn't see anything, so I tried to find my way back out. Had I not tripped over you, I would have never found you."

I started to cry, and Ashley put her arms around me again.

"Shush, you found me Bobby, you saved me, everything is going to be okay, I promise."

"I tried to save you, but I couldn't find my way out and then Maestro found us. He helped me pull you for a bit until I couldn't breathe anymore and collapsed on top of you. I remember thinking that you were dead and then I blanked out. I woke up with an oxygen mask on my face too."

"Miss Hansen," a voice came from behind me. I turned to see another fireman.

"Sorry, I hate to break up the reunion, but you had this on your back when we found you and I don't want it to get lost in all the commotion."

"My backpack, thanks; I totally forgot about it."

"Chief Willis would like to talk to you both," he said, "if you are okay to walk over to his truck."

"Sure, no problem. Give us a minute, would you?" Ashley said.

He nodded and left us alone.

"Are you ready for this, Bobby? I'm a little nervous myself. I'm the one who made breakfast this morning. I really hope that I am not responsible for burning our house down by leaving the stove turned on or something."

"Oh, stop it, Ash; accidents happen, and anyway, I wouldn't blame you if you did, but let's not jump to conclusions. Let's go over and see what he has to say."

I put my arm around her, and we walked over to see the chief. Maestro followed behind. He didn't seem to want to leave our side. Someone had pulled our lawn chairs over beside the truck. The fire chief was waiting there to greet us.

"Hi, I'm Chief Willis. How are you two doing?" he said.

"A little shaken," I replied. "But we are both here to talk about it and that's what counts." A tear escaped from my eye as I spoke. "Sorry," I said, and wiped it away.

"It's okay. You know, you are both very lucky to have gotten out of there. You have a great friend here. What's his name?"

"Maestro," Ashley replied.

He barked.

The chief bent down and patted him.

"He has saved my life a couple of times already," I said. "He is a very well-trained retired sight dog."

"Well, you are darn lucky to have him, or you wouldn't be here. Have a seat; I need to talk to you both."

"Oh... oh, here we go," Ashley whispered. "What have I done?"

"I…" He started to speak, and then she cut him off.

"I made breakfast this morning," she said, "and then we went on a hike. Did I leave the stove on and burn my own house down?"

A tear rolled down her face. I reached over and put my hand on her lap.

"I wish it were that simple," he said.

"What do you mean?" I asked.

"We need to do a proper investigation, but arson is not out of the question."

"What, oh my God, are you kidding?" Ashley asked. "That's not possible; who would do that?"

I got very quiet and just sat there numb. I felt the fear building up inside of me again. I knew, but I didn't want to think about it. It was him; I could feel it. My heart started pumping faster and I was feeling panicky.

"Miss Hansen," the chief said, "are you okay?"

My tears started again. This time they were uncontrollable.

"Bobby, honey." Ashley took me in her arms. "It's going to be okay; we'll get through this."

"I'm very sorry, but I'm not really sure of anything right now," the chief said. "We will take a closer look once the smoke clears and we make sure the fire is completely extinguished so it is safe to go inside and do so."

"Arson? Really?" Ashley asked.

"As I said, we'll know more once we can safely go inside. Unfortunately, we can't allow you to go in until the investigation is over. We will have to cordon off your property."

"Good luck with that," Ashley replied. "We have three hundred and sixty-nine acres from here to the summit."

"Oh… okay… well, maybe just your yard then. Have you noticed anything out of the ordinary, lately?"

"Like trespassers?" I responded through my tears.

"Yes, anything you can think of."

"She means yes," Ashley said, "we have trespassers. We hiked up the mountain this morning to search the forest for signs. Our gate to the mountain trails was found open a couple of times recently, but we always kept it closed. Maestro has been very restless lately and always barking for nothing, or so we thought."

"Did you find anything, Dr. Carter?" he said, "on your hike?"

"Yes, we did. First, we found a snack bar wrapper; and then farther along the train, we came across a recently abandoned camp. We were going to call the police when we got back down."

"How do you know it was recent?" he asked.

"I felt some heat next to the fire pit and dug into the ashes with a poker. There were hot coals underneath, so someone probably had a fire going until the wee hours of the morning."

The chief got on his radio.

"This is the chief. I want everyone to be on the lookout for anyone who looks like they don't belong. Someone may be watching from a distance. We don't want to spook them, so just radio in anything you might find suspicious."

"What's happening? I don't understand," I said.

"Would you girls please get in the truck, just as a precaution?"

One of the other firemen came toward us.

"What's up, Boss?"

"I think it's possible that we may have a guilty spectator. A few of the neighbors have gathered to see what's going on. I would like you to go around and ask them their names, where they live, and if they have seen any strangers around here lately. If anyone seems a little odd, let me know."

"I'm on it."

The chief opened the door and helped Bobby and Ashley up into his truck.

"What about Maestro?" Ashley asked.

"Is there somewhere we could tie him?" he asked.

I gave him a frown.

"Okay, okay, you too, Maestro." He jumped in after us, and the chief closed the door.

"Do you think he is still out there?" I asked Ashley.

"It's possible," she replied.

"That would be crazy, with all the firemen and police around."

"Not necessarily, some pyromaniacs get off on that."

"Pyromaniac, really?" I said. "Oh, come on, Ash; we both know who this is."

"We can't be sure, Bobby."

"Well, I am, so let's just sit back out of sight in case he's out there and can see us."

We sat back and watched as our house went up in smoke and the reality of what was happening sunk in. Ashley looked over at me and saw the tears still trickling down my face. She wiped them away and took me in her arms. Maestro was lying down, exhausted from all the excitement.

Suddenly, there was a commotion... as if there wasn't enough excitement. We heard some noises outside the truck, but we couldn't see anything. We saw Chief Willis running toward the back of it. Maestro jumped up and started barking. I started to get nervous.

"Calm down," Ashley said. "We are surrounded by firemen, paramedics, and police; nobody can get to us."

We were startled by a knock on the window. We turned and were both very happy to see that it was the chief. He opened the door.

"Looks like you have a visitor," he announced.

Dr. Blake came into view. Maestro was very happy to see him and jumped out of the truck, practically knocking him over.

"Maestro… take it easy," I yelled. "Dr. Blake, it's really great to see you. How did you know?"

"I was at work, and I heard about it from the ER. They said that the paramedics were called out to a fire in this area. I asked about the address and realized it was yours, so I hopped in my car and came out. Wow... I really got read the riot act as I came in the driveway."

"Well," Ashley said, "they are thinking it is a possibility that the person responsible for the fire might still be out here watching."

"Are you both okay? You didn't get hurt?" he asked. "As a friend, I can honestly say that you both look like hell, like you've been through a war zone. What exactly happened here?"

Chief Willis gave us the 'all good' to get out of the truck. He was confident that we were out of danger. We sat down in the lawn chairs and told the doc all about it. I also told him about my dreams, and about the bus, and the fact that I thought Tyler was still alive and trying to get to me again. With all the excitement building up inside of me, I just automatically spilled my guts out to him.

He just sat for a moment, analyzing the situation.

"You will need to talk to the detective in charge of this," he finally said. "You will have to fill him in on everything that has happened in the past two years, in case it is all tied in together. Maybe you should call Detective Collins."

"We already did," Ashley said. "We called the other day. He took the time to go over everything from his investigation. He told us that the case was closed, but if we really felt like we were still in danger, he would do some digging on his own time. I will call him again, though."

Dr. Blake nodded in agreement, and then he turned to see who was coming back across the lawn.

We also turned and saw Chief Willis coming back toward us with someone by his side.

"Dr. Carter, Miss Hansen, this is Detective Stone."

I looked him over. I wasn't very impressed. He looked like he should have retired years ago. Dr. Blake greeted them, then excused himself and took Maestro for a walk.

"Hi," he said. "So, you are the owners of this property?"

"Yes," Ashley replied.

"Is there a Mr. Hansen or Mr. Carter?"

"No, there isn't," I said.

The chief whispered something to him, and then he turned and headed for the house.

"Oh, um… okay, um... Chief... no wait," he said.

The chief turned as he walked away. "I have work to do," he said.

Detective Stone turned back toward us and immediately looked down at his notes. He seemed very uncomfortable. He turned back to see where the chief was.

"Is there a problem?" Ashley asked.

He turned and looked at her, speechless.

"What the fuck?" I said.

"I'm sorry, Miss," he said, and looked back down at his notes. "Have you, I mean, has anyone around here ever given you problems, um, you know, about being a couple?"

I was about to explode. "No!" I yelled, "Nobody gives a shit, and you? Does that make it okay for someone to burn our house down?"

"I'm sorry Miss, I didn't mean to…"

"This is getting off to a really great start!" I yelled.

Ashley grabbed me by the shoulders and looked me in the eyes.

"I've got this," she said. "Take a walk, and I will take care of this."

I shook my head, kissed her on the cheek, and turned and walked away, not even looking back at the detective.

I went to join Chief Willis who was standing close to the house. He was outside near the kitchen windows, looking around on the lawn.

"What are you looking for?" I asked.

"Look here," he said. "There was an explosion in the kitchen and this window is broken."

"Yes, I see that," I replied. "I think an explosion would break a window… no?"

"Yes, but where is the glass? There is a little bit here and there, but not enough for the whole window."

"So, where did it go?" I asked.

"I have a sneaking suspicion that it might be on the inside."

"But… how can that be?"

"Did you or Dr. Carter break this window from the outside?"

"Absolutely not!" I yelled. "What are you insinuating?"

"Calm down, Miss Hansen; I'm not insinuating anything," he said. "This window was broken from the outside, before the explosion. So, if it wasn't broken before you went on your hike, then it happened just before the fire."

"You mean you think someone threw something through the window, and that started the fire?"

"I'm thinking it's a possibility."

We walked around the yard together for a bit. When we had gone full circle, I turned and noticed that Ashley was still talking to the detective.

"So, tell me, Chief," I said, "the detective, he's very sexist, maybe a little homophobic, right? I realized it from the short conversation I had with him."

"He's a good man, Miss Hansen, but yes, he's very old fashioned. He is very good at his job, though, and he's fair, no matter who you are. Give him a chance and you will see."

I thanked the chief and went back and joined Ashley. We gave Detective Stone Joe's contact information, along with our own, and he was on his way.

The firemen were still working on the house, but from where we were standing, it didn't look like there was much left to save. They were probably just making sure that the fire was completely out, so it didn't spread to anything else.

Dr. Blake came back and joined us, Maestro at his heels. He offered to let us stay at his house for a few days, which was great, because there was nothing more we could do here, and the detective had said that we were free to go.

I grabbed my pack, at least I had salvaged that, then we headed for Dr. Blake's car. Ashley was in no shape to drive, so he said he would bring us back tomorrow to retrieve Ashley's car.

When we got to his car, Ashley turned and once again looked back at our home. Suddenly, she couldn't hold it in anymore. Tears started cascading down her face and she started sobbing, aloud. I turned around just in time to see the roof cave in, and the gravity of the situation finally hit me too. I turned and took Ashley in my arms and we broke down together.

Dr. Blake put Maestro in the front seat of the car and helped us into the back. He started his car and off we went.

Chapter 62

I woke in a daze. I was feeling disoriented and started to stress. I could barely see anything; it was so dark. I focused hard and tried to look around but didn't recognize any of the dark shapes surrounding me. I heard a strange noise; it was coming from inside the room. I rolled over onto my back and realized that there was someone lying next to me. I gasped.

"Bobby, are you okay?" Ashley whispered.

"Ashley, thank God; it's you."

I turned and put my arms around her.

"I wasn't sure where I was. I heard a strange noise. I thought I was on another one of my journeys."

"It's okay, Bobby. We are at Dr. Blake's house, remember?"

"Oh yes, that's true. Sorry, I was half-asleep. I'm okay now. I just thought, oh, never mind."

I hesitated for a moment and tried to clear my mind of the fear. I thought of my sailboat, and this brought me joy. Then my vision came to mind.

"Oh, you know what, Ash?" I whispered. "I almost forgot to tell you this, it popped back into my head just now, for some reason."

We lay there in each other's arms as I told her about the dream, or flashback or whatever it was that I had, after I passed out on top of her in the burning house. I described how I somehow went back in time and revisited a beautiful sunny day that I spent as a child at the beach with my mother. I described my mom and myself in great detail, and how, even as a child, I seemed to have a great love for the water. I also recounted the conversation they had about my father and his love for the ocean and treasures.

"Wow!" Ashley said. "We never talked about your dad."

"I don't remember him at all, though; it's like he never existed."

"It's amazing, Bobby, how these moments in your past are slowly coming back. You know, even if you don't remember him, the similarities are there. Like you and your own love for the ocean. Now we know where that came from."

I thought about that for a moment, and a smile came across my face.

"Do you remember anything else?" Ashley asked.

Suddenly, I tensed up.

"There it is," I whispered.

"What?"

"The noise I heard before, listen! Oh... see? There it is, again!"

Ashley started to laugh. "It's Maestro, silly; he's snoring."

At the sound of his name, he jumped up.

"Oh crap," she said. "We've gone and woken him. Now he won't leave us alone. We might as well get up. Anyway, I think Dr. Blake is already in the kitchen; I smell coffee."

We had a nice breakfast with the good doctor. We changed out of the pajamas the doc had lent us, got back into our grungy clothing, and prepared to return with him to face the harsh reality of what happened to our beautiful home.

There was already some activity in our yard when we got there. Dr. Blake needed to go to work, so he left us by our car and said goodbye. We watched and waved as he drove off. We slowly turned and looked toward our home in disbelief. It was a complete write-off.

The explosion was probably what did it in. Maestro lay down next to us, also looking a little distraught. Ashley and I both bent down and sat on the ground next to him.

Detective Stone spotted us and started to make his way here. I started to get up so I could walk away, just to avoid a confrontation with him, but Ashley grabbed me by the arm before I had a chance to do so.

Maestro got up and ran toward him. The detective leaned down, and gave him a pat.

"How are you two doing today?" he asked.

"Hello, Detective; as well as can be expected, I guess," Ashley replied.

"Miss Hansen," he said, and nodded.

I nodded back, trying not to make eye contact.

"I'm very sorry," he said, "this must be really painful for you both. I hope that you weren't thinking about going inside to retrieve some of your belongings, because it's not safe for you to go in there yet; the structure isn't sound. Anyway, there isn't much that is salvageable. It's even difficult for us to proceed with our investigation."

He paused, then turned and looked toward the house.

"Oh yes," he added, "Chief Willis told me that you said you were having problems with trespassers, and that you found evidence of this, up on the mountain."

"Yes," Ashley replied. "We noticed that our gate to the mountain trail, which we always kept closed, was left open. Maestro here has been barking a lot more lately in our yard after dark, as if there was something out there. Yesterday morning after breakfast, we headed out to see if we could find; well, I don't know what we thought we would find, but we wanted to see if there were squatters living on our mountain."

"You found an abandoned camp, the chief told me?"

"We did, yes. Then we hurried back down so we could call the police, and well, the rest you know, you're looking at it."

"I see. Well, just so you know, I was talking to your detective friend. We had a very long chat… Umm… Miss Hansen?"

He turned and looked at me.

"Yes?" I replied.

"I just want you to know that I'm very sorry that we got off on the wrong foot yesterday. I'm an old fart, you know, and I'm country folk on top of that. Give me a break, okay? I'm good at my job, though, and I will find out who did this to you, both of you. I do have a request, though. You can say no, but it would help me out a lot.

"You see, my problem is I couldn't find north if it hit me in the head, and finding my way through your forest, well, it's just not going to happen."

"Me too," I said, "but Ashley, well, I think she has a compass stuck up her… ouch!"

Ashley gave me a good smack. That got a laugh out of the detective.

"No offense, Detective," Ashley said as she looked him over, "but the mountain is pretty rugged near the top, and, well..."

"No offense taken at all. I wasn't very keen on it anyway. I'll send a few of the younger investigators up there with you, if you agree to do this."

"What if he is still up there?" I asked.

"Naaa, I wouldn't worry about that. In my experience, with all the law enforcement personnel around here since yesterday, the culprit has vacated your property. The investigators will be armed, though, and they will watch over you, I promise."

"What do you think, Bobby? Can you make it up there again?"

"If you are, I am. I'm not leaving your side."

The detective rounded up a couple of his men, and off we went, with Maestro in the lead.

There were no surprises on the mountain. The climb went pretty well for me the second time around. I was probably running on all the adrenaline that had been building up inside of me. Ashley led the investigators to the area near the stream where we had found the wrapper. They examined the surroundings a bit to see if they could find anything else, but nothing. We regrouped and continued up the trail.

We made our way to the top of the ridge. There was nothing, no evidence up there to show them, but they sat for a while, took a break, and enjoyed the view. We had to pass by there anyway to get to the other trail which led to the abandoned camp.

We continued and got there in no time. It was obvious that nobody had come back to it; it was almost exactly how we had left it yesterday. It was evident, though, that some animals had scavenged through the garbage that had been left behind. The investigators picked up the trash and bagged it to be checked for fingerprints. It was perfectly fine with us. We would have wanted to come back up to clean that mess.

It wasn't long before we were done… and on our way back down. Our journey was uneventful, and I was very happy about that.

The detective thanked us and said that he would be in touch.

We got in our car and headed back to Dr. Blake's house. Ashley passed me her phone.

"Try to see if you can find a restaurant in this area. I am famished after that hike. How about you?"

"I think I'm too exhausted to be hungry," I said.

I turned on the phone. "Oh no, Ashley, it looks like you missed a call. It must have been while we were on the mountain. They left a message, though."

"It's okay, I'll check it later. Find us some food before I pass out."

"Yes ma'am."

I found something that we both could agree on, beer and pizza, so we stopped to have a quick bite. I did find my appetite after all. Ashley checked her message and it was from Detective Collins. He said that he would call us back around three.

My imagination was getting the best of me. I was sure that he had probably found out something about Tyler.

"What do you think he wants?" I said.

"He just found out that we narrowly escaped from perishing in a fire; I'm sure that he just wants to check on us. Don't get your hopes up, honey."

We finished our lunch and headed back to Doc's place with an hour to spare before Detective Collins was going to get back to us.

In the meantime, Ashley started making other calls to the insurance company, for one, and she wanted to cancel all our other services at the house. There was so much to take care of, but I wasn't in a state of mind to be of any help. Ashley was the calm, organized one.

"It's a little after three! He said he would call at three!" I said as I glanced up at the clock.

"So, he's a few minutes late, Bobby; calm down."

At that exact moment her phone rang, and I just about jumped out of my skin. Ashley picked it up and looked at the display; sure enough, it was him.

"Hello, Detective, uh… I mean Joe," she said. "It's really nice to hear back from you."

"Hello Ashley, it's good to hear your voice. Is Bobby around, by any chance?"

"I'm right here; you're on speaker."

"Oh, hello Bobby, I'm in my car, so if you don't hear me well, let me know."

"Sure, no problem," I said.

"I heard from a Detective Stone; he told me about the fire. He said that it was very bad, and that you both were extremely lucky to be alive. I was happy to hear that you were okay. So, Bobby, how many lives did you say you had?" He paused. "But, joking aside, what in the hell is going on? He asked a lot of questions about you both, and I had a lot to tell. He seems like an okay guy, very thorough anyway."

"Well," I said, "we got off on the wrong foot, but we were told that he was very good at his job. He has said his piece, though. I think it will be okay. Is that the only reason you are calling? Did you do some checking up on Tyler?"

"Actually, I have a question for you, Bobby," he replied. "Do you keep in touch with anyone from St. Mary's?"

"Not really… Dr. Blake is here, Carla is gone, and well, I didn't really have any other friends, except for Lou, but we haven't been in touch since Ashley and I moved out here. Why do you ask?"

"What about you, Ashley?"

"No, me neither. I moved there because of the job opening at the hospital. I didn't really get to know anyone with all the hours I was putting in at work, well, except for Bobby, of course."

She winked.

"What about Mr. Fletcher? Have any of you been in touch with him?"

"Recently yes," Ashley said. "A while back, Thomas called St. Mary's and asked how he could reach Dr. Blake. The person took Thomas's phone number and relayed the message to the doc."

"Did he get back in touch with Mr. Fletcher?"

"Yes, he did, and Thomas told Dr. Blake that he had become ill and had to leave town and move in with his sister. He couldn't keep Maestro anymore. He wanted Bobby to have him."

"Maestro is living with us now," I said. "Why are you asking about Thomas?"

"So, Mr. Fletcher knew that you had moved out there near Dr. Blake and that he would be able to reach you?"

"Please stop with all the questions; you're starting to freak me out," I whined.

"Just one more. Did Dr. Blake tell Mr. Fletcher where he lives?"

"I'm thinking that you already know what my answer is going to be," Ashley said.

"I'm thinking it's a yes; am I right?"

"Well, I guess they had to get Maestro here somehow. They had him shipped by a special courier."

"Okay, that's enough beating around the bush," I said. "Could you please tell me what in the hell is going on? I can't take much more of this suspense. You've been fishing around, I can tell."

"I'm sorry; I'm just trying to get my facts straight."

"Tell us about Mr. Fletcher; is something wrong?" I yelled.

"It's a long story, so I need you to relax, Bobby, okay?"

"Alright, alright, I'll try."

"Okay, I'll try to be quick about it. There is a new guy on the force, Phil; he had transferred in from another district. I asked him after you called last time if he could help me go through the files about your case, you know, another set of eyes. He was new here and didn't know anything about it. He came across the name, Thomas Fletcher, and recognized it. He asked me questions about him, and I told him everything I knew. He went into the system and brought up a picture. I looked at it and it was Thomas."

"Something happened to him?" I asked, and a tear rolled down my face. I started to tremble all over.

"I am really sorry, Bobby; I know he meant a lot to you."

"What happened?" I yelled.

Ashley put her arms around me and tried to console me.

"He's dead, Bobby. I would have never heard about it, because his sister lives out of town, but it happened just before Phil was transferred here. Had I not asked him to take a look at the case, I would have never known."

"What happened? I know this is not going to be good. When did this happen?"

"It was about four weeks ago, but there's something else, Bobby."

I couldn't say anything more; I was sobbing uncontrollably.

"Go on," Ashley said.

"Mr. Fletcher was found lying on the floor in his sister's home. Luckily, she was away at the time. He was badly beaten, Bobby, and they said that he died from his injuries. Looks like whoever beat him didn't want to leave any witnesses."

"Really?" Ashley said. "I'm not liking the sound of this. Do you honestly think someone beat up Thomas to find out where we are? That's crazy!"

"Okay," Joe said. "Let's put it in order. Mr. Fletcher contacts Dr. Blake, who gives him his address, so he can send the dog. That was how long ago?"

"Maybe about six weeks," she replied.

"Mr. Fletcher dies from a beating about a month ago, and you, Bobby, have been back from your sailing trip, what, say two weeks now? You called me last week because you thought you saw Tyler, and now your house burns down? I told you before, I don't believe in coincidences."

"What are we supposed to do now?" I cried.

"You are going to stay put. Where are you?"

"We're at the doc's house," I added.

"I want you to call Detective Stone and tell him to get someone over there right now. I should be there in about three hours."

"You're coming here?" Ashley asked.

"I told you I was driving; I'm on my way there as we speak."

"You think he is going to send someone here, just because I ask him to?" I said.

"Tell him that I asked, and that I am on my way there. Tell him to call me if he wants."

"So, you believe me?" I said through my tears.

"I didn't want to believe it when you called me last time, but if I've learned anything, since I've met you, no offense, is that when it comes to you, anything is possible. That is why I started digging around in the case again. The sergeant still wouldn't budge, so I took some vacation time. Now get off the phone and call Detective Stone, and I'll see you soon."

We did as we were told, and in no time at all, there was a knock at the door. A police officer showed us his badge, asked if we were okay, and then took his place outside our door.

"Here we go again," Ashley said. "Never a dull moment with you." She winked.

We called Dr. Blake to let him know what was going on. He was very worried about us and said that he was finished his day except for the paperwork, which he was going to leave till morning. He was going to come straight home.

I sat quietly as Ashley went into the kitchen. She brought us back each a cold one. I took a sip and then started to cry.

"I can't stop thinking about Thomas," I said. "It's my fault that he's dead. I keep imagining him being beaten. He saved my life and now I've killed him."

Ashley put her arms around me again. Maestro seemed to know that there was something terribly wrong, and he jumped up on top of the couch and squeezed in between us. Ashley didn't have the heart to push him down. His best friend for many years had been killed. I wondered if he could sense it. I put my arms around him too and the three of us huddled together.

I lay there for the longest time in a group hug with my dearest friends. I wished that I could just stay like that forever, but I knew that it wasn't possible. I raised my head and saw that Ashley was watching me.

"What are we going to do, Ash?" I said.

"We'll get across this hurdle too, like we always do."

"Don't you get tired of this? Are you not scared of being around me? I'm such bad luck for everyone."

"Don't talk like that. This is not your fault. I'm here because I love you and want to be with you. There is only one ghost left from your past and we have two fine detectives on the case. They won't let anything happen to us; I'm sure of that. Hang in there a bit longer, and after this it will be smooth sailing, you'll see."

Sailing, I thought, and a smile came across my face. I closed my eyes and faded out.

Chapter 63

Maestro started barking and I woke with a scream. Ashley had heard something too and it seemed to be coming from outside the door. We looked at each other, then back at the door. Maestro jumped off the couch; Ashley followed.

"What are you doing?" I whispered. "Get back here."

"I think the guard is talking to someone, not quite sure who, so I need to get closer." She quietly followed Maestro to the entrance. She shushed me and listened. "It's the doc, I think, and he's getting the third degree; I think we should rescue him."

"Are you sure?" I asked nervously.

"Doc… is that you?" she asked.

"Yes, it's me, Ashley. Could you please tell the officer that it's okay, and that I live here?"

Ashley did so, and the guard let him through, "Sorry Sir, just doing my job," he said, and closed the door behind him.

"Hey Doc, would you like a cold one?" I said as I headed into the kitchen for another.

"Here we go again," he whispered sarcastically.

"I heard that," I said.

"I wanted you to. Just trying to lighten things up here, and yes, a cold one sounds good."

"I'm really sorry I have dragged you, once again, back into this."

"Chill, Bobby, you never dragged me into your life. You happened to land in the ER on my shift."

"Can I get another one too?" Ashley asked.

I went back with one for each of us and sat down between them.

"No seriously, this, we did drag you into. We moved out here to be close to you, and I brought my crazy life with me."

"I'm your doctor, Bobby, and your friend. I am going to help you get through this. We thought we had won the battle, but it looks like we still have another round to go." He put his arm around me. "We're going to get him this time."

We sat back and relaxed while Ashley caught him up on every little detail of what had happened this morning. It wasn't long before there was another commotion outside. Maestro ran to the door again. Doc got up this time and went to see what was going on. I sat there, eyes glued to the entrance. He opened the door and greeted Detective Collins. Without even giving it a second thought, I jumped up and ran into his arms.

"I'm so glad to see you," I said. "I feel much safer already."

Maestro was very happy to see him too. Joe took a seat in front of us. We started comparing notes and trying to figure out what our next move would be.

There was yet another knock on the door. Doc got up again and returned with Detective Stone.

"You must be Detective Collins," he asked as he walked over to shake Joe's hand.

"Detective Stone, it's nice to meet you."

"Dr. Carter, Miss Hansen…" he nodded.

He sat, and we filled him in on the discussion we were having. He had a lot of questions for Joe, and vice versa. Our big problem though, and everyone was in agreement, was that we were sitting ducks. Tyler, if it was him, which there was no doubt in anyone's mind at this point, knew exactly where we were. Maybe he was outside on the street even, watching everyone as they arrived. The thought scared the hell out of me.

"Is there anywhere else you can go?" Detective Stone asked, "Family… friends? People that this Murphy fellow wouldn't know about?"

"No, not really," Ashley said. "Besides, I don't think we should put anyone else in harm's way. We just need to stick together. We could just hop a flight and take a little vacation in a secluded place, as long as we could get out of here undetected."

"I don't like it; it's too dangerous. You need protection; what if he finds out where you are?" Joe didn't like the idea at all.

Ashley and I snuggled together on the couch, while the two detectives went back and forth with potential strategies. Doc got up to make some tea. Hours seem to pass, and they weren't getting anywhere.

Ashley's phone rang, and everyone jumped and stared at it.

"He wouldn't," Joe said.

"No way, he doesn't know it. I changed my number when I moved out here."

She picked it up and said, "Hello?"

Ashley put her hand over the phone and whispered, "It's about the boat."

I took the phone from her. "Hello?" I said. "This is Roberta Hansen…"

I looked around and all eyes were on me.

"Yes, I'm really sorry that I didn't get back to you, but something came up…"

I looked away; they were making me feel uncomfortable.

"Yes, I will, but could I call you back tomorrow? It's really a bad time. I will let you know then… Thanks so much for your understanding… okay… yes that's fine… okay then… bye now."

I passed the phone back to Ashley.

"I'm sorry, it was the manager at the marina where I left my boat to get repairs done after the storm. I told him that I would call him back, and totally forgot about it."

Detective Stone looked puzzled. Obviously, he didn't know anything about my sailing. I glanced over at Joe and I could see a light turn on inside of him. A smile came across his face.

"That's it!" he said

"What are you talking about?" asked Detective Stone.

"You need to get back to your boat and go sailing again. How's he going to find you out on the water? Do you think he knows about it?"

"Are you out of your mind?" Ashley said. "She can't go back out there alone. I almost lost her to that storm. And what if he does find her out there all alone? It's too dangerous!"

"Not alone, Ashley," he replied. "I'm sorry, but you're not safe here either. You both need to get the hell out of Dodge."

Detective Stone was really confused at this point, and he couldn't get a word in edgewise.

"Okay… okay… time out!" I yelled. "I'm sorry, Detective Stone; I think we need to fill you in on what Joe is talking about."

"Thanks, Miss Hansen; that would be great. Now what's this about a boat?"

We filled him in and then got back to the problem at hand: our security.

"So, Miss Hansen," Detective Stone asked, "do you think that this Murphy fellow knows anything about your sailboat?"

"I don't imagine so; he didn't even know where we were until Thomas sent us Maestro."

A tear rolled down my cheek, and I started to cry.

"I'm sorry, but Thomas wouldn't be dead if it wasn't for me," I cried.

Joe explained to the detective what had happened to Thomas, and how he thought that Tyler found us.

"Okay, that brings me to my next question," the detective said. "Did Thomas Fletcher know about the sailboat?"

"Not that I know of," I said. "Doc? You were the last one of us to speak with him."

"I don't believe I told him anything about the boat, or where you were, Bobby, for that matter. You wanted to get out of the spotlight for a while, and hell, I didn't even know how to reach you myself."

"I hate to do this, but to be on the safe side, I think I am going to contact Thomas's sister," Joe said. "If Thomas knew anything about your whereabouts, he might have discussed it with her."

He pulled out a pen and pad and jotted down some notes. Detective Stone did the same.

My stomach growled, and we all started to laugh.

"I guess we forgot all about supper; is anyone else hungry?" Ashley asked.

"I'm fine, thanks, Dr. Carter," Detective Stone replied. "I think I need to head out and mull all this over in my mind to see what I can come up with. You girls are safe here for tonight. The guard is not going anywhere, and I'm also putting a car on the street. If he's out there, we will be ready for him."

"Thanks so much," I said. "I really do appreciate everything you are doing."

Joe nodded. "Me too."

They stood, and the two detectives shook hands. "It's nice to have the backup," Joe said. "I'm on my own here. The case was closed, and my boss didn't see any valid reason to re-open it."

"No worries," Detective Stone said. "I've got your back. I can use all the help I can get."

"Thanks, Detective. Well Ashley… Bobby, I'm going to head out too. I booked a room at the hotel in town."

He handed me a card. "This is where I'm staying. You can call me on my cell if you need anything; I'm not far."

"You won't stay with us?" I asked.

"No… you will be okay, you're well-guarded. I need to wrap my head around all of this too. I will be able to think better with no distractions. I probably won't sleep much. I will call Thomas's sister, first thing in the morning. You two need to get some rest. I'll see you tomorrow. Have a good night."

He got up and followed Detective Stone out the door. Dr. Blake led the way and closed it behind them. He went into the kitchen and raided the refrigerator for leftovers.

"I can warm up what was left from last night's dinner. Is that okay with you?" he asked.

"I saw a frozen pizza in the freezer," I said.

"Bobby!" Ashley reached over and smacked me.

"It's okay, Ashley. The girl wants pizza? I'm okay with that," he said.

The pizza didn't take long to cook. We each had another beer to go along with it. It wasn't long before Dr. Blake said goodnight. He needed to get up early.

I followed Ashley into our room. We lay in bed snuggling for the longest time, but sleep wasn't happening. Maestro had no trouble at all; he was lying on the floor next to the bed, snoring his head off. We ended up talking most of the night about how we were going to get out of there. That call from the marina was well-timed. I really wanted to get back to the ocean where I felt safe, and with Ashley by my side, we could sail off into the sunset together. A feeling of peace came over me and I finally faded off to sleep.

Chapter 64

"Hey Bobby, wake up, we're here," Ashley announced.

I yawned and rubbed my eyes.

"Didn't you sleep last night?" she asked.

"Are you kidding? I was too excited. I can't wait to see her."

We got out of the car and walked to the marina office, where a smiling face was there to greet us.

"Miss Hansen…Dr. Carter, it's nice to see you again. I'm sure that you are very anxious to see her, so we won't waste any time. We'll take care of the formalities later."

She waved to someone across the room.

"Take these two lovely ladies out to the dock and show them their boat."

"Which one?"

"Carla."

"Oh yes, I know the one; she's a beauty. Follow me."

I got a lump in my throat when she said her name. Carla and I had talked about sailing the world together. This was my way of doing just that.

Ashley wiped a tear from my cheek, took me by the hand, and off we went.

"Wait!"

We turned and the woman from the desk came running toward us with something in her hand.

"You can't do this without champagne."

She handed us the bottle and two glasses, then turned and headed back to the office. We thanked her and continued on our way.

We were almost to the end of the dock when Ashley stopped.

"Oh my God, she's amazing; look!"

I turned and there she was, in all her splendor, with Carla written in beautiful script. I couldn't move; I was mesmerized. I don't know how long I stood there with my mouth open.

"Come on, girl, we have a boat to baptize."

The attendant told us to make ourselves at home. He needed to head back to the office, but he would come back in a little while. We kept him there long enough to snap a few pictures of us with our champagne and standing right above the script. After that, he was on his way.

"I'd like to make a toast," Ashley declared.

"To you… Bobby, and to Carla, who will always be in our hearts."

I started to tear up of course.

"I wish you many years of sailing into the sunset together."

We raised our glasses in the air, kissed, and then… bottoms up.

"So classy," I said, and we both started laughing.

It was a beautiful day, so we parked our butts on the deck, relaxed, and polished off the bottle of champagne. I reminisced about the fun times that Carla and I shared together. Ashley never got bored of listening to my stories. She smiled as she watched my every gesture and laughed as I told her about all our crazy antics.

"So, do you think you are ready?"

"Are you kidding, Ash? All those classes we took? I'm an expert; you saw how well I was doing. You are pretty good yourself."

"I couldn't do it without you, though; I am not confident enough. You, on the other hand, are a natural-born sailor."

The attendant came back and asked, "Are you girls okay out here?"

"Oh yeah! We can't wait to sail out into the sunset," I yelled back.

Ashley and I started to laugh.

He smiled. "You'd better check the weather forecast first," he said, pointing toward the west. "We are expecting thundershowers tonight."

Just as he said that, we could hear rumbling way off in the distance.

"I think we need to head back to the office before the rain starts," I said.

Ashley grabbed her things and led the way.

"See you tomorrow, Carla," I said. "We will sail away together as promised."

I awoke, and it was still dark. I smiled as I thought about my dream of that wonderful day. I turned to Ashley and she was sound asleep. I snuggled up close to her, closed my eyes, and it wasn't long before I dozed off again.

Chapter 65

It was morning, though it didn't look like the sun had come up yet. There was eerie music playing somewhere in the background, not too far away. I had this uneasy feeling, like something wasn't quite right. Ashley and I had just finished breakfast. The food didn't have any flavor at all. I didn't say anything because I didn't want to hurt her feelings. The clock was ticking very loudly, but Ashley just brushed it off. She said that it was probably just my lack of sleep.

She was buzzing around the house cleaning up. She seemed to be moving in fast forward, or was it me who was in slow motion? I didn't remember Dr. Blake giving me anything to relax me, but that was a possibility. I didn't even see Dr. Blake this morning. I presumed that he had left for work early, but it seemed like he hadn't been here at all, like, this wasn't even his place. I was really confused.

Ashley came over and said something to me, but the words just came at me too quickly and were incomprehensible.

"Ashley! Could you please slow down a bit, you're making me dizzy!" I stopped to take a breath, "I'm sorry, I'm a little fidgety this morning. Sit with me, Ashley. I'm not feeling very well." She did so, and I took her by the hand.

Suddenly, all I could concentrate on was her heartbeat. It was getting louder, and stronger. I had to let go of her hand, because it felt like it was going to explode.

Everything became silent again.

I looked up at her face, and she was smiling back at me.

"Are you okay, Bobby?" she asked.

"Yes, I think so; just stay with me, okay?"

There was a knock at the door. I just sat there looking at it, and suddenly I had no control over my imagination. Ashley got up to answer it.

"No!" I yelled.

"It's Joe; he's right on time," she said.

"You don't know that for sure; it could be anyone."

"Okay," she said, and she pulled out her phone, put it on speaker, and called him. We heard a phone ringing from outside the door.

"Hello?" he said. "I'm outside the door; is something wrong?"

"I'll let you in," Ashley replied.

He joined us in the kitchen. I poured him a cup of coffee.

"Sorry about that," Ashley said. "Bobby got very nervous all of a sudden."

"It's okay. She's a smart cookie, always was. A little too smart for her own good sometimes."

"What? That's not funny, Joe," I said. "This is no time to kid around. We're scared enough as it is."

"Who's kidding?" he replied.

"Stop it, Joe. This is not funny!" I got up from my chair and slowly moved over toward Ashley. He didn't take his eyes off me the whole time.

Ashley just stood there stunned, watching us.

"It's okay, Ashley; he's just trying to lighten things up. Aren't you, Joe?"

He just smiled and nodded, still boring a hole through me with those eyes.

"Have you had breakfast, Joe?" I asked.

Ashley grabbed me by the arm. "Can someone please tell me what's going on?" she demanded.

"I think someone got up on the wrong side of the bed, right, Detective?" I asked. "So, how about that breakfast?"

Ashley was starting to lose it. There was something really strange about Joe, and I didn't like where this was going.

"I'll make him breakfast, Ash," I said. "Why don't you go and see if the guard would like some coffee?" I nodded in the direction of the door, urging her on.

"Good idea," she replied, "maybe he can tell me what in the hell is going on."

As soon as she said that, Joe's frightening gaze turned away from me and over to her.

"Oh no!" I yelled. "Run, Ashley!"

He got up from his chair and turned to face the door. With his back to me, he raised his arms and I watched in terror as he started to float to the ceiling. Everything seemed to be moving so slowly. Ashley was still trying to get to the door, but it seemed to be getting farther and farther away.

"Leave her alone!" I screamed. "It's me you want; let her go."

My words sounded like an old warped record and seemed to keep echoing in my mind. I tried to move but there was some kind of force holding me back.

He started slowly turning around, and at the same time, the transformation started. I watched in utter disbelief as his body started to deteriorate before my very eyes. Joe was no longer there; it was Tyler's rotting corpse. Seaweed started growing out of his body, with long strands roaming around the room.

"Get to the door, Ashley; hurry!" As my still warped words left my mouth, Tyler waved his arm and a stand of seaweed bolted across the room, wrapped itself around Ashley's waist, then lifted her into the air.

"Ashley!" I cried. "You don't have to do this, Tyler. Let her go. I will go with you."

I could hear Ashley screaming.

"Guard… help… please!"

Tyler finally spoke, but the words that came out were barely audible. They were very deep and gurgly as if he was underwater. "Is this who you're looking for?"

Another wave of his arm and a strand bolted across the room again and dove under the couch. I gasped as I saw the guard get dragged out from underneath it by his leg. His limp, lifeless body was dangling in mid-air.

I could see Ashley crying and struggling to get loose. I was hysterical, and my fear was turning into anger.

"Tyler!" I screamed.

He turned and focused his attention on me. His red, evil eyes glared at me as he came closer. I was trembling so much, it took everything I had to get the words out of my mouth.

"Tyler, I beg of you, leave her alone! I'll do anything you ask!"

"You are mine," he proclaimed, "and nobody will stand in my way!"

"No, Bobby! Don't do it!" Ashley screamed.

He let out a roar so loud that it pierced through my mind. Suddenly, another strand flew out in her direction, this time wrapping itself around her neck.

I screamed as loud as I could.

"No… Ashley…"

Chapter 66

"Bobby… wake up... it's okay, Bobby; I'm here." Ashley turned on the light, took me in her arms, and tried to calm me down.

"Oh Ash, oh my God, you're okay. Where did he go?"

"Where did who go?"

"Tyler, he was here. He was going to kill you! He possessed Joe and he killed the guard and…"

"Bobby, it's okay. You had a bad dream, there is nobody here, it's over now."

"Listen to me, Ash, we need to get out of here. He knows where we are. He will find us, and he will kill you. He said that I was his, and that nobody would stand in his way."

"Bobby, you need to calm down. We are not going anywhere till we find out what the detectives have to say."

Ashley took me into her arms again and stroked my hair the way she always did to try to help me relax. Maestro was standing there with both paws up on the bed, wondering what all the commotion was about.

There was a knock on the bedroom door.

I tensed up and started to tremble.

"No Ashley… don't do it," I whispered. "Don't let him in the room."

Maestro jumped off the bed and ran to the door.

"Don't be silly; look, Maestro knows who it is."

"You guys okay in there?"

It was the doc.

"Come on in," Ashley said. "We're fine."

"Hey Maestro… was that you, making all that noise?" he asked.

He bent over and gave him a good rubdown.

"Just so you know, the guard knocked at the door to see if everything was okay. He heard you from out there. Are you alright, Bobby?"

"Bobby had a really bad dream," Ashley replied. "She won't stop trembling. I don't know what else I can do for her."

"May I?" he said, as he came closer to the bed.

Ashley nodded.

"It's okay, Bobby; I just want to see how you're doing."

He reached out, took my hand, and held it for a moment. He put his other hand on my neck.

"Your heart is racing, Bobby; you need to try to relax."

He looked over at Ashley.

"She's borderline in shock. I will need to get something to calm her down. At the same time, I'll go and tell the guard that everything is fine."

I never took my eyes off him as he left the room.

"We need to leave this town and find another place to hide," I pleaded. I trembled so much that I could barely get the words out. "We can't just stay here. Believe me, Ash; the police can't help us."

"We can't leave right now; he might be out there watching," she whispered. "We need to stay put. Joe will figure out a way."

"Joe?" I yelled. "No… not Joe, you can't let him in here! He turned into Tyler in front of my very eyes. I don't want him in here; it's too dangerous."

I was losing it, and poor Ashley didn't know what to do.

Doc came running back into the room.

"I hate to do this, Bobby, but it's for your own good."

Ashley held me down and I felt a prick.

"Here we go again," I sobbed.

"I'm really sorry. It's not enough to knock you out, but it should calm you down a bit. You need to be a little coherent when the detectives come back. Give it a few minutes. You will see that everything will be fine."

Ashley held me close and stroked my hair again. I was whimpering like a little child.

"What are we going to do, Doc?" she asked.

"Don't worry, Ashley. I will stay with you until the detectives come back and we can all discuss together what is best for both of you. As for Bobby, well, she is still my patient, and I need to make sure that she is going to be alright."

I looked up at him and forced a smile. He meant well; he was a really great guy. I watched as he stood up and headed out of the room.

"I'll call the office and rearrange my schedule," he said, "and then I'll make some breakfast. You girls just chill a bit. I'll send Maestro in after you when it's ready. Come on, boy."

Maestro followed him out.

Ashley didn't say anything; she just lay there still holding me in her arms.

"I'm sorry, Ash."

"Shhh..."

"Really, I am. I'm so crazy, I don't know what to think anymore."

"I love you, that's all you need to think about right now, so chill, doctor's orders."

I didn't say another word. I was starting to feel the effects of the shot.

It wasn't long before Maestro came running back into the room.

"I guess that's our cue," Ashley said and gave me a kiss on the forehead. "Smells like breakfast is served."

Soon after we finished eating, the phone rang. The shot must have been doing its job, because I didn't even fret about it. Ashley answered, and it was Detective Stone. I was a little relieved that it was him, and not Joe, since he had nothing to do with my dream. I wasn't sure how I was going to react to Joe. It's incredible that even though I knew it was only a dream, it still seemed very real to me.

"Yes, okay," Ashley replied, "no problem, we will be expecting you."

"What's going on?" I asked.

"Detective Stone is coming over, alone. He doesn't think it's a good idea if Joe is seen hanging around here. He's hoping that Tyler hasn't already seen him."

"Great, but now what?"

"Patience, my love, we just have to wait and see what he has in mind."

"I think we need to just pack our things and get the hell out of here!"

"You're forgetting something, Bobby; we don't have anything to pack."

"That makes it even easier," I said.

"Oh my, I totally forgot about that," Doc said. "You can't leave here in my PJ's. Let me see if I can try to wash your clothes."

He left the room and we went and snuggled together on the couch.

In no time, he was back. "I found two extra-large tee-shirts I haven't worn it quite some time. They will fit you like a dress. You can put them on for now, at least till your clothes are dry."

We went back into the bedroom and got changed.

We heard someone knocking at the front door. We listened, to see who it was.

"Detective," the doc said.

I breathed a sigh of relief, and we went back into the living room to greet him.

"Oh my, Miss Hansen, Dr. Carter, you look, um…"

The doc laughed. "I am trying to get their clothes clean, in case they need to get out of here," he said. "It's all I had to give them."

Ashley looked at me and started to laugh too.

"Oh my God, you look so funny," she said.

The shot Dr. Blake gave me seemed to be really doing its job. I smiled and started to curtsy and spin around.

"You look like a little girl who just raided her father's shirt drawer," she added.

The tee shirt sagged low around my neck, and the sleeves stretched down, past my elbows. I started to get dizzy and stopped spinning. I looked over at Ashley who was watching me with a smile from ear to ear. I stood there for a moment in a daze.

"You, on the other hand…" I said.

Ashley was a sight for sore eyes. The royal blue color of the shirt accentuated her big bright beautiful eyes. The neckline of her shirt hung below one shoulder, just enough to stimulate your temptation. She was so beautiful.

"You look so sexy, my love. I want to just come over there and…"

"Uh… okay, uh…" the detective was feeling a little out of sorts. "I think we need to get on with the business at hand."

Ashley and I just stood there, staring at each other, like there was nobody else in the world.

"Miss Hansen, Dr. Carter… I have something for you."

I turned, and he handed me a bag.

"My wife, the professional shopper, was very pleased when I asked her to do this for me."

I looked inside.

"Clothing for both of you," he said.

"I don't know what to say," I replied.

I pulled out a summery-looking dress and turned to Ashley. She knew what I was thinking, and she gave me a look that said *shut it!*

"No worries," he said. "Now let's get down to business; we have a plan."

We sat back down and listened as he started to divulge his master plan to get us out of there. Ashley looked pleasantly surprised.

"So, where does Joe fit into all of this?" I asked.

I was still a little worried about seeing him.

"He will be waiting in the other ambulance that you will switch to, at the hospital. An undercover policewoman will take your place in the stretcher to be brought into the ER. She will be wearing the same clothing as you, and she actually looks a lot like you."

"What about me?" Ashley said.

"You will travel in the ambulance with Miss Hansen. She will switch with the policewoman and you will follow the stretcher to the ER. You will have to put on a convincing show. Respiratory failure due to smoke inhalation is very serious."

"I am not going anywhere without her," I said.

"Of course not; give me a minute," Detective Stone cut in.

Ashley squeezed my hand and smiled.

"Then, once the new Miss Hansen gets moved from the ER to her private room, where she will be under protective custody as you are here, we will sneak Dr. Carter out disguised as one of the resident doctors, and then she will join you. The staff will be well-informed about the two of you in that guarded room, with only authorized personnel allowed entry. So, rumors will fly, and if Tyler goes in there looking for you, he will know exactly where you are, well, where your look-a-like is."

"That's all fine and dandy, but who's going to be in the ER taking care of these fake symptoms?" I asked.

"Who else?" Detective Stone said as he looked over at Dr. Blake. "I think you need to get yourself to work. Get a team together that you trust. You have about two hours or so. Then Ashley, you dial 911, and again, make it very convincing. Of course, there will be a police escort."

"Wow… I think this could actually work," I said.

"Okay then," he added, "call the marina, and tell them to have your boat ready for this afternoon."

"Woohoo!" I yelled, and I threw my arms around Ashley.

Detective Stone got up and Doc saw him out.

"I guess I'd better get ready for work," he said. "It's going to be another crazy day."

Chapter 67

"911… What is your emergency?"

"It's my girlfriend," Ashley cried. "She started gasping for air, and then she fell to the floor; I can't wake her up!"

It was amazing to watch her; she was a very good actress. She just kept screaming and crying. She answered all their questions as best she could. I had to turn away to stop myself from laughing. Poor Maestro didn't know what was happening. He kept whimpering. I had to distract him as I waited there in silence while Ashley hung on the line with the 911 respondent.

"I hear sirens!" Ashley yelled.

I moved away from the entrance.

It didn't take long before they were knocking on the door. Ashley motioned for me to get down on the floor and get into character.

"They're here!" she screamed. "Got to go, thanks."

She got off the phone without even giving it a second thought and ran to the door. The paramedics had a look of shock on their faces when Ashley flung the door open, practically ripping it off its hinges. She was playing her role very well. The guard showed them in.

"These guys are undercover police officers," he whispered. "You're doing a great job, Dr. Carter; you should get an Academy Award for that performance. Don't stop now, though; the neighbors might look in."

"Well, the show must go on," Ashley whispered back to him, and she started to cry and plead for the paramedics to do something to help me.

They came over to where I was lying on the floor. They huddled around me and made it look like they were trying to revive me. Ashley pulled Maestro out of the huddle. He was very stressed and started barking.

"No, Maestro; calm down."

She couldn't do anything with him, so she put him in the bedroom.

"Bring the stretcher over here," one of the paramedics said. "We'll need to get her to the hospital as soon as possible."

They lifted me up onto it, wrapped me a blanket, and put an oxygen mask over my face. They told me to keep my eyes closed and to not move, as if I were unconscious. They wheeled me out the door and headed for the ambulance. Ashley called back to the guard to let Maestro out of the bedroom as she followed alongside the stretcher, holding my hand and asking questions through her tears.

"What's happening?" she cried aloud. "Why won't she wake up?"

"Looks like respiratory failure!" one of the paramedics yelled. "Probably due to the smoke inhalation from yesterday's fire that you mentioned earlier."

He made sure that the people who had gathered around the ambulance heard him say it. Once in the ambulance, I opened my eyes and saw Ashley sitting there looking at me. A tear rolled down her face.

"This is too *déjà vu* for me," she cried.

That it was. Ashley spent many a day sitting by my hospital bed, hoping that I would someday awaken. This was bringing back the helplessness that she had felt at times. I reached out and wiped a tear from her cheek.

The sirens were wailing as they made their way through the city streets to get to the hospital as quickly and safely as they could. Once in the ambulance bay, the doors flew open, and there she was, the undercover policewoman, getting ready to jump in and take my place. I looked at her in disbelief. She could have been my twin; the resemblance was uncanny. After a quick introduction, she took my place in the stretcher.

Ashley gave me a kiss and got back into her role. The paramedics raced with the stretcher down the corridor to the ER with Ashley running alongside of it.

Joe stepped out of the ambulance that was parked next to the one I was in, along with the officer that was guarding us at Doc's house. I was quickly transferred into theirs and the door closed behind me. We needed to sit tight and wait for Ashley to come back before we could make our getaway.

I examined Joe from head to toe. Part of me was happy to see him, but the other half still remembered what had happened in my dream. I had trouble hiding my nervousness and he could feel it. He asked me what the problem was, and I had to explain. He sat there and listened attentively as I recounted my nightmare.

"Oh my God," he said. "If I were you, I wouldn't want to see me either. Guard, I want you to listen to me, and I really mean this: if you see weeds start growing out of me, don't hesitate, and shoot me on the spot."

I started to giggle at the look that came over the guard's face.

"I'm sorry, Bobby," Joe said. "I know it's not funny, but see, I made you laugh, anyway. Everything is going to be fine, I promise. We will get you both out of here safely; you will see."

I forced a smile. Suddenly, I thought about Ashley, and I was worried about Dr. Blake too. All of the people I loved were risking their lives to keep me safe.

"How long before Ashley gets back?" I asked.

"A couple of hours, maybe; it's hard to tell. Oh here, I almost forgot, you need to change into these clothes."

Joe handed me a bag. It was from the same store as the clothes that Ashley and I got this morning.

"Courtesy of Detective Stone?" I asked.

"Yes, it seems his wife loves to shop; there are some in there for Ashley too."

I looked inside.

"Jeans, tee shirts, and baseball caps, nice." *Now, that is more my style*, I thought.

I changed behind a makeshift curtain, using a stretcher blanket.

We talked for a while about my sailing adventures. The guard said that he had sailed before and loved it very much.

"I don't think that you were aware of this part of the plan yet," he said, then turned and looked at Joe. Joe nodded, and he continued, "But we can't leave you unguarded, even on your boat. I will be joining you."

"Really... no, why?"

"Bobby," Joe said, "Tyler is more dangerous than any of us ever thought. We thought he was dead, but he's not, and he's still after you. It seems like he will stop at nothing to get you back. He's a psychopath, a very dangerous one. We don't even have a clue how many people he has killed in the process. You need to have someone around to protect you until we catch him and put an end to this for good."

"Listen," I explained, "no offense. I'm sorry, it's just that…"

"No apology necessary, Miss Hansen; I promise I won't get in your way."

"Do you have a name?" I asked. "I don't remember if we were formally introduced, or if we were just told that you were our guard."

"Yup, probably the latter. It's Timothy Reed, but you can just call me Timothy."

"Okay then… it's nice to finally meet you, Timothy, and if we are going to be living on my boat together, I guess you should call me Bobby."

Joe's phone rang and we both looked at him. He answered.

"Okay, we're ready."

He hung up.

"Ashley is on her way back. Make the reunion short. She needs to change, and we need to hightail it out of here."

She arrived shortly after the call, dressed up like a doctor with black-rimmed glasses and a file in her hand.

"You didn't have to work too hard to play that role, Dr. Carter," I said, and gave her a quick hug. I handed her the clothes she needed to change into and drew the curtain. In a few minutes, she was ready to go. We buckled up, held hands, and braced ourselves as the sirens sounded and the ambulance sped out of the hospital. It went straight for the highway, and then headed out of town. We were finally on our long journey back to the marina.

The sirens stopped when we were about fifteen minutes away from the hospital. I breathed a sigh of relief. They were making me feel very stressed. Joe got on his phone again.

"We will be there in five minutes," he said.

"What's going on, Joe?" I asked.

"We are going to change vehicles. We can't use the ambulance to go all the way to the marina."

"Oh right, I didn't even think about that."

We stopped on the side of the road behind a fancy SUV with tinted windows, and got out of the ambulance.

I heard a bark.

"Oh my God, Maestro. Are you in there?"

I opened the door and he jumped out and knocked me on my ass. I gave him a major rubdown.

"Courtesy of Detective Stone?" I asked.

Joe nodded.

"I'm starting to like that guy."

Everyone laughed as we got in and got back on the road.

"He's really a great guy," Timothy said, "once you get to know him. He's very old fashioned. It came as a little bit of a shock to him, when he first met you, but he likes you both, and he is doing his damnedest to make sure that nothing happens to you."

"Yes, I think we got off on the wrong foot," Ashley said, "but I could tell that we were going to be friends in the end."

"When he got back to the office the day of the fire," Timothy continued, "he asked me to do some research, to find out everything I could about the two of you. It was interesting reading, Bobby. You were all over the news for a while. I showed him everything that I found, and he immediately put the other cases he was working on aside to take care of this. He feels very bad about everything you have been through in your life, and so do I, by the way. I signed up for this, because of that. Well, I also love to sail... bonus."

He winked.

"That's good," Joe said, "because I wasn't planning on going out there. Water makes me nervous. I never learned how to swim, and anyway, someone has to bring this car back."

"Good excuse, Joe," I said, and we all laughed. "You don't know what you're missing."

"So, Timothy, where did Detective Stone find my twin?" I asked.

"Oh, Jennifer? She's a Rookie on the force. She started about a year ago. The resemblance is uncanny, isn't it?"

"Oh my God, that was my mother's name, and now that I think about it, she even had my mother's eyes. This is too crazy."

"She's really nice too," Ashley added. "I got to talk with her a bit while we were in the room by ourselves, waiting for my chance to sneak out. She loves her job and wants to become a detective."

"It is amazing," I said, "how much she looks like me. Well, as they say, everyone has a twin. Isn't it ironic though, that I spent half my life in jail, and she's in law-enforcement? We are polar opposites."

Ashley smacked me on the arm. "You are not!" she yelled. "It wasn't your fault what happened to you. It was all bad luck. You are a good person too."

"I'm sorry," I said. "I love you too."

She leaned over and gave me a kiss.

"So, tell us about your adventure, Ash," I asked. "In the ER… it must have been pretty crazy!"

"Yes, do tell," Joe said.

"Well, let me tell you all, I might have missed my calling," she turned to me and winked. "I should have been an actress. It was actually pretty exciting."

"Sounds like you had fun," Timothy said.

"I don't know about fun, but yes, it had its moments. It was kind of painful too, a little too much *déjà vu*."

Ashley turned and looked at me again.

She continued, "I ran alongside the stretcher, followed by the police escort, of course, crying and screaming for you to wake up. Dr. Blake and a couple of nurses came running to meet us. The nurses tried to calm me down so they could ask me some questions as we continued into the ER. They transferred you, I mean Jennifer, onto the gurney, and started with the oxygen. They proceeded to check her vitals. Dr. Blake was giving instructions to the nurses and ordering meds and tests. I was still in there, by her side, until they needed to take her for the tests. I was told that I would have to go to the waiting room until they were done. I protested and cried till they almost had to drag me out of there. Believe me, everyone will know that we were there. I stayed in the waiting room, very well-guarded, until they came back with her."

"Good job!" I said. "So, after all that, how did they get you out?"

"Well, she was finally brought back to the ER, where I was allowed to join her again. Miraculously," she winked, "she had woken, but she needed to stay on the oxygen for a while. They found us a room, and we were escorted there under police guard. We went in and the guard took his place outside the room… major *déjà vu*!" she sighed, and a tear rolled down her face.

"Oh Ash," I said. "I'm so sorry you had to go through that. It must have been hard."

"It's okay, Bobby; it's for a good cause. They'll catch that bastard, for once and for all."

"I hope you're right, Ash, I really do, but I know now what he is capable of. How can you be sure that he didn't see you leave?"

"A little while after we got to the room, there was a knock at the door. The guard let a doctor in. I was surprised when I saw her. She had the same color and length of hair as I do and was about the same size as me. She introduced herself and explained that she had come to switch places with me. Martha, the doctor, was going to stay with Jennifer, and I was going to leave as her. She reached into her pocket and pulled out a pair of dark-rimmed glasses like the ones she was wearing and handed them to me. Jennifer helped us do the switch. We weren't twins like you and Jennifer, but with the glasses and the uniform, we were very close. My instructions from Martha were to leave the room and go directly to the ER to have a word with Dr. Blake, as if I was consulting with him about you. After that, I was to casually make my way to the ambulance bay, and then, the rest, you know."

I was skeptical. "So, you really think that you pulled it off? Everyone bought it?"

Ashley took me by the hand, and said, "I do, Bobby, I really do."

"Sounds like everything went off without a hitch," Timothy said.

I got quiet after that. I still felt hunted. That feeling never went away. I watched the road, looking behind us every now and then.

"The exit is right up ahead," I said.

We drove a bit more till we came to a grocery store. We stopped briefly to pick up some food for our trip, and then we got back on the road again. In no time, we arrived at the marina.

We got out of the car and I turned to Ashley, took her hand, and said sadly, "What are we supposed to do? We have nothing but the clothes on our backs."

"Oh, Bobby?" Timothy said. "Remember Detective Stone's wife? Well, she really enjoyed her shopping spree. There are suitcases in the back. Your backpack is in there too. Dr. Blake asked that we bring that back with us when we went to get Maestro, that it was very important to you."

"We have more clothes…oh, and my laptop? You guys have thought of everything," I said, relief in my voice.

"Detective Stone called ahead and took care of your marina expenses, since you haven't had a chance to renew your credit cards after the fire. That, you will have to pay back. Oh, and by the way, Mrs. Stone would like to go out on your sailboat when this is all over with. She wanted me to mention that to you."

"Absolutely," I said. "It will be a pleasure."

We headed straight to the office.

"Miss Hansen, I presume?" The manager got up from his desk. "I have been expecting you. Welcome… come in, please. I have something that belongs to you."

He went into his safe and pulled out the dagger. All eyes were on it.

"I really didn't like having this around. I'm glad you are taking it off my hands. I was afraid of getting robbed. Have you any idea what this is worth?"

"Not a clue. I found it while I was scuba diving and brought it on board."

"I bet you it's worth a pretty penny," he responded.

I thanked him for hanging onto it and off we went to the docks. If we wanted to leave, we were going to have to hurry; the sun would soon be setting. We brought our belongings on board and did a quick check. The sailboat was all cleaned up and ready to go. We said our goodbyes to Joe, and Timothy started to untie the ropes. I got behind the wheel, started her up, and slowly backed out. Timothy jumped on board and off we went. I looked back and saw Joe, still on the dock, waving to us. I felt bad about leaving him behind.

"Nice ride," Timothy said. "Now let's sail off into the sunset."

I started to laugh.

"What's so funny?" he said.

"Nothing much, really; it's just that we will be heading east."

Ashley joined in the laughter.

Maestro seemed a little nervous; he had probably never been on a boat before. He lay down on the deck right next to me and didn't budge. The sun was setting as we looked toward the shore which was getting farther and farther away. Ashley went below deck to unpack, and Timothy stayed up near the bow. He looked very happy to have gotten this gig. The winds were pretty steady, so I cut the motor and we raised the sail. We needed to head south a bit more and then we would drop anchor for the night. The moon was almost full, and the sky was plastered with stars. I could feel the weight of all the stress from the last few weeks slowly rising off my shoulders. I was back in my world, where I belonged, my comfort zone.

"Ashley, what are you doing down there? Come on up and see the night sky; it's beautiful."

She came back up on deck with a bottle of wine and three glasses.

"Let's celebrate our freedom," she said.

Timothy got up and came over.

"Nice, a Shiraz, someone has good taste in wine, but not for me, thanks. I'm on the job, or have you forgotten? As for your freedom, you are not out of the woods yet, as they say."

"Oh, come on," I said, "Join us in a toast."

"Okay, maybe a little sip, just this once."

I watched as he loosened his belt.

"What are you doing?"

"Oh, sorry, I would just like to take this off. I don't think I need it on me right now."

"A gun? You brought a gun on my boat?"

"Of course I did; how do you want me to protect you?"

"I don't like guns. Just keep it away from me, okay?"

"Just let him do his job," Ashley said.

She poured us each a glass. I looked at her and her face was glowing in the light from the moon.

"You look so beautiful," I said as I raised my glass. "To freedom."

Chapter 68

"Beep…beep…beep…"

There it was, that familiar sound again. I was back in the hospital. I listened for the sound of Dr. Carter's voice; she was always there, by my side, talking to me. This was different, though; it didn't seem like the same place. How could I tell? I wasn't sure. It just didn't feel comfortable, I guess. Something was very wrong here.

I was still in total darkness, but I started to hear very faint sounds. I couldn't quite tell where they were coming from. I started to stress. My heart was racing; there was buzzing in my head. My body felt numb. Suddenly, the volume cranked up, and I didn't like what I was hearing.

"Somebody get those handcuffs off her; do you really think she's in any shape to run away? How am I supposed to help her? Everybody out! Get her to the OR, now!"

I was terrified and confused. I couldn't see anything. I didn't know what was happening to me. It wasn't Dr. Blake, I didn't hear Ashley's voice, and I didn't know where in the hell I was. This was not happening…

"She's a murderer," someone yelled. "She killed her foster parents; we are not letting her out of our sight."

"You can stand outside of the OR door for all I care," a woman shouted, "but if I don't get her into surgery right now, she will die, and that's not going to happen on my watch."

Oh my God, no, but I didn't, this is not happening, why am I here? I thought. I didn't want to go back there. What was happening? I tried to move but I couldn't. I wanted to scream…

"Miss Hansen, this is Dr. Jennings. You have internal injuries and we need to operate; can you hear me? Miss Hansen? We're losing her..." she yelled.

I felt a prick in my arm, then something on my face, an oxygen mask, maybe? I tried to speak but nothing was happening. I was starting to feel numb all over. The noises were fading... until there was nothing, not a sound, only the familiar blackness. I didn't like what was happening. I was taking another trip down memory lane.

Chapter 69

I screamed as I felt the sting of the yardstick across my behind. I couldn't bear the pain. She was really upset with me.

"I want my mommy!" I screamed. "I hate you; I want my mommy!"

I fought her, but the more I screamed, the more times she swung that stick.

"You don't have a mommy; you don't have anyone. Nobody wants you. You're lucky that we took you into our home, you little brat, so you are going to have to learn to behave and do as you are told."

I had to stop screaming or this would go on for a long time. I needed to get away from her. She finally stopped swinging and put the yardstick right back up where it belonged, in full view, so I knew what to expect if I ever misbehaved again.

Misbehave? Who had time to misbehave! They were slave-drivers. I had chores to do in the house, in the barn, in the fields, in the woods… everywhere I turned there were more chores to do.

She grabbed me by the arm, pulled me up unto my feet, and told me to go to my room. I obliged immediately; I didn't want to be anywhere near her. I ran upstairs as fast as I could and closed my bedroom door behind me.

I sat momentarily on the edge of my bed, but it was too painful, so I got undressed, put my nightie on, and lay down under the blankets. I tried to remember my mommy and all the fun we used to have together. I couldn't understand why she had to die. Miss Crawford tried to explain things to me. She was very nice. Why couldn't I have stayed with her?

I couldn't sleep; I was in too much pain. All these thoughts kept going around and around in my head.

I lay there for what seemed like hours. I heard a sound. It was coming from downstairs. Suddenly, there was light streaming from underneath my door. I pulled the blankets up around my neck. I counted the stairs as they creaked. I knew exactly how many there were, and I cringed at every one of them. Thirteen, fourteen, fifteen, and then, a moment of silence till my door slowly opened and the hall light lit up my room. He stood in the doorway, looked at me, and shook his head. It was Harold.

"I hear that the old witch got the yardstick out again. You are going to have to listen to her; she really enjoys waving that thing around."

I shook my head; I didn't want him to come any closer.

"I'm not going to hurt you; you know that. I just want to see if you are okay."

He closed the bedroom door and I started to cry.

"Don't cry, my sweet little one. I won't hurt you, I promise."

He came over to the bed and slowly pulled down my blankets. I tried to hang onto them, but he gave me a look, and I knew not to resist.

He sat down on the bed, turned me over, lifted my nightgown, and exposed my backside.

"Oh my, she really went to town this time, didn't she?"

He gently touched me with his fingertips, and I felt a stabbing pain and cried out, so he stopped. Then he got up and headed out of my room. I let out a sigh of relief, but unfortunately, this was not over.

"Don't move; I'll be back in a minute."

I just lay there, blistered butt exposed, waiting for the inevitable. What was I supposed to do? I was a prisoner here, and there was nowhere else I could go.

I heard the stairs creaking again and I knew he was on his way. He came into my room with a bowl and a towel.

"Here you go, darling; this should help."

He put the bowl on the bed next to me and dipped the towel in it.

"It's just cold water; it should take away the sting."

He sat down again. I was getting nervous. He wrung out the towel and laid it on my butt cheeks and I let out a cry again… not that it hurt, but it was cold. With one hand, he started rubbing my back. It was kind of soothing, but I stayed alert because I knew his kindness would come with a price.

"You are so beautiful," he said.

He moved the bowl to the floor and lay down next to me, still rubbing my back.

"You know that I love you, Roberta? I will protect you from her as much as I can. You just have to treat me nicely too."

I could feel his other hand touch the back of my thigh. I gasped.

"Shhh…" he whispered.

He slid it down between my legs and slowly moved up. I could feel his fat ugly fingers pushing up between my lips and the tears started flowing. The pain was unbearable, and though I wanted to stop, I knew better than to scream. I started to feel dizzy, then everything disappeared…

Chapter 70

I awoke, and abruptly sat up in my bed. I was gasping for air. I really hated these nightmares. I lay back down for a moment to try to calm myself. I closed my eyes and took some deep breaths. Suddenly it dawned on me that this was not my bedroom.

"Oh my God; what am I doing here!" I shouted.

I threw the blankets aside, grabbed my clothing that was strewn all over the room, and got dressed as fast as I could.

"Tyler!" I screamed, "what in the hell?"

I found one shoe but couldn't find the other. I opened the bedroom door and yelled, "Tyler, Jesus… where are you?"

"In the kitchen; I made you a nice breakfast," he calmly replied.

"Are you fucking crazy? What do you think you're doing? How did I even get here?"

Suddenly, I got very warm and lightheaded. I could feel my stomach starting to churn. I stopped yelling and put my hand over my mouth.

"Oh no," I mumbled, and then ran to the bathroom.

I barely made it to the toilet, when I started to vomit. My stomach heaved over and over again; it was so painful. Tears were rolling down my face.

Tyler came running into the bathroom.

"Are you okay?"

"Get out!" I screamed. "Leave me alone!"

I lay my head on the toilet seat and tears filled my eyes.

"I'm just trying to help."

"Leave me alone!" I cried.

He left the bathroom, slamming the door behind him.

I cried some more. I didn't know what was going on. I needed to get out of there and go home. What was I going to tell Emma and Harold?

Oh my God, he's going to kill me, I thought. *He's going to kill Tyler too. What have I done!*

I tried to get up; it was slow, but I made it to the sink. I turned the cold water tap on and threw some on my face. I straightened up and looked in the mirror. What a frightening sight. I found a hairbrush in one of the drawers and tried to clean myself up a bit. Not sure why; it wasn't going to make a difference to anyone. I was still going to be in deep shit.

I opened the door and went back to the bedroom to find my other shoe. Tyler came in.

"What are you doing?" he asked.

"I'm looking for my other shoe; have you seen it?"

"No clue; maybe it got left behind."

"Left behind, where?"

"At the lake, don't you remember anything? You got so wasted that you could barely stand up; I had to carry you most of the way here. You were out cold by the time we got here, so I undressed you and put you into my bed."

"Oh my God, where are your grandparents? What are they going to say?"

"They are gone for the weekend, and it doesn't matter; they will understand."

"Are you out of your freaking mind! Why would you bring me here? Why didn't you take me home? You do know that we are both dead right now, don't you? What were you thinking?"

"Maybe I was thinking for a change. Maybe I don't want you to go back there. Maybe I want you to stay with me."

I turned and snarled at him.

"Come on… please..." he begged.

"Stay with you? What are you talking about? I can't stay here. He will send the sheriff out here to get me, or he might even come and do it himself with his shotgun."

"Let him send the sheriff. We'll tell him everything that has been going on over there."

"Are you fucking kidding me? They are best friends. He won't believe a word we say. He thinks we are both trouble…anyway… he'll just drag my ass back over there, and I will be much worse off than I am now."

"I won't let you go; I'm tired of waiting for you. I want you to stay with me."

"I'm not staying. I need to go back to the lake and find my shoe, and then go home and face the consequences."

He turned, and I thought he was leaving the room, but instead, he closed the door.

"What in the hell do you think you're doing?" I yelled.

He didn't say anything; he just guarded the door and never took his eyes off me. I started to get very nervous. Those eyes that were looking at me, well, I didn't recognize them. They looked very dark and evil. I was overcome with a feeling that I was in danger, and I turned away.

I spotted the open window. I thought, well, if things turned bad, I could always jump through the screen. Compared to the alternative, it didn't seem so bad.

"What are you doing, Robbie?" he howled.

His voice startled me, but I was okay; I had a plan. I faced him once again and tried to convince him that I needed to go. He didn't want to hear it.

"You're not leaving here; I won't let you go back to that fucking rapist. What in the hell is wrong with you? I'm trying to protect you."

"Don't you understand? The sheriff is going to come looking for me."

"I don't give a shit about that; let him try! I love you; don't you know that by now? Sometimes I think you love that rapist better than you love me."

I couldn't talk; I just didn't know how to respond to that.

"I know now why he loves you. I saw it last night when I undressed you," he said softly. His eyes brightened, and a creepy little smile came across his face.

I stood there with my mouth open, shocked.

"You are so beautiful, Robbie; your body is flawless. Your ass is incredible, your butt-cheeks fitting perfectly in my hands. I couldn't stop touching you."

I gasped.

"I rolled you over on your back and admired you for the longest time. Those beautiful firm breasts, well, I had to taste them for myself to see why the old bastard loved them so much. Your nipples firmed up when I swirled my tongue around them. You were enjoying it too."

"I was passed out… you bastard… you touched me?"

Tears started rolling down my face.

"Oh… don't cry, honey; there's more. I remember you told me once, that he liked to play a game he called stink finger? Well, I tried it out. I didn't find the name very appropriate though, Robbie, because you smelled awesome. I put my fingers right up inside of you, in and out, in and out, several times. Not only did you smell good, Robbie, you were also delicious. My tongue was craving a little taste too, so I twirled it around your clit several times, then went deep inside you, as far as my tongue could reach. It was pure heaven. You had me so horny, that I came several times."

"I can't believe you did this to me. Who are you? You are not the Tyler that I love. What did you do with him?"

"I am that Tyler," he said as he put his hand down to his bulging crotch. "I was always there for you. You always came running to me when you needed someone to vent to."

"I thought I loved you, but things changed. You have changed, but still you are my best friend in the whole world... Oh my God, you raped me?"

"I always helped you when you needed comforting; you owe me. I can't understand you at all. That ugly old bastard abuses you, and you go right back for more."

"I have nowhere else to go. He has threatened my life over and over again. It's like a prison sentence; I am stuck there till I am at least sixteen. That's why I keep going back. When I turn sixteen, in one more year, I am getting the hell out of here, and nobody is going to stop me, not even you."

"That's not how I see it. When you turn sixteen, we will get married, we will build a beautiful house here on this farm, you will take care of my every need, and we will spend the rest of our lives together."

"You're out of your mind if you think I am going to spend the rest of my life around here; you don't own me! You are just like him! You have shown me your true colors. I will not live in fear anymore!"

"Yes, I do. I think you owe me for all the years that I have let you cry on my shoulder."

He started to walk over to me. I remembered about the window. He grabbed me and threw me on the bed. I screamed, and he put his hand over my mouth.

"What's wrong, Robbie, come on, oh right… I know you like it rough, all those years of abuse."

I bit his hand and he grabbed me by the throat. He swung his fist in the air and it came down on my face. The pain jolted through me. I kicked and screamed as hard as I could. I spotted the lamp on the night table. It was just a little bit out of reach. I struggled a little more with him, sliding myself in the direction of the lamp. I was close enough now, but I had to free my hand somehow. He was holding onto it very tightly.

"Who's there!" I yelled; it was the only thing I could think of. "Help!"

This distracted him, and he turned and loosened his grip. I freed my hand and grabbed hold of the lamp. I mustered up all the strength I had left and cracked it on his head.

I probably could have run out the door, but that window had been on my mind for quite some time. I didn't even think about it; I took a flying leap and burst through the screen.

Chapter 71

I was feeling very groggy, totally drained and disoriented. There was this buzzing in my head. I couldn't move; I didn't even have the energy to open my eyes. I was in a very awkward, uncomfortable position, but as hard as I tried, nothing moved. I listened hard. I didn't hear anything, except for my heartbeat. It was slow, but loud. It was pounding in my ear, almost as if it was outside of me. As for the rest of me, well, it was a total mystery. Pain surged through my body, or what was left of it. I felt crushed and was having trouble breathing.

I had this strange sensation of feeling wet and clammy. I wasn't cold, though, because whatever I was lying on felt warm. Face down and semi-conscious, I was too weak and confused to freak out.

The one thing that was almost unbearable was that smell. It was totally unrecognizable. It made me feel nauseous. My mind was working overtime, just to try to figure all this out.

I felt movement, very little, almost unnoticeable, but something moved. I focused hard, trying to waken all my senses. I tried to move again and open my eyes, but it wasn't happening.

Another movement, but this time there was no question. What I was lying on had moved.

I focused all my energy on my free hand, it felt free, anyway; the other was somewhere awkwardly positioned and throbbing with pain. I desperately needed to try to push myself off of whatever it was that I was lying on.

The heartbeat in my ear was getting louder; it was distracting me. Another movement! It suddenly dawned on me that what I was lying on was alive. It wasn't my heartbeat that I was hearing after all. I wanted to scream. In my head, I was, but no sound came out of my mouth.

I felt a numb tingling in my fingers. My hand, I was starting to feel it. I focused hard on the fingers now, trying to bring life back into them. The tingling seemed to be spreading up my arm, like my body was slowly rejuvenating.

My fingers, they finally moved! *There is hope,* I thought. Oh yes, and again! My hand also started to have some movement.

Suddenly, the thing underneath me jerked and gasped. I started to choke, and my hand automatically came up to my mouth.

At this point, I was sure that I was alive, but the problem was the thing underneath me was alive too. I started to tremble.

I heard something… a whisper… a breath... I wasn't quite sure at that moment. I concentrated hard on the sound.

"Help me," the whisper came again.

I couldn't quite understand.

I rubbed my eyes with my hand. It felt like I was covered in slime. I wiped away at them to try to clean them off. I could see a sliver of light. I kept wiping. I gasped as my eyes opened to the horrific sight in front of me. It was blood. I was covered in blood, and the body I was lying on was also covered in blood.

I heard a gurgling sound.

"Help me, Roberta; please help me."

It was barely audible, but I knew it was Harold. Oh my God, I was lying on top of him. We were both covered in blood. I tried to lift myself up a bit to see him. The blood dripping into my eyes was making it very difficult. I froze when I saw the knife sticking out of his chest, right in front of my face. I couldn't speak. I didn't know what to do. He started coughing and blood was squirting out of his chest wound. I had to look away; my stomach was churning. I closed my eyes; I couldn't believe this was happening.

"Roberta," he whispered. "The knife."

I wiped my eyes clean again and turned in time to see him reach for it.

"Help me, please help me," he coughed, and the blood pissed out of his wound again.

I had to help him; I didn't know what else to do. I pulled myself up a bit and saw his face. He looked so broken, so pitiful. I can't even describe the way I felt. A bigger part of me wanted to try to help him, but that little vengeful side of me wanted to walk out and leave him there to die alone. That was not possible, of course, because I was in no position to even get up and walk away.

I wiped the blood from my eyes again and reached out and wrapped my hand around the knife.

"Please," he begged.

I took a deep breath, tried to gather up every ounce of energy that I had, closed my eyes, and gave it a good yank.

He let out a yell and I opened my eyes again. I looked at the knife still in my hand; it was dripping with Harold's blood. Blood was oozing out of his chest. I managed to free my other hand and place it over the hole to try to stop the bleeding. I looked up at him and he was watching my every move. With relief in his eyes, and a semi-smile on his face, he whispered, "I'm sorry, Roberta, I love you."

That was it. His eyes were still fixed on me but there was no life left in them. He was gone. I should have been dancing with joy, but I burst out into tears.

The pain in my head was getting unbearable. I started to feel dizzy. That buzzing sound was coming back. Everything was starting to fade to black.

"No, you don't; not so fast!"

I heard a voice. Was someone coming to rescue me? I needed to stay conscious. I tried to speak, nothing. I was barely hanging on. I tried to focus. There was another awful smell. My stomach was not dealing well with it. I was fading fast.

"Robbie!" the voice said. "Where do you think you're going?"

The voice was familiar, even the smell. I couldn't quite put my finger on it though. I focused some more.

I felt something on my arm. It seemed to be swirling around it. I felt something tickle my foot, then that same feeling of something swirling around it. My eyes shot open; this didn't feel right at all. I looked around me. There was still blood everywhere. I was still lying on top of old Harold. I wanted to get out of there.

My body felt restricted. I tried to move my legs and arms, but they weren't going anywhere. I couldn't figure out what was happening. I tried to look behind me, but I wasn't able. I felt my legs being lifted, then my hips; oh my God, I was being pulled up, feet first. I tried to scream; nothing happened. I closed my eyes as a wave of nausea came over me. I managed to suppress it.

"Robbie, my love."

My eyes shot open again. The sight before me brought along another wave of nausea. I was hanging upside down, my arms and legs bound with seaweed. I tried to get my hands free.

"Don't even think about getting away from me this time; I told you that I was coming back for you. You are mine."

Tyler's rotting corpse was floating up near the ceiling. He had red, evil eyes and a wicked smile. Seaweed was sprouting from his body and covering the whole room. He started to laugh with his deep horrifying voice as he swung me from side to side in front of him. "We will live happily ever after, Robbie."

That evil laugh echoed through the room. His mouth opened, and a strand of seaweed shot out and wrapped itself around my neck. I tried to scream again but choked as the seaweed's grip tightened. I tried to fight, but I was hanging upside-down at his mercy. I wasn't going to last much longer. I kept gasping for air. The lack of oxygen was taking its toll. I felt lightheaded, and that buzzing started in my head again. My eyes blurred, and I could barely see anything anymore. I started to fade out, but he shook me, and the seaweed loosened its grip around my neck. I started to cough, and then my voice started to come back.

I needed to get out of there. I took a deep breath and screamed as loud as I could. Tyler kept laughing and I kept screaming…

Chapter 72

I kept screaming but Tyler's demonic laughter was so overpowering, and it just kept echoing through my mind. I wanted desperately to free myself, but this monster I was fighting against was much too powerful… I stopped fighting and just kept screaming…

"Bobby, wake up… Bobby, honey… Wake up, it's just a dream, Bobby, come on. Stop screaming. Open your eyes… it's me, Bobby; you're okay."

It was a trick. Tyler was trying to deceive me; I was sure of it. I was afraid to open my eyes…

"Bobby, stop please… Listen to me. We're on our boat: you, me, Maestro, and Timothy. Open your eyes, honey. You'll see it's just a dream; you are safe."

I heard barking; no, it couldn't be. I felt something wet slide across my face.

"Down, boy!" Ashley yelled.

I stopped screaming, jumped up, and opened my eyes. I was having trouble breathing and I wasn't quite sure where I was. Ashley was trying to console me.

"It's okay, honey; I'm here."

Suddenly, there was banging on the cabin door, and I started screaming again.

"Are you guys okay in there?" he yelled. "How in the hell do you open this damned thing?"

"It's okay, Bobby, honey; it's just Timothy. You're safe."

I started to cry, and Maestro started barking.

"We're okay, Timothy," Ashley said. "Bobby was having a bad dream. I'll be out in a few minutes. Maestro, calm down, boy."

She pushed him off the bed.

"Everything is going to be okay, Bobby. I won't let anything happen to you; I promise."

Ashley took me back into her arms and rocked me gently, stroking her fingers through my hair. I kept my eyes open, fearing that I might return into the hell that I had just come from. I concentrated on Ashley and her every movement and every sound. She kept speaking to me, gently reassuring me that everything was going to be okay.

"Ashley," I whispered.

"Yes, Bobby, I'm here."

"I had the worst dreams."

"I know, honey."

"It was all different parts of my life that flashed before my eyes, and then Tyler wrapped it all up with his decaying body. He won't stop till he has me, you know. I think I should get you back to shore and leave here without you. He will kill you too, I know he will, like he has killed everyone else that has gotten close to me."

"I'm not going anywhere; we are going to get through this. We have Timothy, Joe, and Detective Stone on our side. He will not get away this time."

I held onto Ashley as tightly as I could. I was so afraid of losing her.

"Is it okay, Ashley, if we go on deck?" I whispered. "I really don't want to go back to sleep. I think sleeping is my worst enemy right now."

"Let's do it," she said.

She took me by the hand and led the way.

"We are coming up, Timothy," she said.

She opened the hatch, and there he was, gun in hand, and swinging it around all over the place. Suddenly, there was a splashing noise and he pointed the gun in that direction.

Maestro started barking.

"Something is out there," he said. "Right after you started screaming, it started jumping and splashing around."

"Fred!" I yelled. "Fred, is that you?"

I went port-side and looked overboard.

"Fred?"

He jumped in the air again, and I knew right away that it was him. I kicked off my flip-flops and without hesitation, I dove in.

"Bobby!" Ashley yelled, as I splashed down into the water.

It wasn't long before Fred and I were reunited. We snuggled and slow-danced together in the moonlit waters. I thought that I would never see him again. He must have heard me screaming and came to my rescue. I was overjoyed as I hung onto his fin and we swam around the boat. Ashley followed us from port to stern to starboard to bow and back to port again. She couldn't see us very well and was getting nervous. Timothy was totally freaking out. Maestro never stopped barking. I looked up on board, saw their panicked state, and started to laugh.

"Okay, Fred, the party's over for tonight. I better get back in the boat before they both have a heart attack."

Ashley put down the ladder and watched as I climbed back up. She reached out and threw her arms around me and held me close. Timothy started scolding me.

"How am I supposed to protect you. Are you crazy, jumping overboard in the middle of the night; you don't know what's out there?"

"But, it's just…"

"No buts, you can't just run off when I'm trying to keep you safe. You need to give me a heads-up at least."

Ashley let go and smacked me on the behind, then she headed for the galley. "Come on, Maestro."

"I'm sorry," I explained, "but I thought I would never see him again. I just got very excited; I wasn't thinking. I promise that I won't do it again."

Ashley came back up with a towel, threw it at me, and then leaned over the side of the boat.

"Fred!" she yelled. "We meet again."

Fred swam to the side of the boat. Timothy watched in awe.

"Where did he come from, I mean, how do you know him? He has a name?"

"It's a long story," I said.

Ashley turned and headed back to the galley. "I'll make some coffee; I don't think anyone will be going back to sleep now."

Maestro sat next to me and looked overboard at Fred. He didn't do anything, just watched curiously.

I started to tell Timothy the story of how Fred and I met and the adventures we had together.

All eyes were on Fred, but Fred's eyes were on Maestro. He was just as curious.

Ashley came back up with coffee.

"You know that we're talking about you, right Fred?" she said.

At that, he dove into the water. Moments later, he came flying up into the air and splashed down, and then he came back up laughing.

Timothy backed away from the side and Maestro started barking again, as if he wanted to play too.

"Okay, Fred, thanks for that; you're quite the joker," Ashley said.

We all laughed.

We sat and had our coffee while Maestro and Fred got acquainted. It was funny to watch them; they seemed to be hitting it off.

I looked toward the east and pointed out the beautiful orange glow coming up over the horizon. It paved the way to a spectacular sunrise.

We spent the morning scuba diving. It was Timothy's first time. He was a natural. It took a lot of coaxing, but after a while even Maestro jumped in and joined us for a swim. It was funny to see Fred and Maestro, nose to nose, trying to get more personally acquainted.

Around mid-afternoon, the wind picked up a bit and we raised the sails. Timothy suggested that we keep moving. He thought it would make it more difficult for someone to track us. With the beautiful weather, there were a lot of boats on the water. Timothy kept note of every one of them to make sure that we weren't being followed.

The day went by without any news from Joe or Detective Stone. I found a nice place where we could drop anchor and stay for the night. Fred followed along and brought some of his friends with him. We all jumped in and had a quick swim with them before supper. Maestro stayed on board this time; I think he found it a little challenging getting back up into the boat last time.

We got back on board and dried off, then I joined Ashley in the galley and helped prepare supper… sliced chicken, Caesar salad, and beets. Timothy, again, took note of all the boats anchored nearby and Maestro sat quietly at his feet.

We ate on deck and relaxed with a bottle of wine until the sun went down, presenting another spectacular sunset.

Chapter 73

I woke to what I thought sounded like a phone ringing. I sat up in bed and looked around. Ashley wasn't there. She must have gotten up early and gone on deck. I opened the hatch and Maestro greeted me.

"Did I hear a phone ring?" I asked.

"Shhh..." Ashley whispered. "It's Joe." She was leaning into Timothy to try to hear the conversation.

I sat down and joined them, but I was getting very frustrated. There is nothing worse than hearing one side of a phone conversation. Especially when it's, 'Really?' and then there is the ever so popular, 'Oh no!' Oh, and don't forget the 'Unnnn... hunnnn...' really dragged out for your pleasure.

"What in the hell is going on?" I yelled. "Can you at least put him on speaker phone?"

"Please do," Ashley said. "It sounds serious. You are driving us crazy!"

"I'm sorry; I wasn't thinking," he said apologetically. "I just got on the phone. Give me a second, hang on Joe."

He fumbled with his phone a bit. "Okay, we're on speaker."

"Ashley, Bobby, it's Joe. How are you two holding up?"

"We're okay; what's going on?" I asked. "Did you catch him?"

"No, Bobby, not yet. There is something, though. Someone broke into Dr. Blake's office late last night."

"What? Oh my God, is he okay?"

"He's fine, Bobby; he wasn't there."

"Oh right, what was I thinking."

"Was there anything…" Ashley started to say something, and I cut her off.

"It was Tyler!" I yelled. "I know it!"

"Yes, Bobby, I think you're right, because the drawer with your file was left open."

"He is going to find out that I am not there."

"Not to worry, Bobby; Dr. Blake has been doing a great job of this. He has been keeping a fake file ongoing on your supposed progress."

"I'm sorry to interrupt, but I don't like this one bit," Ashley said, and she reached over and took me by the hand.

"Well, I think it's good," Joe replied, "because we know for sure that he is here."

"They can't keep this charade going for much longer," Ashley added. "At some point, in real life, Bobby would recover from her smoke inhalation. He's not stupid. That is probably why he looked for the file. He's suspicious."

"Listen, Ashley, I understand your concern, I'm just telling you what I know; we can speculate all we want. We really don't know what he is up to, but we know that he is here and that he didn't follow you out to the coast."

"What next?" I said.

"Well, Ashley's right. We can't keep your double in that room forever; we'll have to get her out in the open where he can see her. Set a trap or something, and see if he falls for it."

"I still don't like it," Ashley announced. "I don't know... I have a bad feeling about all of this."

"Give him a break, Ashley," Timothy replied. "He's just trying to do his job. I've got this; I am keeping track of every boat that is around us. They come, and they go; nobody has stuck around for very long or followed us."

"Thanks, Timothy, but her fears are legitimate," Joe said. "He has evaded us before. All I can say, girls, is that you can rest assured that we are using every resource possible to track him down."

"What if he gets wise and disappears again?" I said.

"We'll set the bait and give him twenty-four hours. If nothing happens, I'm heading out your way; we won't take any unnecessary chances."

"How will you find us?" I asked.

"I know exactly where you are. Timothy's phone has a tracking device. I will find you; don't worry."

"Easy for you to say," Ashley said, then she got up and went down into the galley.

I watched her as she disappeared below deck. Ashley had spent enough time with Tyler to know what he was capable of. She had told me about the times they had spent arguing about my care, and how he obsessed over me, not wanting anyone else to get close to me. She knew that he was dangerous. Reading people and getting inside their heads, after all, was her expertise. But she, along with everyone else, had underestimated to what extent, until it was too late. He was just that good. Ashley had always felt a little guilty about that, I thought, *and she still does to this day.*

"Ashley?" Timothy yelled.

"It's okay," I said, "I'll go down and check on her. Goodbye, Joe, keep us informed okay? Come on, Maestro."

I followed Ashley below deck and found her sitting on the bed with the jewel-covered dagger in her hand. Tears were dripping down her cheeks. Maestro lay down at her feet. I sat down next to her and put my arm around her.

"And... what do you plan on doing with that?" I asked.

"I'm sorry, Bobby; I should have known how dangerous he was, I..."

"Stop it, Ashley, nobody knew, this is not your fault."

"I won't let him hurt you, I promise. I will kill him first."

"You won't kill anyone; we have Timothy, remember?"

I took the dagger out of her hands and put it under the bed.

"I love you, Ash. The police will find him and then we can go on with our lives. We can sail around the world and do anything we damn well please. This nightmare will be over soon."

I gave her a gentle push and she tipped over onto her back and forced a smile. I got to my knees and straddled her, then I leaned over and looked into her eyes. I could see the glistening path left behind from the tears that were running down her cheeks. I held Ashley's head in my hands.

"We will spend the rest of our lives together. You, me, Maestro, oh, and umm... don't forget Fred."

I winked and leaned in, just close enough to lick the salty remains left behind, and then I pressed my lips against hers. I felt Ashley's hands grab my shoulders as she pulled me in, even closer. I could feel the fire building up inside of me. I tried to resist, but I couldn't hold back any longer. I reached down and took hold of Ashley's shirt, releasing our kiss just long enough to pull it up over her head.

We connected again. This time, I pushed my tongue deep between those luscious lips of hers. My hands slowly made their way down her neck and chest, and then stopped at her beautifully firm little breasts. Ashley moaned, which excited me even more. I couldn't wait to get my mouth on them. I drew back just a bit, and licked my lips with my tongue, then slowly moved it down Asley's chin, and then her neck, anticipating pure ecstasy. I reached her breast and then made my way to her nipple, which was perfectly erect. I put my mouth around it.

Ashley moaned and squirmed again. I felt Ashley's hands push my head into her breast; she loved when I sucked them very intensely. My hands slowly moved down her sides, my mouth never letting go of her delicious nipple. I followed the waistline of her shorts until I came to the button. I slipped it through the hole and slowly pulled down the zipper.

"Oh my God," Ashley whispered, "you drive me crazy."

I let go of her still very erect nipple, and continued licking my way downward, zig-zagging from side to side. Ashley giggled and moaned some more. I was burning up with desire and couldn't hold back any longer. I ripped Ashley's shorts right off her and tossed them across the room. Then I stopped, just for a moment, to admire this beautiful woman who was lying there naked in front of me. Ashley's face was flushed, her eyes were partly closed, and she had that look on her face that said… 'Take me, now.'

I ever so gently spread her legs apart.

"I'm… going in," I said, as I plunged into the tantalizing delight laid out before me.

Ashley let out a yell…

We heard footsteps, "Are you guys okay in there?" Timothy yelled and pulled open the hatch.

"Oh shit… I'm sorry… Jesus…" he slammed the door shut.

"What in the hell?" I yelled.

"I'm sorry, I heard some yelling; how am I supposed to know?" He was still struggling with the hatch, trying to close it properly.

"How do you work this fucking door anyway, Jesus?"

"Just leave it," Ashley said, then she started to laugh hysterically. I fell onto the bed next to her and joined in.

"Oopsie…" I whispered, "we should have thought of that."

"We? I didn't know you were going to ravage me, or I might have," Ashley winked, and gave me a kiss.

"That was amazing, my love."

Chapter 74

I heard rumbling and opened my eyes. I looked over at Ashley, who was still sound asleep. We had such a wonderful time yesterday, scuba diving, swimming, drinking, and dancing, no wonder she was still passed out.

The boat was rocking slightly, and I could hear footsteps on deck. I quietly got out of bed, put some clothes on, and went up. Maestro followed behind.

"Thank goodness you're up," Timothy said, "I didn't know what I should do. Look to the west, a storm is coming."

"It doesn't look that bad," I replied. "I'll go back down and check the radar."

I tried to very quietly make my way back down, but Ashley heard me and rolled over.

"Good morning, beautiful," I said.

"Oh my God, I drank too much; what time is it anyway?"

"Time for you to get up, sleeping beauty."

"What was that?" she said as she sat up.

"Thunder," I replied. "I'm checking to see how bad of a storm it is."

"Oh no!" she said and jumped out of bed. "What are we going to do?"

"We are going to get out of its way, if we can. Get dressed and put some rain gear on."

I checked the radar, and saw the blob moving across the screen. It didn't look too bad, but it was coming right for us. I grabbed my gear and went back up. I went to the helm and started the motor. There was no wind yet, so the sails were of no use to us.

"We are going to head southeast," I said, "to try to get out of its way. Sit down and hang on; the waters might get a little rough."

Suddenly there was a big splash.

"What was that?" Ashley yelled.

Maestro started barking.

"Calm down; it's just Fred."

We watched for him and he came back up to the surface again.

"Hey Fred!" I yelled. "Looks like there's another storm coming."

He responded with a nervous squeaking sound.

"What do you think we should do, Fred?"

He replied.

In disbelief, Timothy watched the exchange of conversation between Fred and me.

"Okay guys... looks like Fred is going to lead us out of here."

He dove into the water, came back out with another big splash, and then off he went.

Timothy stood up as I proceeded to follow Fred.

"What? Are you kidding?" he said.

"Not at all. Take a seat and keep Maestro with you. I trust Fred with my life."

Fred had gotten me out of that tropical storm, and I had no doubt that he would get us clear of this little one. I took my eyes off Fred for a moment to see how Ashley and Timothy were doing. She didn't look so well. All of that partying last night and the alcohol she consumed was not going to fare very well with rough waters. Poor

Maestro wasn't looking very brave either. He lay with his head down between Timothy's feet.

"Hey Timothy," I yelled over another crack of thunder, "you might want to hang onto Ashley if she has to lean overboard; she's looking kind of pale."

With that, she turned, leaned over the side, and projectile-vomited into the water. I felt so bad, but there was nothing I could do to help her.

I looked ahead to track Fred again. He had veered a bit more to the south, so I followed his lead. I looked behind us and I could see the black clouds slowly catching up. Another crack of thunder, and then the rain came.

I glanced at Ashley again, sitting there, head between her knees, and Timothy hanging onto her. He didn't look so well, himself. I was on my own here; good thing I had Fred.

Lightning streaked across the sky, and the wind started to pick up.

"Timothy, you need to get over here and grab the wheel," I yelled, "Just to hold it steady while I try to raise the sails."

"I can help you with that," he answered.

"Okay, then help Ashley over here, and she can hold it. You okay with that, Ash?"

"I can do that," she said softly, just before she threw up again, this time all over the deck. Maestro got out of the way just in the nick of time.

"You sure?"

She nodded her head and crawled over to me, Maestro following behind her.

I grabbed a cloth and wiped her face a bit. Ashley sat at my seat and just collapsed onto the wheel.

"I got this," she whispered and pointed to the sail. "Let's raise that thing!"

It didn't take long; Timothy really kicked it into gear. Must have been all the adrenaline. I thought that he was secretly shitting his pants from fear, but Timothy proved me wrong and he pulled it together. After I gave him the A-Okay, he went back, sat down, and braced himself.

The rain was pelting down hard on us now. I took my place at the helm and glanced up ahead. Fred was still leading the way. I kept Ashley by my side, thinking that she was safer with me. The waves were getting high, but the boat had picked up a lot of speed and was plowing right through them with no problem. I glanced at Timothy, who was hanging on for dear life.

"Are you okay?" I yelled.

He sent me a thumbs up, but I wasn't reading that at all from the expression on his face. He looked like he was terrified but trying to act brave. To be honest, I was quite nervous myself. It was *déjà vu* for me. It didn't come close to the tropical storm that I survived, but it sure brought back the tension.

Another slight turn and we seemed to be slowly moving inland, which was a good thing, because the storm was definitely heading out to sea.

Ashley was sitting on the floor with her head on my lap and both arms wrapped around my leg. I reached down and stroked her hair. I felt bad for her; booze and waves are not a good combination.

Thunder exploded, and lightning lit up the sky again. Ashley screamed, and Maestro started barking.

"It's okay, Ash; we're almost there. I can see a clearing in the sky, up ahead."

I took a deep breath and yelled as loud as I could, "Come on, Carla, we can do this."

As suddenly as those words came out of my mouth, the rain stopped. I looked up ahead and I could see the sun coming through the clouds.

"Thank you, Carla," I yelled, and my eyes swelled with tears.

"Thank you!" I whispered again and smiled.

"Woohoo!" Timothy stood up and put his arms in the air. "Woohoo," he yelled again.

I started to laugh, and Ashley lifted her head.

"Are we okay?" she said, with every ounce of energy she had left.

"We're good, Ashley, really good. Carla and Fred were helping."

She looked up at me and smiled.

"Be sure to thank them for me," she said, and then she leaned over and vomited again.

I helped her up onto my seat, took her rain gear off, and tried to clean her up. Maestro decided to go sit with Timothy.

"I'm so sorry," she said. "I've made an awful mess."

"It's okay, Ash; don't worry about it."

We brought down the sail and anchored.

Fred jumped up into the air and said his goodbyes.

"Thanks again, Fred," I yelled, then off he went.

I watched as the storm headed out to sea. The sun felt warm on our soaked bodies. Ashley lay her head back and closed her eyes. She seemed to be getting the color back in her cheeks.

I glanced over at Timothy and saw that he was looking toward the shore with his binoculars.

"Anything interesting?" I asked.

He didn't answer.

"Timothy!" I yelled.

"Hang on," he said. "Looks like there is a craft coming toward us."

I turned and looked. Sure enough, it was coming straight for us, and fast. I started to get nervous. I didn't take my eyes off it.

"No worries," Timothy said, "It's the Coast Guard."

I breathed a sigh of relief. We watched as their boat pulled up next to ours. There were two officers on board.

Maestro started barking at them.

"Are you folks okay? We saw you come out of that storm."

"We're good," I replied.

"George!" the other guy from the vessel called out, pointing to the side of my boat.

The officer turned in that direction, then looked back at the three of us.

"Are you sure that everything is okay? Your friend doesn't look so well."

He pointed to Ashley, who was passed out at the helm.

"The waves didn't agree with her," I replied. "She threw up all over the place. She's fine, now. She's just resting."

"Do you mind if I come on board?"

"Why?" I asked.

"Just to check on her. Do you have a problem with that?"

"Be my guest," I said.

"Is your dog dangerous?"

I shook my head. "It's okay, Maestro."

Timothy spoke up. "I'm a police officer," he said as he pulled out his badge. "Is there a problem here?"

"Not at all," the officer said as he boarded.

He looked at Timothy's credentials.

"You're way out of your jurisdiction. What is your business here?"

"We are on a little vacation," I interrupted.

I gave Timothy a dirty look. We didn't need people finding out who we were or what we were doing out here.

I walked over to Ashley, Maestro by my side.

"Ash, honey, wake up. We have company."

She slowly showed signs of life.

"What?"

"Are you okay, Miss? I'm with the Coast Guard; we're just making sure that everyone is fine."

"I'm good; what happened?"

She tried to get up and almost fell.

"Nothing happened, Ash," I said, "They just saw us come out of the storm and came to check on us."

"Oh, the storm… right…"

"I'm just going to take her back down to our bed to sleep it off," I said, "Come on, Ash; you need to rest."

"Is this your boat?" the officer asked.

He addressed his question to Timothy.

"It's mine," I replied.

"Can I see your registration?"

"Really, what is this?" I yelled.

"Just show him," Timothy said.

"Okay, I'll be right back!"

I brought Ashley down and came back up with my papers. He examined them thoroughly.

"Looks like everything is in order, Miss…?

"Hansen, it's on the registration." I gave him a dirty look.

"Oh… and… Miss Carter?" he said, pointing to the galley.

"Yes, it's ours."

"Who is Carla?" he asked.

"What?" I was shocked at the question.

"Your boat, it has the name Carla on it."

"She was my best friend. She died, and I named the boat after her. Is there a law against that?"

"No, I guess not," he said, "but someone pointed you out to us and said that they had heard that someone was looking for their boat that was stolen, and the only thing they could remember about it was that it had the name Carla painted on it."

"Well, it's not this one, so, thanks for your concern, but we have a vacation to get back to, and I have to check on my girlfriend. If we see the boat, we'll be sure to let you know. Come on, Maestro."

I turned and went below deck. I could overhear Timothy talking to them for a few minutes longer and then their engine revved and off they went.

After checking on Ashley, I went back up on deck.

"What do you make of that?" I asked Timothy.

"I don't know; do you think it's a coincidence?"

"Are you kidding? I don't believe in coincidences, and neither does Joe," I said. "Maybe you should give him a call?"

He nodded and reached into his pocket for his phone.

"Oh shit," he said. "It got wet!"

He opened it up and pulled the battery out.

"It's not so bad; I'll just leave it in the sun for a bit and it should dry out okay."

I shook my head and went back down. Ashley heard me and rolled over. She reached out her hand, and I lay down next to her. I put my arms around her, and she closed her eyes again. I was doing enough worrying for both or us, so I kept this to myself. She just snuggled and didn't say a word.

I was starting to stress, though. I didn't like this one bit. Two boats with the name Carla on it? No way; this didn't feel right at all under the circumstances. I got thinking about Dr. Blake. I was sure that he wouldn't have anything in his files that said that I owned a boat with Carla written on it. Why would he?

It was driving me crazy, just lying there below deck, so I decided to go back up and help keep an eye on things.

I gently woke her. "Come on, Ash. I'll set you up on deck; the weather has turned beautiful. The fresh air will do you good, Maestro too, come on."

I helped her up and prepared the cot. Timothy was busy taking note of all the boats that surrounded us. That was good, but the only thing I wanted to do was get out of there.

"I think we should lift anchor and move on," I finally said.

"Yeah, I've been thinking the same thing," Timothy replied. "We've been spotted and reported to the authorities. Word will travel fast, if someone is out there looking for us. We'll keep moving, at least until my phone dries out and we can contact Joe…let's get the hell out of Dodge."

We raised the sail and did just that.

Chapter 75

Hours went by and we decided to put down anchor and take a break. Ashley, fully revived now, was below deck, getting a lunch together for us. She still didn't have a clue about the fact that someone was looking for a boat with the name Carla on it. I didn't want to worry her while she wasn't feeling very well. I decided to fill her in after we got done eating, so she could be on her guard too.

Ashley listened carefully as we recounted the conversation that we had with the Coast Guard. She vaguely remembered them coming on board.

"Do you think he is out there looking for us?" she asked.

"I don't know, Ash, but I am not taking any chances."

There wasn't much boat traffic where we anchored, which was great, except for one vessel that slowly cruised by, waved at us, and continued on its way.

"It's working!" Timothy said after he put his phone back together. "I have a missed call; it's from Joe."

"When did he call? Did he leave a message?" I asked.

"It looks like it was early this morning, and yes he did, hang on. I'll retrieve the message, and put it on speaker."

"Timothy, why aren't you picking up your phone, damn it? I hope I'm not too late. Bobby… he knows… he has the picture of you and Ashley on your boat, standing right above Carla's name… the one that was taken at the marina. Nobody noticed after the break-in that the picture was missing. Dr. Blake realized it last night. I don't imagine that he's around here anymore… he's gone to look for you, I'm sure. You've got to keep moving! Don't stop for anything… answer the fucking phone, damn it! I'm on my way to find you."

I just stood there with my hand over my mouth and looked over at Ashley.

"Oh my God!" I cried. "He's coming after us."

Reality was hitting home. Ashley took me in her arms and held me close.

Timothy started dialing his phone. "I'm calling Joe back."

Maestro started barking and ran to the other end of the boat.

"I'll get him," Ashley said, and took off after him.

I turned toward Timothy and waited anxiously for Joe to answer. It kept going to his voicemail. Timothy redialed again and again.

"Well, he did say that he was on his way," I said. "There's not much more we can do, so just leave him a message and hopefully he will get back to us."

Timothy called again and did just that.

"What do you think we should do?" I asked after he was done.

"You're not going to like it," Timothy replied, "but I think we need to ditch this boat, leave it at a marina somewhere, and rent a car. He's looking for the boat. By the time he finds it, we will be long gone."

"I don't know. What about Joe; how's he going to know where we are?"

"He's following my phone, not the boat, remember? There is a tracker in it, and anyway, we will let him know what we are doing when he calls us back."

"What do you think, Ash?" I asked.

She didn't answer.

I turned my head and tried to look around. "Where did she go? Ashley?" I called.

"I think that she went after Maestro."

"Ashley?"

I stood up, turned, and then froze. I couldn't move or speak; it was like time had just stopped. There were no waves, no wind, no sounds, nobody was moving… I couldn't understand what was happening. My mind, though, it was definitely working. I felt like I was in one of my crazy dreams. I guess I was just hoping it was a dream, and I was going to wake up any minute. It wasn't happening, though, and I knew it wouldn't. This was real… I needed to get a grip… focus… I took a deep breath...

"Tyler!" I yelled.

Timothy jumped up and raised his gun.

"I've got this," I told him, without taking my eyes off of Tyler.

Maestro had been tied up with the ropes from the sail, and he was squirming, trying to get loose.

Tyler wore diving gear and was armed with a spear gun. Ashley was trying to say something, but he had his hand over her mouth. I gasped as he aimed the spear at Ashley's stomach.

"Tyler, you don't have to do this!" I cried.

I tried to stay calm, with not much success. I could see the fear in Ashley's eyes as they overflowed with tears.

"I can take a shot," Timothy whispered.

"Are you crazy? He will kill her!"

He was getting nervous and very fidgety with his gun.

"Put it down!" Tyler yelled.

I took my eyes off of Ashley for just a moment.

"Do as he says, Timothy," I begged.

"He will kill her anyway, and then he will kill us both," he replied. "We can't let him gain control."

I looked back at Ashley. She started struggling again. She managed to pull his hand off her face long enough to yell, "Shoot him!"

"No…" I screamed. My mind was running in slow motion. Tyler was yelling, Ashley was yelling, Timothy… I didn't know where to turn. I wanted to scream, but nothing came out. I felt paralyzed again, as Timothy's arm straightened out and he braced himself. I watched helplessly as his finger tensed up on the trigger. I turned back to Ashley, who was still yelling.

"Shoot him..."

The words dragged on for so long that I thought they would never stop echoing.

My ears exploded from the blast that came from Timothy's gun, and my eyes followed the bullet as it slowly made its way toward Tyler, who was raising the spear gun in our direction. As he did so, he pulled Ashley in front of him, and launched a spear. That moment seemed to last forever. I still couldn't move. I watched, in desperation, as Tyler took cover behind Ashley and the bullet pierced right through her body. She flew back, almost knocking Tyler overboard. He let her go and she fell on the deck.

"Ashley!" I screamed. "Oh my God... no!"

I wanted to run to her, but Tyler, who stood there with an evil grin on his face, raised his spear gun toward us again.

I turned to Timothy just in time to see the first spear pass through his body. He went down. I could hear him moaning in pain. I didn't know what to do. I looked back at Tyler, who was still pointing the spear gun at me, and wearing that evil grin.

"Finally, you are mine!" he yelled.

"Kill me!" I screamed. "Kill me, you bastard!"

He hesitated, still smiling, and then lowered the spear gun.

"No, I don't think so. I have better plans for us; after all, we were supposed to sail the world together, or have you forgotten?"

I just stood there speechless, staring at this madman in front of me... this monster. I half-expected the seaweed to start growing out of him, but I knew that this wasn't a bad dream. It was real. I shook it off and then closed my eyes for a second.

The sound of Timothy's moans brought me back. Tyler hadn't moved. He just stood there, staring at me with those evil eyes.

I turned to Timothy.

"Oh my God, Timothy," I whispered. "What can I do?"

"Never mind me," he said, so quietly that I could barely understand.

I could hear the pain in his voice, though.

"Take my gun…" he whispered. "Shoot him, and then try to get to Ashley," he whispered, "I'm so sorry, I…"

He let out a painful cry, and then, there was nothing. The tears started filling my eyes. I could barely see. I was on my own. Nobody could help me. I wiped my eyes and cleared my vision, just in time to see that Tyler had moved forward a bit.

"You need to move away from him, Robbie," Tyler commanded, pointing the spear gun in my direction.

I looked back down at Timothy.

"Robbie," Tyler yelled, "don't even think about picking up that gun. I'm coming over there, so move it!"

I didn't say anything as I stepped aside, watching his every move.

"That's right, keep moving," he said.

I moved along one side of the sail and he on the other, till we were on opposite sides of the boat.

"That's a good girl," he said. "Do as you're told, and maybe I won't hurt you."

I hesitated, my eyes still glued to him. I watched as he reached Timothy's side. He bent down and picked up the gun.

"This might come in handy," he said. "Go ahead and check on your girlfriend; I know you want to. If she's still alive, she won't be for long; I'll make sure of that."

I didn't want to let him out of my sight, but I needed to see if Ashley was okay. I turned and saw poor Maestro, all tied up and squirming and whimpering. I noticed a loop of rope that was loosening up around him. I didn't really want him to get free in case Tyler killed him too, but I was all alone against this monster and I needed all the help I could get. I casually tugged on the rope with my foot as I walked by.

"Stay, Maestro; don't move," I whispered.

I kept going until I got to Ashley.

"Ash!" I cried and knelt down beside her.

I put her fingers on the side of her neck and felt a pulse. It was very faint, though, and she was unresponsive.

"Don't leave me, Ash, please; I love you."

I gently raised her head and held her in my arms. I rocked her ever so softly.

"Don't leave me, Ashley; I can't live without you."

There was so much blood. I didn't know what to do.

"Tyler!" I screamed. "You have to help her! We can't just let her bleed to death!"

"I don't have to do anything!" he yelled. "The stupid bitch deserves to die. She took you away from me. We would be together now, if she hadn't come along."

I felt powerless... I had nobody... I was better off dead. I was not going to spend the rest of my life with that psychopath.

"If she dies, you will lose me too," I yelled back. "I will kill myself. I will have nothing left to live for."

He watched me as he fiddled with that damn gun.

"Get away from her!"

He pointed the gun in our direction.

I laid Ashley down gently and got in front of her. I was trembling but trying to look strong.

"No! You'll have to shoot me first!"

"I will kill you too."

"No… you won't; you didn't go through all this shit to kill me. If you let her die, you will be left with nobody. I swear, I will kill myself."

I saw a movement in the corner of my eye. I took a quick glance; it was Maestro.

"I will stay!" I said with emphasis on the word stay, for Maestro's sake, "if you let her live. Please help me; we need to stop the bleeding."

I watched as he got up. He leaned over and yanked the spear out of Timothy's lifeless body. He held it out in front of him and watched as the blood dripped from it.

"If you do anything stupid, I will drive this thing straight into her heart."

He pointed it toward us.

"I promise," I cried. "Come on, Tyler, help me please; she's lost so much blood."

I watched as Tyler laid the spear down and put the gun in his back pocket. He bent over and grabbed hold of Timothy's upper body. He had a little trouble but managed to lift his arms high enough to get them over the railing. He turned and gave me the evil eye. I stood there, shocked, with my hands over my mouth and trying not to scream. He turned around again and tried to lift the rest of him enough to toss him overboard. He was struggling.

"Bobby…"

I heard something. I thought it was my imagination.

"Bobby…"

I turned slowly, and saw Ashley move.

"The dagger," she whispered.

I bent down next to her.

"What are you doing?" Tyler yelled.

"I'm just checking on her. Can you do that later? We need to help her."

He stopped what he was doing and turned toward me.

"Put pressure on the wound," he said. "You've been around hospitals enough; you should at least know that much."

"I need some rags," I yelled. "There's too much blood." I looked around. "Oh, never mind."

I pulled my shirt up and over my head and used it to try to stop the bleeding. Tyler was watching my every move.

Ashley moaned.

"Ash?" I whispered.

Nothing, she didn't make another sound.

I turned, and Tyler was walking over, spear in hand.

"What are you doing?" I yelled.

"Coming over to take a look. Do you want my help, or not?"

"Not with that spear in your hand!"

He put it down, then continued toward us. I gave him a little space, keeping a close watch on him. He took a moment to admire my shirtless body.

"Don't you hurt her!" I warned.

"I won't; I'm just going to look at the bullet wound."

He rolled her over.

"Be careful!" I yelled.

He used my shirt to wipe away some blood so he could see it better.

"Looks like the bullet went right through her," he said. "She might live after all."

He put his hand up to his right shoulder.

"Isn't that interesting… same place as mine."

He started to laugh.

"I don't see anything funny, here. You're out of your fucking mind. We need to get her out of the sun. She's burning up, and we need to get her to a doctor!"

He gave me a shove and walked back to the helm, where Timothy was still hanging over the railing.

"You can take her below deck if you want, but I'm not helping you get her down there; and as for getting her to a doctor, well, that's not going to happen."

"Bastard!" I yelled, and he laughed some more.

I turned to check on Maestro. He was nowhere to be seen. I was very concerned that Tyler might see him and hurt him, but it seemed like he had forgotten all about him. Maestro probably managed to get loose while Tyler was busy checking on Ashley. He had probably found a good place to hide.

I turned back to Ashley. She was out cold. She looked like her life was draining out of her. I got down on my knees and started to cry. Ashley was my life; I couldn't lose her now.

I laid her wounded arm across her chest and I tried to get my arms under her to lift her. It didn't take me long to realize that was not going to work. I thought for a moment and came to the conclusion that the easiest way to get her close to the hatch, at least, was to gently drag her by the feet. I threw some water on the deck to make it slippery and proceeded to do so.

I glanced at Tyler, and he just sat there watching me and playing with that stupid gun. It made me very nervous. I didn't trust him at all. There was no telling what he would do next, still… I continued.

I finally made it to the hatch; it was open. Now my next problem was how to get her down to the bed. I turned again to check on my psychopath with that freaking gun. He was not looking at me anymore; he was looking toward the shore. I turned back to Ashley. Her eyes were open, and she was watching me.

"It's okay, Ash," I said quietly so Tyler wouldn't hear. "I'll take care of you. Everything will be okay."

Ashley whispered something but I couldn't understand. I glanced down the steps and saw something move. I was very happy to see that Maestro had made it safely below deck. I turned back to Ashley. Her hand was motioning me to come closer. I did, and she whispered again.

"You have to kill him."

I watched as she struggled to get the words out.

"It's your only way…" she paused to try to take a breath, "out of this," then she closed her eyes.

Tears started to fill my eyes. I turned to see what Tyler was doing. He was still looking toward the shore. I started to wonder what he was looking at, but I didn't want to leave Ashley's side. I took another look below deck. Maestro was halfway under the bed. I looked back at Ashley.

She had opened her eyes again, "Kill him, Bobby," she whispered and nodded.

Next thing I knew, Maestro was climbing the steps. I couldn't believe my eyes. He had found the dagger that I had tossed under the bed and had it in his mouth. He put it down in front of me. I was stunned. I turned to look at Tyler again, just as he started yelling.

"Fucking hell, will they ever leave me alone?"

He got very agitated. He resumed trying to toss Timothy overboard.

"Get your ass over here and help me!"

"Do it yourself!" I yelled back.

"Start the motor, then; we need to get out of here… now!"

I didn't move. I looked past him and saw what looked like a boat in the distance. Suddenly, there was a splash.

"Timothy!" I screamed. "Why did you have to do that?"

"Did you want to keep him as a souvenir? Now, get your ass behind the wheel and get us out of here."

There was another splash, and then another.

"What in the hell?" Tyler blasted.

"Fred!" I yelled.

He was back, and he brought some friends. They kept jumping in and out of the water. Tyler was freaking out. He kept yelling. I turned and looked at Ashley and she had the dagger in her hand.

"Now's your chance!" she whispered.

Maestro barked in agreement. I took it from her.

"I've had enough of this shit," Tyler yelled. "You're all dead!"

I turned and saw him raise the gun and point it toward the water.

Fred and his friends were still jumping around out there, so he started shooting all over the place. He cursed again when he ran out of bullets and tossed the gun overboard.

I continued watching as he reached for the spear gun.

My mind went blank for a moment and it brought me back visions of that awful dream I had, the one where Fred had a spear through him. I gasped as I came back to my senses and saw Tyler standing there calmly, weapon raised.

"Come on, you little bastard. I won't miss you with this."

At that, Fred jumped up out of the water.

"Nooo..." I screamed as I jumped up and went for Tyler, dagger in hand.

Things seemed to be in slow motion again.

"Nooo…!"

The spear shot out. I watched, still moving, as it pierced through the air, barely missing Fred. Tyler turned toward me just as I dove into him, dagger-first. I felt the blade crack through his ribs and the warm blood flow out over my hand. He screamed with pain as we flew overboard together. He never took his eyes off me. It seemed like we would never hit the water… like that moment was frozen in time. I saw a faint smile come over his face, as we plunged beneath the surface.

I let go of the dagger and watched as he drifted away. Still, his gaze never left me. I stayed there and watched him, holding my breath for the longest time, making sure that he didn't start moving.

Finally, I turned to go back to the boat and Fred came along to greet me. I grabbed his fin and off we went. He led me up to a slow-moving vessel. I paused at the surface to catch my breath, still hanging onto Fred, and then I looked up. It was the Coast Guard vessel from before. Joe reached out, pulled me on board, and laid me down. I was totally exhausted. I looked across to the other side of the boat and saw poor Timothy.

"You found him," I said.

"Your dolphin friend has been very busy," he replied. "Oh… here he comes again, and it looks like he's got the catch of the day, dagger and all." He looked back at me and smiled. "I believe that your nightmares are finally over, Bobby… good job."

"Ashley!" I yelled, as I came back to my senses. "Joe, you've got to get to her. She's on the boat; she got shot!"

He helped me up as their vessel parked alongside my boat. We boarded, and I ran to Ashley's side. She greeted us with a smile.

"Oh Bobby, thank God you're okay," she whispered, "I was so worried when I saw you fall overboard."

"I got him, Ash, and we have the body to prove it." I leaned over and gave her a kiss.

Maestro barked.

"You saved me again, Maestro; I love you too." I patted his head.

I lay down next to Ashley with Maestro on the other side. I held her close, never wanting to let her go. The Coast Guard was towing us to shore where there was an ambulance waiting.

"I love you, Bobby," she whispered, then tears started flowing down her cheeks.

My eyes were also filling up and my vision was starting to blur. I was getting very lightheaded. The daylight was fading slowly, being replaced by blackness. The sound of the ocean was being replaced by that buzzing noise in my head, and then, once again, that very familiar sound.

"Beep…Beep…Beep."

About the Author

Deborah has always referred to herself as "A jack of all trades and a master of none."

She has worked in restaurants, bars, and department stores. She has cared for children and the elderly, worked in farming, construction, hairdressing, and drafting, and even operated her own florist shop. Her most rewarding job was raising two beautiful children.

She enjoys painting, music, writing, nature, and outdoor adventures including hiking, kayaking, and the occasional rock climbing, parachuting, and scuba diving.

Like many of you, she has lived a challenging life. Many traumatic experiences still weigh heavily on her soul, the most recent of which is the loss of her daughter and grandson. Deborah has also conquered personal challenges. As part of the Cancer Research Society Kilimanjaro Challenge, she raised $11,000 for cancer research. After five days of climbing, she summitted on October 28, 2013, a day she will never forget.

She, like her protagonist Bobby, is a survivor who finds the strength to keep going. Deborah finds peace today living with her husband in the Quebec Eastern Townships, surrounded by lakes and mountains.